MEET JAKE TANNER

Born: 28.03.1985

Height: 6'1"

Weight: 190lbs / 86kg / 13.5 stone

Physical Description: Brown hair, close shaven beard, brown eyes, slim athletic build

Education: Upper Second Class Honours in Psychology from the University College London (UCL)

Interests: When Jake isn't protecting lives and finding those responsible for taking them, Jake enjoys motorsports — particularly F1

Family: Mother, older sister, younger brother. His father died in a car accident when Jake was fifteen

Relationship Status: Currently in a relationship with Elizabeth Tanner, and he doesn't see that changing, ever

By The Same Author

The CID Case Series
Toe the Line
Walk the Line
Under the Line
Cross the Line
Over the Line
Past the Line

The SO15 Files Series
The Wolf
Dark Christmas
The Eye
In Heaven and Hell
Blackout
Eye for an Eye
Mile 17
The Long Walk
The Endgame

The Terror Thriller Series
Standstill
Floor 68

WALK THE LINE

By Jack Probyn

ISBN: 978-1-80520-006-2

First Edition

Visit Jack Probyn's website at www.jackprobynbooks.com.

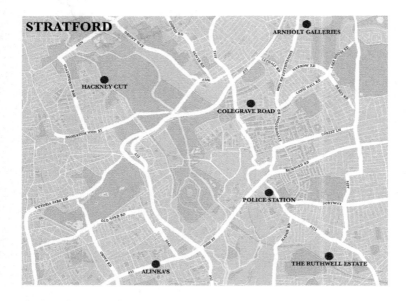

| PART 1 |

CHAPTER 1

THE BLACK DOOR

Steven and Jessica Arnholt weren't afraid to share the darker, seedier side of their relationship with others. In fact, it helped. When it came to the bedroom – and what happened behind the four walls – there was nothing that they kept hidden. Tonight, however, was different. Jessica wasn't ready for what was about to come her way, and when her husband asked whether she was, she lied. In his hands he held two glasses of red wine, the liquid as dark and deep as blood. One glass for him, one for her.

'Thanks,' Jessica said, taking the glass from him and placing it down on the desk beside her. She rolled up the sleeves of her blue tartan shirt and sat on the chair, tying her long, auburn hair off her face and into a ponytail. 'What time's he coming?'

Steven checked his watch. A long, sinewy forearm and skeletal fingers extended through the red tartan shirt he wore – the same brand and material as hers. His skin looked a ghostly white against the red.

'In about five minutes,' he replied.

'Is the room set up?'

The sides of Steven's mouth flickered. He took a sip of wine and licked his lips, wiping the excess from his skin. 'I finished it earlier. Let me show you.'

Jessica took his hand and travelled with him through the gallery.

On the left wall was a new piece of artwork that she didn't recognise – which now explained where Steven had been disappearing to for the past three days. Jessica paid it little heed though, as there were more important things to focus on than admiring his work and realising he wasn't having an affair. Her mind was too distracted. She felt apprehensive. Nervous. Afraid. She'd experienced a night like this before – countless times, in fact – but she had a feeling that tonight was going to be different; the full moon was on show and she knew, particularly for Steven, it would awaken the beast. His beast.

Steven came to a stop by a heavy black door that led to the basement. He lifted the handle and pushed. A black wall stared back at them, lit only by the dancing light of the candles that hung intermittently on the wall. Jessica went first. Her feet landed delicately on the steps and she held on to what holdings she could find on the brick, using it for guidance. As she reached the final step, a deep red swathed her.

What had, hours ago, been her husband's art room was now his dungeon. Along the back wall was a row of what Steven liked to call 'his toys'. Dildos. Whips. Beads. Spankers. Blunt objects. But there was a new addition. To the right of the other objects were a set of kitchen knives. She daren't ask what they were for... not yet anyway; she was too absorbed by the magic of the entire room. Her body tingled at the sight of it all.

In the centre of the space was a large table, with four chains placed in each corner. It had been crafted to her exact measurements, and they allowed no room for manoeuvre: once she was locked in, she was locked in until released. On the right-hand side of the room were two poles, and at the top of them, another set of chains; one for each hand – or foot, depending on Steven's preference.

Jessica took another sip of wine.

'What do you think?' Steven asked.

'It's nice. I sense plum with a tiny kick of cherry... right?'

'Not the wine,' Steven said, puffing out a small laugh. 'I meant the room. I think it's the best it's looked in a long time.'

Jessica pointed to the blades hanging from the wall. 'What are those for? Do you want him to kill me?'

'Don't worry,' Steven said, placing a hand on her shoulder. 'They won't do anything other than make you sore. They're blunt. I wore them down earlier while you were at work.'

'They better be. I don't want him to kill me.'

'He'll do exactly as I tell him. And exactly as you'll let him.'

She looked him deep in the eyes. They had turned a darker brown than usual. And that was when she knew his sadistic tendencies had begun to consume his mind and body. It wouldn't be long until his entire personality changed.

'Yes, master.'

Steven opened his mouth to speak but was cut off by the sound of a doorbell ringing on the gallery floor. Saying nothing, both Steven and Jessica headed upstairs; Steven pulling Jessica by the arm, stretching her skin as he gripped her tightly.

The harsh fluorescent light blinded her as she climbed the final step. On the other side of the gallery window was Lester Bain, their victim. He was a small man, balding, and the little hair that remained on his head was the colour of straw. She'd never bothered to ask how old he was, but she was certain he was either in his late thirties or early forties, though Lester's physique belied his real age. He had the body of a twenty-year-old. Sculpted. Muscular. It was clear to see he looked after himself. It was just a shame that he repulsed her as soon as he touched her.

Lester gave a quaint little wave as the light from inside the gallery illuminated his face.

'What are you waiting for?' Steven asked her. 'Open the door, you stupid bitch. We can't leave him waiting too long.'

'Yes, master.' Jessica bowed her head, placed her glass on the desk and opened the door for Lester.

His aftershave was strong, but she'd become immune to its power. Lester entered the building and removed his shoes – it had been a common courtesy he'd insisted upon the first time they'd all met.

'Jessica, my darling,' he said, kissing her on the lips. His hand wandered down her body and found its home on her breast. He squeezed hard.

'Lester!' Steven called from the other end of the room. 'Don't get too carried away with yourself. We have to wait. Trust me. It'll make it all better.'

'Is tonight *the* night?' Lester asked, his voice endearing, like a child's.

Steven nodded. 'The very one. We wanted to surprise you. I hope you're prepared.'

'I've waited three long months for this.'

Steven raised a glass. 'Red? Or we have white if you'd prefer?'

Lester released Jessica's breast as though it were an inanimate object that he held no emotional attachment to and started towards Steven. 'Red please.'

Jessica closed the door behind them and locked it. She gave one final look at the world outside – the normality of it all; the world that had no idea what would go on behind these four walls; the world that would judge them if they did know. There was no turning back now.

Steven called her name. She turned towards him and then rushed over. Her masters were standing in front of a five-foot-wide painting.

'I was just showing our guest my new work,' Steven said.

'I think it's wonderful,' Lester added.

'He's a talented man, my—'

Lester slapped her across the face with the back of his hand, knocking the glass from her grip. It smashed into hundreds of pieces, wine spreading across the floor, soiling her shoes as well as Lester's white socks.

'Now look what you've fucking done!' Lester screamed in her face. 'What have I told you about talking out of turn? Go and clean it up now.'

Jessica immediately complied. She rushed through another door that led into a kitchen area, grabbed some cloths, a dustpan and brush, and returned to the gallery. As she bent down to pick up the glass and mop up the wine, she eavesdropped on their conversation.

'As I was saying,' Steven continued. 'I wanted to go for something slightly different. I wanted something that would make a commentary on life.'

'I have to say, it's hyperreal. I'd love to feature one in one of my properties,' Lester said. He tilted his head and glanced at Jessica on the floor. 'At a nominal fee, of course.'

'Naturally.'

Lester returned his attention to the painting. 'Now, you know I don't know much about art – and I would say, in my immodest opinion, that it looks a lot like all your other works – but this one is my favourite.'

'My art shows the perfection of life. The order. The normality of it. The *banality*. A complete contrast to our little secret.'

'Speaking of little secrets,' Lester began, 'The Community has just reached fifteen thousand members. We hit the figure earlier this afternoon.'

'If that isn't something to celebrate, I don't know what is!'

Steven and Lester's glasses clinked together while Jessica carried the filled dustpan and sodden cloth back to the kitchen area. She returned empty-handed.

An awkward moment fell on the three of them as both men stared at her. Lester's eyes bore into her skin, and the sensation that he was undressing her with his eyes – which, she knew, he was – made her feel even more apprehensive. In the few months since they'd started their Communion with Lester, it had only been foreplay. Handjobs. Blowjobs. Heavy touching. All of the stuff that Steven allowed her to perform. But now Steven determined that they had teased Lester enough – it was time for the Full

Communion. Intercourse. She didn't want it, but she had no say in the matter. She was submissive, and it was Steven's choice. But of all the other Community members they'd been with, Lester was the first that made her skin crawl. There was something different about him – something she didn't like.

'Well?' Lester was the first to speak. 'What are we waiting for? Shall we begin?'

Steven checked his watch. 'I think it's about time.' He turned to the black door and gestured for Lester to move first. 'Please. Follow me.'

CHAPTER 2

BETRAYAL

Lester was hard. He could feel it all ready, bulging in his trousers. His palms were turning moist, and a thin film of sweat had formed at the crease of his neck.

Steven opened the big black door that Lester had come to love in recent months. His pulse skipped.

'After you,' Steven said. 'I'll give you the tour while Jessica gets ready. I've prepared it a little differently this time.'

Lester grinned. 'Now you've really got me excited.'

He crossed the threshold into the stairwell. As he descended the steps, he let his imagination loose. He imagined tying her up, pinning her tightly so she couldn't move, whipping her, beating her until he drew blood, penetrating her, not knowing when to stop, not knowing if to stop, not knowing how to – all manner of depraved things.

He reached the bottom of the steps and observed the apparatus hanging on the wall and dangling from the ceiling, his mouth agape. It was everything he'd imagined it would be. More. Beyond his wildest dreams.

'You approve?' Steven asked, placing a comforting hand on Lester's back.

'Yes,' Lester said, almost chuckling with excitement.

'I wanted to tailor it to you and your preferences.'

'It's... it's a work of art.'

Steven puffed out another laugh and adjusted his glasses on his nose. 'It's my day job for a reason.'

Lester moved about the room and paused by Steven's toys. He reached for the blades that dangled from the wall.

'You know, I've been thinking about your wife for many weeks now. I've been planning this in my head from the first moment I contacted you.' Lester's finger ran up and down the knife's edge.

'I sharpened that one earlier. The others are blunt. I want you to use it on Jessica. Gentle, but not too gentle. Heavy, but not too heavy.'

'I'm sure I can find the happy medium. And she consents?' Lester asked, stabbing his finger on the tip of the blade. He made a mental note of which one it was.

'She will do as I tell her. I told her they were blunt. If she knew they weren't she'd refuse. It's better she finds out this way, while her emotions and excitement are up – that way she can't get out of it. Once we begin, she's all yours.'

'This just keeps getting better and better.'

Lester moved along the wall and grabbed a paddle. He ran it over the palm of his hand, the blunt spikes massaging his skin and teasing his sensory reflectors into action. He finished admiring the sensation and then pointed to the large desk in the middle of the room. 'Where's the camera? I want to make sure this gets thoroughly documented. For all our records.'

'Don't worry, it's under the table. I was going to record it myself this time from a distance. You won't even know I'm here. After all, it is *your* special day.'

'Perhaps we should get you involved as well? Add to the tally?' He was enjoying what he was hearing, and he couldn't wait to begin.

'We'll see. If the timing's right, then maybe I'll join you. But you've been good to us – you've really helped us *improve* – so it's only fair we repay you like this.'

'You know, S has recently added a new level of points. I think—'

Lester was silenced by Steven's finger. 'Hold that thought. I'll go and get her ready, and then you can test them out on her. Sound good?'

Lester nodded emphatically.

'Wait right here.'

With that, Steven turned and disappeared up the stairs. Lester appreciated that. It added to the excitement and tension of the situation. But then a thought occurred to him. If Jessica was preparing upstairs, then should he prepare downstairs? No. He would wait. He would make her undress him. Yes. That was the best way. He was looking forward to that. Her touch. Her skin. Her lips around his cock. *Jessica.* He shivered thinking about her. He wanted her – wanted her more than anything. More than his next breath. He wanted to lay next to her. Wake next to her. Be next to her. Every minute of every waking day. It wasn't fair that Steven had her. It wasn't fair that he could do all those things whenever he wanted, and Lester couldn't. He bet they didn't even fuck. Not like he and Jessica did when they were together in his mind. He bet they had lost the chemistry and the romance and the spark in their sordid relationship. *The curse of sadists and masochists,* he thought, chuckling.

Lester checked his watch. Only a minute had passed, but it was beginning to feel like ten. As the seconds moved by, he grew impatient.

He stormed up the steps, climbing them two at a time, and as he was about to open the door onto Steven's art gallery, he heard their voices, hushed, panicked. His hand caressed the handle, and he kept it there, pressing his ear against the door.

'I don't feel comfortable.' It was Jessica's voice. She sounded different. More concerned, like it was missing that hint of sexiness and aggression Lester had grown accustomed to.

'I don't care. You'll do as I say.'

'Pineapple,' Jessica said.

'What?'

'Pineapple. That's our safe word. I'm using our safe word. I want out.'

'Listen here,' Steven said. 'You're going to go through with this right up until the moment I tell you to stop. The longer you go for, the more points we get.' Steven quietened his voice. 'Think about it. With this, we'll be able to overtake him on the leader boards, and then we can *finally* dispose of him. For good. All we'll need to do then is get rid of Christopher, and then we'll be at the top of the table. Untouchable. I've had a look online and Christopher's already overtaken us – it's a Friday night. He's getting busy. We can't let him beat us. We do this, we go to the top.'

'How do you want me to do it?' Jessica asked, her voice trembling.

'The blades. The one on the far right is sharp enough to slice his throat.'

'You told me it was blunt! What if he uses that one on me!'

'Relax,' Steven said. 'I won't let it get that far. There's cleaning chemicals and a bag underneath the table to tidy it up afterwards. It'll be fine. I promise. Now take your knickers off and hurry up. He's waiting.'

Lester's body turned cold. He couldn't believe what he'd heard. His hand tightened around the handle until his knuckles turned white and the metal dug into his palm. They were going to betray him. They were going to use his rank and status to heighten their own so they could pass him on the leader board. Worse still, they were going to fucking kill him!

Aware that they were on the other side, about to open the door, Lester rushed down the steps quietly, grabbed the blade from the far right on the wall and slid it in the waistband of his jeans, feeling the cold metal of the weapon press against his skin.

The door opened overhead, and he heard the sound of footsteps approaching. Adrenaline coursed through his veins. He shook with excitement.

'Lester?' Jessica asked softly. 'You ready?'

'Oh, you bet,' Lester said with a grin on his face. His hand gripped the blade's handle tightly.

As he did so, Jessica appeared. She was naked, but her hair had been let loose and dangled either side of her square shoulders, falling over her supple breasts and covering her nipples. The red light in the room cast an almost demonic aura around her slender frame, illuminating her brown eyes and turning her lipstick an even darker shade of crimson. She looked like a goddess with a naughty side, an ephemeral figure that would haunt his every waking moment for the rest of his life – for all the right reasons. She reminded him of a model, someone who made it their life's mission to entertain and tease and flaunt. And then he saw it: the dimples in her cheeks that only ever came out during Communion. They were like light bulbs that she could just flicker on and off at ease.

Lester moved around the table so that it separated them both from him. He pulled the back of his shirt over the knife's handle to shield it from view. Jessica advanced towards the centre of the room.

'Where do you want me?' she asked, placing her hands by her curvaceous hips.

Lester stuttered before he answered. He was panicked at the unearthly sight of her, but if he was going to do this, he needed to maintain a clear head.

'On the table. I want to tie you up.'

Jessica did as she was told and climbed atop the table's surface. Her body lay flat and her breasts spread softly either side. Her ribcage and flat stomach inflated gently in tandem with one another as she breathed. Lester moved around the bottom of the table and chained Jessica's ankles. Her skin felt warm under his. He imagined the blood coursing through it – and how, soon, it would be spilling all over the floor.

'Wait!' Steven called, his voice echoing around the room. He stood at the midpoint of the stairs. 'Don't start until I get the camera. I don't want to miss any of it.'

Lester looked up at him and smiled. 'Trust me – you won't want to miss a thing.'

Steven pulled up at the table, bent underneath and produced a video recorder. Heavy. Professional. If all else failed with the knife, then Lester mused that he could use the camera as a battering ram to open the man's skull.

Steven pressed a button on the device and held it close to his face.

'Ready whenever you are,' he said.

'Are you recording?' Lester asked.

Steven gave the thumbs up.

It was time.

Lester moved to the top of the table and clasped the remaining chains over Jessica's wrists. They shut with a satisfying *clink*. Now she was locked in, unable to move. Next, Lester moved over to the wall of instruments and pretended to deliberate. He went straight for the blade furthest on the right, which he knew was blunt. He pulled it from the wall and returned to Jessica, standing beside Steven. He slapped the flat side of the blade against her stomach. As soon as the metal hit her body, she groaned like she always did. Nothing unusual about that. But then, as she realised what was in his hands, her eyes widened, and he saw fear stretch across her face; her glance darted towards Steven and the camera.

Lester moved the blade over her body, tickling her with it, and left it resting on her nipples. The closer it got to her throat, the more she shook and writhed; the more her breathing increased. Smiling, he flipped the blade, so the blunt edge was against her skin, then he hovered over her chest and held it against her neck. Beside him, Steven moved around and held the camera close to them both at Lester's waist height. *Perfect!*

With his free hand, Lester reached for the small of his back, closed his hand around the sharpened blade and buried it deep in Steven's neck. A fountain of crimson burst from his carotid artery and showered Jessica's body. Piercing screams filled the air as Steven slumped to the floor and dropped the camera. Lester's gaze followed the man as he lay there hopeless, defenceless, holding his throat and gasping his last breath, squirming on the concrete as he drowned in his own blood.

Within seconds, he was dead. But the screaming still persisted. Lester stared down at Jessica on the table. Her movements were frantic, but it was all futile. She spat Steven's blood out of her mouth and tried to blink away the splatter that had got into her eyes.

'No! Please! No!' she said in between chokes.

Lester silenced her by holding the blade against her throat. 'Quiet!' he shouted at her. 'You think you can try to kill me and get away with it?'

'What are you going to do to me?'

Lester pressed the knife's point into her skin, drawing a droplet of blood. 'Everything I've always wanted to. And then some. And then some more after that. It's going to be a long night.'

Lester bent down and picked up the camera from the concrete. He wiped some of Steven's blood from it and placed it on the table, then he undressed, mounted Jessica and picked it up again.

He grinned as he looked at her, then slid inside her.

'You have no idea how long I've been waiting to do this.'

CHAPTER 3

SNITCHING

Jake Tanner was working for the name of the badge, not the name on it.

He was already in the office by 7 a.m. He was an early bird, keen to make his mark known, his face seen, and his presence felt by his new team. He was a member of the Metropolitan Police's Major Investigation Team based in Stratford's police station, Bow Green. The team was a small unit of between five and ten officers of varying ranks. In the short time that he'd been there, Jake had seen dozens of new faces recycled through the team like they were in a revolving door. There were, however, a select few who seemed to be permanent, like fixtures in the walls.

As Jake sat there at his desk, looking at the Metropolitan Police Service emblem emblazoned on his screen, he smiled. It had taken a while for him to move across to the new team – months of transfer requests and interviews – but now he was finally here, he felt like he was a part of something different. Something bigger and better than anything else out there. He was making a change to London, and he was changing lives. He loved his job, regardless of the tedious and monotonous work he'd been doing for the past few months. Paperwork. Filing. Forms. He'd read the first few lines of the MG11 witness statement form so much that he was beginning to recite it in his sleep. He supposed that was a good thing if he was going to develop as a detective.

Jake loaded up a form he'd been working on the night before and continued filling it in. It was almost another hour until he saw someone else appear in the office. Lindsay Gray. She was the civilian facilities manager for Bow Green, and she was usually the first one to show her face in the office. She was in her mid-fifties and, after retiring a few years ago, she'd soon realised that her love for the job was too much – that she had to rejoin the force in some capacity. She had been a member of the Major Investigation Team throughout her career, and so she made sure that she could be around the atmosphere as much as possible while also serving the rest of the teams in the building. Her desk was in the corner of the MIT room, kept out of the way but not out of earshot. More often than not, she'd join in with some of the banter and heated discussions the team had while they were settling in for the mornings and getting ready to go home for the evening. Jake liked her. She was a friendly face, and she always carried a smile as though it wasn't a burden. For that, he respected and admired her. In many ways, she reminded Jake of his own mother, which he believed was the best compliment he could pay her.

'Morning, mate,' she said as she slung her bag over the back of her chair. 'Coffee?'

'Kill for one, if you wouldn't mind,' Jake said, leaning across the desk for his mug. Dried coffee stained the rim and bottom of the ceramic, and a dribble ran down the side. 'One s—'

'Don't worry. I know how you like it.'

Jake thanked her and continued working while she disappeared behind him. When she returned, she placed it on his desk then hurried to hers. He took a sip, grimaced at the bitter taste and placed the mug back on the desk. It definitely wasn't the way he liked it, but he didn't have the heart to tell her.

'Did you have a good evening?' Jake called across the office. 'How was the—?'

Before he was able to finish, he was interrupted by the sound of the office door opening. The remaining dozen officers from the team filtered in with one addition joining them. They were laughing and cajoling one another, holding coffees from the local shop round the corner in their hand. Jake observed them as they came in. They were all present, not one of them missing. It was 8:45 a.m., and they'd all been due to start over an hour ago. At the head of the group was Jake's senior officer, and the head of the Major Investigation Team, DCI Liam Greene. He was a small man – a few inches south of six foot – who wore his ego on his sleeve and never took kindly to being ridiculed. Yet whenever Jake had tried to get to know him, he was standoffish and rude. Liam wasn't afraid to do what it took to get the job done and he regularly made sure everyone in the team knew where they stood. There was an air of intimidation about him too. Though Jake supposed it was perhaps because he'd only been afforded the opportunity to speak with his boss a handful of times since joining MIT, that he felt nervous around him. Beside Liam was DCI Hamilton, the commanding officer responsible for the efficiency of the Missing Persons Team on the floor beneath them, who'd decided to accompany them on the morning's coffee run. Both men were in their early forties and were beginning to grey at the top and sides.

'Where have you lot been?' Lindsay asked, rising to her feet. She sounded like an unimpressed mother whose children had come home late from playing outside.

Liam stood in the doorway of his office with his hand planted on the handle. 'We went out for a group breakfast, all of us. To celebrate. Our heads are feeling a little worse for wear.'

She placed her hands on her hips. 'Where were our invites?'

'Well…' Liam paused to look at Jake and then back at Lindsay. 'Neither of you were here when we found out the good news.'

'Which was?' Jake asked, taking another sip of his coffee and then immediately wishing he hadn't.

'You haven't heard? Benjamin Pryce has been found. Alive and well. A little shaken up but he'll live.' Liam pointed across the room to Hamilton. 'Our resident child molester over there found him and returned him home safely.'

Hamilton replied with a middle finger. Without saying anything else, he ducked into the debrief room in the far-right corner of the office, grabbed something from his desk and stormed out, charging towards Liam.

'That reminds me,' Hamilton said, brandishing a pair of scissors in his hands. 'A bet's a bet.' Then he grabbed Liam's tie and snipped it from the top.

Laughter erupted around the office.

'I win,' Hamilton said as he raised the loose tie in the air triumphantly to the sound of cheers and applause.

'I deserve that one,' Liam ceded. 'Same bet on the next one? First to crack the case gets bragging rights for a week?'

'Or they get a go on the other's missus!' DS Drew Richmond shouted. He was Jake's immediate supervisor and had been part of Major Investigation long before anyone else. He was one of the oldest fixtures in the office.

'Or we could all get a go on yours!' Hamilton shouted to another barrage of laughter.

'At least that'll make one of us,' Drew replied.

'You'll have to join the queue on that one, fella.'

'Right you lot, back to work,' Liam said, clapping his hands together. 'The AC's coming down later today, so anyone not doing anything will get their balls pinched.'

At that, DCI Hamilton left the office to return to his team, and the rest of MIT stuck their heads down. Before long, the sound of typing and clicking replaced the laughter. It was back to work, business as usual.

Before Jake was able to join them, Liam arrived at his desk. In the distance, a phone rang.

'Busy morning, Jake?' Liam asked, perching himself on the edge of Jake's desk.

Jake shook his head. 'Not particularly, sir. Just the usual.'

'Good. Anyone asks, we were here on time, all right? Kind of reflects badly on all of us – including yourself – if anyone learns otherwise.'

'Yes, sir. Of course.'

Liam patted Jake on the back hard, reinforcing the need for secrecy.

'There's a good lad.'

'Guv!' a call came from DC Pete Garrison, another member of Major Investigation. He was Jake's equivalent and was more than happy to spend the rest of his career behind a desk. He was the workhorse of the unit, constantly filling out applications and forms and all the other monotonous stuff in the background without anyone else in the team realising he'd done it. It didn't take long for Jake to realise that he didn't want to live a career like that. Instead, he wanted to be out on the front line, policing the streets and putting people who were capable of insidious things behind bars where they deserved to be.

Garrison rose to his feet with the phone still in his hand. 'We've got one. Double whammy. Art gallery. Uniform are already there.'

Excitement welled in the office at the words, and Jake felt his own adrenaline surge a little. This could be the opportunity he needed to prove himself, rather than remain sidelined in the office like he had done for too long.

'Excellent. Nice work. Send me the address. DS Richmond...'

'Sir.'

'Get your stuff. We're going.'

As Liam started off, Jake called him back.

'Sir? Sir – can I come?'

Liam shot him a glare.

'For the experience?'

Liam pondered the request a moment, scratching the underside of his chin. 'Why not? At least that way I'll know you won't be snitching on us.'

CHAPTER 4

A DAY IN THE LIFE OF A TEENAGER

Jake slammed the door of Liam's green Volvo C30 behind him. Rain lashed at his face, hammering his eyes and eyebrows, quickly soaking his hair. He pulled the collar of his blazer over his ears, but it made no difference.

'Hurry up,' Liam called back to him. Standing beside him was Drew, smirking at Jake's discomfort.

They had parked up a hundred yards from the crime scene, behind a tailback of other emergency response vehicles. In the distance was a police officer standing behind a white tape. Dressed in a fluorescent waterproof coat, and with a plastic protector around his cap, rain slicked off his body and onto the ground. Jake, Liam and Drew approached the man. In his hands he held a clipboard, a pen and a sheet of paper that was rapidly becoming sodden. The three of them signed in on the attendance log and moved over to the back of the forensics van, where they donned their forensic suits. The suit consisted of a hood, gloves, face mask and overshoes, and it was one size fits all. Jake had to step into it fully clothed, tucking his tie into his shirt and making sure the metal clip was securely fastened. He pulled the suit's zip to his neck and tucked little wisps of damp brown hair into the hood before letting the elastic snap against his forehead. The material was thin and coarse and, within a few seconds, began to chafe against his skin.

A few feet from the scene's entrance was a figure, blending into the backdrop of the white walls and other scene of crime officers who were coming and going from the building.

The three of them approached her. Liam extended his hand and introduced himself.

'Poojah Singh,' the figure replied, shaking Liam's hand. 'Forensic pathologist. I'm in charge of this lot.' She nodded to the two SOCOs who had just emerged from the building.

'Aren't we supposed to be here before you?' Liam asked.

'Not when you see what's inside,' Poojah replied.

'Sounds interesting. What have you got for us?'

'You'd best see it for yourself. It's a messy one.'

Jake didn't like the sound of that. This was the first time he'd been to a major crime scene since Luke Cipriano and his mother Candice had died in the middle of a small park while locked in one another's grip almost a year ago. The images of that afternoon in Southampton were still heavily ingrained in his memory, sometimes giving him sleepless nights.

The four of them headed into the art gallery. Jake observed the artwork that hung on the wall. Magnificent. Intricate. Vibrant. Some of the pieces were as wide and tall as his bed at home. Jake didn't know much – or indeed anything – about art and wasn't the type to pretend he did either, but he could appreciate a good painting when he saw one. The most striking was a painting of a faceless figure holding a gun against his chin. Behind the figure was a halo of blood and brains scattered across a wall. The piece was titled: *A Day in the Life of a Teenager*.

'We've got two victims,' Poojah said, her voice disappearing further away from Jake. He hadn't realised it, but they were walking in the opposite direction, venturing deeper into the gallery. 'Both IC1. Recovered wallets and driving licences confirm their identities as Steven and Jessica Arnholt.'

'Anything else?' Liam asked.

'Just searched his name online, guv,' Drew added, holding his phone in his hand. 'His website biography says he's an artist and an art dealer.'

'Makes sense. And Jessica Arnholt? Anything about her?'

Drew lowered his phone and shrugged.

They came to a stop at the end of the room in front of a pitch-black door. Jake observed an investigator to his left scoop up fractured pieces of glass and swab the floor with a cotton bud before placing it in a tube and then an evidence bag.

'The bodies are down here. I'm warning you – I've been doing this job for a while now and this is the nastiest thing I've seen. Prepare yourself,' Poojah said.

Jake didn't think that he could. He didn't want to let his imagination run away with itself. There was only so much training that could have prepared him for a dead body, and, as he stared blankly at Poojah, it all disappeared out of his mind.

Without saying anything else, she disappeared down the first step. Startled, Jake followed at the back of the queue and entered into the stairwell. A dark red hue swathed the walls, and as Jake walked down, he brushed his fingers along the bricks for support. He looked down at his feet, watching his every step, lest he slip and fall.

'The stairs have been wiped clean,' Poojah said. 'There's no trace of anyone ever setting foot on them. The team are still making their way around the rest of the crime scene, so we won't be able to intervene too much.'

'Anything we can do to help,' Drew said. As he reached the final step, he stopped abruptly. 'Jesus fucking Christ!'

Jake froze behind him. His eyes widened and his pulse stopped.

Before him, spread on a large table, was a dead body, illuminated by a demonic light hovering over the torso. The head had been removed and placed a few inches above the figure's chest, standing upright so that it peered down the length of the body. The hands and feet had been amputated and positioned either side of the head, pointing outwards, away from the body. Dark purple patches the size of watermelons dotted the victim's thighs and back. Incisions, three inches wide, had been made up and down the stomach, and two circular holes had been punched in the chest where a pair of breasts had once been. The word LIAR had been inscribed on the woman's stomach, a small bead of blood dotting the I. A pool of thick blood, now congealed from the exposure to the air, covered the entire table, and small puddles had formed at the foot of the four corners where the excess of blood had fallen over the edge.

Jake's eyes moved around the room. To his left, on a wall, was an array of sexual instruments all crusted with blood. Each and every item looked as if it had been used during the killings in one way or another. To the right of the room, dangling from two chains, was another body. It was taller, longer and skinnier. The head had also been removed, and there was a small red hole in the crotch where his penis had been sliced off. Scene of crime officers surrounded the body, moving it slightly as they set to work.

The sight made Jake retch. The massacre was the worst thing he'd ever seen. Bile rushed from his stomach and pained his throat. He threw his hands over his mouth, vomited a little, then sprinted up the stairs and out of the gallery. By the time he reached the building's entrance, the vomit was already spewing over his fingers. It landed hard on the concrete outside and splashed on his suit and onto his face. The acid burned the back of his throat and his body ached. He vomited again. This time he wiped the excess on his sleeve, then changed into a brand-new suit and returned.

Jake composed himself when he returned to the massacre a minute later.

'You good?' Drew asked him, slapping him jovially on the shoulder. 'This your first time?'

'Experiencing something as morbid as this, yeah,' Jake said.

'The first time's always the worst.'

'Always,' Liam echoed. 'You'll get used to it sooner or later. And if you don't... well, perhaps you're in the wrong place.'

Jake looked at Liam sternly. 'I'm not going anywhere. Just a couple more months to go and then I complete the training.'

'We'll see.' Liam turned to Poojah. 'What do we think happened here?'

'Your guess is as good as mine,' Poojah replied. 'Jessica and Steven were either interrupted during some alone time by happenstance, or this was some sort of threesome gone wrong.'

'I'd say this is about as far wrong as you can go,' Drew added.

'Who found them?' Liam asked.

'A woman named Elisa Talbet. She found them this morning when she came to speak with Steven about a painting she wanted to buy.'

'Where is she now?'

'With one of the uniform, answering some preliminary questions in the car. I think she wanted to get away from the rain for a bit.'

'OK.' Liam faced Drew. 'When we're done here, I want you to speak to her. And then get one of the team to take a statement.'

'Yes, sir.'

'Anything else you need to tell us?' Liam asked Poojah.

'We've seized Steven's laptop, mobile phone and a digital camera upstairs. They'll be sent away to IT forensics later.' Poojah paused and pointed to a camera stand beside the table. 'This one doesn't have a memory card in it, and we've not been able to recover it. So potentially whatever was on that one is now missing.'

'Whatever kinky things these guys were into, perhaps they weren't afraid of documenting it. I wish I could get my wife to do that,' Drew said, but nobody listened.

Poojah folded her arms across her chest. 'We've also found multiple semen and saliva deposits all over the bodies, as well as fingerprints about the place. I think whoever is responsible for this tried to clean up after themselves but didn't manage as thorough a job as they'd liked.'

Liam and Drew nodded. Liam was the first to speak. 'Estimated time of death?'

Poojah hesitated. 'Erm…'

'No rush.'

'It's difficult to say…'

'Want me to start doing your job for you?'

'Excuse me?'

'You need me to spell it out for you?'

Poojah huffed and placed her hands on her hips. 'My *estimate* is at least eight hours. Given the stage of decomposition the body is at – the purple blotches on the thighs and back, and the final stages of rigor – I'd say you're looking between 10 p.m. and 2 a.m. last night. But don't take that as gospel until I know more.'

'Maybe the killer decided to have some fun with them while they were dead,' Drew remarked.

Again, nobody paid him any heed. It was usually the way whenever Drew said something or even offered his opinion. It wasn't because people didn't like him – although Jake was sure there were people in the office that felt that way – it was because the things he said were generally inappropriate and unprofessional.

'Any eyewitnesses come forward other than Elisa?' Liam asked.

Poojah shook her head. 'That's your job,' she said, with a smirk.

Liam chuckled. In the months that Jake had been with Major Investigation, he'd learnt something important about Liam: that the man was charming and had the power to disarm anyone he was speaking to. Jake didn't know how he did it, but he had seen Liam get out of a handful of sticky situations in the past. Perhaps it was because he gave whoever he was talking to the chance to act superior, just as he'd done with Poojah now, acting as if she were in charge of the investigation, as if she was the one with all the information and the answers and the burden of trying to find the killer. Perhaps it was that disarmament that enabled him to speak to people any way he wanted.

'Thanks for your help, Poojah. You've been great,' he said.

'If there's anything else you need, you know where to find—'

'What's in the bag over there?' Jake asked, pointing to a gym bag on the floor by Steven's body. His outburst took all of them by surprise, and he looked at them apologetically, realising that he'd spoken out of turn.

'I'll give you a few guesses,' Poojah said. 'One of the items in there is Steven Arnholt's head. Another is his severed penis. Any other questions?' Poojah asked, and when there was no answer from either of them, she continued, 'If we find anything new, I'll be sure to keep you updated.'

Poojah gave them a small wave and then resumed her work by

Jessica's dead body. Jake gave it one final look, the image scarring his memory, before he climbed back up the stairs.

'What you thinking, guv?' Drew asked Liam as they returned to the gallery floor.

'I think some fucked-up stuff went on in there, Drew. That much I'm certain of. And I can't afford to lose another tie.'

Drew chuckled. 'You not got any loose change anymore?'

As soon as he'd said it, Liam's eyes bulged and then he quickly turned his attention to Jake.

'Tanner,' Liam continued, 'you're in charge of the house-to-house enquiries. Get yourself some experience doing that. See if anyone noticed anything, or if anyone has anything they want to talk to us about. OK? I'm trusting you.'

Jake nodded.

'I won't let you down, sir.'

CHAPTER 5

TENACITY

The doorbell sounded almost as loudly on the inside as it did on the outside. Jake held his pen and notebook at the ready, clutching it against his chest to protect it from the rain. He had already been to five other properties along the road and none of them had witnessed anything, none of them had heard anything, none of them were any the wiser that a murder had taken place a short distance from their house. And now that he was at the house furthest away from Steven Arnholt's gallery, it was looking less likely that he would return to Liam and Drew with anything at all.

The front door opened and he was greeted by a man wearing a grey Adidas tracksuit. Stains soiled the front of his trousers and the top of his hoodie. Whiffs of tobacco laced with a thin hint of marijuana stroked Jake's face. The man's lips were lined with a thin layer of black hair – the only sign of facial hair he had – and there was a large mole next to his left eye. His face was red and he looked flustered, as if Jake had just woken him up.

'Yes… Yes? How can… I help you?' the man stuttered, chewing on his fingernails.

Jake flashed his warrant card. 'I'm with the Major Investigation Team at Bow Green station, sir. We're investigating an incident concerning two individuals down at Arnholt Galleries.'

'Here?'

'Yes, sir. Might I ask you a few questions?'

'Bad, bad, bad,' the man replied. 'Don't like questions. Not supposed to answer questions.'

Jake pressed the pen to paper. 'That's fine, sir.' He scribbled the property number at the top of the page. 'They're nice and easy. And they won't take too long.' There was no response. 'How about we start with an easy one… What's your name?'

'Archie. Archie Arnold. Archie is my first name, and Arnold is my second name.'

Jake scribbled as he asked the next question. 'And do you live alone, sir?'

'Yes,' Archie said, glancing over his shoulder and into the house.

As Archie finished answering the question, a figure in the background moved from one room to another.

'Are you sure?' Jake asked, pointing towards the figure in the distance.

'Yes. Friend. She's a… a friend. Friend. Friend.'

The figure in the distance came into view. She wore a full face of make-up, a miniskirt, high heels and a blouse that was opened halfway down her chest, revealing her cleavage. A thick streak of red flashed through her hair. She grabbed a handbag from the floor and hurried out of the door, keeping her head low and her hair over her face. Jake stepped aside to allow her through. As she scurried past him, he caught a glimpse of a tattoo on the underside of her wrist. It looked like a barcode, and underneath it was a number inscribed on her skin. Nine.

'A fond friend, is she?' Jake asked, finding some amusement in the situation. He struggled to suppress a wayward smirk.

'I found her at a phone box!' Archie said, his demeanour immediately becoming defensive and afraid. Jake noticed his eyes widening slightly.

'Excuse me?' Jake asked.

'I'm sorry. Don't tell anyone. Please don't tell anyone. I met her at a phone box. Diamond Geezers. Friend. On the corner of High Street and Carpenters Road. Don't tell anyone. Don't tell Diamond Geezers.'

'You've lost me.'

'Sorry. I'm sorry. Sorry.' Archie scratched the side of his head and continued chewing his nails. 'What did you… Why are you… Bad. Arnholt Galleries? Steven… Jessica…'

'Ah! Yes,' Jake said, readying his pen on paper, forgetting everything Archie had just told him. 'Are you friends, or familiar, with either Steven or Jessica Arnholt from Arnholt Galleries, sir?'

'Are they OK?'

'I'm afraid I'm not at liberty to say yet, sir.' Jake chided himself.

'How long have you lived in the area?'

'Years. Many years. Lots of years. Nice house.'

'Did you ever have any interaction with either of them?'

Archie shook his head.

'Speak to them in the street? Say hello? Wave at them?'

Archie shook his head again.

'Did you see anything suspicious last night? Any sounds that might have disturbed you after 10 p.m.?'

Archie nodded. 'Yes. Something. Loud. Very loud. Really loud.'

'What?' Jake said, a glimmer of hope flowing through him.

Archie hesitated before responding. 'Man. Little girl. He was black. She was white. Looked bad. Don't like bad things.'

Jake sighed silently. He was running headfirst into a dead end.

'Thank you for your time, sir,' Jake said, underlining Archie's name on his rain-splattered notebook.

'Friend.'

Jake reached into his pocket and produced a business card. 'If you remember anything, give me a call. Or email. I'm available all the time.'

'Weekends?' Archie said.

'Including weekends,' Jake replied with a forced smile.

'Good. Friend.' Archie sniffed Jake's business card and closed the door.

For a while, Jake stood there, unsure how to make sense of what had just happened. He had given five business cards out already, and out of all of them, Archie had been the most unusual recipient. There was something so perplexing about the man that Jake couldn't quite place his finger on. His appearance? No. His attitude? No. His mannerisms? Perhaps. Jake didn't know, but he knew it was a lost cause trying to figure it out.

Closing his pocketbook, Jake turned his back on Archie's house and started towards Liam and Drew. Both senior officers were talking to a young woman who wore a light purple, skintight hoodie and jeans. She was jittery, constantly moving from side to side, and she rubbed her arms fervently. By the time Jake arrived, Liam and Drew were finishing up.

'Please wait for one of our colleagues to take you back to the station,' Liam said, shaking the woman's hand and passing her one of his own business cards. Beneath it, reflecting the sunlight that was just beginning to break through the cloud, was the zero of a ten-pound note.

'Who's that?' Jake asked.

'The witness,' Drew said.

'Any luck?'

Drew shrugged. 'Not much. She found them dead in that room

when she realised the door had been left open. She wandered in, saw them and came straight back out again. We were the first people she called. And her alibi checks out – she showed us the emails between her and Steven about organising the viewing of a piece of his artwork. But I'll speak with her when we get back to the station.'

Jake nodded. Then he watched Elisa wander over to a police car on the other side of the outer cordon. As she walked, her head darted from left to right and she continuously rubbed her forearm and the back of her neck furiously.

'Is she all right? She doesn't look it.'

'Her?' Liam said, stepping in Jake's field of view. 'No. Probably just nervous. Shock.' He extended his hand and took Jake's notebook from him. He leafed through the pages. 'Any luck with the H-to-H?'

Jake shook his head. 'Nothing useful, guv. Just some guy telling me about how he saw a little girl walking with a man. Oh, and I think he might have had a prostitute in his house when I got there.'

'You get a lot of that here,' Drew said, pointing to the row of houses on the street opposite. 'And drugs. They love them. That's the problem with these types of places, being so close to the estates. They've got so many distractions.'

'Could this be drug-related?' Jake asked, thinking aloud.

Both men looked at him perplexed.

'You saw the bodies in there, right? No drugs have been recovered, and that certainly isn't your typical drug kill,' Liam began. 'Don't worry about it. We'll find something.'

Jake didn't like to dismiss it straight away, but it made sense.

'What now?' he asked, taking the notebook back and clasping it tightly.

'I want you to head back to the station. Help Garrison set up the MIR. You can be our eyes and ears back at HQ. Anything comes in, you let us know straight away, OK?'

'And what about you two, sir?'

'DS Richmond and I will be responding to your calls. We'll take care of the interviews, don't worry,' Liam explained.

Jake cleared his throat before responding. 'With all due respect, sir, if it's all the same to you, I'd rather not. I'd much rather get out there and speak to friends and family. Maybe help you as FLO. I'm not going to learn anything or develop if I'm sat behind a desk all day.'

'Or you could go back to the station and do as you're told,' Drew interjected.

Just as Drew was about to continue his tirade, Liam held him back, an arm pressed against his chest.

'I can deal with this, thanks, Drew,' Liam said.

Jake felt his shoulders relax slightly. He had been meaning to get that off his chest. He hated doing nothing – or, at least, for it to look like he was doing nothing. He wanted to be out on the front line. Making a difference. Solving crimes.

'I admire your tenacity, Jake,' Liam said, holding a finger in the air. 'You've got balls. I think it would be good for you to join in on some of the fun stuff. Drew, I want you to go back to the station and bring us up to speed on everything. Get one of the uniforms to take you back along with Elisa. We'll stay here until then. Jake – would you mind going back to the gallery quickly? I just want to speak with Drew for a moment.'

'Of course, sir. Thank you, sir.' Jake wandered off, a smile widening on his face.

CHAPTER 6

TEST THE WATERS

There was something so harmless and inoffensive about Jake Tanner that it instantly made Drew suspicious of him. Perhaps it was the fact that he'd trusted almost no one in the fifteen years he'd been a police officer – and those people he *did* trust, he could count on one hand: Liam and Pete. Or perhaps it was the fact that, in his years of experience, he'd learnt to distrust the good cops, the ones who tried hard at everything they did, because they always had an ulterior motive. He had come close to being accused of being a bent cop in the past, and he would do everything in his power to make sure it didn't happen again.

Drew watched Jake wander off, waiting until his colleague was out of earshot. He gave a quick recce of those around him and made sure he couldn't be heard by anyone.

Then he shoved Liam on the arm.

'Are you serious?'

'What?' Liam replied abruptly.

'You're going to let him get in on this? Why's he piping up all of a sudden?'

Liam raised his finger in the air and pressed it into Drew's chest, instantly dismissing him.

'I've been forced to change the shift patterns so there's more crossover with his and ours. And I never said he was getting *in* on anything. He's just helping with our lines of enquiry. You know, the job you *used* to do.'

'It's too close to home, Liam. What if he starts getting curious and ruins everything?'

'He won't. I'll make sure of it.'

'How?'

'You don't need to know how.'

'I do when it concerns me. I don't want to get another grilling.'

'It concerns you just as much as it does me.'

'We came too close last time.'

'Of all people, I think I know that the most. Trust me, all right?'

Drew stopped as a uniformed officer swaggered past them. He waited until the man had disappeared before continuing.

As he spoke, he kept his eyes on Jake, who was busy talking to a SOCO, writing notes in his pocketbook as he did so.

'You reckon he suspects anything?'

'No. He's not had the time to. Besides, look at him... he's like fucking Bambi. Innocent. He doesn't have a fucking clue what he's doing.'

Drew scratched his head. 'He might have been watching us. Listening in. Reporting.'

'Reporting to who?'

Drew shrugged and massaged his chin to calm himself down. 'I don't know. Anyone. The IPCC.'

'Shut up – you're being paranoid.'

Liam paused to observe Drew. He felt Liam's searching eyes like needles all over his skin. Was that just an off-the-cuff remark, or did Liam know the reason behind his paranoia?

'Have you been using again?'

'No,' Drew lied.

'Because you know that if there's anything that connects us to Steven and Jessica's murder, then we're both done for. All right?'

Drew held his hands in the air.

'Relax. Relax. I'm clean, all right? It's just...' He pointed at Jake. 'He's making me on edge. For weeks he's been hiding in the background and now a big case comes up, all of a sudden he wants in.'

'It's fine. Leave him with me.'

'Can he be trusted?' Drew asked.

'We'll have to test the waters. That way, we'll find out.'

CHAPTER 7

GOLDEN SHMOLDEN

Images of Jessica Arnholt's mangled and dismembered body lying upon the table haunted Jake. He closed his eyes in an attempt to eradicate them, but it was no use. They were permanently etched into his brain, stained in indelible ink that even the most powerful form of therapy wouldn't remove.

Jake and Liam were stationed outside the Arnholt Gallery. They had left the SOCOs to do their job while they waited for Drew to do his. It took a long time for him to get back to the station and pass on the address for Steven Arnholt's parents. Apparently there had been an issue with the computer systems at the station and Drew had needed to wait till someone from IT fixed it for him.

'According to the bloke it was just a case of switching it off and on again,' Drew said on loudspeaker just as Liam ignited the engine.

'You can be a complete tit sometimes,' Liam said, pulling out onto the main road and swinging left.

He hung up and switched on the sirens.

Jake and Liam sat in silence for most of the journey. Not out of choice; Jake had wanted to speak with his boss – get to know him a little better – but even though Liam had taken his side with Drew, it hadn't changed how intimidating Jake found him. That, and the fact Liam was the type of guy who would only permit someone to talk to him so long as he spoke to them first. And if anyone tried to deviate from that pattern, he would scold them for it.

It took them less than ten minutes to drive to Steven's parents' address, a few miles down the road from the crime scene. That was a luxury Jake could appreciate – his own mum's house was about fifteen minutes from his. Not too far in case of emergency, not so close she'd be over all the time. And that was just the way Jake liked it.

Liam slowed the car to a halt outside the Arnholts' drive and pulled the keys out of the ignition. As they paced towards the door, Jake noticed Liam hadn't locked the vehicle.

'Sir,' he said, pointing to the car.

'We shouldn't be here too long. I doubt they'll be much help anyway. Plus, I mean, look at it.' Liam fanned his arms around the vicinity; the road was littered with expensive cars and motorbikes that looked like advertisements for German engineering, 'I can't see anyone round here trying to rob my shitheap, can you?'

Jake shrugged.

'I want you to lead this one, Jake. I'll step in if there's any issues, all right?'

'What?'

'You're the one who wanted to get some experience under his belt, right?'

Jake nodded. 'Right.'

'Then this is all on you.'

Jake exhaled deeply as Liam knocked on the door, and together they waited. Jake stood with his hands folded in front of him by his waist, slowly breathing away the nerves. Giving death messages -- telling someone that their relative had just passed away and that they were never going to see them again – was one of the hardest parts of the job. It was a torment that he hoped he never had to endure personally. Elizabeth, his wife, had always told him that that was the one thing she dreaded every day when he was at work: the dignified ring of the doorbell, the solemn-faced police officer standing in front of her, the tenor of his voice as he informed her that Jake was dead and that she was left to raise her child – soon to be children – alone. The thought made him check his phone. He thought he'd felt it vibrate. False alarm.

As he pocketed the device, Jake chewed on his bottom lip, wondering how he should pass on the news. He knew how he'd want it: hard and fast, like ripping off a plaster. With all the facts. That way there would be no time for his mind to process the information and allow his emotions to get the better of him.

The front door opened and there, dwarfed by the white door, was Steven Arnholt's mother. She was wearing a patterned blouse with thick black buttons. Her hair was parted down the middle and her face rouged with make-up, her fingernails matching the colours of her lips: bright pink.

'Mrs Arnholt?' Jake asked, flashing his warrant card.

As soon as she saw the emblem on his badge, her face dropped. Carefully, almost cautiously, she nodded.

'May we come in?' Jake asked.

'Y-Yes. Of course.' Mrs Arnholt stepped aside to allow them through. She was visibly shaking, and Jake waited in the lobby for her to close the door behind them. 'This way p-please.'

A sound came from overhead. 'Who is it, sweetie?' Footsteps rushed above and then down the stairs. They stopped as soon as Jake and Liam came into view.

Jake had his ID at the ready. 'Good afternoon, sir. We're from Bow Green Major Investigation Team.'

'Is this about Steven?'

'I think it's best if we sit down, sir.' Jake turned to Mrs Arnholt. 'Ma'am.'

'Please, call me Julie. And he's Tristan.'

Jake nodded and followed Julie into the living room. Three sofas circled the forty-inch television that hung on the wall. There was a large coffee table with a vase of lilies positioned in the middle. Jake sat down. To his left was a row of patio doors that led out to the garden. From where he sat, he could see a wooden chair swing by the back fence.

'Can I get you both a drink?' Julie asked as Tristan sat opposite them both. 'Tea? Coffee?'

'I'm fine, thank—'

'Coffee. Please. Three sugars. Lots of milk,' Liam said, smiling.

Jake shot him a look filled with disdain.

'Sure,' Julie said shyly. 'I won't be a moment.'

She was right. Less than a minute later she returned with three mugs on a tray. Jake was grateful to see her; the silence between the three of them had been awkward and he was beginning to run out of things to look at. Julie placed Liam's mug in his hand and set the rest on the coffee table.

'So…' Tristan began. 'What is it we can help you with, officers?'

Julie's hand found Tristan's on his lap and squeezed.

'Mr and Mrs Arnholt, there's no easy way for me to say this…' This was it. This was the moment he delivered the devastating news that he hoped, as a parent, he would never have to receive himself. 'Steven and Jessica were murdered last night in Steven's gallery.'

Julie gasped in shock and threw her hands to her mouth. Tristan massaged his hands together, fighting the emotions behind his tear-filled eyes.

'I'm terribly sorry to have to give you this news. And I know it's a lot to take in, but there are a few questions we'd like to ask.'

Julie tried to speak, but her words were extinguished by pain and grief. On the arm of the chair beside him, Jake saw a box of tissues. He reached across and handed them to Julie.

'Thanks,' she said, grabbing one and dabbing her eye delicately so as not to disturb her make-up.

'H-H-How did...' Tristan trailed off. 'How did it happen?'

'I'm afraid that's not entirely clear to us at the present moment.' Jake reached into the breast pocket of his blazer and produced his notebook. 'I was wondering if you could tell me about Steven and Jessica's relationship? How long had they known each other?'

'About... seven years or so, I think. They met on holiday in the States. Steven was out there for work. He had just sold a painting to a gallery in New York and invited us over to celebrate.'

'So you met her there as well?'

Tristan nodded, and Jake made a note in his book.

'And... how long have they been married for?'

'Nearly five years,' Julie added, clutching the tissue paper in her hands. 'He proposed to her in New York.'

'Nice,' Jake said.

Beside him, Liam leant forward and placed his empty mug on the coffee table. Jake could smell the acrid stench of coffee on the man's breath.

'What were your first impressions of Jessica?'

'Lovely,' both of them replied at the same time.

'There wasn't a bad bone in her body. She always treated us with so much respect and kindness. We always loved having her come round – both of them!' Julie broke into another flurry of tears. This time she cared little for her make-up and smeared it across her face. By the time she was finished, black shadows had bloomed underneath her eyes, making her look like The Joker.

'Did Steven mention anything to you about what he was doing last night?'

Tristan shook his head. 'The last time we spoke to him was last week or so.'

'Can you think of anyone who might want to hurt him? Any art deals he may have done in the past that had gone wrong or where someone didn't get the bargain they'd hoped for?'

Tristan shook his head.

'Did he ever mention feeling threatened by anyone? Did he ever say anything about someone following him or wanting to...?' Jake let the sentence hang in the air, allowing Tristan and Julie to finish it for themselves.

'No. No,' Julie said, her words laced with turmoil. 'No one. Nobody would want to hurt our precious Steven. He was kind and generous and loving and so helpful to everyone he met.'

Jake continued to write in his book as Julie spoke, looking up at her intermittently to demonstrate to her that he was still listening. As he scribbled, he felt his phone vibrate against his leg. He pulled the device out and stared at the screen. Nothing. Another false alarm.

'The only trouble Steven would ever get himself into was at school when he didn't do his work. Now he's an adult. He doesn't do any of those sorts of things. He's sensible,' Tristan added. Jake didn't know whether Steven's dad was being naïve on purpose, or whether that was something he truly believed, but Jake made a note of it nonetheless.

Julie grabbed for the box of tissues, realised they were all gone and stood up to get some more.

'Julie!' Liam said, leaning forward to grab his empty mug. 'If you wouldn't mind, I'd love to have another coffee, if that's all right. I'm feeling really thirsty for some reason. Same again please.'

Julie's face contorted in shock as she slowly reached out to take the mug from Liam. Jake stared at his senior in disbelief. What was he playing at? Inviting himself another drink like that? Did he have any sense of decorum or respect?

'Of course…' Julie hesitated. 'Three sugars, wasn't it?'

'That's the one. And lots of milk.' Liam leant back into the chair and placed his ankle on his knee.

Jake opened his mouth, but the words were stolen from him. He looked at Tristan as if to say, 'I'm sorry for my colleague's behaviour', and then he cleared his throat. 'As I was saying…' He hesitated, losing his train of thought. 'I… I have to ask you this because it's pertinent to the circumstances surrounding his death… but did Steven – or Jessica – ever mention any particular interests they had?'

'What?

'Did they… ever declare any sexual fantasies they had? Did they ever open up to you about that sort of stuff?'

Jake sucked in his breath as the shock registered on Tristan's face and, out of awkwardness, he pressed at his phone's home button, just to check it again. Still nothing.

'Do you have children, Officer?' Tristan asked.

'Yeah,' Jake said. 'One.'

'How old?'

'Two.'

'So you've not had to deal with them growing up yet?'

Jake shook his head and scratched the small scar on the side of his face – the one that stopped any hair from growing around it.

'Well, let me tell you something then,' Tristan began. 'Perhaps as a word of advice. As a parent, I cannot think of any conceivable situation where you might ask your child what they like to do in the bedroom – where they like to do it and how they like to do it. That's between a man and his wife, and it should stay that way. No! Of course they didn't tell us anything like that, because that's a deeply personal thing. If you force your children to share those sorts of details with you, I don't think you should be a father.'

Julie returned with another mug of coffee and Jake watched her place it down on the table. He squirmed as he repeated in his head the question he'd just asked.

'I... I'm sorry.' Jake pulled his phone out again, hoping, praying that there was a notification that would pull him out of this awkwardness. But there was still nothing. 'I think we've got everything we need—'

'Yeah. I agree. It's time for you to leave,' Tristan said, almost animated, his arms communicating as loudly as his voice.

Jake lifted himself off the sofa and pocketed his possessions. Liam downed what he could of the coffee before rising to his feet. Then he brushed himself down and led the way out. Jake apologised to both Julie and Tristan again, gave them his condolences and then left their house.

As Liam and Jake returned to the car, Jake couldn't help feeling terrible. And angry. Not at Julian and Tristan – no, their behaviour was completely warranted – but at Liam. He was acting almost childish, insolent.

'Seriously, guv?' Jake said, closing the door behind him.

'What?'

'The coffee. Really? *Two* cups.'

Liam slipped the keys into the ignition and started the car up. 'You see, Jake, there are a few things you still need to learn. The most important being that people will take you, as a police officer, for granted, so you have to take a few of their things for granted also. Case in point: people abhor us when the media or social media says we're doing something bad, or that we've not been performing up to their exceptionally high expectations of us. But people will crave us and love us when they need us. When their house gets burgled. When they need us to find their missing child. Nobody thinks they'll ever need our help – Christ, nobody purposely *wants* it – but they only appreciate us when they pick up that phone, dial 999 and we come running to help them. So, now and then, you have to take back what you can – you have to make the most of those few opportunities.'

'Like drinking all their coffee?'

'Precisely.' Liam slipped the car into first gear. 'I'd have taken a couple of snacks if she'd offered them to us. But you've got to start small, and then work your way up.'

Jake scoffed. He'd never heard of such blatant disregard for the Code of Ethics that they, as police officers, were supposed to live by. It was unfathomable.

'I... I don't know what to say. How can you... What about the Codes?' He paused a beat. 'How long have you been an officer?'

'Ever since you were a little boy, son.' Something changed in Liam's expression: his face straightened and he pointed a finger at Jake. 'You don't need to lecture me on the Code of Ethics. I've seen them and studied them for long enough to know what they are. Besides, you weren't exactly as holy as can be either.'

'What do you mean?' Jake asked, pulling out his phone to check it again.

'*That*,' Liam said, pointing at Jake's mobile. 'You were on it non-stop. Checking it every few seconds. Hardly makes the public feel confident in us, does it, if you aren't even listening?'

Jake looked down at the phone in his hands. The screen illuminated again, but it was just a Twitter notification.

'Sorry,' he said. 'It's just that Elizabeth, my wife... She's pregnant. We're due in the next couple of weeks, and I've been keeping an eye on my messages in case she goes into labour and I need to be with her.'

Liam's face lit up and he shook Jake's hand.

'Pregnant? That's excellent, mate. Congratulations. Well done. Good to see the old swimmers are working all right – or, in your case, young swimmers. I'm really pleased for you. Why didn't you say anything earlier?'

'I... I... There was an email about it the other month...'

'Mustn't have got it. Must have slipped through the net. Never mind. Right, well, I know where we're headed next,' Liam said, pulling away from the kerb.

'Where?'

'Pub with the boys. We'll round them up on the way. We'll go to one of my favourite locals. To celebrate.'

Jake's mouth fell open. 'But what about Steven and Jessica Arnholt? There's still a mountain of work to do.'

Liam dismissed him with a wave of the hand. 'It'll be all right. I'm the SIO, MLO, FLO and EO, so I make the decisions, and whatever I say goes. If anything goes tits up, it's on me. And there's nothing we can do about it now anyway. Forensics will take a while to come in, and when they do, that's when we'll kick ourselves into action.'

'But what about the golden—?'

Liam moved his hand closer to Jake's face, cutting him off. 'Golden shmolden. You don't need to worry about that right now. I

37

can tell you're a little tensed up and in need of a heavy drink. Correct me if I'm wrong?'

Jake remained silent, more out of disbelief than choosing to answer Liam's question.

'Then it's sorted,' Liam continued. 'We'll find the killer. All in good time.'

He stopped at a set of traffic lights. 'You're a good egg, Jake. We like good eggs in MIT. Not bad eggs. We don't have any time for bad eggs. If you want to become part of the team – *properly* – then we need you to be a good egg. Understood?'

Jake hesitated for a moment. This was what he'd been waiting for – a chance to feel like part of the team – and Liam was handing it to him on a plate.

Jake nodded before he reached out and grabbed it.

CHAPTER 8

ROVER

The pub was called The Head of the House. Jake had been there once before, when he was a testosterone-fuelled eighteen-year-old on a pub crawl with the rest of his university friends from the Ski and Snow social club. It had been the final stage of a journey that had seen them crawl the length of London from west to east – which had then left them all with the burden of trying to get home to the UCL campus in central London. But for Jake, the night was a blur. He had drunk far too much in a short space of time and had forced the group to cut their night short. All he could remember was that the drinks here were cheaper than anywhere else and they tasted ten times stronger. And he would always remember that morning after where he'd nursed the worst hangover of his adult life.

Liam and Jake were waiting at the bar. Jake rested his arms on the counter and then instantly lifted them off. It was sticky and damp, rings of beer and alcohol mixer soiling the surface.

'What you having?' Liam asked him as he flagged down the bartender.

'No, no. It's fine, guv. I can't drink.'

'Why not?'

'I'm driving—'

'Bullshit!'

'And I've got Elizabeth—'

'You can treat yourself to one, at least. Come on, Jake. You've earned it. I respect people who put themselves forward like you did today. Too many people expect things to come to them, but you went out and grabbed it. Consider this a part of the initiation on your first outing with the lads.'

Jake hesitated for a moment. A part of him – a big part – wanted to have a drink. He was thirsty, he hadn't had one in a while and he wanted to take the edge off a little bit. It had been a disturbing and stressful day. But he knew the dangers of drinking on the job. At first, it was just the one. Then, as the workload and stresses began to mount, one bottle was close on the heels of another. Followed by another. And another. He didn't want that to happen; he had a family and a loving wife to care for. Not only that, but he knew Elizabeth would berate him for spending money they didn't have fuelling an unhealthy and debilitating addiction.

The bartender arrived in front of him and Jake snapped himself to attention.

'Afternoon, Maggie,' Liam said.

'All right, Liam. Who's this then?'

'Jake. Some fresh meat for you.'

Maggie smirked, flashing a set of brown bottom teeth. 'I like 'em fresh. At least his face will make a welcome change to Drew and Pete's ugly mugs.'

Liam and Maggie chuckled to one another, but after a few seconds, the laughter died down and she focused her attention on Jake again. 'What you having then, newbie?'

'Foster's please,' he said, swallowing.

'Two pints of piss for the fresh meat and a Guinness for the old meat, coming up.'

'Two?' Jake asked, looking at his manager, his brow creased.

'Tradition. The first round is always double when it's your first outing with us,' Liam said, tilting his head at the freshly poured pint of Foster's Maggie had placed in front of them.

The liquid fizzed and small bubbles spat out at the top. Maggie placed another glass beside the first. Liam paid and then they headed to the nearest table.

'When is everyone else coming?' Jake asked.

As they rounded the side of the bar, he got his answer.

'Guv!' somebody shouted from behind them.

It was Drew, seated with some of the Major Investigation Team and a couple of the guys from Missing Persons. They each had a beer in their hand and, after Jake made a quick count at the empty glasses on the table, he realised they were already one drink down.

Jake and Liam wandered to the table and sat next to one another. Beside Jake was DS Richard Clifton, a bald man – out of choice rather than anything hereditary – with a bottom lip that stuck out further than his top. He was a member of the Missing Person Team, and from what Jake had experienced of him around the building, he was a calm and respectable human being. For a start, he was the only one who seemed to make a conscious effort to talk to him in the lift or sometimes in the canteen, or – and Jake thought it odd every time he remembered this – in the bathroom.

'Congratulations, fella!' Clifton said, shaking Jake's hand. His breath was dampened with the smell of alcohol.

Everyone else around the table congratulated him, raising their glasses in the air.

Drew, seated opposite, leant into the middle of the table and grabbed a full glass of stout. 'Sorry, Liam. We didn't realise you'd already ordered, so we got you your usual.' He placed the glass in front of Liam, spilling some of the contents over the side, then looked to Jake and said, 'We didn't know what you'd like, so we got you a Stella.'

'You're going home to your wife after this, right?' Garrison asked, holding a glass a few centimetres under his lips.

The table erupted with laughter and Jake found himself chuckling too. It wasn't his usual banter, but if he was going to fit in, he was aware he'd have to make a sacrifice or two. Jake took a sip of the drink, avoiding any opportunity to answer the rhetorical question. Fortunately for him, someone else responded.

'You can tell McVitie's on the drink again,' Drew said.

They called him Pete 'McVitie's' Garrison because his favourite brand of biscuits was McVitie's. At every opportunity, he would have a packet of digestives or hobnobs either on his desk or in his hands. From Jake's observation, it was the only nickname any of them had for one another.

'It's easy for him to talk about wife beaters when he's the one who's going to die alone,' Clifton said.

Garrison shot Clifton the finger.

'I'll be retiring before you've even got your dick wet again, son,' Garrison said.

The group erupted.

'Here we go,' Drew said, rolling his eyes. 'Retiring. Retiring. Retiring. You don't fucking shut up about it. It's re-*tiring* for the rest of us.'

Garrison ignored the jibe and turned his attention to Jake.

'Come on, mate,' he said. 'You've got three to finish now. You're not leaving until you've downed them all.'

'I'll be here all night,' Jake said, before taking a long swig of his first. By the time he put it back on the table, less than half the glass remained. The sudden intake of alcohol sent his head spinning.

'So,' Liam began, touching him on the back. 'When's the due date?'

'Twenty-eighth, sir.'

'Got a name?'

Jake shook his head.

'My mum was called Ellie,' Liam began. 'Delightful woman. Best you've ever met. And I mean that. Absolute trooper. She wouldn't take anything from anyone. She had a fire inside her, but she had a soft side to her as well. Something to think about.'

'I'll think about it, guv,' Jake said, taking another swig.

'Come on, Jake. We're off duty now. There's no need for that *sir* and *guv* bullshit. If I like you enough, I might let you drop it completely. Perhaps I'll even let you call me by my nickname.'

'Nickname? I didn't know you had one,' Jake responded.

'Rover,' Drew added, taking another sip. 'Lunar rover. Mars rover. He's into space and all that. Aliens. Star Trek. Star Wars. Oh, and he always dreams about owning a Range.'

'Thanks for that, Drew,' Liam said, scowling at him for the outburst. 'One day you'll be able to call me that, Jake. Christ knows it took Richmond a long enough time.'

'Gradually breaking down those barriers.' Drew winked.

'I'd aged by a few years at that point. I just decided to give in, in the end.' Liam hesitated. 'Is this your first child?'

'Second.'

'Many congratulations to you,' Garrison said. He lifted his beer in the middle of the table and called for a cheer. Everyone gave one, and the rest of the patrons inside The Head of the House turned to face them. Jake could feel their judgemental looks slicing into him, but he didn't care; he was enjoying the banter and camaraderie with his new-found colleagues and friends.

Garrison downed his pint and slammed it on the table upside down. 'Jake, do you know what I've just realised.'

'What?' Jake replied, suddenly feeling anxious. His mind raced and tried to think of things he'd done wrong recently… if any.

'This is your first time down here with the rest of us… and Drew. Do you know what that means?'

Jake didn't respond.

'It's time for twenty-one questions. This way we'll get to know the real Jake Tanner.'

Oh, God, Jake thought, preparing himself for a barrage of embarrassing and, he assumed, deeply personal probes.

Drew was the first to go. 'How long have you been a police officer?'

Almost instantly, his question was met with a cacophony of deep groans and complaints.

'That's a shit one, you tit,' Garrison said. Jake was beginning to learn that he was the loudest – as well as the eldest – of the group. The patriarchal one. The father figure. The one who, despite the lower rank, kept everyone on the straight and narrow.

'What?' Drew replied defensively. 'It's important.'

'Go home,' Liam shouted. 'You're shit at this. Nobody let him back in please. I've got one: what's your deepest darkest secret?'

The table went silent, save for the sounds of Clifton's heavy and wheezy breathing.

Jake paused for dramatic effect. He knew the answer straight away, and he had no intention of telling any of them.

'They call it a secret for a reason.'

'Give over!' Liam said, rolling his eyes and leaning back in his chair in disgust. 'You've got to tell us something. You could lie and we wouldn't even know. Although…' He leant closer to Jake. 'I'm exceptionally well trained in the art of deceit. And I can tell if someone's lying to me. Consider this your first warning.'

Liam's gaze remained fixed on Jake, and Jake was unable to tear his eyes from him. He didn't doubt for a second that Liam was lying, and that his warning was entirely credible.

'I've got one,' Garrison said, bringing Jake's attention back to the table. 'What's your biggest fear?'

'Failing my family,' he said instantly. 'Not being able to provide for them. Everything I do is for them. Everything. They're my world, and I won't stop until they're happy and provided for.'

'You two been practising these questions or something?' Garrison asked, wagging his finger in the air between Jake and Liam. 'It's just that your answer seems to be well prepared.'

'Like fuck we have,' Liam said, jumping to Jake's defence. 'The man knows what he wants in life. That's good—'

'No, no,' Drew added. 'That's not what we asked. That's a different question entirely.' He swallowed a mouthful of beer before continuing. 'What do you want in life, Jake?'

Jake was stumped. He hadn't thought about it. Well, he had. But not deeply. He knew on a superficial level that he wanted all the nice things – toys, cars, house, pet – but on a deeper, personal level… he hadn't thought it through.

'I suppose…' Jake said. He needed to be honest, not only with himself, but with Liam and the rest of the team if they were to accept him as one of their own. 'I suppose I want justice. My dad died in a car crash when I was fifteen. He crashed into a tree. Dead instantly. But someone else was to blame. They jumped out in front of him, caused him to swerve. But they were never prosecuted or anything. We were just left to survive without him, a massive hole in all our lives.' Jake needed a sip and so took one. Everyone around him paid attention. 'That's why I want to be out there on the front line. That's why I want to be able to stop people from hurting other people, like I did with The Crimsons.'

A moment of silence fell over the group as they drank from their glasses. All except one. Garrison.

'Haven't you heard?' he asked quietly, as though speaking any louder would rouse the armed robbers from their invisible hiding places.

'Heard what?'

'The Crimsons... Danny and Michael... their trial... it's all falling through.'

Jake froze; his body turned cold and he became deaf to the ambient sounds of laughter and chatter around the bar. Then he swallowed, his mouth dry. Images of Danny and Michael Cipriano flashed in his mind. Their faces. Mocking him. Laughing at him for all the hard work and effort he'd put into arresting them, only to have it overturned less than twelve months later.

'You're – you're joking, aren't you? I mean... I...'

'I thought you'd have heard?'

Jake shook his head.

'Yeah,' Garrison continued, 'I don't know the ins and outs of it, but they're getting let out of remand. Think it has something to do with CPS... I heard they're not offering any evidence on Friday's court hearing. Wouldn't be surprised if they somehow managed to bribe a couple of the jurors in advance as well. I've heard a lot of bad things about them – both those in Surrey Police and the Cipriano brothers.'

Jake shook his head in disbelief. He was lost for words.

'Sorry to be the bearer of bad news there, mate.' Garrison paused; beside him, Drew burped and a cloud of yeasty breath floated towards Jake's face. 'I know you fought hard to nick 'em and get 'em locked up.'

'It's fine,' Jake said. He finished off his drink and placed it on the table, then checked his watch. It was six thirty. Where had the past hour gone? Paranoid, Jake looked at his phone. There was a message alert from Elizabeth on the home screen. Panicking that it might be something important, he opened the message and read. She just wanted to know when he was coming home. He sent a response telling her he was on his way.

Jake lifted himself up, staggered as the alcohol rushed to his head and leant on the back of the chair for support.

'You all right, mate?' Liam asked.

'Yeah.' Jake nodded. 'Yeah. I'm going. The missus is calling. Sorry. I'll – I'll see you later. *Tomorrow.*'

'Are you OK to drive?'

Jake gave the thumbs up. 'Never better.'

He said his goodbyes and then wandered to the car. His mind was awash with concern. He couldn't shake the images of Danny and Michael Cipriano – the men he'd fought hard to capture – and how, soon, they would be free to roam the streets like normal civilised human beings.

As he stepped outside, a rush of cold air slapped him in the face. It was then that he realised he was in no fit state to sit in the driver's seat, let alone drive, so he hailed a cab. On the journey home, he made a vow.

It was a simple one – one that he wasn't going to drop until it was completed.

Jake was going to send The Crimsons back to where they'd come from.

CHAPTER 9

MEDICAL ASSISTANCE

An incense candle burned beside him, its orange tip receding further and further down the stick. Wisps of smoke clawed and sank in the air, seemingly at random, as the air around him shifted.

Lester was in his dining room, sitting at the table. In the kitchen behind him, a microwaveable chilli con carne was heating up. The repetitive sound of the plastic container bumping into the machine's window slowly grated on him.

Lester inhaled, breathing in the sweetly scented air. Camomile. His favourite. He had bought himself a selection once as a treat, and after burning through all of them, he'd decided this daisy-like smell was the best. Now, whenever he went to the shops for supplies and provisions, he only ever bought that strand. After every Communion, he would burn one. It was a part of the ritual he'd created after his first ever experience in The Community. But tonight was different. Since he'd slaughtered Jessica and Steven, he'd burned four, non-stop. It helped soothe him, cleanse him, rid him of what he liked to call 'The Nasties'.

The microwave pinged, and Lester removed his dinner and threw it onto a plate, oblivious to the searing heat on his fingers, then grabbed a knife and fork and returned to the table. He opened his laptop beside him and opened up TorBrowser. Once the connection to the private server was made – finally linking him with the Dark Web and all its illicit activity – Lester loaded another piece of software called TorSearch. It was riddled with every manner of depraved activity. Terrorism. Human trafficking. Paedophilia. All of which Lester had no intention of becoming involved in. But the Dark Web was host to his second home, the lifestyle he'd adopted after stumbling across it by accident one afternoon: The Community.

But before he could allow himself to delve into the website, he had some tasks he needed to complete. The first: eat. He hadn't eaten anything since before his meeting with Steven and Jessica, and he was ravenous. He turned his attention to his microwaved meal, scoffed it within a few minutes and then placed the empty plate next to his laptop, wiping his mouth clean with the back of his hand.

Next on the list was to make a call to S. It had been a long time since he'd spoken to his friend, and he was eager to speak with him again. Lester removed his phone from his pocket and dialled.

The phone rang. And rang. And rang. Until eventually there was a response.

'Lester,' the voice on the other end said. It was weak and raspy.

'S,' Lester replied. The sound of S's voice excited him.

'I was expecting to have heard from you by now.'

'Something came up.'

'Oh?'

'I've been hiding all day. I couldn't risk calling you too soon.'

There was a pause.

'How was it?'

Lester licked his lips as he inhaled deeply. He thought of what had happened less than twenty-four hours ago. Steven. Jessica. Her body. Her head. Her cunt. Her skin. Her blood. Her flesh. It titillated him. His body tingled.

'Perfect,' Lester replied. 'Couldn't have gone any better.'

'You have evidence?'

'Yes. A video of the entire thing.'

'Did it last long?' S asked.

'Like you wouldn't believe. A few hours. The longest it's ever been. It was the purest experience of my life.'

That was true. It had been, and since then, he'd been trying to relive it as he masturbated in the shower, conjuring images of Jessica squirming and screaming as he raped her to help him climax. But it had been no use. The experience was far removed from the real thing.

'What happened?' S insisted.

Lester smirked as he stared at the computer screen. 'I killed them. They're dead.'

Lester paused, expecting a reaction, but there was only silence.

'I want to know more,' S eventually said in his softest voice.

'Before you send the footage.'

'They were plotting to kill me. They wanted to overtake me on the leader board, but I got to them first. I slit Steven's throat while he was recording. Jessica was tied up. She couldn't do anything other than accept everything I gave to her.' Lester hesitated as he reminisced; the blood rushed to his groin. 'She was mine. All mine. It was perfect. Exactly what I had been waiting for. I did everything to her that I could think of. And then I cut her head off. You know, I've never had a blowjob from a severed head before – two severed heads, even.'

'I don't believe you.'

Lester suspected a hint of jealousy in his master's voice.

'It's the truth. It's all on the footage. I documented every aspect for your enjoyment.'

Lester opened The Community home page and logged in. His password was fifteen characters long and contained a combination of letters, numbers and symbols. It was a password he would never forget.

'Do you know what this means for your score?'

A smirk grew on Lester's face. 'It means I'm untouchable.'

'Perhaps I will have to create another league for people like you.'

'There is no one else like me,' Lester said, pride oozing through him.

'Of course there are. We just haven't found them yet.'

'We?'

'If all goes to plan, you can help me. But it will have to be a select few. Ten. Twenty. I'm already conscious that The Community is getting too big. We can't afford for word to spread about this new one.'

'Would you become a member?'

S chuckled down the phone. 'No. You know those days are long behind me. I did my time.'

'I remember. I remember. It would still be good to have you as part of The Community – officially, that is, collecting points. You could impart some tips,' Lester said.

'And you'd be happy for me to share that, would you? Considering I've taught you everything there is to know?'

'Hmm. Actually. No. No, fuck that idea.'

Lester scrolled through The Community's home page. He skimmed the members' posts and only enlarged a few of the images that caught his eye.

'How many points do you feel you deserve for Jessica and Steven then?' S said after a while.

Lester paused before replying. At the top right of the screen was his profile – icon-less and discreet – and beneath that was his score.

Lester was currently sitting top of the leader board with fifteen thousand points. Second place had twelve thousand.

'Jessica alone was worth 1000. You can vouch for that. And as for Steven... well he was just an add-on, so... 250?'

S said nothing. In the background Lester heard the sound of a keyboard clicking. He stared at the screen and within a few seconds the number that appeared underneath his name changed. It adjusted specifically to what they had discussed. An extra 1,250 points.

Lester revelled in the distance that separated him and second place. He was winning – for the first time ever in his life – and he wasn't going to stop there.

'What's next?' S asked.

'I've got something planned. You'll just have to wait.'

As Lester was about to hang up, S called his name.

'Erm... Don't send me just the usual five minutes,' S said. 'I... erm... I want everything. The whole night.'

Hook. Line. Sinker. The apprentice had become the master.

'As you wish,' Lester said and rung off. He wandered to the kitchen to pour himself a glass of milk and returned to the table.

He began browsing through The Community again, searching through profiles, reading the posts and comments more intently now. He did have something planned. Something big. Jessica and Steven weren't enough. They had hurt him. Betrayed him. Made him feel small. It wasn't about the points. It was about his ego and his vanity. He needed to feel adored and abhorred both at the same time – that was the only way he could get control. And, more importantly, that was the only way he would be able to relive the experience of Steven and Jessica.

While he'd been sodomising Jessica's dead body, he'd realised something. He loved Jessica. *Loved* her. It wasn't lust; it was love. And now that she was gone, he would never be able to love her again. There was a hole left in his heart for her – a hole that was filled with copious amounts of rage at how easily she had betrayed him.

And he needed to find someone to fill that hole, to dissipate that anger.

Lester moved the mouse to the top of the news feed, typed in the name Jessica and waited for the results to populate. Community members with the same name appeared on the page. At the top was Jessica Arnholt, and for a moment, Lester was tempted to view her profile, download her pictures so he could masturbate over her one last time – and then he realised he had the video. He changed his mind.

He clicked on the second profile and inspected her image. She was pretty. *Very* pretty, in fact. She had long, flowing brown hair, deep brown eyes and her smile was radiant. Her name was Jessica Mann, and her profile picture was of her in a hospital, smiling vehemently at the camera. The caption beneath her picture read, 'My favourite thing to dress up in is my uniform. I can be a nurse during the day and at night.'

As soon as he finished reading that, Lester became aroused. Jessica Mann was suitable. She looked very similar to Arnholt – eerily similar – and that was what he wanted. If he was going to relive the experience, it had to be as close to the original as possible.

Lester's eyes fell on her score on the leader board. Fiftieth out of fifteen thousand. Commendable. But he could make her better. And her last points were from a few nights ago, so she was still fresh and active.

Lester clicked on the message icon beneath her name. Then he typed out a message, hovered his finger over the enter button and waited.

After a brief moment of deliberation, he sent the message.

It read: *Hi, Jessica. I'm in need of some urgent medical assistance.*

| PART 2 |

CHAPTER 10

ALINKA'S

Shadows stretched across the street as birds awakened and sang from their perches amidst the branches overhead. A slight chill nipped the air, aching the joints in his fingers and the muscles in his nose. Cars sped past him, picking up some of the spray from the rain that had fallen all day yesterday and the night before.

Lester was perched on the edge of a bench outside Jessica Mann's house. He'd found her address through a variety of contacts he'd made on the Dark Web, who were always keen to help him out in exchange for some of the footage he had from his previous Communions. He sat leaning forward, his elbows resting on his knees, with his head down and his hat pulled over his eyes. It had been several hours since he'd messaged her, and he hadn't heard anything since. He was beginning to worry. What if she'd taken one look at his profile and decided against meeting him? Lester decided that all she needed was a little push, a little incentive. Something that would encourage her to respond, and then if there was still no response, he would have to take matters into his own hands.

Lester was dressed in his smartest outfit. A light blue Hugo Boss shirt, with the top two buttons undone revealing his pasty chest. A thin navy Guess blazer and matching trousers. A pair of Christian Louboutin jet-black shoes that were so clean he was almost certain he could see the reflection of his face in them. And a set of Mont

Blanc cufflinks that finished the ensemble. The outfit had cost him in excess of two thousand pounds, and he always made an effort to wear it on special occasions. Funerals. Weddings. Christenings. And, more commonly, when he was meeting another Community member for the first time. His father had always taught him one thing that stuck with him: that first impressions were everything. And if there was one thing Lester loved more than making first impressions count, it was leaving a *lasting* impression, whether it was via his outfit or his unique personality.

A few minutes of nothing passed, save for a few joggers running past him, synchronising their exasperated breaths with their heavy steps. The sight of them reminded him that he still needed to do his exercise routine for the day; he had been forced to miss it yesterday because he'd spent too much time thinking about Jessica and Steven Arnholt's still-warm skin under his. The routine consisted of twenty push-ups, twenty pull-ups, twenty bicep curls and then twenty squats. It was a routine he'd started when he was a teenager and it had stuck. And the outcomes hadn't been too bad either. He was satisfied with his body, his physical presence in the bedroom. And he especially loved the compliments he received from other Community members. The way they massaged his muscles. The way they touched him, arousing every corner of his body. He couldn't afford to let it slip.

After another ten cars and two joggers rushed by, the door to Jessica Mann's small semi-detached house finally opened. Lester recognised her instantly from her profile. She was even prettier in real life – taller, slimmer, more striking than her picture suggested. In fact, she looked a lot more like Jessica Arnholt than he'd originally envisaged. And that excited him.

Lester followed her for the next half mile, keeping his distance and separating himself from her on the other side of the street. Her hair swayed left and right in its ponytail as she walked, and the bag on her side bounced against her hip. Lester admired the way her figure moved in tandem with her hair. It was almost too perfect.

As they approached an independent bicycle shop on the street corner, Jessica slowed. Lester matched her pace and held back. He watched her cross the road and enter a coffee shop called Alinka's. Home of artisan coffee. Whatever that meant.

This was it. His opportunity to acquaint himself with her for the first time. His opportunity to make the best first impression he knew that he was capable of.

Lester leant against a nearby lamp post with his hands resting by his side. His palms were beginning to sweat as he waited. He watched through the building's vast windows as Jessica ordered her drink.

It was time.

Placing his hands in his trouser pockets, Lester crossed the junction with little heed given to the cars and taxis and buses zooming up and down. As he skipped onto the kerb, he removed his phone and looked down at the screen just as Jessica came out of Alinka's. She was on the phone too, answering a call. Neither were looking where they were going, and Lester had no intention of stopping.

A few feet from the entrance, they collided. Lester dropped his phone on purpose, allowing it to smash to pieces on the concrete, and Jessica's cup flew from her hands. The muddy-brown liquid soiled the knock-off phone Lester had bought second-hand online, destroying it completely, and splattered across the ground.

'Oh my God!' Jessica exclaimed. 'I'm so sorry. Are you OK?'

Jessica touched his arm and then bent down to the ground. She picked up the phone using her thumb and forefinger. Coffee dripped from the corner.

'Oh my God,' she repeated. She hung up her conversation and pocketed her phone. 'I'm so sorry. Your phone... I... I didn't...'

'It's OK,' Lester said, attempting to disarm her with his smile.

'But it's broken.'

'It's fine. Honestly. It's not mine. It's a company phone. My work pays for it.' He took it from her. 'So you can do what you like with it. Snap it in half if you want. It's useless anyway.'

Jessica stared at the phone for a moment and then the ground. Lester followed her gaze.

'What were you drinking?'

'Chai tea.'

'Let me get you another one.'

Jessica shook her head. 'No. This was my fault.'

'Well, I'm not going to ask you to buy me a brand-new phone – especially when it isn't mine in the first place. Come on – let me buy you another drink.'

'Let me. Please. It's the least I can do.' Jessica bent down, picked up the cup from the ground and started back towards the coffee shop.

Lester wasted no time in following her. As they entered, he moved to the side of the space and found a pile of napkins. He wiped down the phone, wrapped a few sheets around it and then placed it back in his pocket.

'What would you like?' Jessica asked as he joined her in the queue.

'Chai tea. Same as you.' He sniffed the air. The aroma surrounding her was delicious – a perfume he wasn't familiar with. Fruity. Sweet. Different to the Chanel that Jessica Arnholt had been wearing the other night. If everything went to plan, he would have to buy her the same one. The experience needed to be perfect, immaculate, exact.

Jessica smiled and turned her back on him. She gave the barista the order, told him her name and then shuffled along with him to the other side of the till.

'Listen,' she said, turning to him. 'I'm sorry, again, about your phone. I didn't mean to... I – I didn't see you. You came out of—'

'What did I tell you? It's cool. Nothing to worry about. I'm just glad I didn't get any on my suit.'

'Won't your manager be annoyed? Won't they have to get you a new one?'

Lester shook his head. 'No, I don't think he'll be annoyed.'

'How do you know?'

'Because I am my manager, and I'm pretty sure I can't be annoyed with myself for too long. And I certainly can't be annoyed with you – after all, it wasn't your fault. All mine. That's that.'

Jessica smiled and her cheeks flushed. Her gaze fell to the ground and she readjusted the bag on her shoulder so that it sat against her hip.

'Well, thank you,' she said.

Lester extended his hand and he introduced himself.

Jessica took it. 'Nice to meet you. Jessica.'

Before he could respond, the barista called Jessica's name and placed the two cups on the counter before them. Lester took his and handed Jessica hers.

'Now we're even,' he said with a smile. 'You no longer have to feel guilty about anything.'

They left Alinka's, and as they exited, Lester headed left, and Jessica right.

'Well, I'm this way,' he said.

'And I'm this way,' she said, pointing in her direction.

'See you,' he said, and started off.

He made it two steps before he was called back.

'Wait,' she said. 'Sorry. This is going to sound completely strange and weird and stalkerish. But... do I know you from somewhere? You look vaguely familiar...'

Lester smirked at her and licked his lips. The scent of her perfume was beginning to grow on him. Maybe he would let her get away with it.

'I don't think so.' He shrugged. 'I'd remember a beautiful face like yours.'

Jessica blushed, sipped her drink, apologised, and then left.

Lester waited a while and watched her go before heading home. His operation had been a success. She had recognised him. And he had planted the delicate seed of curiosity inside her. All he needed to do now was let it grow.

CHAPTER 11

PINKY PROMISE

As soon as the kettle stopped boiling, Jake poured the steaming water into his mug and stirred. He had deviated from his norm and opted for three heaped spoons of coffee. It was needed. His head ached and his eyes were sore. Sleep had mostly escaped him last night – he'd managed four hours at most. And now he was beginning to feel the effects of it. But it wasn't the alcohol that had caused his restlessness. No, the effects of that had worn off after the cab journey home. That was one of the good things about living nearly an hour away from the station, even if it was a minor consolation to the cost of the cab ride home. Instead, Jake's mind had been plagued with thoughts of The Crimsons, of Danny, of Michael, of their trial, of their inevitable – and imminent – release back among the British public. It was a tragedy, a major lapse in the judicial system, and, as he lay there staring at the ceiling in the early hours of morning, with the soft sounds of Elizabeth's breathing beside him, he decided he was going to investigate it.

As Jake set the spoon face down on the kitchen counter, Elizabeth entered, her dressing gown wrapped tightly around her, emphasising the swell of her stomach.

'You came home late,' she said sternly, resting against the fridge.

'I know,' Jake replied, wiping the coffee stain on the surface away with a piece of kitchen roll. 'I was with the guys from work.'

'Drinking?' Elizabeth moved across the room and sat down at the island in the centre of the kitchen. The chairs were at a comfortable enough height for her to slip away easily when she needed the toilet, or as soon as her back started to ache. In her hand she held a letter.

'Only a few,' Jake said, sitting opposite. He watched her place the letter back on the table upside down so that he couldn't read what was written on it. He didn't have the heart to tell her how much it had cost him to get home – and how much it was going to cost in getting another cab into work. 'They wanted to celebrate our pregnancy. They only found out last night.'

'You've been working there for months!'

'I know. But I'm beginning to fit in a little bit more. They're talking to me about things other than work now, which is nice.' Jake gulped the rest of his coffee as Elizabeth placed her hand on his.

'I told you they'd come round eventually. Anyone would be lucky to have you as a friend. You're a half-decent guy when you're not being a sarcastic arsehole. Hell, I know because I married you, though it took me a while to warm up to you. And you said yourself that they were a close-knit team.' Elizabeth wrapped her fingers in his and squeezed. 'I just don't want you to become someone you're not to try to impress them.'

Jake burped and swallowed the stench of coffee away. 'I won't, Liz. Trust me.'

'Pinkie promise?'

'Pinkie promise.'

The two of them entwined their baby fingers and squeezed. It was a long-standing tradition of theirs. When they'd first met in a coffee shop during their second year of university, Jake had made her pinkie promise that she would return his set of highlighters. Ever since, the routine had stuck. It was their little thing, and it was a reminder that there was still trust and honesty in their relationship. The pinkie promise was a sacred vow that neither of them ever wanted to break.

Elizabeth's hand fell onto the letter again.

'What is it this time?' Jake asked, already aware of what might be inside.

'Another bill,' Elizabeth replied.

'Which one now?'

'Take your pick. Internet, phone, television. They're all going up.'

Jake sighed. Now he really felt guilty about the drinks last night. 'Can we look at other providers?'

'I will do today.' Elizabeth averted his gaze and glanced down at the table, deep in thought. Jake observed her, admired her. After a few more seconds, she turned her attention back to him, rubbed her stomach and asked, 'We're going to be all right, aren't we?'

Before Jake could answer, Maisie, his two-year-old daughter, waddled into the kitchen from the living room dressed in her Peppa Pig pyjamas, wiping the sleep from her eyes. 'Daddy!'

Jake bent down to pick her up and held her in his arms, then gave her a kiss on the cheek and buried his nose into her skin. Maisie giggled, and Jake smiled along with her. Her happiness and innocence and ebullience was infectious. It was irreplaceable, and he couldn't wait to experience the same feeling with the new baby.

'How did you get down here?' Jake asked her, glancing at Elizabeth quickly.

'Stairs,' Maisie replied.

'Sorry,' Elizabeth added. 'I must have left the child lock off.'

Jake turned his attention back to Maisie. 'You're a very clever girl for coming down the stairs on your own, aren't you? Mummy and Daddy will have to be a little more careful in the future... How is my angel this morning?'

'Sleepy!'

'Sorry for waking you up last night. Daddy got home late.' He hesitated and looked at Elizabeth. 'And how's my big girl doing?'

She scowled at him. He knew she hated that name, but he thought it was rather fitting.

'Tired as well,' she said, shuffling onto the edge of the seat and hopping down. She rounded the island and traipsed up to his side. 'Please keep your phone on loud today. I don't want anything to happen and not be able to get a hold of you.'

'Don't worry. I've got a charger on my desk and one in the car. The only way I won't answer is if my phone breaks... or I die.'

Elizabeth's face dropped at the end of his sentence and she slapped him playfully on the shoulder.

'Don't try to be funny,' she snapped.

'Are you still seeing your mum today?' Jake asked.

Elizabeth nodded, squeezed Maisie's cheeks and moved to the sink. She turned on the tap and started washing the dishes.

'She's coming over early.'

'Will she still be here when I come home?'

'Don't worry – she'll be gone.'

Jake set Maisie on her feet. 'Good.'

'You know, you should be a little more grateful to her when she's around.'

'Why's that?'

'You know why. You wouldn't be in this position if it weren't for her.'

Jake paused a beat. 'I'll think about it,' he said.

He spent the next few minutes preparing his bag for work and made lunch – tuna and sweetcorn sandwiches, his favourite. By the time he was done, Elizabeth had finished washing the dishes and was preparing to feed Maisie her breakfast.

'Guess what I found out yesterday,' Jake said, pouring Maisie a glass of water.

'What?'

'The Crimsons.' Jake paused. 'Their trial's falling through.'

She shook her head in disgust. 'That's ridiculous.'

'I know. The lads at work told me last night. I'm going to find out what's happened. I'm going to stop it if I can,' Jake said, handing Maisie the plastic cup of water. His daughter took it and guzzled it down in one.

'How do you intend on doing that? These are dangerous people, Jake. I don't want you getting hurt or involved in anything risky.' She placed her hand on top of her stomach. 'Not now. Not ever.'

'I won't,' he said.

'Promise me.' Elizabeth held out her little finger.

Jake gazed at it, contemplating. He didn't want to promise her that what he was about to get involved with would be safe. But he also didn't want to lie to her. Or worse, worry her.

'I'll be safe,' he said, curling her finger around hers. 'I promise.'

CHAPTER 12

PART OF THE TEAM

Lindsay Gray was already in the office by the time Jake got there. He didn't like being the second to arrive, even if she was a completely separate entity to the Major Investigation Team. He wanted to show dedication and determination. Sometimes, when he was sitting at his desk – during the dullest parts of the day, or during his lunch breaks – infrequently fantasising about his future career, he imagined what his managers and colleagues would say about him, how gracious they would be in their praise.

'Jake was a stellar officer. He was always the first in the office and last to leave.'

'Never met an officer who worked as hard as Jake did.'

'He always gave everything to his work.'

If he put in the hard work now, it would set him up for all the glory later.

'Morning, soldier,' Lindsay said to him as he wandered past her.

The kitchen area was old and bleak. It still contained appliances from the eighties – all of which hadn't been safety checked in over a decade and posed a considerable risk to every member of the team who used them. There were other, more important things to spend the budget on, and kitchen appliances wasn't one of them.

There, Jake made himself another coffee and returned to his desk. He loaded up the Police National Database and entered Danny

Cipriano's name in the search bar in the top-right corner of the screen. As he hovered his finger over the return key, the office door opened. The sound distracted him. It was Liam, carrying two cups of coffee in his hand. He nodded to Lindsay in acknowledgment and strode straight towards Jake.

'Thought you could do with one of these,' Liam said, handing him the drink. 'You didn't look too pucker before you left yesterday. You feeling all right this morning?'

'I've felt better.' Jake placed the cup on the table.

'Lightweight. You're only twenty-five. What's wrong with you? You should be able to stomach more than a couple of pints,' Liam said, chuckling. 'When I was your age, I was out on the piss almost every night.'

'My days of heavily drinking are long behind me,' Jake said.

'Wife and kids'll do that to ya.' Liam drank from his coffee and held it in the air, staring at it as if it reminded him of the bottom of the glass he'd drunk from last night. 'Probably for the best. You don't want to rely on it. That's when you know things have got bad.'

Jake didn't know what to say. For a brief moment, he pondered asking what was inside Liam's plastic cup – he carried it with him almost everywhere and always held it close against his chest – but then he thought better of it. He didn't want to insult the man who was finally beginning to accept him, and he certainly didn't want to burn the bridges they had just started building together.

'Hey,' Jake said, lifting the coffee almost triumphantly, 'cheers for the drink.'

Liam placed his hand on Jake's shoulder. 'When you're part of the team, we look out for each other. Remember that.'

Liam started off. He stopped by his office door and gripped the handle. Then he checked his watch and called to Jake.

'Two minutes. I want you in the MIR.'

MIR was the acronym for the Major Investigation Room, the hub of all police activity relating to a major crime. It was where the team pooled their resources together and focused on the strategy of their investigation. While Jake and Liam had attended the crime scene, Garrison had started setting it up.

Jake glanced around him at the rest of the office. 'Where's everyone else?'

Liam opened his mouth but was cut off by a sharp buzzing sound. The remaining members of Major Investigation entered sluggishly, and headed straight into Investigation Room 2. Jake lifted himself out of his seat, deleted what he had typed into the search bar and joined them, cup in hand.

'Morning,' he said, and as he entered, he was greeted by a round of applause.

'Here he is!' Garrison said, seeming even livelier than he'd been last night. In his hand he held a chocolate digestive, while two more rested on top of his notebook. 'The man of the hour. Get home all right then?'

Jake sat beside him. At the head of the small room was a whiteboard. Beside it, on either side, were corkboards with images of Steven and Jessica's faces, along with the house numbers of the neighbours Jake had spoken to. It was the summation of their work, and it was looking bare.

'Jake?'

Jake looked at him and realised his colleague had asked him a question. 'Yeah. Sorry. Two hours. It took me nearly two hours to get home. Double what I can do on my own. I swear the cabbie took the longest route imaginable.'

'Shambles. He probably wanted to rinse some more money out of you. You could have had a couple more in that time, and it probably would have been cheaper.' Garrison nudged him in the shoulder.

'Not unless he knew his missus was going to chop his dick off if he did,' Drew said. He was sitting behind them, with his arms folded high up on his chest.

'At least he's got someone who can chop his dick off,' Garrison said, jumping to Jake's defence. 'Unlike you, you lonely prick. When was the last time you saw your wife?'

Just as Drew was about to retaliate by throwing a fake punch at Garrison, Liam entered. At once, the air fell still, and the atmosphere dropped. The teacher had just entered and commanded the attention of the classroom without saying a single word.

'I'll make this one brief,' Liam began. 'We've all got a lot to be getting on with. It's been more than twenty-four hours since Steven and Jessica Arnholt were murdered, and we've not had a single strand of evidence. Forensics on the DNA and laptop and mobile phone found at Steven's art gallery will take a little longer to come in I've been told. Something to do with a number of personnel changes within the team. Seem they're a man – or should I say woman – down.'

Liam moved to the corkboard on the right and pointed to a house number. 'Thanks to Jake's detective work, we've got a potential suspect. A Mr Archie Arnold. Steven and Jessica's neighbour down the road. Now, we've not got any evidence linking Archie to the murders, but Jake had a sneaky suspicion there was something not quite right about him, and he's been on our radar in the past for drug-related offences. I think it's something we should look into and exploit if we can, bring him in for further questioning.'

Liam paused to finish the last of his drink.

'Today's tasks are simple. I want Garrison to bring Mr Arnold in. And Drew, in the meantime, I want you to widen the search online. Build a victimology report and start looking into Steven and Jessica's online profiles, activities. Find out if there's anything we can learn from them. That laptop is likely going to be the greatest source of evidence when we eventually hear back from forensics. But I don't want us to rely on that to then find out it's completely useless. When Garrison gets back, I want you sitting in on the interview as well. And, finally, Jake' – Liam pointed to another face on the board – 'Steven's an art dealer, so that means he must have an agent or an accountant somewhere. Someone he speaks to regularly. Someone he trusts more than his parents. Find them. Speak with them. Learn all you can. Go.'

CHAPTER 13

WORK IN PROGRESS

Liam browsed aimlessly through his emails. Darkness encompassed him, save for the blue artificial light emanating from the computer monitor. The lights were off. The blinds were shut. And he was where he liked to be: in the dark. And today, in particular, he was in extra need of it. His head was spinning and he felt like there was a tonne of bricks crushing down on him. He could almost feel his brain cells dying. It made him nauseous and delirious, the sensation starting to make its way down his throat and into his stomach. And, worse still, he was out of alcohol to abate the sensation. There was none left in his reusable Starbucks cup. He pulled the desk drawer by his leg open and saw there was none left in there either. He had been slacking; he had forgotten to stock up on his last visit to the convenience store.

Before he could think on it further, someone knocked on the door.

Liam let out a little groan. Who was it and what the fuck did they want? He rubbed his temples with the palm of his hands, hoping to alleviate some of the pain swimming in his skull.

'Come in,' Liam said weakly.

The door opened and Drew entered.

'What's up?' Liam asked, avoiding the streak of light that flooded into the room. 'What can I help you with?'

Drew stepped inside and stopped behind the chair that was on the other side of Liam's desk.

He opened his mouth but hesitated. 'You all right, guv? You look a little bit pale. And it's really dark in here.'

Drew turned on the lights despite Liam's best efforts at waving him away from the switch. Liam threw his hands to his eyes to shield them, but it was no use. A harsh burst of white disorientated him. He tried to blink it away, muttering under his breath as he did so.

'I... I'm fine. Hungover, that's all.'

'Let me get you some water.'

Liam protested but Drew was having none of it. Within seconds, his colleague returned with water in a mug.

'You're not very good at listening, are you?' Liam said, setting the cup down. He had no intention of drinking it. 'Now, what do you want?'

'Tanner. What's the latest with him?'

'I've sent him out today on his own. We'll see how well he copes.'

'I wasn't talking about—'

'I know what you meant.' Liam sighed. 'You know the plan with Archie, right? Play it cool with him for a little while. Don't do anything yet. Just make him aware of where he stands. Use the drug angle if you have to. And make sure he doesn't see my face.'

'Guv,' Drew said, nodding in acknowledgement. 'And Jake?'

Liam dipped his head. 'He's a good egg. I told him that yesterday. I told him we don't like bad eggs here. We introduced him to the team last night over drinks. This morning I bought him a coffee. I'd say give him a few more days, a few more home comforts, and then he'll be on side.'

'Completely?' There was apprehension and concern in Drew's voice.

'It'll take time to fully break down his barriers. He's a work in progress. And we all love a challenge. There's a good man inside him – I can see it. A willingness and keenness to succeed. That's just the rookie in him. The dedicated police officer. We were all like that once. Just give him some time and he'll realise what it's really like. That it's not all sunshine and rainbows; that there's a darker side to policing. But if you see any suspicious behaviour, come and let me know.'

CHAPTER 14

REMAND

As Jake made his way out of the building, across the car park and towards his car, he held his phone to his ear, listening to it ringing on the other end.

'Hello?' the other person answered eventually.

'Danika? It's Jake. Jake Tanner.'

'Jake! Oh my God, hi! How are you?' She sounded excited to hear from him, though he didn't believe it – she hadn't bothered to contact him once since they'd last seen one another.

'Things are going well. Elizabeth's pregnant again. We're expecting soon.'

'Oh, Jake, that's fantastic! How soon?'

Jake unlocked his car door and slid in. 'She's due in the next couple of weeks.'

'I'm so pleased for you,' Danika replied. 'You must be thrilled. Do you know what you're having this time?'

'A little girl.'

'Beautiful. You'll be outnumbered.'

'I'm just looking forward to any future boyfriends I might get to intimidate,' Jake said, and the two of them chuckled.

A part of him missed her voice, her laugh, her personality; her tenacity, her dedication, her drive to work hard and outperform everyone else in the team. They had first met back when they were bobbies on the beat over three years ago. And since then, they had endured the stresses and pressures of becoming qualified detectives with one another, and, more recently, on their first case as trainee detectives, they'd been caught in the middle of The Crimsons' final heist in Guildford. For Jake, Danika had been instrumental in helping him bring them down. She had been his eyes and ears throughout the entire operation, and without her, he remained adamant that it wouldn't have been a success.

'How's life in Guildford treating you?' he asked.

'Boring. Not a lot to do here. Not a lot of incidents to respond to. Few robberies. Thefts. Car jackings. Pub stabbings. The odd kidnap. That seems to be about it. Nothing too exciting.'

'Sounds like more than most. What were you expecting?'

'Probably not as much as you're getting up in London, eh?'

Jake avoided the question and moved the conversation on. He didn't want to make it about him. 'I've been meaning to get in touch, but I've just been really busy.'

'Likewise,' Danika said, although he could sense the lie interlaced in her voice. 'I can imagine you're swamped with homicides and rapes and drug deals and everything?'

Jake chuckled half-heartedly. He knew there was a line between the confidentiality of a case and the trust of a friend, but he wasn't prepared to cross it.

'Suppose you could say that. The workload's definitely increasing.' Jake hesitated for a moment. He had a favour to ask, but he wasn't sure if Danika still needed warming up. 'How's the family?'

Danika had married into a strict family. Both she and her husband had been police officers, but after her husband had been thrown off a building, an incident that had rendered him disabled, their marriage had begun to fall apart. Jake supposed there was a reason Danika had continued to work for Surrey Police rather than return to her home borough in Croydon.

'Tony still won't let me see the kids. I've not seen them in five weeks. They've gone to his parents. He says I'm too unstable and unfit as a mother to look after them. But he's no better – he's in a worse state than me.'

'Dan... I'm... I'm so sorry. That must be horrible,' Jake said, at a loss for words. 'And it was all because of that one night?'

Danika hesitated before responding. It was clear this was a sensitive topic of conversation for her, but Jake wanted to know the details – he wanted to satisfy the hunger of curiosity inside him. Besides, the other part of him cared for Danika; they had spent years together, and he wanted to make sure she was safe – physically, mentally and emotionally.

'Yes and no. That night with Mark was a mistake. I hope I never have to see him again. But there were other things wrong with the relationship before that. The whole Mark thing didn't help.'

'Is he still with Surrey Police?'

'You didn't hear? He resigned a couple of months back. Nobody's seen or heard from him since. I thought you would have known.'

'Right. No. I hadn't. Turns out I'm learning a lot of new things lately.'

'It also transpires that he was fucking Pemberton as well – *kako zoprno!*' she yelled in her native Slovenian.

Jake smirked; he'd bought her a thesaurus for her birthday once as a tool for her to develop her English skills, and it was clear to see she had been using it, but she always reverted to her own language whenever she got angry.

'You know what the worst thing about it is?' she continued. 'He not only ruined my marriage, but he also ruined Pemberton's too. Her husband left and now she's got the kids alone. I think there was an army of angry husbands gunning for him at one point.'

'I... I... I don't know what to say.' Jake paused while he considered what to ask next, buckling his seat belt at the same time. 'What about your parents? Are they speaking to you?'

'There's no coming back from my decision, Jake. It's been made.'

'Well,' Jake said, 'if you need anything... anything at all, then you can call me. If you need a witness or someone to testify against your husband, then you can ask me. I want you to have custody of the kids.'

'No,' Danika said. Her voice was soft and weak, almost devoid of all hope and life. 'As much as I miss them, I don't want the kids. In a way, Tony's right – I can barely look after myself. I'm never home, and I'd never be able to care for them in the way they need. I wouldn't be the mum they deserve.'

'You always were job pissed, weren't you?'

'You're not much better,' she retaliated. 'The kids are happy at their granny's. That's all I care about. I just want to be able to see them, that's all. Make sure you don't make the same mistakes I did, Jake.'

Jake took a moment to reflect. About his children and their relationship with their grandparents. About how he had Elizabeth at home to look after them and care for them, About how little he was home. About how he wanted to be able to watch them develop. About how he didn't want to miss the important stages in their lives – their first steps, their first words, their first laugh, their first smile, their first day at school, their first romance. So far, he'd missed almost all of those for Maisie, and she was only two years old. But his situation was much better than Danika's. And that put things into perspective for him.

'I'm so sorry, Dan.'

'It's fine. I'll be all right. Thank you.' Danika sniffed through the phone. 'What was it you wanted?'

'What?'

'I know you weren't calling just for a chat, Jake.'

Now hardly seemed like the right time to talk to her about Danny and Michael Cipriano, but he had questions he hoped she'd be able to answer.

'I'm sure you've heard already…'

Danika paused before replying, 'Depends on what it is you're talking about.'

'It's over. Their case. It's collapsing. The CPS.'

Another pause.

'Danny and Michael?' she asked tentatively. 'Really? I… er… I had no idea. I'd heard something mentioned but didn't know it was about that.'

A uniformed officer walked past Jake and hopped into a police vehicle outside the station's entrance.

'You didn't hear anything about it in the office? No one in the team's been talking about it?'

'No, Jake. Sorry.'

'They must have said something. What about Bridger? Is he still there, pulling all the strings? He must have had something to do with it. I wouldn't put it past him – he's the reason our first interview on Michael couldn't be used in court. I trusted him to follow the procedures to the letter of the law, especially considering he kept giving us that bullshit about not needing to be reminded of them because he was such a fucking superstar.'

'Come on, Jake. You know that's a sensitive subject. Nobody's allowed to mention it around here. And he's always so busy I hardly see him.'

'Dan, this is serious. This is the group that killed four innocent people, including one of our own. You've got to help me here. I don't know how, but I'm going to make sure they stay locked up.'

Danika hesitated again, and for a moment Jake thought she'd disconnected. There was silence. Not even the sound of office chatter in the background. Not even the sound of her breath rustling in his ear.

'Danika? Dan? You there?' Jake looked at the dashboard. He had been sitting there for ten minutes.

'I'm here… There's… There *is* something. But I don't know… No, I can't.'

'Yes, you can, Dan. What's holding you back? I know you want them to rot in prison as much as I do. It's where they belong.'

'You can't say anything. I'm not even supposed to know about this.'

'I promise.'

'The other day I heard Bridger talking with someone over the phone about Danny and Michael. I overheard Bridger say that once they were let out of remand, both the brothers were going to be entered into the witness protection scheme.'

CHAPTER 15

WILD URGES

Steven Arnholt's agent was called Nathan Hewitt. He was a heavy, overweight man with leopard-print glasses and a button nose. He wore a navy suit – without a tie – and a brown leather watch. His suit trousers were tight against his legs and too short – about three inches of his blue polka-dot socks were visible between the top of his shoes and the bottom of his trousers.

Jake had arrived at Nathan's office unannounced. Drew had forwarded on the address to his email and Jake had rushed there as soon as he was finished with Danika, careful not to add any more suspicion to his inactivity outside the police station. Talking to Danika had been a big risk, but it was a necessary one – one that he couldn't neglect any longer.

'Thank you,' Jake said as he stepped into the centre of the room and cast his eye around his surroundings. The office was small, almost the size of Jake and Elizabeth's bedroom, and was situated in the centre of a street filled with off-licences and cafes. 'Nice little place you got here.'

It wasn't. Jake was just being polite. It was, in fact, a shithole. There was nothing inside the office save a desk, two chairs, a small bench with a synthetic leather cushion, situated by the window, and a lonely plastic plant that looked as if it had been bought second-hand at a car boot sale. There was no indication that Nathan was an art dealer anywhere. At the very least, Jake had expected to find a painting on the wall, a masterpiece hanging over a printer or even a small portrait resting on the desk in a small frame. But there was nothing.

'I've worked hard to get it where it is,' Nathan said, smiling. As the corners of his mouth rose, the light overhead caught the thin, blonde hairs on his top lip.

Jake raised his eyebrow. 'Well, I think you've done a good job. Must have shelled out quite a bit.'

Nathan found his seat and gestured for Jake to sit opposite. As he touched the hard plastic chair, Jake instantly knew he'd made a bad choice in accepting the offer.

'So,' Nathan said, leaning forward. He sat with his hands locked together, his elbows perched on the edge of the table. 'Are you in the art business? Are you looking to sell or buy?'

'No,' Jake said, shooting Nathan's smile down abruptly. He reached for his warrant card and introduced himself. 'I was wondering if I could—?'

'I didn't do anything.' Nathan leant back in the chair and his body constricted; his shoulders moved closer to his chest and his hands fell between his legs.

'I'm not saying you did.' Jake substituted his ID for his pocketbook and paper. 'I was just wondering if I could ask you a few questions about one of your clients?'

'Oh, God. What's Elijah done now?'

Jake made a note of the name for someone at the station to check out later on. 'I was referring to one of your other clients: Steven Arnholt… and his wife, Jessica.'

Nathan's brow furrowed. 'What about them?'

'Were you close with the two of them?'

'Steven was my first-ever client. He trusted me when no one else did. I knew Jessica before Steven.'

'Did you set them up?'

Nathan shrugged. 'I suppose you could say that. I introduced them to one another. They took the rest from there – I can't take credit for that. He's an incredible artist.'

As they spoke, Jake made notes in his pad. 'How did you introduce the two of them?'

Nathan hesitated as he collected his thoughts. 'It was a dinner. I was throwing a big party. We'd just sold one of Steven's biggest artworks to a gallery in America for a large sum of money. I wanted to celebrate. My wife and I invited our friends and Steven invited his. Jessica was a friend of my wife's, and then… well, you know the rest.'

Jake glanced at Nathan's finger – at the lack of wedding ring –

and noted the observation.

'How long have you been with your wife, Mr—?'

'I thought this was about Steven and Jessica?' Nathan said defensively.

'It is. Forgive me.' Jake paused and shuffled himself into a more comfortable position on the chair. 'How would you describe Steven and Jessica's relationship? Happy? Sad?'

'What is this about, Detective?'

Jake ignored the question and continued. 'Did you ever hear about any arguments they may have had? Steven ever complain to you that he wasn't happy in the relationship? That he was, perhaps, looking for… *something else?*'

The tension in Nathan's shoulders eased and he relaxed. 'What is this about? What's happened to them?'

Jake exhaled deeply. Then he explained to Nathan, in the possible briefest terms, what had happened to both Steven and Jessica, making sure to leave out all the gory details.

'My God…' Nathan said, wiping sweat from his top lip. 'I can't believe it. Who did this?'

'That's why I'm here. We need you to help us.'

'Sure. Anything. *Anything* I can do to help. I'll answer everything you need me to.'

'Thank you,' Jake said, nodding. He cleared his throat before continuing. 'Did Steven ever come to you with any fears or concerns that someone may have been watching him, or that someone may have wanted to hurt him?'

Nathan's head shook violently. His saggy jowls wobbled from side to side. 'No. No. Nobody comes to mind.'

'What about drugs, was he involved in those at all?'

'No. I mean, yes. I think so. Only recreationally. He took them to get his creativity. But I never heard him complain about money or saying that he owed anyone any debts.'

Jake made a note and moved on.

'What was Steven and Jessica's personal life like?'

'I… I… I don't know. Steven never talked that much about it.'

'Did he have any other friends?'

'Yes. No. Well, yes. Only a couple. He mentioned a couple of people he met online, but I never really listened that much.'

'Did he see them a lot?' Before Nathan could answer, Jake continued, 'How would you say his time was divided up – in percentage terms? Between you and his other friends?'

'It's difficult… seventy me. Thirty the others. That I know of.'

'So would you say that you and he were close? You trusted one another.'

Nathan's head dipped slowly.

'And, if you don't mind me asking,' Jake said, 'what is your current relationship with your wife like?'

'How is that relevant?' Nathan said before he removed his glasses and wiped his forehead with the back of his sleeve.

'You want to help us find the killer, don't you?'

Nathan nodded, placing his glasses back on his face and pushing them to the top of his nose.

'Good. Then please answer the questions. Anything you tell us – no matter how small or trivial – might help us find whoever did this.'

Nathan looked to the carpet then chewed his bottom lip, and for a moment Jake thought he looked different. No longer was he a man of blind arrogance and confidence. No longer was he exuding ignorance. He was small, insignificant, aware of the realities of the world.

'We've not been together for a few months now. She wanted to go on a break.'

'Why?' Jake asked, cutting straight to the point.

Nathan allowed a long, slow breath to whistle through his lips. 'She found me with Jessica one night.'

Jake stopped writing. The pen almost slipped and fell out of his grip.

'Could you... elaborate?' Jake asked, trying to process the information.

'Jessica and I slept together one night. Imogen, my wife, found us going at it in Steven's gallery.'

Jake sat up straighter in his chair.

'What about Steven? Did he find out?'

'He was the one who organised it. He saw how unhappy Imogen and I were, so he thought he'd help me out.'

'By letting you sleep with his wife?' Jake asked loudly. An unwelcome image of himself walking in on Elizabeth sleeping with another man – a friend, a colleague, a stranger – flashed in his mind and he instantly dismissed it, willing it to never come true.

'You don't understand,' Nathan began. 'Imogen and I were struggling. He said it would help. And it did. For a bit. In fact, it was really good. I needed a release and had done for some time. I don't know if you've seen her, but Jessica is... was something else. Smoking hot body. Smoking hot personality too. Steven was a lucky man. But all that fun stopped when Imogen found us. Steven and I didn't speak about it that much afterwards.'

'How did he convince you into going along with it?'

'Steven was... Steven was convincing. He knew what would tip me over the edge. He saw Jessica as a trophy wife. Most men that came across her did. And he knew that, so he exploited that aspect of her. But she didn't seem to mind. She seemed to enjoy it. Apparently they'd done it before.'

'With who?'

'I don't know. They never said.'

'How many times had they done this before you?'

'I don't know.'

Jake pressed the pen to his lips and bit the end. His mind was whirring, splitting off into a myriad network of tangential possibilities. Who were this couple? Why were they so intent on letting other people into their relationship? And who else had they added to the list of threesomes?

Nathan's voice brought him back to the present.

'I'm sorry,' Nathan said, pushing his glasses up to the crown of his head and wiping at his eyes. 'I don't want to discuss this anymore.'

Jake sucked in a breath.

'Was this a sexual fantasy for Steven, do you know?'

'I said no more.'

'Was it a sexual fantasy?'

Nathan hesitated. 'Yes. I think it was,' he said, sniffing hard and wiping his nose and upper lip with the back of his hand. 'He had a lot of bizarre and wild sexual urges. I never judged him on it – he's entitled to like what he likes. Everyone is. But there was something different about what he was into.' He paused. 'He said there was a large group of people that were all like-minded and into the same sort of things. He said there was a community of them that would regularly meet up and do all manner of things to one another. Steven even invited me to join, but I refused. Now... I'm sorry, but I'm going to have to ask you again to leave. I don't want to answer any more of your questions.'

As Jake left the office, he was certain he'd seen a knowing smile form on Nathan's face. Either there was something he wasn't telling him, or he was secretly reliving the experience he'd had with Steven and Jessica.

CHAPTER 16

WELCOME TO THE COMMUNITY

A draft of cold air bristled against Lester's cheeks as he opened the front door to his house. It concerned him. The air should have been warm, just above room temperature. It should have been still. Exactly the way he'd left it. Which meant there was a draft coming from somewhere in the house – one that had no right being there.

As he crossed the threshold, his body tensed and his hand clenched into a fist. Carefully closing the door behind him, he threw the keys into a small pot that dangled from the wall. He stormed into the kitchen, darting to the drawer nearest the door and rummaging through the contents. Wrapped in his fingers was the seven-inch kitchen blade he'd stolen from Jessica and Steven Arnholt's gallery. Cleaned and polished, it served as a memento of his time with them both.

Gripping it tightly, he started searching the house. First he moved into the living room, peering around the door. He was half expecting someone to be there, but there wasn't. A part of him wanted to find someone. So he could make them wish they'd never trespassed onto his property. He had a taste for blood now, for slaughter, and nothing was going to stop it. Even though he knew the points would be unofficial and wouldn't increase his score, it would still be a whole lot of fun.

After making sure the ground floor was clear, he headed

upstairs. His feet whispered along the steps, his breathing flat. His pulse stayed at sixty.

As he reached the top of the stairs, he stopped. Held his breath. Listened.

Silence. Except for the sound of wind whistling past an open window. It was coming from the bathroom.

Before going to the bathroom, he checked the rest of the bedrooms and the study. Everything was as he'd left it.

He turned his back on the bedroom and stared at the white door of the bathroom, which was slightly ajar. Again, he stopped to listen. Still nothing.

Lester approached the bathroom, keeping the blade pressed against his leg. With his other hand stretched out, he pushed the door. The hinges gave way and creaked, and as the door bounced against the back wall, he rushed in, his body taut with the onset of adrenaline.

He exhaled deeply, dejected. It was empty. In front of him was an open window. He must have left it open himself.

'Idiot,' he chided. 'You stup—'

Something distracted him – the sound of movement. His gaze darted behind him. On the floor, scratching its head against the door frame, was a cat.

'What the fuck are you doing here?' he said, lowering the knife and easing his grip around the weapon.

He bent down to pick up the feline, but it scuttled away into his bedroom. He chased after it, peered beneath the bed and yanked it out by its collar. The cat hissed and squealed at him. He held it aloft, disarming its claws just like he had done when he was child. Moving towards the bathroom, he tightened his grip around the cat's body and held it out at arm's length.

As he entered the bathroom, Lester placed the cat on the window's edge. There was a fifteen-foot drop between the window and solid ground, which, bizarrely, beggared the question of how it had got in in the first place. But right now, Lester didn't care about that. His only concern was how it would get down. And he had the perfect answer.

Beneath his house, to the right, was a main road. A couple walking their dog meandered along, arm in arm, talking with one another. He hated the sight of them and their wide smiles. He imagined they had a shit sex life. That it was boring. Uneventful. Tasteless. Then he imagined what he'd do to the both of them in one night. How he'd show them things they'd never known were possible. The thoughts excited him, and he struggled to tear himself away from them, like a violent and aggressive STD that kept coming back.

The cat distracted him, slicing his forearm and drawing blood with its sharp claws. Lester squeezed tighter, making sure the animal sensed that it was in imminent danger. He leant against the wall, held his arm out of the window and then launched the cat like a dart. Its arms and legs flailed about as it soared through the air.

After what felt like a long time, it eventually landed on its back and barrel rolled onto the road. It staggered to its feet, disorientated, stumbling then collapsed to one side, where it lay perfectly still for a few moments. Lester held his breath as he watched it struggle; he willed it to cross the road and get run over.

But nothing happened. There were no cars. The road was empty.

The cat was lucky. It had narrowly escaped death. But if Lester saw it again, it wouldn't be so lucky.

He switched the knife into his other hand and headed downstairs, then opened his laptop and signed into The Community. It was the first thing he did every time he came home, when there weren't stray animals breaking into his house. After a few seconds, his profile loaded and there, in the top-right corner, underneath his name, was a small red notification above a message icon.

Jessica.

Lester read the message, and as soon as he finished, he masturbated aggressively over Jessica Mann's news feed, pressing the knife into his leg and stomach for extra stimulation. A few minutes later he was finished and decided to leave the mess in his trousers. There were bigger things to worry about.

Jessica wanted to meet him. She had read his initial message last night but forgotten to reply. But after this morning's incident she now remembered where she recognised him from. It was a date. Her place. Tonight – 9 p.m. After her flatmate would be gone.

It would be just the two of them in less than seven hours' time. Now they could solidify their relationship with a Communion. Now Lester could relive the experience and unbinding he'd felt with Jessica and Steven the other night.

Welcome to the real *Community.*

CHAPTER 17

GOING FISHING

'Thanks for agreeing to this,' Drew said as he placed a set of folders on the table. 'It's really going to help our investigation.'

'Good. Good. Helpful,' Archie Arnold said, sitting upright with his arms placed flat on his knees. 'Just a few questions?'

'That's all it is,' Garrison said beside Drew. 'Just a few questions. Nothing serious. We just want to follow on from what our colleague asked you the other day.'

'Detective Constable Jake Tanner. I liked him,' Archie said.

'Good. We're warming to him too,' Drew replied

The three of them sat in Interview Room 3. Garrison had been to pick up Archie and then driven back to the station. Apparently he had no means of getting himself to the station and had a phobia of public transport.

The interview room was cold and poorly lit. Drew's decision. A mild intimidation technique he'd learnt from an old colleague when he was just starting out. The majority of the time it didn't work because the general public were becoming more and more educated about their rights and the sorts of conditions they should be kept in, but on the infrequent and, arguably miraculous, occasion that his technique did work, its success was evidence enough for Drew to warrant continuing with it.

Drew pretended to start the recording and then paused for a

further ten seconds, staring at Archie in complete silence – another trick he'd learnt from the same colleague.

'How much can you tell us about Steven and Jessica Arnholt, Archie? Were you good friends with them? Meet up at the weekends and go for a little picnic? Get them to read you bedtime stories at night?'

Oh, this was going to be good. He was going to enjoy this.

'I didn't know them that well,' Archie said. 'Honest. Promise.'

'Are you sure?'

Archie nodded.

'You didn't have little sex parties with them? Take a few drugs with them to help take the edge off, calm the nerves?'

'Bad. Drugs are bad. Stay away from drugs,' Archie said, gesticulating with his hands. 'Honest. Promise.'

'But prostitutes are fine?' Garrison remarked and then retreated back into his seat.

'Are you sure, Archie? I reckon there's a bookie out there willing to give good odds on that. Five to one maybe?' Drew paused. His eyebrows rose.

Archie's rose as well, mirroring Drew's expression. Then Archie began to bite his finger.

'I'd say those are quite good odds, considering,' Drew added.

'Considering,' Garrison said, nodding to Archie. 'So what more can you tell us?'

'Drugs, bad. Scary. Stay away from drugs.'

Drew sighed heavily as he leant forward on his seat. They were getting nowhere. It was time to turn up the heat. 'Where were you on the night of the seventeenth?'

'Indoors. Watching television. *University Challenge*, my favourite.'

'All night? From eight till eight in the morning? That seems to me like a really long time. Wouldn't you agree, DC Garrison?'

'I would, DS Richmond, I would. I know for certain I'd get bored. Maybe even go for a walk if I wasn't feeling tired yet. Which... funnily enough, is what we've got an eyewitness saying you did. They saw you walking up and down the street. They said they saw you leaving your house at around midnight and going into Steven and Jessica's art gallery at a similar time to when they were murdered. And then they saw a prostitute entering your house shortly after.'

Garrison hesitated and Drew watched the man lick his lips. Their eyes locked before he continued. 'Really good odds on that one as well. Maybe even better at two to one.'

For a long moment, Archie said nothing. He continued to bite his finger until he drew blood. All three men in the room knew what was happening, even if it did take Archie the longest.

'Archie...' Drew insisted. 'Anything you'd like to say to that?'

'It's not true. Honest.'

'Really? So what were you doing last night?' Garrison asked.

'It's fine,' Drew interrupted, adjusting his tie. 'We can always have another meeting if necessary. Perhaps you can tell us if you know what happened to Steven and Jessica Arnholt? Their killer is still out there, and there would be quite a significant reward if we were able to find them. Of course, nothing financial, but you would feel a great sense of pride and servitude if you were able to supply us with a name. Perhaps it was someone you know.'

Another brief moment passed as the room fell silent. Drew heard the sound of his breath as he inhaled sharply. 'You're being such a massive help to our investigation, and you don't even realise it yet.'

'Finished?' Archie said, standing up. The chair screeched against the floor.

'Sit down,' Drew said sternly.

Beside him, Garrison hefted himself out of his chair and stood between Archie and the door. There was no escape. His task was simple: sit down, shut up and answer the questions.

Tentatively, Archie sat down. He placed his forearms on the arms of the chair.

'We can either make this really simple or really difficult for you, Archie,' Drew began, casting a quick glance at the recorder to make sure it definitely was switched off.

'Bad. Bad things,' Archie said, his voice quiet.

'We own you. We own your area. But we don't like it when you lie to us. We know you were scoring last night, and we know you had a piece of skirt with you. You don't need to be embarrassed about it in front of us. We don't mind. But if you want your continued supply – of both the pussy and the packet that it came in – you'll do as we tell you.' Drew made a slight nod to the finger Archie had been nibbling. 'I'm curious... is that a symptom of the drugs, the disability or a nervous reflex?'

Archie observed his finger as though it wasn't actually his – as if it was an inanimate object he'd picked up from the table.

'Ouchie,' he said. 'You made me hurt myself.'

'Not as much as we can do if you don't listen to us. If you want your little friend to keep bringing his drugs round for you on your estate, then we'll continue to make sure you're well looked after, and that you get a competitive price – whether you're on the outside or on the inside. Although, I heard you already get good rates given your circumstances.'

'I... I... Why are you telling me this? What if I tell?'

Drew smirked. 'We're confident it won't come to that. Besides, who are they going to believe? A disabled junky, or two esteemed police detectives who have contributed years of hard work and dedication to the service? I think I know the answer, don't you, DC Garrison?'

'I do,' Garrison said, nodding.

'Archie,' Drew continued, pausing to swallow and clear his throat. 'You see, our new relationship can be mutually beneficial.'

'Explain,' Archie said.

'If you help us with our investigation, we can work something out for you. Discounted rates. A major stake in the operations. A higher position of power. Of course, those three tiers are heavily dependent on the work you do for us... should we require it.'

Archie kept his attention on Drew. 'What do you need me to do?'

'Nothing, for now. You'll only be required if our investigation doesn't make any progress.'

'Fishing. Going fishing.'

'You'll be bait, yes,' Garrison added. 'We can either use you to take the rap or – and I'm assuming you'd prefer this route because the other one isn't so inviting – you can find a suitable replacement. Someone who can take the fall for it instead. But that decision depends almost completely on us. So you'd better impress.'

'And...' Archie hesitated. 'No. Say no. I refuse. I tell everyone. I tell the police... I tell Tanner!'

Another smirk grew on Drew's face. He really was enjoying this. And he wanted it to continue. 'You can try, but it wouldn't be worth the time or the effort. DC Tanner is with us. You really think we'd have a member of our team that doesn't follow the same path as us? Stupid.'

'No. Say no,' Archie repeated.

Drew leant back in his chair, crossing his arms. 'Since we've been here, Archie, we've had a couple of our officers sneak into your home and find everything with your DNA on it. Clothing. Bath towel. Hairbrush. Toothbrush. I'm sure we'll be able to find some semen deposits on your socks as well. All it takes for us is to be a little bit pissed off and we'll plant that evidence all over Steven and Jessica Arnholt's body. It won't take much for us to persuade someone to re-examine the evidence, and... wait! What's that? They've found something. Something they overlooked before. DNA implicating Archie Arnold at the crime scene during the time of the deceased's murders? Wow, incredible. Miraculous. God bless modern science.'

Archie's face contorted as he absorbed what was being said. He was fucked, and everyone in the room knew it. Drew had just delivered the final nail in the coffin. And it felt euphoric.

For a long while, Archie didn't respond. And then, as Drew scowled at him, tears formed in his eyes and streamed down his face. Archie leant forward, resting his elbows on his knees, and began to weep loudly.

Drew didn't want to stay and watch this bullshit; he rose out of his chair and slid it flush against the table.

'Nice doing business with you, Archie,' he said, moving to the door. 'You can find your own way home.'

CHAPTER 18

CONGRATULATIONS

As soon as Jake returned to the office and sat down at his desk, his phone vibrated. It was an email notification that had been sent to his personal account from Danika. He opened the message. There was no subject header. Instead it only contained a series of screenshots taken from HOLMES. The body of the email read:

Case number 05/E9/22312/09. This is all I can do for you. Hope you understand.

Jake did. She had broken countless procedures and regulations in sending him the documents, not to mention getting access to them in the first place. As he hovered his finger over the first image, he couldn't help feeling guilty about it all. She had potentially risked the career she was just beginning to make for herself so that she could help him. It was nonsensical and foolish. The entire Crimsons trial had been plagued by corruption from the outset, and asking Danika to do some of his dirty work made him just as bad as the bent cops who were trying to get Danny and Michael Cipriano out of jail in the first place. If he wanted to get to the bottom of their trial, then he was going to have to play by the rules. That's what they were there for.

Jake swallowed as he tapped open the first image attachment. It was a screenshot of Danny Cipriano's personal file. Danny's mugshot was in the top right of the page, followed by some brief information about him. Date of birth. Height. Weight. But before Jake could read any further, he was interrupted.

Drew and Garrison wandered past his desk and stopped either side of him. At the sight of them both, Jake locked the screen using the side button, but as he set his mobile down on the table, the movement wakened the screen, flashing an image of him and Elizabeth on their wedding day. Drew peered over and glanced at it.

'That the wife?'

Jake snatched the phone before Drew could and quickly pocketed it. 'Yeah,' he replied.

'She said anything?'

'Nothing yet.' Jake chuckled nervously. 'Still waiting to hear from her.'

'Well, let us know when something happens.'

'Of course,' Jake said.

'Be careful what you wish for,' Garrison added. 'This one'll be stealing your missus if he gets near. He's a deviant. Bit of a predator.'

'Fuck you, Pete,' Drew spat, and then the three men laughed awkwardly.

As the brief laughter died down, a body exited the interview room to Jake's right. Jake recognised Archie immediately. That face. That hair. That tracksuit. At the sight of Jake, Archie waved. Surprised, and feeling obliged to reciprocate, Jake waved back. Wandering behind him, escorting him out, was a uniformed officer. After quickly losing interest in Jake, Archie meandered across the office and then headed out of the building.

'How'd it go with him?' Jake asked, turning to Drew.

'Oh... you know. Wasting police time apparently. Doesn't look like anything will come of it.' He faced Jake. 'We'll still keep our eye on him though. If anything crops up I'll let you know, all right?'

'Yeah,' Jake said, his mind elsewhere. 'I appreciate it.'

Jake was distracted. He was thinking about the email. He wanted to read the rest of it, but first he had to get rid of these two loitering behind him.

After the door closed behind Archie, Liam appeared from his office and headed over to the three of them.

'Nice little mothers' meeting?' he asked. Before any of them could respond, he pointed at Jake's computer monitor. 'You haven't even opened it yet?'

'Opened wh—?' Jake snapped his head round to face his computer. Resting against the screen was a card. Jake reached for it and opened it. Sparkles and glitter and confetti fell onto Jake's lap, and in his hand was a Congratulations card. The inside of the message wished him good luck on the imminent arrival of his baby girl and everyone in the office had signed it, including DCI Hamilton and the rest of the Missing Persons Team.

'That was my idea,' Liam said, slapping Jake on the shoulder. 'Before anyone tells you otherwise.'

Jake was speechless. He had never received anything like this before – not even before Maisie was born, and during that pregnancy, he was so excited he hadn't been able to shut up about it.

'I don't know what to say,' he said. 'It's so kind. Generous. Thank you.'

'I'll buy you a pack of digestives when I'm next in the shops,' Garrison said over his shoulder.

'We didn't know when you were going off, so we thought we'd give it to you now.' Liam reached behind his back and produced another envelope. 'This is for you as well.'

'What is it?' Jake asked.

'A lollipop.' Liam shot him a scowl. 'Open it and find out, you idiot.'

Liam took a step back and whistled for everyone in the office to come over. They did, and as they stood there watching, Jake felt the pressure of their eyes on him. The tension. The heightened sense of anticipation.

'If you don't do it,' Garrison said, 'then I will.'

Jake wasted no time in opening the envelope. Inside was a thin wad of notes. The papers felt heavy in his hands, and the smell of old money wafted up his nose.

'There's about five hundred quid there. The team had a bit of a whip-round before you got back. We know it's not much, but it's something to help you out if you need it,' Liam said, coming back to Jake's side. 'You can buy the little'un something nice. Or maybe yourself.'

A lump caught in Jake's throat.

'I... er... I... This is too much,' he said. 'I can't accept this—'

'You can, and you will,' Drew said. He extended his hand and Jake shook it. 'Congratulations again, mate. Pleased for you.'

The rest of the team shook Jake's hand and patted him on the back before leaving to get back to their work. After he was left alone, he sat on his chair slowly and stared at the money. Then he smiled to himself; not because of the extra cash which covered the costs of the cabs, but because now – *finally* – he felt part of the team.

Feeling inspired about his work and colleagues, Jake forgot about Danika's email and began to create a profile of the killer. There was a large whiteboard behind him. He grabbed a pen and began to scribble on it. He noted everything he could think of – anything either Archie, Steven's parents or Nathan had said to him.

In the middle of the board, he circled one word: Community.

'What's that for?' Drew asked beside him.

Jake snapped the cap on the end of the pen. 'When I spoke with Steven's agent, he said that Steven and Jessica were into threesomes, and that they were part of a group. I feel like the killer was a part of the same group. They invited him over, started to have a little bit of fun and then something went seriously wrong.'

'Have you run a search on local paedophiles or sex rings or anyone on ViSOR?'

'Not yet.'

'Probably worth a look before you start doing anything else. At least then we'll have a list of names we can investigate.'

Filled with the excitement he always felt when investigating, Jake immediately got to work. He was one of the few MIT detectives who had been trained and authorised to use ViSOR – the Violent and Sex Offender Register. It contained a list of people who had been convicted of sexual-related offences in the UK. The parameters for Jake's search were location and date of conviction. Stratford, and anyone in the past five years.

Shortly after running the search, he had a list of names.

Ten.

None of them began with 'Lester'.

CHAPTER 19

JESSICA

Lester rang the bell and then placed his ear to the door. The bong echoed on the other side, followed by the sound of a glass being set down on a surface and footsteps drawing closer.

When the door opened, Jessica Mann smiled brilliantly at him, flashing a set of incandescent teeth. She wore a tight, strapless black dress that came to a stop just above the knees. Her chestnut brown hair hung loose, the ends teased into tight curls. She wore a full face of make-up, accentuating her cheeks and eyebrows, and her eyes had been shaded black, giving her an air of mystery and intrigue that Lester adored. The Jessica Mann in front of him was a completely different woman to the one he'd stumbled upon earlier.

'You look nothing like your profile picture,' he said, holding the bottle of wine that he'd brought with him.

'Is that a bad thing?' she asked. She stepped aside for him to enter.

'On this occasion, quite the opposite,' he replied, thinking of how much she looked like Jessica Arnholt. He looked down at the bottle to distract himself. 'I hope you like Pinot.'

'It's my favourite.' She shut the door behind him and pointed to the kitchen at the other end of the hallway. Beside the kitchen door was a steep set of stairs. As Jessica brushed past him, he felt her hand brush against his groin. She continued down the corridor nonchalantly.

They moved into the kitchen. Jessica grabbed two glasses from a cupboard, took the bottle of wine from Lester and poured. As he waited, Lester observed his surroundings. The kitchen was immaculate and modern. Clean. White. The perfect colour to remove bloodstains from.

'Nice place you have here,' he said. By the dining-room door to his left, a cat entered with its tail extended. 'I hope you didn't go to all this effort just for me.'

Jessica passed him his glass of wine. 'You're lucky my housemate is a clean freak. She claims she has OCD, but I just think that's an excuse to be anal about everything – working in a hospital doesn't help.'

'So what does that make you then? The messy one?' Lester drank. The wine was warm and tingled his chapped lips, but it was smooth going down his throat and left a sweet aftertaste in his mouth. Not bad for £7.

Jessica drank too, and as she placed the glass down on the surface, she said, 'I'm messy beyond your wildest comprehension.'

Lester smirked. He was hungry. Ravenous. The monster that he'd discovered as a child was hungry, and he wanted nothing more than to rip her clothes off, tear her in half and fill himself with The Nasties. But he had to wait. He needed to conduct a sweep of the house first; with Steven and Jessica it hadn't been necessary because he knew and trusted them from his previous visits. But this was new territory for him, a new partner, a new Communion, and there was no knowing what was going on behind the scenes. Whether he was being set up to be overthrown on the leader board. Or, worse, whether she was secretly working for the police and setting him up for an almighty fall.

Lester's eyes fell on a photograph on the window bay.

'I hope we won't be expecting a boyfriend to join us?' Lester asked, looking at the photo of Jessica wrapping her arms around a man's shoulders with a girl beside them.

Jessica leant against the oven, folded her arms and legs over one another and sipped. 'No,' she said, turning her attention to the photograph. 'That's my flatmate's brother – he lives in Scotland. And that's my flatmate with us.'

'Oh?'

'Yeah. You're a very lucky man.'

'Oh?'

'It took me ages to persuade her to get out of the house. She was called in to do an extra overnight shift, but she told them no. I convinced her it was good for her to go. She needs the money.'

Lester's concerns rose.

'Does she know I'm here? She knows I've come over?'

Jessica placed her glass down on the counter and approached him. She stroked his arm and squeezed his muscles the same way she'd done when he'd bumped into her at the coffee shop.

'Relax,' she said. 'She doesn't know a thing. If she did, she'd ask a thousand questions. It's all good. Our secret is safe. Trust me. I can make you relax.'

Jessica leant in for a kiss, but Lester held her back. His urges were so strong it took every fibre in his being to refrain.

'What's the rush?' he asked. 'We've got the wine. We've got the time. Let's take things slow. I want to make it last the whole night.'

A smirk grew on Jessica's face. He was disarming her with his charm, and he knew that he was impeccable when taking this approach.

'I'm beginning to understand why you're the best,' she said, wandering back to her glass, picking it up and heading into the living room.

'Be careful, Miss Mann – flattery will only get you so far,' he said.

'I'm prepared to do whatever it takes to get me all the way.'

The living room was clean and tidy. In the corner was a flat-screen television with PlayStation remotes resting beside it. Plush, grey two-man sofas faced the television as if worshipping it on a shrine. Artwork hung on the wall, and for a moment, Lester observed it, but he became distracted by something else: Jessica finding herself a seat on the sofa. As she sat down, she flipped one leg over the other slowly, flashing her underwear and giving Lester, he presumed, the opportunity of looking up her skirt.

Lester slid onto the sofa, joining her. He drank some more of the wine and ignored the thin layer of excited sweat forming on his back.

'Did you paint that yourself?' Lester asked, nodding to the art on the wall. It looked familiar.

'I'm about as artistic as a tortoise with a hairpin for a brush. I'm shit.' She paused. 'No, it's a piece of art from a local dealer. Steven Arnholt? Have you heard of him?'

Lester tensed up. He opened his mouth to speak, carefully calculating his words, but nothing came out. He sipped his drink to stall for time.

'I thought I recognised the artwork,' he finally said.

'It was given to me as a present.'

'Present?'

'They're part of The Community too. They're CandidCouple. They gave it to me for putting on a *stellar performance* – Steven's words, not mine. I haven't heard from them recently. They usually like to meet up once a month or so. You should try them. They taught me things I could never have imagined.'

A deep grin grew on Lester's face and he gripped the glass in his hands tightly, testing its strength. 'I can teach you even more.'

'I wouldn't have responded if it weren't for your high score. I'm looking to learn *a lot*.'

'It will only work if you're a good learner.'

'I'm fast too.'

'Even better,' Lester said. He finished off the rest of his drink and placed the glass on the carpet. 'Do you have anywhere we can go?'

Jessica nodded. 'My bedroom. I've kitted it out especially for tonight. It's a rarity a Communion happens in my room. It's usually at the other party's. Somewhere better, with lots more room to play in.'

'For my particular methods, we don't need a lot of space.'

Jessica ascended the steep staircase, followed closely by Lester. They came to the landing and made a right turn. Lester took a quick glance at the other bedroom and the bathroom, which were visible through their open doors. He deemed it safe to proceed. There was no one there, and there was nothing immediately suspicious about the house either. But that didn't mean there wasn't anything suspicious about Jessica.

'What about in your flatmate's room?' Lester asked, just as Jessica entered her own. 'It looks bigger. Plus it feels naughtier.'

Jessica shook her head violently. All her flirtatious behaviour had disappeared like a random star in the night sky. 'No. I couldn't do that. Her room is off limits. She doesn't even let me in during the day when she's here, let alone when she's not.'

'Come on,' Lester said, edging closer towards Jessica's flatmate's room. 'She won't know if we're careful. We've got time to tidy up if we make a mess. Come on, Jess – it'll make it more exciting. You get more points if you do it somewhere different to normal.'

'Really?' Jessica's eyes widened.

'Didn't you know? You get an extra hundred for doing it somewhere other than your Designated Communion Area. That's why they make you enter that information when you sign up.'

Jessica shook her head. 'Those bastards. They didn't tell me that. If I'd have known earlier, I could have got nearly a thousand extra points.'

Shrugging, Lester said, 'Shame. You'd be nearer me on the leader board.' He crossed the threshold into the flatmate's room and peered inside. 'Now you've got the opportunity to get an extra two hundred.'

'Two hundred?'

'I know the founder. I can work out a deal.'

'Why don't we go to yours? You've already got enough points.'

No, I don't, he thought. In his mind, the gap between him and second position wasn't large enough. It was just over three thousand, and that, Lester knew from experience, could be achieved in as little as five Communions. But that would require some depraved activities – the likes of which had only been committed by one person: him.

'Why do you think I'm here?' Lester started. 'I've got a high score to maintain. The moment I let that slip, the moment I fall to second… third… fourth… I can't let that happen.'

For a long moment, Jessica neither said nor did anything. She seemed to be stuck in an internal conflict. Lester knew the answer before she did. He knew that she'd concede defeat and agree to it. He knew that she wanted – no, *needed* – those extra points that he could get her. He knew that she strived to climb the leader board.

Becoming a member of The Community was like a drug. Once you'd got a small taste for it, you wanted it more and more. It became an obsession. An addiction. Except this one didn't eat away at you and make you any less of a human being. If anything, it had the opposite effect. It built bonds between people, relationships. And Lester was the living, breathing version of that obsession.

'Fuck it,' Jessica said. 'I'll deal with her tomorrow. Right now, I want you.'

Jessica tore across the landing, grabbed Lester's collar and threw him down on the bed. She slammed the door shut and crawled atop him. Lester was instantly hard, and he fought the urge to remove his trousers.

He didn't want that old pleasure anymore. No, he was after something else. Something new. Something that, until recently, he'd never thought possible. The other night, with Steven and Jessica, he'd experienced a completely different level of sensation. He had been at one with their dead bodies – more than he could have ever said for someone living.

Jessica pulled her dress up and slammed her body down on his crotch, which made Lester groan in pain.

'I thought you were the masochist?' he said through struggled breath.

'I was, but now I want to flip sides.'

'You can't.'

Jessica hefted herself from him, wandered out of the room and returned a few seconds later. She held a whip and handcuffs in her hands.

'I'm going to do to you what Steven and Jessica Arnholt did to me.'

There it was. Those names again. The ones he didn't want to hear. The ones that made him suspicious. The ones that incited paranoia every time he heard someone else mention them.

Jessica removed her dress, placing the whip and handcuffs on the bed. Lester propped himself up on his forearms and looked beside him to the bedside table. There was nothing there he could use as a weapon. Deciding on a better plan, he undressed himself, flinging his clothes to the floor, and hopped off, naked from the waist down.

'What are you doing?' Jessica asked.

Lester pretended to lunge for the whip on the bed with his left arm. He anticipated Jessica's reaction – she reached for it just as quickly – and, using his right hand, punched her in the jaw. She yelped and collapsed to the ground. Her hand flew to her mouth. Within seconds, it was bloody.

'What are you—?'

Lester punched her in the face again, this time with the left. Her head recoiled and smashed on the floor. Lester straddled her, pinning her to the ground. She clawed at him as she began to choke on her own blood.

Lester punched her one final time, almost incapacitating her. Jessica's eyes rolled back in her head as it lolled from side to side. Then Lester gripped her throat in his hands. It felt small, thin, narrow, like a rolling pin. He applied his body weight onto her neck and squeezed simultaneously. She gasped and wheezed for air, clawing at his face, trying to force him to stop.

Her efforts were futile. Lester was hungry, The Nasties were on their way, and he had no intention of giving up. Nothing could stop him now.

Nothing.

He grinned at her as the life gradually left her body.

'It's all a part of it,' he said, dribbling with excitement. 'Think of the points.'

Jessica gasped but nothing came out. More blood and phlegm rolled down her throat and she coughed it back up.

Lester increased the pressure, and then, within a few minutes of struggling and fighting back, Jessica Mann was dead.

And now she was his to play with for the next eight hours, until her flatmate came home.

He picked her body from the carpet and slumped it onto the bed.

'Oh, Jessica,' he said. 'I've been so looking forward to this.'

| PART 3 |

CHAPTER 20

PLAYING BY THE RULES

Lester delicately closed the door behind him so as not to disturb the still silence and tranquillity of the street. He wiped his fingerprints free from the handle using his sleeve and wandered to the edge of the front porch. In the distance, the hubbub of city life reminded him that he was invisible. A mask amongst millions. Just another ordinary individual going about his life without any interference, cloaked by anonymity in the early hours of the morning. There was no reason to suspect him of anything. Unless… unless he'd made a noise during Communion. Unless somebody heard him defiling Jessica Mann's body.

No, that was a ridiculous thought. It was impossible. He'd been quiet. He'd made sure Jessica didn't even have the chance to scream before he beat her to death. Everything was fine, he convinced himself. But it wasn't over yet. He still needed to get home.

Lester pulled his flat cap lower over his face and meandered along the pavement cautiously, keeping his head down and his eyes focused on the slits in the pavement in front of him. As he swayed his arms through the air, he realised something. His hands were still covered in Jessica Mann's blood. Keeping one by his side, and the other by his face, making it look like he was rubbing his nose or scratching his cheek, he licked the blood clean. The taste was delicious. Metallic. Tangy. Sweet, like Jessica's perfume had been.

Jessica Mann had been good fun and a good ride. But she was nothing compared to Jessica Arnholt. There was still something missing. Something he couldn't quite place. He had even smashed a few of Mann's teeth out and removed her tongue to make the blowjob more satisfying. But it hadn't worked. Maybe it was him. Maybe he was the one at fault. Something psychological, something in his brain that was prohibiting him from enjoying himself as much. Maybe he was trying to encapsulate the experience too perfectly. Maybe next time he would need to relax more, worry less and be more carefree about it all. Maybe he needed to let The Nasties completely consume him.

Lester made a left turn at the end of the street. Twenty yards away, approaching him with its lights beaming across the road, was a police car, illuminated in fluorescent yellow and white by the street lamps on the pavement. At the sight of the vehicle, Lester panicked. His foot caught on a disjointed pavement slab and he tripped, his body flopping onto the concrete, skin tearing away from his palms. He let out a little groan and hoped the patrol vehicle hadn't seen him.

But then the driver pulled the car to a stop and rolled down the window.

'You all right there, mate?' the driver asked.

On the passenger side of the car a uniformed officer exited the vehicle and started towards him. Lester's pulse quickened. He picked himself up and then brushed himself off, keeping his back to the police officer.

'You had a little too much to drink tonight there, mate?' the officer asked, hovering a few feet from him.

Lester readjusted his hat, pulling it further over his eyes. He shook his head.

'No,' he said, standoffish.

'Where you headed?' the officer asked.

'Home.'

The officer took a step forward and Lester froze. In his pocket, he held the blade he'd used to dissect Jessica's body, another memento, along with the others secreted in his coat. He gripped the weapon tightly and readied himself to plunge it under the officer's armpit. He didn't want it to come to that, but he was physically strong enough to be able to inflict such damage. He just needed to catch the officer unawares. And be able to deal with the other one.

'You going to be all right? You didn't twist your ankle or anything?' The officer took another step forward, and Lester inched his hand out of his pocket.

'I'll be fine,' he said, starting away. 'Thanks though, Officer. I feel a lot safer when you're around.'

Lester hurried out of there. That had been a close one. There was no knowing how much of his face the officer had seen. He just hoped it wasn't enough for him to be able to identify him.

Lester sped home on foot. It took him half an hour to complete the two-mile journey. And as he walked, he darted his gaze left and right, searching for any signs that the police car was suspiciously following him.

There was nothing, save for his own paranoia wracking his nerves.

Once he was home, Lester locked the door behind him and headed straight upstairs. The window in the bathroom was locked. He undressed and then jumped into the shower. He enjoyed the cold water streaming over his muscles. They flexed as the shock set in, and then he relaxed. Torrents of water travelled down his face and into his mouth. He panted heavily. The sin was releasing from his body. Thin streaks of blood mixed in the water that pooled by the drain, swirling as it waited to descend the plug.

He stood there for five minutes, allowing himself to be cleansed. After he'd finished, he climbed out of the tub, wrapped a towel around his waist and carried his soiled clothes to his bedroom. Throwing them on the floor, with his other hand, he reached inside his trouser pocket and removed a plastic freezer bag.

Blood smeared the walls of the bag. He moved to the chest of drawers in the corner of the room. Resting atop them was a large empty jar. Lester opened it, decanted the contents of the freezer bag inside the jar and discarded the bag to the bin by his feet. Staring back at him was Jessica Mann's severed tongue and fingers. It had been an old ritual from when he was a child. He couldn't recall exactly how old he was when he'd first killed, but he knew it was early in his development. It had started with birds and rats that he'd trapped in the garden, slowly growing more severe as the size of the animals increased. And eventually he'd started receiving sexual gratification from it. The sensation had reached new heights when he'd slaughtered Whiskers, the family cat. Growing up, he'd hated the way the cat had hissed at him and clawed him for no reason, drawing blood at the slightest scratch. So he decided to seek revenge and remove its tongue and paws. That way there was no chance the animal would be able to intimidate or hurt him again. And there was the same parallel with Jessica Arnholt. He had removed her tongue too. Now she wouldn't be able to harm him with her words again – those fateful words that had invoked fear within him and awakened The Nasties after she'd let slip that they were going to kill him. Now both Jessica Mann and Jessica Arnholt had been silenced for eternity. They could never speak out about their injuries. And they could never reveal his identity.

Lester grabbed a bottle of disinfectant from inside the drawer and wiped his thumbprint clean from the glass until he saw his distorted reflection staring back at him. Then he dressed himself and headed downstairs to the kitchen to burn his camomile candle. The sun was creeping over the horizon, which meant it was nearly time for breakfast. There was a full day ahead of him, and he didn't feel like sleeping; the euphoria of the past six hours – two hours shorter than he would have liked – was all the energy he needed to keep him awake for the rest of the day.

As the time reached 6 a.m., the alarm on his phone vibrated. He stopped it and called S. It was the earliest that S would be awake, and if there was one thing Lester knew about the man he adored – yet had never met – it was that he did not like to be woken up before his prearranged time.

'Another one?' S asked, answering almost as soon as the phone had begun to ring.

'Yes,' Lester said. He was dressed in jogging bottoms and T-shirt. To an outsider, he looked like a normal person – someone who had a normal job, with a normal life – and that was just the pretence Lester wanted to maintain.

'Send me the proof.'

'Check your messages.' Lester had videoed and photographed his time with Jessica Mann. He had sent them to S on the way home. 'They should already be in there. But it doesn't have quite the same production value as Steven Arnholt's camera.'

There was a moment's pause as S confirmed receipt of the files. He breathed heavily through the phone, and as Lester waited, he opened his laptop, logged onto The Community and checked the leader board.

'What the fuck is this?' Lester said.

'What?' S replied. His breathing was heavy, almost aroused.

'You know exactly what. Second place. The gap. It's five hundred points. How? Overnight?' Lester's breathing increased as rage began to scorch his body.

'He's catching you up.'

'Bullshit. In one day? Impossible.'

'Twenty-four hours is a long time.'

Lester was shaking his head in disbelief as he spoke. 'If he was playing by the rules, he would have to Communion with twenty people in twenty-four hours…' Lester hesitated. 'But he's not playing by the rules, is he?'

There was another pause. Lester bit his lip in anger.

'Don't ignore me,' Lester hissed.

'He came to me. He wanted to know how to improve. What was I to do? You two are front runners to become part of the separate league. If he's getting the better of you already, then you need to up your game.'

Lester stared at the screen.

'Fine,' he said. 'I will.'

CHAPTER 21

TROPHIES

For the second time in the space of three days, Jake donned a forensic oversuit. This time it was an even tighter fit, and the material chafed his wrists, ankles and neck. He and the rest of Major Investigation had received a call early morning, alerting them of a murder less than a mile from Stratford Central Station.

'What've we got?' Jake asked, waiting outside the house in the middle of the street. Drew, Garrison and Liam all struggled to fit their suits over their shoes and bodies. The street had been cordoned off and a perimeter set up around the block.

Poojah, the pathologist, exited the house and wandered across to them. 'Similar to Monday's. Female, IC1, mid-twenties.'

'Name?' Liam asked as he pulled the zip up to his chin.

'Housemate identified her as Jessica Mann. Driver's licence confirms that. Her NHS card says she's a trainee nurse,' Poojah explained.

'Jessica…' Jake repeated. 'Too much of a coincidence?'

Liam scoffed. 'I've been in this job too long to know there are no such things as coincidences.'

'She was pretty too,' Poojah said.

'Was?'

Poojah didn't respond.

'Think you might need another sick bag, Jake,' Drew said to a chorus of chuckles coming from Liam and Poojah.

Beside them, Garrison was the final one to suit himself up. The four of them – Liam, Drew, Jake and Garrison – followed Poojah into the house. Scene of crime officers swarmed the downstairs area like flies, zooming from one corner to another with total disregard for the new arrivals. Several of the SOCOs were in the middle of taking photographs of the living room, dining room and kitchen at the end of the corridor. Jake climbed the stairs and felt the air temperature drop. There was a frostiness in the atmosphere, worsened by the absolute silence, and Jake sensed every one of them was preparing themselves – physically and mentally – for what they were about to see.

As they entered the bedroom, the sight made Jake immediately want to gag. A load of bile – this morning's breakfast – bubbled in his stomach, ready to come up. But he fought it, swallowing the sensation back down his throat. He wasn't going to fall ill to the same attack he had last time.

For a long moment he stood there, transfixed at the sight in front of him. He wanted to tear his eyes from it, but he couldn't. An invisible, impenetrable force was keeping him there.

Jessica Mann's arms and legs were spread to the four corners of the bed. Her hands and feet had been dismembered, and a gap about two inches wide separated them from the rest of her body, as though they were missing components of a model that required some screws to tighten them in place. Jessica's head had been removed too and was in an upright position, staring out at them, like a lighthouse. Her eyes were open, but they were vacant, hollow, ghostly white. A large incision had been made along the length of her body and its contents had been emptied, including her blood.

Jake took a step forward. Then another. And another. As he crossed the threshold into the room, he was hit by the putrid stench of rotting flesh, decaying organs and the surprising smell of cleaning chemicals.

'Jesus fucking Christ,' Garrison said. This time it was his turn to vomit. He sprinted out of the bedroom and barged past a duo of investigators on the landing, knocking a camera to the ground and splintering the glass lens. Then he disappeared down the stairs and out of the house.

Jake sympathised with him.

'Do we know what killed her?' he asked as his eyes fell over Jessica's body again.

'The decapitation couldn't have helped,' Drew said sarcastically. Jake couldn't determine whether he was being sarcastic playfully, or whether he was just being a dick; either way, Jake thought it was unnecessary and unprofessional. The least he could do was show a little respect to the deceased.

Poojah shot Drew a scowl, easily visible through her hood and face mask. 'Early inspection shows bruising on her cheeks and temple, which could suggest that she was bludgeoned to death. There do, however, seem to be more bruises on the neck, which would indicate strangulation – but they could be post-mortem. It's difficult to say. With this type of killing, as well as the other one, I'd say it's evident that strangulation has been used as a form of sexual pleasure. But it would be remiss of me to tell you definitively. You'll have to wait for my report.'

Jake continued to observe Jessica's body, leaning forward and peering into the gaping hole of her stomach. It was empty and looked as though half of her blood had been suctioned up through a hoover. The bed sheets surrounding her were surprisingly devoid of blood, and looked as though an attempt had been made to clean them. He swallowed and wiped his top lip. 'Dare I ask what's gone on there?'

'Two possibilities. Her organs have either been removed and disposed of somewhere. Or whoever's responsible for this has ingested them. The incision marks are sloppy, like the body was hacked at.'

Jake looked at her in pure disgust. 'Cannibalism?'

Poojah's dark eyes gave nothing away. 'I've never seen it, but I know the symptoms. If I had to make an educated guess, I'd say he started to cut the organs out of the body, but then changed his mind and used his teeth instead. There are marks consistent with that on the inside of her stomach.'

Just as Jake was about to respond, Garrison returned to the conversation. The colour had left his face and he rested his hand against his stomach, massaging it gently. A small chorus of cheers concerted amongst the group.

Jake waited until the commotion was over before he addressed Liam. 'What now then, boss?' he asked.

Liam turned to Poojah and asked where the witness was.

'One of your guys took her to the station. She was inconsolable,' she said.

'Any other witnesses?' Liam asked.

'None, sir.'

'He's getting cleverer…' Liam began but was cut off by Drew.

'What's the significance of the missing body parts?' he asked, pointing to Jessica's fingerless hands. 'And why'd he remove the tongue?'

'Liar,' Jake said without realising. 'Liar. Jessica Arnholt had that inscribed on her chest, didn't she? So she must have lied to the killer in some way or another, and removing her tongue is a way of silencing her, making sure she never lies to him again or speaks out about him.'

'A jaded ex-lover?' Drew asked.

'Possibly. Either that or it's something more spiritual. The tongue symbolises sensuality. Taste. Feeling.' Jake scratched the side of his face, drawing on the memory of a psychological case he'd studied in university. 'And that's what this whole experience is for him. It's about connecting his soul with the person he's killing. He did the same to Steven and Jessica Arnholt as well, and maybe he's getting a taste for it – literally. He tested the waters with it the first time, and now he's not going to stop until he's satisfied his cravings, like an urge for a piece of food, or a drink when you're really thirsty. With Steven and Jessica he just cut them off... with Jessica Mann, he's upgraded to the consumption of his victims.' Jake hesitated. 'As for the fingers...'

He drew a blank.

Poojah carried on for him. 'Each finger supposedly represents a different part of your body. Heart. Brain. Bladder. Perhaps he's cutting them off because that's what he wants to eat next.'

There was a moment's pause as Drew, Liam and Jake considered the theory.

'But he didn't eat anything on Steven or Jessica Arnholt,' Liam said.

'It's not uncommon for killers to take objects as trophies,' Jake added. 'But where he goes next... I don't know. Unless we can find the link. But his modus operandi is developing – it's becoming more severe. And I don't think he's fully realised what he's capable of.'

'I'd rather we find him before he makes that discovery.' Liam thanked Poojah, ordered her to send him the report as soon as possible and then the four of them headed for the stairs. As they exited the house, they each undressed out of their scrubs and signed out of the attendance log.

'Tanner,' Liam began, 'I want you to head back to the station. Speak with the housemate. Find out what she knows. We'll be right behind you.'

Jake nodded, hopped into his car and drove off.

CHAPTER 22

THE LION'S DEN

Drew waited for Jake to disappear down the street.

'What's the latest, boss?'

'What do you mean?' Liam replied, placing his hands in his pockets.

'Tanner. Is he on side?'

'You saw him take the money. He was chuffed. Had a smile on his face for the rest of the day.'

'We just need to tell him where it came from,' Garrison added.

'Which reminds me,' Liam said, taking a step back. He removed his hand from his pocket and massaged his chin. 'How are we coming along with Archie?'

Drew looked at Garrison sheepishly.

'He's on side, guv. We sat him down yesterday and had a little chat with him. He's aware of where he stands. He's ready to roll over at any point.' Drew hesitated. 'But we need to be cautious of him.'

'Why?' Liam snapped. A scene of crime officer swaggered past with a camera in his hands, and the three of them immediately fell silent. After the white scrubs had rounded out of sight, Liam continued, 'What's the matter with him?'

Drew looked at Garrison and then the ground before replying. He scratched his thick black hair as he spoke. 'He's... well, he seems tight with Tanner for some reason. I don't know how, nor do I know why, but when they saw one another yesterday, Archie waved to him. And during the questioning Archie said that he liked Jake, that he was nice.'

Liam rubbed the bridge of his nose, deep in thought. 'Did you not warn him of the consequences of his actions?'

'We couldn't have made it clearer, guv,' Garrison added.

'Right,' Liam continued, 'well, with the way this is going, it's looking less and less likely we're going to need Archie. Not unless he knows anyone who likes to fuck dead people and eat them. But we need to find another way we can get Jake on side. We need to show him where that money came from.'

'It's too soon to start pumping him full of drugs,' Drew said with a smirk. His attempt to make the others laugh was met with muted, cold stares. His smile dropped and his expression turned flat.

'What do you have in mind, boss?' Garrison asked.

Liam opened his mouth to speak but was distracted by a large white van skidding to a halt forty yards away from them, on the other side of the perimeter. Three individuals, dressed casually, alighted the vehicle. One of them carried a large pole with a microphone boom on the end of it. The other held a large video camera in his hand. The final person to leave the vehicle was a well-dressed woman, wearing a pinstripe jacket and pencil skirt that reached just below the knee.

'Here we go,' Liam said.

Drew spun on the spot and glanced at the personnel setting up beside the van. He knew who they were. They all did.

'Tanya Smile... Wow...' Drew said, grateful he didn't voice the other thoughts he had in his head about her.

Liam checked his watch. 'Three hours. That didn't take long. They're getting better.'

'Or we're getting worse,' Garrison said.

'Leave it with me,' Liam said. 'I'll go and do my thing.'

'Be careful,' Drew added just as Liam started off. 'We know how you like to behave in the lion's den.'

CHAPTER 23

BEST BEHAVIOUR

Tanya Smile was a formidable opponent. At least, that was what he wanted people to believe. He had encountered her many times in his career, at several meetings such as this; at a crime scene where he was further behind the pace than he should have been. Further behind the pace than the public would have liked to hear. Further behind the pace because he was relying on others to do the job – and, indeed, the dirty work – for him.

Liam sauntered towards her and sniffed his collar; the thin scent of aftershave he'd sprayed this morning was still fresh on the fabric. As he approached, he checked Tanya out before addressing her: the black hair, curled at the bottom just south of her ears; the thick black glasses; the long legs he stared at for longer than was socially acceptable; the mole on the side of her neck that she tried to cover with make-up at every opportunity. As he arrived, the cameraman held the camera against his eye and the sound recording artist hovered the microphone over Tanya's face, issuing her with instructions.

'Don't worry,' Liam called to her, holding his hands in the air in surrender. 'I'll save you the time of trying to find me. I'm right here.'

Tanya spun on the spot. At the sight of him, her pupils dilated and her lips parted, revealing a set of almost perfectly white teeth that had been bought with money – and lots of it. She brushed her hair behind her ear, and in a single move, she had disarmed him. It was his Achilles heel, and Liam sensed that she was trying hard to suppress a smile of her own.

'DCI Greene. You can be a hard man to reach at the best of times,' she said, gesticulating for the cameraman to lower the device before giving Liam her full attention.

'It depends what mood you catch me in.'

Tanya placed her left hand on her hip. 'What mood have I got you in now?'

'A facilitating mood.'

Tanya's eyes widened. She turned to face the cameraman and motioned for him to leave the two of them to it. After he left, she returned her focus to Liam. 'What front-page news have you got for me?'

Liam rolled his eyes and chuckled, then edged closer to the white tape that separated them. 'Come on, Tan. You know that's not how it works.'

'Yes. I know. Have I ever let you down before?'

Liam raised his eyebrow. 'Let's not hang around long enough to find out the answer to that question.'

'What do you need from me?' Tanya asked. They were almost shoulder to shoulder.

'Something a little unorthodox. We've got a newbie in the ranks.'

'How long's he been *with* you?'

'That's what we're trying to work out,' Liam said. 'You're going to help us.'

'How?'

'I need you to pile on the pressure. Kick up a fuss about it. Call us out. Call me out. After you've done that, we'll see how the newbie reacts,' Liam explained. His eyes darted left and right, searching for wandering ears.

'That really is an unusual request,' Tanya said, rubbing her right nostril. 'You reckon it will make a difference?'

'He's a good egg, but if this guy turns out to be a rat, then rooting him out is better than finding this serial killer. We've got a backup solution for that.'

They both paused as a liveried police car drove past. Liam watched and gestured at the driver as it went.

Tanya touched him on the arm, bringing his attention back to her. The touch lingered longer than it should have – especially in public.

'What's in it for me?' she asked, rubbing the same spot on her nose again.

Liam shrugged, avoiding her gaze. 'The same as usual. Maybe a little extra... *gratis*, obviously. I'm sure we can work something out.

It depends on how well you can execute your part of the plan.'

Tanya smirked and squeezed his forearm playfully. 'I'll be on my best behaviour.'

'I'm counting on it. And tell your boyfriend that—'

'He's not my boyfriend,' she protested.

Liam carried on heedlessly. 'Tell him I'm still waiting to hear from him.'

'That lazy bastard. What's he done now?'

'He's still got a shipment to sell. And he needs to let me know if he's having issues shipping it. If he's not the right guy for the job then I n—'

'No!' Tanya said, touching his arm again. 'He is. Honestly. He is. I'll speak to him. Leave it with me.'

'I will,' Liam said. 'Now, have you ever heard of an organised crime group called The Crimsons?'

CHAPTER 24

COFFEE SHOP

'Please state your name,' Jake began.

'Rebecca Langton.'

'What's your relationship to Jessica Mann, Rebecca?'

'She was my flatmate.'

'And where were you last night?'

'At work.'

Jake reached for a closed brown folder on the desk beside him. He pulled out a sheet of A4 containing information on Rebecca Langton. It was the combination of a quick personal profile he'd drawn up of her on his own, combined with the brief question and answers the officers at the crime scene had noted down in order to establish her as a credible witness.

'Homerton University Hospital,' Jake said, more as a statement than a question.

'Yes.' Rebecca nodded. 'I worked the night shift. Six till six. I found her when I came home.'

Jake closed the folder and placed the sheet on top of it. 'And did you notice anything suspicious about Jessica last night? Was she acting strangely? Different in any way?'

'Come to think of it, yeah. She was... I don't know. I think she was... she kept telling me to take the night shift.'

'Were you not supposed to?' Jake removed a pen from his pocket and began to scribble on the top of a new page in his notepad.

'Well, yes and no. I'd agreed to do overtime a couple of weeks ago, and they called me asking if I could do the night shift. I told them no because... well, because I was feeling lazy and I couldn't be bothered.'

'And Jessica told you to take the shift?'

'Well... no. It wasn't quite that simple. I needed the money as well. She just kept trying to convince me to get out of the house.'

'Did she mention why? Did she say anything about having someone over for a meal or a drink? A date?'

Rebecca shook her head. 'She didn't tell me anything.'

Jake hesitated for a moment. 'What about during the day? Did she message you about anyone in particular? Anyone suspicious? Anyone that caught her attention at all?'

Rebecca contemplated for a moment. 'I think she mentioned something about a man...' Rebecca reached for her phone. 'Do you mind if I check?'

'Place it on the table so I can watch you do it,' Jake said, making sure to cover his own arse if need be.

Rebecca did as she was told, unlocked the device and opened her messages. She tapped on the conversation with Jessica and scrolled to the top of the chat. The time stamp on the messages dated it more than twenty-four hours ago.

'For the recording, I am reading the messages on Miss Langton's phone.'

Jake read them and then, when he found a message that struck him as odd, he stopped.

'OMG,' he recited aloud, 'just met the weirdest man outside the coffee shop! I bumped into him, spilt my drink and then I bought him another one, but I felt like I knew him from somewhere, but I couldn't remember where.'

Jake scrolled and read the message underneath.

'OMG! Now I know where I remember him from! I think I've seen him online.'

Jake stopped reading and slid the phone back to Rebecca. He swallowed.

'Did Jessica ever mention anything to you about online dating?'

Rebecca shook her head. 'Not really. I think she was a member of Match.com but she never openly told me about any of it. She was quite private like that.'

'So you can't think of anyone that would want to hurt her?'

'Sorry. No. Jessica was a loving, caring person. The only person she ever hurt in her life was herself – she was renowned for putting other people first. I suppose that's why she became a nurse.'

Jake slid the folder off the desk, placed it under his arm and said,

'Interview terminated at 11:07.' He switched off the video recording and then explained to her what would happen next. 'You've been a great help, Rebecca. Thank you. Someone will be through shortly to escort you out, and these are my contact details if you remember anything else.'

Jake slid a business card across the desk, got up and moved to the door. As he pulled it open, one final thought occurred to him.

'Oh, one last thing – the coffee shop. Do you know which one she's talking about?'

'The same one she always goes to. Alinka's. On the edge of Tomlin's Grove.'

CHAPTER 25

ARTICLE

Jake returned to his desk filled with excitement and optimism. He was one step closer to finding the killer. He had a clue. He had a lead. And he had a chance to prove to the rest of the team that he was capable of carrying out the investigation while they weren't there. He unlocked his computer and logged in. As he was about to research the coffee shop on the edge of Tomlin's Grove, a notification appeared on his phone. It was from the BBC News app. He tapped the notification and loaded the article.

It was about Danny and Michael Cipriano. Their faces – images taken from their mugshots when they were arrested – were plastered at the top of the page.

Career criminals Danny and Michael Cipriano, formerly known as leading members of the organised crime group The Crimsons, are being released from jail where they were previously held on remand. The brothers were originally charged with manslaughter, several counts of armed robbery, possession of firearms and murder. After much deliberation, the Crown Prosecution Service are expected to offer no evidence at their forthcoming plea and case management hearing this Friday, which would mean they will be released.

Jake's body turned cold. It was official. They were getting out.

Friday. Two days away. That meant he had little time to act, little time to do anything. And what made it worse was that it was now headline news. But why? Why had it taken so long for the news to report it given that they'd been following the trial from the beginning? It was one of the biggest cases the country had ever seen, and they were only reporting it *now*. It didn't make sense. He checked the author's name – Tanya Smile – and made a mental note of it for future reference. He would have to follow up with her soon.

Before he was able to dwell on it any further, Liam, Drew and Garrison returned from Jessica Mann's crime scene. Drew opened the door so hard that it bounced off the adjacent wall. The sound of continuous typing and mouse-clicking stopped abruptly.

Liam pointed at Jake and called from across the room. 'Tanner – debriefing room. Pronto.'

The three men turned and wandered into the debriefing room in the far corner of the office. Jake rushed in behind them, grabbing a pen and paper before he went. There was something serious and worrying in Liam's voice. And his suspicions were confirmed as he sat down. He was greeted with silence and muted stares. Jake's mind raced with paralysing and nauseating thoughts. What had he done? Had they found out about his interaction with Danika regarding The Crimsons? Was there a conflict of interest? Were they going to remove him from the case?

The door shut, and Liam walked into the centre of the room. His face was placid, and, in his arms, he carried a laptop. He set it down on an empty table and opened it up. A few moments later, he spun it round and displayed the screen to Jake and the team.

'We're up shit creek here, guys. And I don't see any of us with a fucking paddle.'

On the screen was a news article from the BBC. A thumbnail of a video was at the top of the page, and Liam was in the shot. Jake squinted to read the article.

'Three dead in suspicious Stratford murders,' Jake repeated, leaning forward.

Liam scrolled down the page.

Jake peered at the monitor. 'Three bodies have turned up dead in the East London area of Stratford. The police are treating the murders as connected. They send out their thoughts and condolences to the families of those affected and are doing everything in their power to catch the individual – or individuals – responsible. The senior investigating officer in charge of the investigation, Detective Chief Inspector Liam Greene, said, "At this moment in time, we are no closer to finding the person responsible for this attack, and it does not look likely we will be able to either. Perhaps we'll have to wait… until another arrives." The message here is clear: can we trust the police to keep us safe? Or will we have to do it all ourselves?'

A deafening silence echoed around the room. Fortunately, Drew broke it by swearing and giving the computer screen the middle finger.

'Exactly,' Liam retorted, slamming the laptop shut. 'No paddle. And things are only going to get worse if we don't do anything about it. We've got pressure coming in from all sides, guys. And it won't be long until the Assistant Commissioner's filling the boat from the inside. If we let too much water get in, we'll sink.'

Jake raised his hand and spoke before anyone gave him the opportunity. 'Sorry, guv. I don't mean to play Devil's Advocate here, but why did you tell the press that we're nowhere near finding the person and that we're going to have to wait until another dead body comes up?'

Liam placed his hands on his hips, sighed and looked to the floor. 'You've still got a lot to learn, Jake. You can't believe everything you read in the papers. They took those words from other responses I had and put them like that to make us look bad. They're a bunch of fucking wolves, just looking for the next pay check.'

'Surprising from the BBC, that,' Garrison added.

Liam hesitated before responding. 'I've had to call a press conference this evening, so they can all get what they need in time for the ten o'clock news. There'll be a lot more than just the BBC there, trust me. And I need to be able to give them something concrete.'

Liam paused as he scanned the room. Jake's skin went cold as he waited anxiously for Liam's gaze to fall on him. Eventually, it did.

'What are you working on at the moment, Tanner? How was the interview with Jessica Mann's flatmate?'

Jake shuffled on his chair. 'Productive. She didn't know anything about Jessica meeting up with anyone, but—'

'How was that a productive interview?' Liam snapped.

Jake twisted his neck left and then right, ebbing the tension away, before responding. 'Rebecca said that Jessica bumped into someone randomly. Someone that she thought she'd met before but couldn't quite work out where.' Another pause. 'Then she remembered she'd seen the guy online. On a dating website. That's what connects this all up. Steven's agent said that Steven and Jessica were part of an online community where they met up and did stuff with one another. It's the same with Jessica Mann. Whoever's behind this is targeting women with the same name, who look a *lot* like one another. If we can find the dating website, we can find the killer. We just need to do that before he kills again... or runs out of

Jessicas to murder. Whichever comes first.'

Liam nodded and called the meeting to a close, ordering everyone to get back to work. Drew and Garrison were the first to leave, followed by Jake. As he returned to his desk, his phone vibrated against his leg. It was another email from Danika.

In the past twenty-four hours he'd tried his best to force any notion of The Crimsons and Bridger from his mind. Steven Arnholt, Jessica Arnholt, Jessica Mann – they were his priority right now. But as he read the contents of the email, Jake knew that that would have to change.

Without having a chance to sit down, Jake grabbed his blazer and his car keys and headed out of the office.

'Where are you going?' Liam asked from the doorway of his office.

Jake had hoped nobody would notice his disappearance, although he knew it unlikely.

'Out,' he said. He didn't know what to say, and he was beginning to feel like a defiant teenager who had just tried to leave the house without his parents knowing. 'I'm going to follow up a lead quickly.'

'What lead?'

Jake stuttered.

'Arch – I mean the coffee shop where Jessica Mann bumped into the killer. I want to speak with the manager. See if he saw anything. And then I'm going to speak with Archie Arnold again. Something about him doesn't seem right.'

Liam shot a sideways glance to Garrison, who was only a few feet away from Jake.

'I'll be as quick as I possibly can,' Jake added.

'Fine,' Liam said, nodding slowly. 'Go.'

CHAPTER 26

FOLLOW HIM

Liam turned his back on Garrison, closed his office door behind him and lowered the blinds halfway, put them back up to the top again, and then down a quarter, leaving them there. He moved to his desk, opened up his computer and loaded Gmail. The three of them used a covert account to communicate when they didn't want any of it to be traced or monitored by the IT department. Each had the login details, and each were able to access the inbox via a secure browser.

Liam clicked on the plus in the top left of the screen and opened a draft email. He waited until the blank email saved itself in the Drafts folder.

He gave it a few more seconds and waited for the others to sign in. There was no notification letting him know that they were viewing the same screen as him, so he had to use his intuition and experience.

Staring at the keyboard, breathing heavily, Liam sighed. Then he typed.

Follow him.

CHAPTER 27

ANGEL

Jake headed west on the M25 and then south on the A3. His foot stayed glued to the accelerator, swerving in and out of traffic, bullying other drivers out of the fast lane. He was in a rush, and he was up against time. According to Danika's email, Bridger was leaving the country in the evening and wouldn't be returning for a few months. It was too much of a coincidence that he was escaping at the same time as Danny and Michael. There was still so much he needed to confront him about, questions he needed answered, suspicions he needed confirming that he didn't care if he dropped everything to do with the serial killer. There was no knowing when Bridger would return. *If* he would return. And Jake couldn't afford to wait till then. By that point it would be too late. There was too much at stake.

It took him thirty minutes shy of the hour and fifty that his satnav said it would take to make it into Surrey; it was just after lunchtime and the roads were surprisingly empty.

As Jake passed the BP services on the A3, a few miles outside of Guildford, he called Danika via the Bluetooth on the dashboard. He had done the journey enough times to know he was only fifteen minutes away.

'Where is he?' he asked as the speedometer reached 80mph.

'Jake, I wasn't expecting you to get here right away,' she

whispered. 'He's still here, but he's finishing early so he can get his things ready.'

'When's he leaving the office?'

'I have no idea. I'm not a mind-reader.'

'Can you stall him?'

'I can try, but—'

'Please, Dan. If I miss him, it's over. All of our hard work will have been for nothing. We can't let him get away with this. I just want to speak to him. That's it.'

There was a long pause on the line. Jake checked the signal level to make sure he hadn't lost her.

'All right,' she finally said, 'leave it with me.'

'You're an angel.'

CHAPTER 28

COMING CLEAN

Surrey Police Headquarters at Mount Browne had been Jake's second home for a brief time during the beginning of his spell as a trainee detective constable. The building was grand, made from Victorian stone, and the grounds surrounding it were velveted with luscious green grass and oak trees that sparkled in the sun. It was the complete antithesis to Bow Green in Stratford: grey, dreary, derelict, unkempt.

A part of Jake wished he was still a member of the Surrey team. But now he was finally settling into the Major Investigation Team, he didn't want anything to jeopardise that.

Jake killed the engine on the outskirts of the car park that ran across the north ring of Surrey Police HQ. He had made it in just under the fifteen minutes, his journey assisted mercifully by empty roads and obedient drivers pulling over as soon as they saw him roaring behind them in their mirrors.

He opened the car door and exited, and as he did so, something in the distance caught his eye. It was a figure, just leaving the building. Jake was fifty metres away from the entrance, but that didn't matter – he knew the walk.

Dani, you fucking hero, he thought as he locked the car and started towards Bridger.

The seasoned sergeant carried a laptop satchel over his shoulder and a carrier bag in his right hand.

Forty metres separated them. Jake prepared himself to launch his attack on Bridger. But then something alerted him, and he suddenly changed his mind. Confronting him here was wrong. It was too public, too out in the open. It needed to be more private, somewhere Bridger would be more prone to telling him the truth.

Jake watched as Bridger headed to his car, slung the bags into the boot and started the ignition. There was no time to dawdle, so he rushed back to his own car and followed, keeping a covert distance between them.

As he pulled out of the station car park, he was frightfully aware that he couldn't afford to lose Bridger. Under any circumstances.

Jake checked the time on the dash. It was nearing 1 p.m.

Bridger headed east, out of town and out of Guildford. They drove through country lanes, winding left and right, swerving in and out, peaking up and troughing down. Throughout, Jake kept his distance, his mind working overtime as he tried to figure out the right time and place to pull Bridger over.

And then the decision was made for him.

As they entered the outskirts of Farnham, Bridger turned left down a narrow, unmade road that was sheltered by leaves and overhanging shrubbery. The brake lights flashed and then stopped. The car bounced up and then down again as Bridger depressed the handbrake and killed the engine.

This was it. It was on.

Before stepping out of the vehicle, Jake unlocked his iPhone and opened the built-in Dictaphone app to record their conversation. As Jake alighted the car, Bridger froze at the sight of his former colleague.

'You?' Bridger said, his face contorted.

'Were you expecting someone else?' Jake replied, carefully placing the phone in his pocket.

'No. Nobody. Just surprised to see you, that's all.' Bridger's Adam's apple convulsed as he swallowed. 'You look... good. MIT looking after you?'

The sides of Jake's lips flickered into a smile. 'You've not changed. Good to see. Although I think you've gone a bit greyer around the edges.'

'And you wider.' Bridger nodded at Jake's waist.

In recent months – since Elizabeth had become pregnant again – Jake had put on some weight. Perhaps it was stress eating. Perhaps it was comfort eating. Maybe a combination of the two. But he was always too tired to cook anything when he got home, so they usually settled on frozen food instead. Their finances weren't complaining either, as the meals were often Jake's favourite Cs: cheap and cheerful.

'Why are you here, Jake?' Bridger asked. 'I assume it's not for a catch-up, otherwise you would have done that back at Mount Browne.'

Jake paused to look around him. They were standing in a wider stretch of the road that allowed drivers to pull over so other cars could pass. Gravel lined the side of the tarmac and a patch of nettles sat inches away from his hand, swaying in the light breeze. 'Is this where you used to meet up with The Crimsons? Organise your little activities together?'

Bridger's smile disappeared and his face dropped. 'You heard the news then?'

'I think it would be better if Danny and Michael Cipriano remained where they are. They're a threat to society. We can't allow them to get out. Who knows what they might do next?'

'There won't be a next time.'

'How do you know?' Jake readjusted the phone in his pocket so that the microphone was pointed outwards. He hoped it would improve the audio quality.

'Because I know these things. They're not a danger to anyone. They don't want to hurt you anymore, Jake. They never did. It was all in your head. It was all business.'

'Is that what it's called now? Business.'

Bridger smirked and continued to stare at Jake. A long moment passed between the two of them, and the only noticeable sign of movement was a twenty-four-wheeler lorry that ripped past behind them.

'Why are you really here, Jake?' This time there was a tense edge to Bridger's voice. Jake hadn't heard it before, but it didn't sound welcoming.

'I want to know how you've done it.'

'You still pissed I'm on the payroll? Still angry that no one believed I was a bent copper?'

'Enough people did,' Jake replied.

'But not the right people to do anything about it.'

'I know what you've done, Bridger. I know you were the one responsible for everything that happened that day. Stalling until the forensic and bomb squad arrived with that bullshit story about the car crash on the motorway. Leading us away from finding the keys that killed Candice. Lying to me about getting that interview with Michael approved by a chief super. I know about it all. And I know that you had Mark Murphy helping you along the way too. But nobody listened to me. And now I want to know how you're helping them get out of prison – how you've managed to convince the CPS to drop everything. Who did you have to pay? Or is it the other way round?'

Bridger threw his hands in the air. 'What makes you think I had anything to do with it?'

'You're still working with them. I know you are.'

'You have no proof.'

'It's staring me right in the face,' Jake said, pointing to Bridger's car. 'Brand new car. Jaguar XKR. Must have set you back quite a bit. Especially on a sergeant's wage. What'd that cost? Fifty... sixty grand?'

Bridger gave a slight nod. 'In today's money.'

Jake was slowly knocking the barriers down – he could sense it. He was feeling confident and decided to go for a stab in the dark.

'And for a man in as much debt as you, that's quite a little treat for yourself. You pay all in cash?'

'How did y—?'

Jake found it hard to suppress his smile. 'I didn't, but you just confirmed it for me. Have you declared that you're in debt?'

Bridger didn't reply.

'Because, and I'm sure you're aware of this – after all, you were the one badgering on at me about how excellent you are – it's a police officer's duty, under paragraph four, Schedule 1 of The Police Regulations Act 2003, that you shall not wilfully refuse or neglect to discharge any lawful debt. Not to mention, Article 9 of the Code of Ethics—'

'You still believe in that ethics bullshit? Ha! You're even more naïve than I thought, Jake. Nobody's followed that for years – for as long as I've been a police officer.'

Jake chose to ignore him and continue. 'Under Article 9 of the Code of Ethics, it is your duty as a police officer to report financial problems you may be having, as you are – and in your case it seems highly likely – at greater risk of becoming involved with organised crime. I'd say you already tick those boxes.'

Bridger switched. His expression dropped and he charged towards Jake. Within seconds, the domineering man towered over him, giving Jake little time to react. Bridger extended his hand and grabbed Jake's shirt, his breath blowing into Jake's face. They'd been locked in the same entanglement before, but this time felt different. They were no longer colleagues anymore, they were no longer working on a case together, so there was nothing stopping Bridger from punching him in the face and beating him up.

'You don't know what you're fucking talking about, Tanner. Who told you? How'd you find out?' Bridger hissed.

'I didn't. I just told you – you confirmed it for me.'

'Who's your source?' Bridger stabbed him in the chest with his finger. 'Who's supplying you with this information?'

'Nobody. But it sounds to me like you're afraid,' Jake said, and Bridger took a step back. 'Who are you afraid of, Elliot?'

'Nobody.'

'Let me help you. Tell me everything and I can make this better. If you're in trouble – or if you're in deeper than you ever imagined with whoever you're working for – then we can work together to fix it. You just need to tell me what's going on.'

There was something different in Bridger's face. His eyes. The colour had changed; his pupils had dilated. It was clear to see that he was afraid. That there was something deeper lurking beneath the surface.

'You're chatting out of your arse, Tanner,' Bridger said, clenching his fist and hovering it a few inches from Jake's chin. 'You don't know what you're talking about. You don't know what you're getting involved with.'

He began to pace from side to side. 'I had nothing to do with The Crimsons last year, and I have nothing to do with them now. And I certainly don't have anything that *you* need to know about regarding my personal financial circumstances. Fuck you. I'm not bent.'

Jake took a moment to breathe and collect his thoughts.

'You've told yourself that lie for so long you're finally beginning to believe it, aren't you?'

Bridger bit his top lip. 'Fuck you! I've had enough of this. I'm out of here.' He threw his hand in the air and stormed towards his car.

The door was open halfway when Jake yelled back at him, his voice echoing up and down the road.

'You're not going anywhere, Bridger,' he said. 'You don't think I've got evidence, but I do. That's called good old-fashioned police work – something you never gave me credit for at Surrey Police. So stop and pay attention.'

'What can you possibly have? I've been immaculate.'

'Evidently not.' Jake removed his phone and pretended to scroll. 'There's a document.'

Bridger said nothing.

'It contains everything implicating you,' he lied. 'The funds you received and decided to deposit into your account. Large sums of money. Phone calls between you and The Crimsons. Phone calls between you and some other unregistered pay-as-you-go mobile numbers. Text messages telling you what to do. Voice recordings.'

Bridger's eyes widened. 'If you've got all of this then why are you here? Why haven't you gone to the IPCC or Professional Standards?'

'Because you and I both know that takes time. Time we don't have, not if I'm going to get them back on remand. It's not too late for you to turn yourself in and make amends for what you've done.'

Bridger shook his head frantically.

'I can't do that. This thing's bigger than you, Jake. It's done. Leave it. Danny and Michael Cipriano are getting off. It's too late. You win some, and you lose some.'

'Tell me everything, Elliot. You can make it stop. Bring back the evidence against them. Make sure they get sent down for life.'

'Do you know what they'd do to me if I did?'

'Who, Elliot? Who?'

'All of them. They'd find me. They'd make sure I don't talk.'

'Then tell me everything now. I can help you. Tell me what happened!'

There was a long pause. It was broken by a car passing them on the other side of the road, giving them both a wide berth. Jake's gaze followed it as it eventually disappeared down the mile-long road. He thought the number plate looked familiar. But before he could think about it any further, Bridger distracted him. The man stood with one hand on his car door, his breathing growing heavy, his other fist clenched – then he turned his back on Jake and paced up and down the road, clutching at his hair.

Nerves wracked Jake's body and his fingers trembled. He'd come this far. Wasted all this time. He hoped it wouldn't be for nothing.

'Fine,' Bridger said, coming to an abrupt stop a few metres away from Jake. The bonnet of Jake's car separated them. 'Everything. I'll give you everything. But first I want some assurances.' He held out his hand. 'Give me your phone.'

Fuck. He was about to give up the only thing he was relying on to use as evidence, even if Jake had lied to him and coerced him into confirming things without realising it.

'No,' Jake said. 'Elizabeth's pregnant. I need to keep it with me in case she calls.'

Bridger shook his head. 'Should have thought about that before you came down here. Now give me the phone. We're going for a walk.'

Jake glanced at his screen. In the top corner, the red banner that indicated he was recording had disappeared. Then the screen lit up with Liam's name glaring at him.

Shit!

Before he had time to process that Liam was calling him, he panicked, repeatedly tapped the red button and rejected the call. After the phone returned to the lock screen, he passed the device to Bridger. Bridger then threw it onto the seat in Jake's car.

'Follow me,' Bridger ordered, already wandering down the road.

They came to a stop a hundred metres away from their vehicles, well out of range of any audio recording devices. As they turned to face one another, Jake felt afraid. Vulnerable. Isolated. As though he was about to be ambushed and placed inside the back of a van, only to end up halfway across the country tied to a chair in the middle of a desolate warehouse.

'I did it, all right?' Bridger began. 'I did it. Danny, Michael, Luke – I helped them. I had been drafted in a few days before the robbery and was told there would be three brothers looking to rob a jewellery store, and that the woman who had been kidnapped would be in on it too. It was my job – with Murphy's help – to make sure they got out of the country. In exchange they'd give me a cut of their takings. Fifty grand, all in all.'

'Candice died,' Jake said, his voice soft. 'You helped kill her.'

'No,' Bridger said, shaking his head. 'I knew nothing about that. I had no idea the spikes and the live charge would be in there. I was told they would be dummies. They said nobody would die. Nobody would get hurt.'

'You still agreed to do it even though you knew who they were?'

Bridger hung his head low. 'I didn't... I didn't know anything about them. I wasn't in a position to say no, anyway. They had leverage. They knew who I was. They knew I was struggling financially, and they threatened to expose me.'

'And you couldn't let that happen?'

'I still can't.'

'What do you mean?'

'I've still got to deal with this. It's not finished. I made a promise to make sure they'd never serve time in prison. But that was under the provision that they keep up their end of the bargain and keep their mouths shut. But they couldn't even do that. When they were inside, they started talking to people – especially Danny. He loved the attention. He started talking about the people they were dealing with, about the people who put us in contact with one another. And I knew what was going to happen to them if they said too much.'

'How?'

'I'd seen it before.'

'Who?'

'Murphy.'

Jake's eyes widened. He scratched the scar on the side of his face. 'Murphy's dead?'

'Why do you think no one's seem him for a while?' Bridger asked, his expression emotionless.

'Danika told me he left after what happened with Pemberton.'

Bridger shook his head. 'Mark got cocky, started opening his mouth wider than he should to people he shouldn't have been talking to in the first place, and then he just disappeared. Nobody saw him. Nobody heard from him. I couldn't let the same happen to the brothers, and I knew it would if they continued mentioning names, so I fucked up their trial and entered them into the witness protection scheme instead. At least that way they'll be able to give some dirt on other gangs and organised crime groups that they usually saw as competition. But once they set foot in those houses, I'm done. I'm out of this all.'

'And you think they're safe in the WPS?'

'So long as they keep their mouths shut, they'll be fine. But that saga's nothing to do with me anymore.'

Jake hesitated, licked his lips.

'So where are you going now?' he eventually asked.

'Away.'

'Why?'

'I need to get away.'

'Will you be coming back?'

Bridger shrugged.

'Why are you telling me all of this, Elliot? Why now, after so many months of keeping this to yourself?'

Bridger looked to the ground and sighed. 'Because… because you're a good police officer, Jake. I knew from the moment I met you. But consider that a warning. That nothing you do now will be able to stop it – it's too late. The brothers are getting out, and you need to move on and forget that part of your life.'

'It's not that easy,' Jake said, defiant.

'You're going to have to, because, during the rest of your career, you're going to learn something else. And it's better you learn it now, here. This is bigger than you. The MPS and every other force in the country is not the golden pipe dream you thought it was. Everyday people lose their livelihoods because of dodgy dealings and dark meetings. You need to open your eyes to everything, Jake. It'll be better for you if you do. And it'll be even better if you turn a blind eye to it.'

'How can you say that? Somebody's got to put a stop to them.'

'And that's you, is it?

Jake shrugged.

'So you're happy to get yourself killed in the process? It's not worth it. Trust me, I've tried. And if you need more reminding, look what happened to Murphy.'

At that, Bridger nudged past Jake and headed back to his car.

'What about you? How do you know the same won't happen to you?' Jake called back.

Bridger clasped his hand around his door handle, turned to face Jake and said, 'The only way that's going to happen is if you tell anyone.'

Jake froze in the middle of the road as he watched Bridger step inside his car, start the engine and drive past him, keeping his eyes on the road ahead as though Jake didn't exist. He watched Bridger's car dissolve into a small dot.

After it disappeared at the end of the road, Jake stood there for a moment longer, still stunned, still reeling at the events of the past ten minutes. At what Bridger had told him. At what the implications of it were. At how Bridger had blackmailed Jake with his own life into keeping his mouth shut.

You clever son of a bitch, Jake thought, too much in disbelief to think of anything else. His mind tried to process and comprehend everything Bridger had just told him, but it wasn't working. Instead, the information lay on the surface like oil on water.

Jake blinked himself back to reality and returned to his car. He grabbed for his phone and looked at the lock screen.

Four missed calls. All from Liam.

'Shit!' Jake slammed his palm on the steering wheel.

Before he could do anything else, Liam called again. For a moment, Jake stared at the device, frozen. He was too far past the point of no return now, but he knew that it would only get worse for him if he didn't pick up.

Jake pressed the green button.

'Tanner' – he sounded pissed – *'where are you?'*

'Guildford,' Jake said without thinking.

'What are you doing down there?'

'Archie wasn't at his address. I spoke to a neighbour and they said he's got family down in Guildford and that he was visiting.'

Liam sighed through the phone. 'Get yourself back to the office. The wolves should be arriving in just over an hour, and so should you.'

CHAPTER 29

TRIP

Bridger's adrenaline was at an all-time high. He'd never felt both so afraid and so elated at the same time. He was glad he'd told Jake everything; it had weighed him down for too long and it felt right to finally get it off his chest. But that truth had come at a cost. He'd compromised his position, and his entire credibility. How could The Cabal trust him now to carry on? How could they believe he was still on their side? The only thing he could do was trust Jake to keep his mouth shut. His life now depended on it.

Bridger pulled onto the A3, sticking his foot to the floor. He was heading for Southampton Airport where he would be able to get an internal flight to Manchester, and then a long-haul flight to Mexico for the foreseeable future. Everything was ready. Travel. Accommodation. Everything.

But his progress came to a halt when his phone began to ring. It wasn't his smartphone. It was the burner phone he kept in the back of his pocket. And that could only mean one thing – it was only ever used by one person.

Bridger answered. Waited. Held his breath.

'What just happened?' the person on the other line asked him.

'Nothing. I—'

'Don't bullshit me, Elliot.'

'I'm not, I—'

'What did Tanner want?'

Bridger squinted, avoiding the harsh sunlight above.

'I don't know. I—'

'What did Tanner want?' the voice repeated.

Bridger slowed the car along the A3 and pulled into the hard shoulder so he could concentrate on the call.

'He wanted to know everything.'

'*Everything*?' the person on the other end asked.

'Everything.'

'What did you tell him? Your next few words must be considered very carefully. They may be your last.'

Bridger knew the threat wasn't idle.

'I told him nothing.'

'Are you sure?'

'Yes. But you could have given me a heads-up about the article in the BBC. I saw it at the office, and everyone started asking me questions. I had fuck-all time to prepare anything,' Bridger explained. The car jostled gently each time a car whipped past.

'That was a test.'

'For me?'

'For Tanner.'

'And… did he pass?'

There was no response. That was the only answer Bridger needed.

'I promise you I didn't tell him anything,' Bridger began, feeling as though he needed to keep on talking in order to defend himself. 'He has no evidence to support anything.'

'I hope for your sake that you're telling the truth. It will be a shame to see you suffer a similar end to Murphy. Remember him? I liked him. I like you more, but don't think that makes me any more likely to be lenient if you double-cross us.'

'Yes…' Bridger said, lost for words.

'Are you looking forward to your trip?' the voice asked.

Bridger gripped the steering wheel until his knuckles turned white. They knew what he'd done. Of course they knew. It was impossible to hide it. They knew everything. And now there was no escape.

He needed to do something about it. But what? He couldn't run. He couldn't hide. The only other option was to stand up and fight. Alone. With no one readily available to support him.

'I don't know where you got the impression you could leave so soon. The brothers aren't out until Friday. There's still a lot for you to do.' The voice hesitated on the other end. 'But you already know what *I* have to do as well now, don't you?'

Bridger slipped the car into first and roared back onto the dual carriageway.

'I do,' he said. 'I do.'

CHAPTER 30

SOUR

Liam rung off and placed the burner phone in his bottom drawer, then grabbed the new bottle of whisky he'd bought earlier in the convenience store – he fancied a different spirit today – and poured three measures into his reusable cup. After screwing the bottle lid back on, he held the cup in his hand, swirled the contents and sipped.

The drink soothed and warmed his throat, leaving behind a slight burning sensation. Liam pressed his tongue to the roof of his mouth and swallowed. His body shook. He exhaled heavily. It felt good. Tasted good. It had been long overdue. Something he'd needed for a while. Something to fight away the pain in his body and the rising sea of nausea that drowned him every waking moment of the day.

A part of him just wanted to down the bottle in one go and pass out like he'd done last week before Drew had found him in his home. Drew had come to pick him up for their weekly football practice at the five-a-side pitch but had found Liam in a comatose state instead. But Drew hadn't been that much better off either. When Liam eventually woke up, Drew was sniffing, rubbing his nose and bouncing off the walls. The only difference between their vices was that Liam had a genuine reason for his, whereas Drew was just a fuckwit who'd snorted a bit too much Charlie one time and realised he'd developed an instant liking for it.

Liam sealed the drawer shut and sighed heavily. The call he'd just received was one he'd never thought he would. And now he had a task he never thought he'd have to action.

He wandered over to his office window and tapped on the glass. Drew and Garrison's heads rotated.

They knew what to do.

Returning to his desk, Liam dragged his finger along the woodwork. He woke his computer up and opened the Gmail inbox.

He created another draft and waited until it saved on the screen.

He tapped his leg furiously in anticipation. He needed to psych himself up.

The cursor flashed in front of him, mocking him, teasing him to type his message.

Eventually, he did.

OUR GOOD EGG HAS GONE SOUR. SERVE HIM.

CHAPTER 31

GAME CHANGER

Lester wiped himself clean. He'd just masturbated for the third time in the past two hours. And each time was becoming more and more painful than the last. But it was taking him longer to ejaculate. And that was what he wanted. He needed to build up his sexual stamina. He wanted to prolong the moment before ejaculation, making it last as long as was physically possible. Jessica Arnholt and Jessica Mann had been over too quickly. He'd been too excited for both of them. And now that he had second position chasing his heels, he was feeling the pressure. He was going to need more points if he were to sustain his prowess.

The scoring system was simple: the longer you lasted, the more you got. Obviously, that was all dependent on the type of sexual act you were committing, but Lester had been at this long enough to know what he needed to do in order to gain the maximum number of points while still enjoying himself and being comfortable with the result.

Even if it meant he couldn't piss properly without it stinging, Lester was determined to make himself last as long as possible. His penis would heal, but his dignity and pride would never recover. Shortly after he'd joined The Community and enjoyed Communion with a few members, he'd tried to treat it like a game, a workout – a situation where he either gave it his everything or nothing at all.

There was no in-between.

Lester flushed the tissue down the toilet, washed his hands and returned to his laptop. He'd been searching all day for another Jessica. But The Community had been less than helpful. Although there were a handful of other Jessicas, their appearance was too different, too far from the original. And he wasn't prepared to sacrifice the points – and his adoration for his newfound desires – for someone who looked completely different. No matter how close second position was behind him. No – the third Jessica needed to be tall, slim, brunette, with brown eyes. Anything other than that simply wouldn't do. The game had now changed. So would he.

He was slowly becoming infuriated. It was just past lunchtime, and his laptop was opened on the leader board. Live updates filtered in after the server refreshed every ten minutes. And in the past four hours, second place had managed to gain another five hundred points. The gap was closing. And time was running out.

He needed to broaden his horizons. Go further afield. Even if it was against the rules and conditions of the league. If he was going to prove himself to S, then he would need to go rogue, find someone outside of the circle.

He grabbed his jumper from the back of the chair and headed out, adjusting his penis against his leg. He knew exactly where to go.

CHAPTER 32

DIAMOND GEEZERS

Carpenters Road bustled with life. Cars sped up and down the busy street. Oddly, the sound of tyres rolling on the tarmac soothed him. Perhaps it reminded him of when he was younger and his parents would drive them to the nearest caravan site for their family holiday where they would beat him, and his mother would sexually abuse him in the back of the van while his dad watched. Perhaps it reminded him of the time he'd burned a stray cat alive in his garden and his parents had called the police, and he'd been taken to the station in the back of the saloon. Or perhaps it reminded him of the time he'd been in the back of the car with his mum and dad on the way to the hospital, driving at double the speed limit, and he'd pulled his trousers down and pissed everywhere before both of them had ended up launched through the windscreen after crashing into a truck. All of those instances were examples of happier times, exciting times – times where, in those split seconds, he was outside the chaos of his shit life and able to enjoy of it what he could.

Lester was standing on the side of the road with his flat cap pulled over his face and his head kept down. Twenty metres ahead of him was a phone box. He wandered up to it, opened the door and shuffled in. He reached inside his pocket and found a 50p coin.

He'd used this place before. If ever there was an issue with his burner phone and he needed to contact S, he would come here. It was isolated, discreet, untraceable and, more importantly, unused. He was certain he hadn't seen anyone use a phone box in over five years, but that didn't stop him from feeling grateful that they still existed.

Above the phone was a corkboard. Local taxi and trade business cards were pinned to it, offering discounts and loyalty schemes for frequent users. But there was always one that caught his eye – one that was different from the rest.

He grabbed it.

The card was a dark rouge colour, and the silhouette of a naked girl with golden stars over her crotch and nipples, standing in an evocative pose, stared back at him. The company was called 'Diamond Geezers' and there was a mobile number on the bottom of it.

Lester slotted the money into the machine, dialled the number and waited. He swayed from side to side and cautioned several glances out of the windows, lest he see anyone he knew. His hand shook slightly as he held the receiver against his ear.

'Hello,' a person on the other end answered. It was a man, and he sounded rather dismissive in tone – almost disinterested.

'Hi… er… I was… I was wondering what sort of services you provide?'

'You got any odds you'd like to recommend?'

Lester froze. Confused, he sheepishly said, 'Yes?'

'One moment please.'

The line went blank, and for a moment Lester thought he'd wasted 50p. But then, after a few seconds, the line eventually returned. This time it was a different voice, gruffer than the first.

'What's your heart's desire?' they asked. He had a thick foreign accent that Lester placed as either Russian or Eastern European. 'Black girls. Asian. White. Fat. Slim. Young. Old.'

Lester was taken aback. He hadn't expected to be able to choose from such a wide selection. Everything had just changed in that moment because now he could perfect his choice.

'White,' he began. 'Tall. Slim.'

'Yes.'

'Young. Brown hair.'

'How young?'

'Mid-twenties.'

'Hmm… That's not as young as we offer. Anything else?'

'Yes!' Lester shouted, allowing the excitement to get the better of him. 'Her name must be Jessica.'

'What?'

'Her name,' Lester repeated. 'It *must* be Jessica. She must be called Jessica, or I won't have her.'

There was a pause. Sweat permeated through his skin.

'Ah, yes. I have found the perfect girl. She is one of our most popular. You will like her. But you will have to get her quick. She is very busy.'

'Tonight? Can she make tonight? I'll pay whatever you need.'

'Five hundred pounds. Jessica. One night. Tonight. She will do everything.'

'Everything?' Lester repeated. He bit his lip and licked his teeth.

'Everything that your heart desires.'

'You've got yourself a deal. All cash. Tell me her address.'

'No. She will come to you. All part of the s—'

'Listen,' Lester interrupted, 'send me her address. Tell her I'll be there at 9 p.m., and I'll pay you a thousand pounds. If you let me do this, I guarantee you I'll come back and I'll buy more of your girls for one night.'

The man on the other end hesitated. It was a long while before he spoke again.

'OK. I tell you the address. One thousand pounds. All cash. One night. Everything?'

'Everything.'

CHAPTER 33

STRATFORD KILLER

'About fucking time you got here. Where've you been?'

Jake was out of breath. He'd just sprinted from his car to the station, then up five flights of stairs to the press conference room.

'Traffic,' he said to Garrison as they stood in the hallway.

The sound of muffled and distorted discussion came from the other side of the half-open door beside them. Jake peered through and saw Liam and the Assistant Commissioner sitting at the head of the room. There was an empty space next to Liam. Behind them was a large dark-blue wall with the Metropolitan Police Service emblem emblazoned upon it. Their faces flashed intermittently as the press and news outlets took rapid photo bursts of them.

'They're waiting for you,' Garrison said, giving him a slight nudge on the shoulder.

'What?'

'Drew was meant to be doing it, but he got called away. Now it's your time to shine.'

Before Jake could register what Garrison had said, his colleague opened the door and ushered him in. At once, the cameras and photographers flashed and blinded him. Dazed, he stumbled to the table and pulled out a seat next to Liam.

They exchanged a quick glance as Jake sat. His boss made no effort to hide the frustration in his expression.

Liam leant behind Jake and whispered in his ear. 'I hope you've got something to feed them with. They're fucking starving.'

Jake's gaze flitted from left to right, at the various people in the room who were looking to him for answers he didn't have. His body went cold, and his skin turned to gooseflesh. Out the corner of Jake's eye, Assistant Commissioner Richard Candy raised his hand. The action commanded the attention of everyone in the room, and silence quickly fell, save for the sound of arses shuffling on seats and gentle spluttering of people clearing their throats.

'Thank you,' Candy said, lowering his hand. 'Thank you for your patience and being here. We will now begin.' He snorted before continuing. 'On the seventeenth of May, Steven and Jessica Arnholt were killed in a brutal and sadistic manner. Their families have been informed and the art gallery where they were killed is still an active crime scene. Their killer remains at large, although we have several suspects and witnesses who are cooperating with the service and local authorities to assist in finding the attacker.'

Candy took a small pause to swallow. 'Last night, on the nineteenth, a young adult female – Jessica Mann – was killed under similar circumstances. Again, her family and friends have been informed and our Family Liaison Officer is working closely with them to help them get through this tragic and difficult time. We are almost certain that this is the same attacker.'

Jake watched intently as AC Candy turned his head slowly, like an owl, casting his ominous gaze across the room. 'We will now take questions.'

Almost as soon as Candy had finished, the room erupted as the starving news reporters waved their hands and begged to be picked first. The flashes started, immediately blinding Jake. There were so many of them he didn't know where to look. He struggled to keep his eyes open. This was the first press conference he'd attended, and he hoped that, if they were all like this, his experiences of them would be few and far between.

'Assistant Commissioner – do you think the killer will strike again?'

'What links these two murders? What makes you so sure they're connected?'

'Who are your main suspects? What leads do you have?'

'What will—?'

'Who do—?'

'Why is—?'

It was relentless. The toing and froing. The talking over one another. The constant bombardment of words and flashes and sounds from every angle. Jake struggled to hear himself think.

A civilian press officer appeared to Jake's left. She was smartly dressed and had her hair in a bun. In her arms, clutched tightly against her chest, she carried a tablet. She pointed her finger to the crowd. Everyone fell silent. The reporter she'd elected to speak first waited patiently until the furore died down. At least now there was some sense of decorum amidst the animosity he'd witnessed only a few moments ago.

'Nina Partridge, ITV News – what leads do you have ongoing at the moment? And how close are you to finding the killer?'

The room fell quiet as everyone waited for a response. At first, it didn't come. And then Jake figured out why: Candy and Liam were staring at him – as, by now, was the entire room.

Jake looked out at the sea of people, lost. And then a dizzying sense of claustrophobia washed over him, as though the four walls were closing in on him. Public speaking had never been one of his strongest suits – he'd sweated profusely during a high-school presentation once and almost fainted, and had never quite recovered socially – and every time he was in front of a large crowd, his anxiety amplified exponentially. What made this occasion worse was the fact that he knew his responses would be broadcast on national television, enabling him to persecute himself with the tiniest of mistakes. He swallowed, trying to ignore the layers of sweat now forming on his palms and the back of his neck.

They were waiting. And they weren't going anywhere until they had a response.

'At this moment...' He choked and cleared his throat. 'At this moment... we are unable t-to confirm what leads we have, as these are s-sensitive to the nature of the case.' He rubbed his fingers in his palms, and as he found the words coming out, he managed to relax a little. 'We anticipate having the case resolved and the killer apprehended s-shortly.'

As Jake finished, another flurry of activity came from the journalists. The woman to Jake's left elected another candidate to speak, and the room fell silent again.

'Dayna Roberts, Channel 5 News – what do you think about the killer being dubbed the Stratford Ripper? How can you be sure it *is* the same killer? And what links the two murders together?'

Jake waited, hoping that either Liam or Richard would answer. They didn't.

He rubbed his palms together.

'W-We have n-no comment regarding the nickname Stratford K-Killer. To do so would feed the killer's ego. The murder of Jessica M-Mann has certain nuances that correlate with the deaths of Jessica and S-Steven Arnholt. For the sake of public discretion, I will not go into details, but there are certain c-characteristics that connect the two crimes.'

'And what will you do if the killer strikes again?' asked Dayna Roberts.

This time, Jake didn't even wait for the others to answer; he knew they wouldn't.

'Nothing is going to hinder our investigation. There is no knowing whether the killer will strike again. Of course, we hope they won't, but if they do, we will be armed with more evidence and more passion to catch them.'

'So are you saying that there's a lack of passion right now?' someone in the crowd asked. She stood up and introduced herself as Tanya Smile from BBC News. 'Is that why you've not found the killer yet – you don't "care" enough?'

'N-No. That's n-n-not what I... I didn't... I didn't mean...' Jake was choking. He'd slipped up and there wasn't a visible exit anywhere near him. 'I believe... I feel... I know there is lots of passion—'

'Too much? Is it clouding your judgement?' Tanya continued.

Jake could feel her words scathing him like a searing stick.

'Are you the right man for the job? Are you the right team? What's going to happen to the two Jessicas and Steven – are you going to let their murderer run free because you don't *care* enough?'

Jake blinked frantically, blocking out everyone in the room. He hoped they would go away, but they didn't; every time he opened them, the reporters and cameras and flashes were still there, burning into his retinas. He sensed their vitriolic stares boring into him as their minds concocted tomorrow's newspaper headlines.

'Hopeless: the case, and the cops on it.'

'When they don't care, why should we?'

'Stratford Ripper petrifies police's passion.'

Jake felt Liam's hand touch his shoulder.

'That's enough, ladies and gentlemen,' AC Candy said in the background, his voice drowned out by the excitement generated by Jake's inadequacies. 'That will be all for today. Thank you for your time.'

Liam grabbed Jake by the arm and hefted him out of his chair and out of the room

'Nicely done, mate,' Liam said, touching Jake's shoulder again, although this time less violently as they breached into the corridor. 'Made us look competent enough. I suppose now all they'll think we do here is stand with each other's dicks in our hands!'

Candy tore through the door and slammed it behind him. It was just the three of them. Jake's breathing echoed around the walls.

The Assistant Commissioner raised his finger in the air. 'I'm lost for words. Liam, you brought me here under the impression that this investigation was in good hands. But never in my career have I seen someone make a mistake as big as that and continue to dig fucking deeper and deeper. Strike one, DC Tanner. Strike one.'

Candy tore off down the corridor and made a left turn into one of the connecting rooms. Jake waited for the door to close before he protested.

'You could have helped!' he said to Liam. A few inches separated them, and Jake sensed Liam's anger and resentment oozing through his pores.

'You're the one with all the evidence. The whole point of you sitting in there with us was so that you could tell them about Archie Arnold, and you couldn't even manage that.' Liam paced from side to side, stopped and placed his hands on his hips. 'What did you find anyway? Any info?'

Jake shook his head. He'd been preparing for this. On the way back from his encounter with Bridger, he'd come up with a plan on what to tell Liam.

'Nothing,' Jake said. He swallowed and waited, expecting a reaction. There was none; so he continued. 'Archie Arnold wasn't there. I found his cousin and they said he'd already moved on. I tried to look for him but couldn't find anything.'

'So what were you doing all that time you were there?'

'Looking for him…'

'Unsuccessfully.'

'Yes.'

'Jesus fucking Christ, Jake. I thought you were going to be good at this. I'd heard such good things about you. When I saw your name land on my desk with those transfer requests, I thought "here we go, someone who can actually make a difference to the team". I thought you were keen, eager to prove yourself and to succeed—'

'I am,' Jake said.

'Don't interrupt me.' Liam raised a hand, dismissing Jake. 'I thought you were going to become a fully functioning member of the team, capable of pulling your own weight while everyone else is handling theirs. But you've let me down. Big time.'

Liam paused, reached inside his pocket and looked at a text message. 'Right,' he continued, 'I want you to stay behind tonight. I want you to be the last one in the office. You've got a lot of making up to do.'

CHAPTER 34

NEED

Night was nearing. But Lester couldn't wait for the cover of darkness. He was too impatient. He needed to get out – now. He needed to engage in Communion. His score was rapidly losing its strength in the polls, and he had some making up to do. Even if his next victim wasn't strictly a member of The Community, he was sure he would be able to come to some sort of arrangement with S later. The old man was as depraved as him, and he was confident S wouldn't have any reservations about viewing the evidence. It was only fair if he gave him points in return.

In his hands he held Jessica's address on a piece of paper. He shuffled his fingers around the edges, enjoying the stinging sensation as the edge cut into his skin now and then.

Lester checked his watch. There was still an hour to go.

He pondered whether or not she would mind if he was early. Fuck it. What did it matter? She was still going to be naked either way by the end of the night – what difference did it make if he caught her like that a little sooner than planned?

It was time.

Lester closed his laptop, grabbed his wallet and keys, and headed out of the door. He was on his way to Clapton, a few miles away near Hackney Marshes. He had planned the route beforehand – a few minutes after speaking with the Eastern European man who had given him Jessica's address, in fact. He would have to get the Overground service from Stratford Station to Hackney Central, and then walk the rest of the journey. It would take thirty minutes in total, and he would still be there with plenty of time to spare. It was risky being out in the open. Exposing himself. It went against everything S had ever trained him to do. Anonymity was the mask of deceit and corruption, S had always told him. And now he was breaking the cardinal rule. But he couldn't deny The Nasties raging within him. He couldn't deny the beast that had already developed a taste for his lascivious tendencies. The feeling was too strong, and he couldn't wait for it to take hold of him again. He'd already prepared with his masturbation and exercise routine. Now his testosterone was at an all-time high.

Lester arrived at Stratford Station a few minutes after leaving his house, purchased his ticket and wandered jauntily up to the platform. It was deserted, save for a teenager wearing a hood and carrying a gym bag over his shoulder. A set of earphones were plugged into his head and he tapped away at his phone screen. Lester moved to the other end of the platform, as far away from the kid as possible, keeping his head low, and waited for the train to arrive.

Nine minutes later, he pulled into Hackney Central where he started the next leg of his journey: a twenty-minute walk to Jessica's address. The station was quiet. The air was quiet. The streets were quiet.

He would be there in no time.

As he left the station, he threw his train ticket into the bin.

He had no further need for it.

CHAPTER 35

L DY CO K

Jessica the Prostitute lived in a river boat along the Hackney Cut. She was stationed at the north end of Hackney Marshes, one of Hackney's green lungs, and Lester had made it there within twenty minutes of leaving the station.

He was standing in the middle of the bridge that crossed the river, watching, waiting, observing. The area was empty, desolate, and there was nobody in sight – as he'd expected at this time of night. The river wasn't much of a river; it was a few metres wide, at best, and was littered with weeds, reeds, plastic bottles, crisp packets and other pieces of litter people were too lazy to put in the bin. Skeletons of branches and leaves hung overhead, almost covering him in complete darkness. Jessica's canal boat was long – Lester estimated about seventy feet – and poorly maintained. From what he was able to see from the low light of the setting sun that peered through the branches, the fascia was decrepit and falling apart. Mountains of rust had begun to form on the underside, and the name of the boat was missing a few letters. It read: L DY CO K.

From his vantage point, he was able to discern where the living room was, the kitchen and also the bedroom. At the far end, middle and near end, respectively. Lights were on in each of the rooms, and he noticed a shadow flicker past the windows as Jessica moved about her home, teasing him from the other side of the curtains.

Lester had had enough of waiting. It was time to pay her a visit.

He crossed the bridge, wandered along the gravel path and then pressed his ear against the boat's door. The thud of music emanated from behind, but as soon as he knocked, it stopped. There was a long pause. Then he knocked again.

This time the door opened. Jessica was wearing a dressing robe pulled tightly around her body. It was a thin material – either silk or nylon – and Lester glimpsed her nipples through it. They made no impression upon him. He observed the minutiae of her face. She wasn't anything like the other two. She was still tall, slim and had brown hair, but there was something different about her face – something that he couldn't quite decipher. Perhaps it was the nose. The eyebrows. The intricate pores and whiskers on the top of her lip and cheeks. But… either way, it was too late to back out now. She was good enough.

'Jessica?' Lester asked.

Jessica retreated a little. 'Steven?'

'Yes,' he lied. 'That's me.'

'Have you got the money?'

Lester gasped. 'Already? We haven't even got to know one another yet.'

'I like to make sure my clients have the money first. It makes good business sense.'

'Now *that* I can agree with,' Lester said, smiling. He reached for his back pocket, produced his wallet and pulled out a cheque. It was made out for five hundred pounds. 'Half for you. Half for the man who made the deal. That's what we agreed.'

'A cheque. Seriously? I thought these were extinct,' Jessica said, swiping it from him.

Lester snatched it back from her and said, 'Fine, don't have the money then.'

She grabbed it back, almost tearing the top of the paper. 'Don't have the sex then.' Jessica placed it in the cleavage of her top and invited Lester in. He ducked as he entered, and he felt the boat sink under his weight.

'You're early,' she said. 'I was just putting my make-up on.'

Lester stood awkwardly in the narrow corridor. It was so small it felt like the walls were closing in on him.

'I don't mind. I won't be seeing much of your face anyway.'

Jessica pulled him into the bedroom, to the left. The room was red. The curtains were pulled and there was a plush red throw draped over the duvet. A mirror hung from the ceiling.

Lester pointed to it. 'Is that for your pleasure or mine?'

'Both.' She dropped her robe and pushed him onto the bed. 'How do you like it?'

'Wild.'

'I can handle that,' Jessica said, winking at him.

Lester lifted himself off the bed and stood. 'Where's your bathroom? I want to drain the beast before we begin.'

'It's... er... down the other end, past the kitchen. On your right.'

Lester gave her a smile before he slipped out of the bedroom. He wandered carefully along the length of the boat, keeping his eyes wide open in search of a blade. It had become another habit of his, using his victim's weapons against them; that they should trip and fall at the mercy of their own swords. In his mind, it was oddly poetic.

A few seconds later, Lester found one in the kitchen, resting on the surface beside a couple of peeled lemons and a jug of water. It was small – much smaller than he was used to – but it would suffice. If it was sharp enough to skin a lemon, it was enough to slice a throat.

Lester bypassed the kitchen and went into the toilet. There, a toothbrush had been abandoned on the sink, with toothpaste stains left on the mirror. He waited there for a moment, pretending to go for a piss. After thirty seconds, he flushed, pretended to wash his hands and left.

Carefully closing the bathroom door behind him, Lester glanced up the length of the boat. Jessica was out of sight, the sound of rustling coming from within the bedroom. He tiptoed along the hallway and dipped into the kitchen, grabbed the knife and sheathed it in his trousers, before starting back to the bedroom.

'Everything ready?' he asked, leaning against the door frame.

'Ready when you are.' Jessica perched herself on the edge of the bed and tapped the duvet for Lester to join her. 'What would you like to do first?'

'I have an idea in mind.'

Lester crossed the threshold into the room – this was it: there was no going back now – then grabbed Jessica by the shoulder and forced her onto all fours. She gave a slight yelp as Lester's force overwhelmed her. Most of his Communion encounters had been surprised by his sheer strength, and it was flattering to know that this Jessica was no different.

He climbed onto the bed and reached behind his back. As his hand grabbed the kitchen blade and removed it from his pocket, Jessica glanced back at him. Her eyes widened as they fell on the demonic blade – the way it reflected the room's sensuous light. Jessica was first to react. She kicked her leg out, colliding with Lester's balls. He flew off the bed and smashed his back against a wooden wardrobe. In an instant, Jessica clambered off the bed, grabbed her robe from the floor and dashed out of the bedroom.

Lester regained his composure and chased after her. She was already outside the boat by the time Lester was on his feet, and he knew that he needed to be quick. The low light would soon mean that visibility was poor – and under the blanket of trees, it would be non-existent.

Lester disembarked from the boat and chased after Jessica. She'd made a left turn and was running along the riverside. She cried out in pain as the stones underfoot tore through her skin. It slowed her down massively, and within seconds, Lester was upon her.

He reached his arm around her waist from behind and plunged the blade into her neck. He'd buried the knife so deep into her throat that, despite its length, it looked as though it had come out the other side. For a short while, Jessica struggled, but it was over within a few seconds. His hands and arms were covered in her blood, and her body felt heavy against his. Dead weight. He expunged the blade from her neck and let her body drop to the ground. It landed with a dull thud.

Lester paused to look up and down the path. It was empty; there were no late-night dog walkers or doggers to disrupt him. He was faced with two options. One: drag Jessica to the bedroom and do everything he'd planned for her there; or two: save the hassle of dragging her back to the boat and do it here for the sheer heightened enjoyment of it.

Lester opted for the latter option.

Before beginning, he removed Jessica's tongue from her throat and placed it in his pocket. He saved the fingers for later.

Now, he could begin.

CHAPTER 36

REG 13

'How much longer are you going to be?' Elizabeth asked.

Jake sighed through the phone. 'Hopefully not long. I'll try and get done as quick as I can, but when you've got the worst serial killer since Jack the Ripper in your borough, there's just so much that we have to do.'

Jake scanned the office. It was 10 p.m., and by now the office had cleared out. Save one. Drew. And for the past hour, Drew had done nothing but sit and pretend to work on his computer. It didn't take a genius to work out that he was only there to further Jake's punishment for his earlier mistake.

The fallout from Jake's poor judgment during the press conference had been immense. Within hours, lies had spread like venom that the police were disinterested in the case and were putting their feet up until the next body arrived. But the reality of the situation was that they were doing everything they could, that they were working as fast as they could. Although… as Jake sat there staring into space, he questioned whether that was necessarily true. Had *he* done everything possible? Had *he* worked his arse off to get closer to the killer? No. He'd spent a few hours of the day chasing after Bridger, focusing his efforts on The Crimsons when he had no right to. And that wasn't good enough. Especially now that Bridger had left his life in Jake's hands and he could no longer get anywhere near Danny and Michael Cipriano without putting Bridger's life at risk. He had no choice but to focus his entire efforts on the Stratford Ripper. But how?

The implications of his blunder would undoubtedly be severe to his career. Through his mistake, he'd changed the public perception of the Metropolitan Police Service. If the public couldn't trust Jake and the rest of the team to find the killer, then who would? But it wasn't just the public who now couldn't trust them – it extended further than that. Up the higher echelons of the Met. How could he focus while all that paranoia was going on his head?

'Jake,' a voice called. 'Jake.'

It was Elizabeth. She was slowly bringing him out of his reverie.

'Jake, are you there?'

'What… er… yeah, sorry.'

'This is the second night in a row, Jake. Please don't be too late,' Elizabeth said. 'I miss you. Maisie misses you. She wanted you to read her to sleep tonight.'

Jake's heart warmed. 'I'm sorry, Liz. Really, I am. I'll try and get home as soon as I can.'

'Fine. I'll see you when I see you. Text me when you're on your way.'

And that was that. Elizabeth rung off and left Jake with the sound of the disconnected tone ringing in his ear.

In the corner of the room, Drew sneezed, lifted himself out of his chair and moved towards the printer. Jake eyed him suspiciously.

'You going to be much longer?' he called across.

Drew ignored his question. Instead, he grabbed the paper from the printer, stapled it in the top-left corner and wandered over to Jake.

Then he placed the documents on Jake's desk.

'What's this?' Jake asked, holding the paper in his hands.

'A Regulation 13 notice,' Drew said as he walked back to his own desk and grabbed his car keys. 'If it was up to me, you would have had it a long time ago, so you should count yourself lucky. You know the drill. Ten days to respond. Get your evidence ready. Get your police buddy prepared. And I suppose we'll see you at your performance meeting. Have a good evening, Jake. Say hi to the missus for me.'

| PART 4 |

CHAPTER 37

DISEASE

Jake rattled on Liam's office door repeatedly until his knuckles hurt. He was furious, and his emotions were only amplified by his tiredness; he hadn't slept a wink last night. An hour, max. The other six had been spent tossing and turning, staring into the ceiling, then at Elizabeth. She was already asleep by the time Jake got home. She apparently hadn't stayed up much later after their phone call.

As he'd stared at her, he'd started to consider the implications of the notice. It was a regulation notice for his performance, which meant he was in immediate breach of the Code of Ethics and Police Performance Regulations Act – the one that he'd lived by for so long. It wasn't career-ending, he knew that – the worst-case scenario was a Written Improvement Notice – but he also knew that it would be on his record, and that it would tarnish his chances of transferring to a separate team or any future promotions he wanted to put himself forward for. He'd only been in the service for a few years, and he couldn't believe he was already being given a Reg 13. It was embarrassing and made him feel worthless, useless, like a piece of shit. He'd let everyone down – Elizabeth, Maisie, their unborn child, his mum, them all – and never before had he felt so small and insignificant. His career was just beginning, just starting to develop and flourish into what he'd hoped it would be. And now he'd been handed this.

Jake's knuckles rapped on the door again, knocking even louder this time. Liam's blinds were pulled shut, and there was still no answer.

'What are you doing?' a voice called from behind him.

It was Drew.

'Where's Liam?' Jake asked, turning to face his colleague.

'DCI Greene, to you,' Drew corrected. 'He's not coming in today. Something's come up.'

'How do you know?'

'Because there's this beautiful little thing called trust. Perhaps you've heard of it?'

Jake ignored Drew's abhorrent sarcasm and hurried away to his desk. He threw the regulation notice on the table and his head into his hands.

'You know, if that's what you want to talk about, then you and I can discuss it,' Drew said.

'I'd rather not,' Jake replied, keeping his head down.

'You want to know what it's about. I can tell you do. Why else would you be slamming on Liam's door at eight in the morning when you know full well he never gets here until nine.'

'I'd rather wait until he gets here,' Jake snapped.

'Didn't you hear me? I just told you he wasn't coming in today. Not trustworthy *and* deaf... oh dear, what are we going to do with you?'

Jake slammed his hands on the table. 'What could be more important than Steven and Jessica Arnholt... Jessica Mann? Hmm? What could be more important than this?' Jake waved the Reg 13 in the air.

Drew's face contorted. He bit his lip and shook his head. 'You don't get it, do you?'

'What?' Jake said, still exerting an air of defiance.

'Not everything is about you. I don't even understand why you need to speak to him about it – you'll find everything out during the meeting.'

'I'm going to appeal it, you know.'

'You won't. You can't appeal until after a decision's been made. You should know that; you read all the regs like they're your friends.' Drew wandered behind Jake and stopped on his other side. 'They're not going to help you when you really need it though, are they? They're not going to help you when you're dying from a vicious and vindictive disease that doesn't give two shits about who you are.'

Jake paused a beat.

'Liam's dying?'

Drew didn't respond, but that was answer enough for Jake.

'I... I'm sorry, I... I didn't know.'

Drew returned to Jake's right side. 'There's a lot you don't know about any of us. If you carry on the way you are, things will stay that way.'

Drew turned his back and disappeared through a set of heavy double doors. Leaning back in his chair, Jake exhaled deeply. This was worse than he'd first thought.

But before he could dwell on it for too long, his phone vibrated. He answered immediately.

'Is everything OK?' Jake asked without giving Elizabeth any breathing space to speak. 'What's the matter? Is everything all right?'

'Jake, Jake, Jake,' Elizabeth began, speaking between heavy, exasperated breaths after every word. As soon as Jake heard that, he knew it wasn't going to be good news. 'Your mum's taking me to the hospital now.'

'What? Oh my God, why? Are you having the baby?'

'I don't know. But I'm in a lot of pain—' She groaned down the phone as if to prove her point.

'Right. OK. Fine. I'm coming to the hospital now. Tell my mum to call me when you get there.'

CHAPTER 38

FALSE ALARM

Jake pulled up outside Croydon University Hospital and sprinted to the entrance's sliding doors, forgetting to lock his car. The hospital was a few miles from his house, but even further from the station. It had taken him just over half an hour to race there – with the added help of his blue lights ninety per cent of the way. Once inside, Jake rushed to the front desk, flashed his ID and was finally led to Elizabeth on the maternity ward.

He was out of breath and his cheeks flustered. Nerves had plagued his entire body in the time it had taken him to get there – the unknown, the uncertainty of it all – and nobody had bothered to give him an update, so he was only able to think that the worst had happened. But, as soon as he saw Elizabeth resting on the bed, he relaxed a little.

'Are you OK?' Jake asked as he entered her room. He pointed at her stomach. 'The baby?'

Elizabeth flinched as he approached her.

'Jake – what are you doing here? What about work?'

'Work can wait. You're my priority right now. What's going on?'

Elizabeth took Jake's hand and squeezed it, setting off his nerves again. The last time he'd received a touch like that in a hospital was from his mum as she told him his dad had passed away.

'Nothing. Everything's OK. My stomach hurt but the doctors

checked the baby and it was all fine. The baby's healthy. I'm healthy. There's nothing to worry about.'

Jake perched himself on the side of the bed beside her ribs. He clutched her hand in his and squeezed. 'Oh, Liz. I was worried sick. Why didn't you call me sooner?'

'I didn't want to disturb you. I know you're stressed at work. I didn't want to add to it.'

'Nonsense. I would have stopped what I was doing, no problem. Everyone at work's aware of the situation. You know that.'

She shook her head and loosened her grip on Jake's hand. 'No, I don't. I've not seen you these past few days. You haven't spoken to me about it – any of it, in fact. You've been too busy. I heard you come home last night. You were crying, weren't you? I heard it all, but I was too tired and pissed at you to do anything about it. Are you going to tell me what it was about, or am I supposed to just stay in the dark about that too?'

Jake hung his head in shame then looked around him. The room was empty save for one other patient in the corner who was sleeping.

'I know,' he said. 'I've been shit. I know that. I'm sorry.'

Then, as Jake finished, his mum stepped into the room. She held Maisie in her arms.

'Daddy!' Maisie called, reaching out for Jake. He took his daughter from his mother and held her in his arms. He beamed, a reflection of his daughter's expression, and kissed her on the cheek. His body tingled with warmth and happiness, and an ear-to-ear grin grew on his face, as though all thought of their discussion moments ago had flown out of his mind and never happened.

'What are you doing here?' Jake's mum, Denise, asked.

'When my wife calls telling me she's going to a hospital, I think it's generally expected that I turn up,' Jake snapped.

'It's lovely to see you too, son.' She leant in, gave Jake a kiss on the forehead and spread her arm around his back. Her sarcasm instantly shut him down.

A brief pause flittered about the room.

'I spoke with the doctor,' Denise began. 'They just want to run a few more tests. Make sure everything's OK. And then they'll discharge you—'

'I'll take you home,' Jake interrupted.

'Er, OK,' Denise continued. 'That's fine with me. Are you staying here now?'

'Yes,' Jake said, nodding. He squeezed Elizabeth's hand. He hated it looking like his and Elizabeth's marriage was on the rocks. His mum and his dad's marriage had been the ideal. Smiles. Laughter. Embracing one another. Always talking. Always spending time with one another. Always being there for one another. Jake had wanted to model his relationship with Elizabeth on that, but as he was learning, it was much harder to do than he'd originally planned.

Denise smiled. 'Would you like me to stay a little while longer?'

'Yes!' Maisie screamed, clinging to Jake's shoulder.

'No, you don't need to—' Jake began.

'Yes,' Elizabeth interrupted. 'Please stay. I'd like you to.'

'Anything, my dear.'

Jake watched as his mum rounded the front of the bed and positioned herself on Elizabeth's other side. As Jake opened his mouth to speak, his phone vibrated. He rolled his eyes and sighed. Then he let go of Elizabeth's hand, placed Maisie on the floor and stepped out of the ward. He held the phone to one ear and buried a finger in the other one.

'Tanner.' It was Drew, and from the way he spoke Jake knew it wasn't good news.

'DS Richmond,' Jake said, exercising common courtesy now that he'd been served with his Reg 13.

'There's been another one.'

'Another one?' Jake said, raising his voice. Nurses and cleaners that meandered up and down the hallway stopped and turned to face him. 'Where?'

'Hackney. The Hackney Cut. By the marshes. It's not a pretty one, I'm told.'

'I don't know if I can—'

'You don't have a choice. Hurry up and get here.'

Drew rung off.

Jake swore in a whisper and pocketed his phone. How was he going to explain this one? After everything he'd just said to Elizabeth. There was going to be a lot of making up to do.

Jake returned to the ward, feigning a smile, but he knew both of the women in his life could see right through him. He approached Elizabeth's bed and opened his mouth to speak but was interrupted.

'Let me guess – you have to go?' Elizabeth asked softly.

Jake hesitated before responding. 'I'm sorry, Liz.'

'It's fine. I understand. I knew this was what I was getting myself into when I agreed to marry you. But don't think I'll forget – I'm already making a list.'

Jake chuckled. 'I'll keep my phone on at all times. If anything happens, let me know, OK?'

Elizabeth nodded.

Jake turned to his mother. 'Make sure you look after her.'

'She's perfectly safe with me.'

Jake bent down beside Maisie, who was now playing with a plastic cup on the floor. He kissed her goodbye and paced away.

As he hopped into his car and started the engine, Jake pictured the day where his second little miracle would be born, and how he would have all four of his favourite girls in one room.

The thought inspired him. But for now, he had other priorities.

CHAPTER 39

TROUBLE IN PARADISE

'Her name's Jessica-Anne Hart,' Drew began. 'Thirty-one. Single. Her humble abode was that river boat up there.' In the distance, a hundred yards away, was a rectangular box bobbing from side to side on the water.

Rain lashed at Jake's face, his thin mac offering him little protection from the elements, while the river torrented and splashed over the edges of the bank into the shrubbery and bushes.

Jake looked down at his feet.

Buried beneath the weeds, lying on her front, was the serial killer's latest victim. Her head was still attached to her body, but there were obvious attempts to decapitate it; inch-thick and wide cuts had been made, exposing cartilage and the unmistakable dull white of bone. More incisions had been made across the rest of her body. Cross-hatched. Zig-zagged from left to right. A mosaic pattern of flesh and blood. And a long incision had been made from her buttocks through to between her legs.

'Out of all the ones we've seen over the past few days, why do I feel like this is the worst,' Jake said, feeling his body begin to retch again.

His statement was met with silence.

Garrison whistled to Jake's left. The man was accompanying a SOCO as they sifted through the dense weeds by the riverbank.

'Drew,' he called, 'come over here, mate.'

Drew bounded over to Garrison, leaving Jake behind with Poojah.

'What happened to her?' Jake asked, stepping closer to the body, his foot almost slipping on the wet grass.

'Steady,' Poojah said, chuckling. 'Given her current position, it's difficult to say. I wouldn't be able to tell you if she drowned and bled to death.'

'Would you say these injuries are consistent with the others?'

Poojah nodded. 'In terms of MO, yes. She's missing her fingers and tongue, but her head's still attached – though there was no lack of trying. But the rest of her limbs are in place and she's not been torn open like Jessica Mann was.'

Jake contemplated for a moment.

'The other murders have been cleaner, calmer, taken place in the security and sanctity of someone else's home. They were private affairs... but this feels more open, more public. Maybe there was a struggle. She cottoned on to what he was up to, tried to escape but then he caught up with her.' Jake crouched down by the body and inspected her wrists. 'Are these ligature marks?'

Poojah nodded.

'Supports the theory,' he said. 'Maybe he knocked her down, killed her and then decided to tie her up as a metaphor, to symbolise that she couldn't evade him anymore.'

'The lacerations on her skin look as though they were born out of frustration.'

Jake stretched his legs. 'A hack job. He took his aggression out on her body rather than doing what he wanted to do with it.'

'Not necessarily,' Poojah replied. 'The body's been in water for several hours, so it's possible that any semen samples have washed away.'

At that point, Drew and Garrison returned.

'How are we doing on witnesses?' Jake asked them.

'A dog owner found her on her morning walk,' Garrison said. 'Uniform are scanning the local area for any other witnesses. No houses anywhere nearby. Only an industrial estate a few hundred yards in that direction, but it's covered by trees so nobody could have seen anything.'

'Do we know what she did for a living?'

At first, Drew didn't respond; instead, he glanced up at the river boat and then back to Jake. 'If you can call it a living...' He bent down by her side, pulled a plastic glove from his pocket and donned it over his right hand. He reached for Jessica-Anne's left arm and flipped it over, revealing the underside of her wrist. Tattooed over her veins was a barcode and a number. Fifty-three.

'What is that?' Jake asked, staring at the barcoded lines on her skin. As he looked at it, he recalled images of the woman who had fled Archie Arnold's home on the day he'd conducted his house-to-house enquires. She'd had a similar tattoo but with a different number.

'Why would he kill a prostitute?' Jake asked, more to himself than the others around him.

'What do you mean?' Drew replied.

'All the previous murders were people from this online community that they're all a part of. But now he's killed someone outside of his own ecosystem, his own comfort zone.'

'Perhaps he's run out of Jessicas to meet up with.'

'It doesn't make sense,' Jake said, again, more so for himself than anyone else.

'Nothing makes sense to you, does it?' Garrison intervened.

'I'm just saying,' Jake said.

Garrison shot Jake a stare that quickly shut him down.

'I hate to say it,' Drew said, 'but I think he might be right. This attack feels more sporadic, more unplanned, more violent. When can we get samples back to the lab and verified? I want to know if this really is the same killer.'

Poojah's face contorted. 'I'd like to say within twenty-four hours, but these past few murders have completely drowned us.'

Drew chuckled. 'If you can do it in twenty-four hours then I'll treat you and your team to lunch. How many are there?'

Poojah looked up and down the riverbank. 'Thirteen in total.'

'On second thoughts...' Drew said. 'Maybe just you then. And you can tell everyone how grateful I am.'

She chuckled behind her mask. Then she crouched by Jessica-Anne's body and snapped a few more photos.

'Come on,' Garrison said. 'Let's get out of here.'

Without saying anything further, Drew and Garrison started off towards the river boat. They left Jake on his own. For a moment he was suspended, not sure whether to follow or stay.

He huffed, then decided to walk after them. As he did so, Poojah made a derisive noise.

'What's that?' Jake asked, his temper flaring.

'Is there trouble in paradise?' she asked as she rose to her feet. 'Yesterday you were all pally, and now look at you. One of them say something to upset you? Or was it the other way round?'

Jake squinted and threw his hands into his pockets.

'There's nothing wrong. Nobody's said anything to anyone.'

'If you say so.'

CHAPTER 40

THETOPDOG

Jake knew how to use a computer, but he didn't have a working knowledge of how one worked. His experience stretched as far as opening Task Manager on his Windows PC when things stopped working – and when that didn't work, he tried the old adage of turning it off and on again. He was grateful, therefore, that the force had its resident digital forensic technicians to help them hack into victims' phones and laptops. If it were left down to him during a technical malfunction or a glitch, then the investigation would stumble and fall. So when Roland Lewandowski, MIT's dedicated DFT, emailed Jake summoning him to his office, Jake was filled with excitement. Roland was a technically gifted individual and had spent his whole life around computers – from the day he was first able to use his fingers. The team relied on him, and on the two occasions Jake had seen him work, both instances had been a success.

Jake tapped his knuckles on Roland's door. He entered as soon as he heard a response.

'Ah!' Roland yelled, rising out of his seat as he caught sight of Jake. 'My good friend, how are you?'

Roland was a larger-than-life character with a larger-than-life stomach. His diet consisted solely of beer and curry, and whenever Jake saw him around the building, he was always eating a snack or packet of crisps from the vending machine in the canteen.

'Things are well,' he lied. 'Things are well.'

'That's good to hear. Elizabeth?'

'Fine. Baby number two will be with us soon.'

'That's excellent, my friend.' Roland embraced Jake and slapped him heartily on the back. 'When do you leave?'

'Paternity starts in two weeks' time,' Jake said as they let go of one another.

'Part-timer.' Roland winked. 'I'm glad you came down. There's a lot I need to tell you.'

Jake grabbed a seat and sat opposite. 'I'm listening.'

Roland reached behind his desk and grabbed a plastic evidence bag. Inside it was Steven Arnholt's laptop. Roland pulled it out of the bag and placed it on the table. Jake held his breath.

'It took me a while, but—'

'You can say that again...'

Roland raised a fat hand in Jake's face. 'Listen. I consider it more of a test of my skills when I'm faced with a challenge this hard. Whatever this person had on here, they were intent on making sure nobody else found it.'

'And did you?'

'I said it was hard, not impossible.'

Jake scurried round the side of the table and came to a stop beside Roland, leaning closer to the screen. His body trembled with excitement. This was the first piece of solid evidence they were going to get. And it meant they would be closer to the killer.

The home screen loaded, and Jake was met with an image of Steven and Jessica smiling fervently at the camera. In the background was the Grand Canyon. They looked happy, untouchable, as though there wasn't a morsel of evil anywhere near them. How their lives were completely separate beneath the layer of the photograph. Jake supposed that was what photos were: a hyper-real representation of life – someone's, anyone's – that wasn't minutely close to reality.

Roland moved the cursor and opened a piece of software called TorStream, breaking Jake from his reverie. The software icon was a dark circle with a yellow camera in the middle. Jake had never seen it before, and as Roland clicked on it, he rubbed his thumb on the underside of his fingers in anticipation.

'It's the Dark Web,' Roland said, beginning a running commentary of what he was doing. 'There are various applications and software out there that get you to different parts of the Dark Web.'

'Different parts?'

'Yeah. So if you like little children, you'll use one programme. If you like beheading people, another. Terrorism, several. And so on.'

Jake blew through his lips.

Roland continued, 'This particular one gets us to some sort of sadistic and sordid sex-gang culture – not too far from the child porn ring.' Roland tapped the mouse a few times and the images on the screen changed. 'I thought you'd want to see this first. I trawled through Steven's browsing history. The problem is, because it's the Dark Web, it constantly deletes browsing history and buries it deep within the web so you can't find it.'

'But you did?'

Roland grinned. 'Everything leaves a trace, Jake. You wouldn't be here otherwise.' He tapped the mouse again, and the screen loaded up a web page. The header across the top was black with red writing, while the rest of the page was predominantly red interspersed with injections of black and white.

'The Community?' Jake said, reading the banner.

'That's one word to describe it,' Roland retorted.

'What's that supposed to mean?'

Pointing at the screen, Roland said, 'Look.'

The web page was a blog-feed filled with thumbnails of pornographic images, and to the right-hand side of them, snapshots of comments that other users had made. At the bottom of the page was a leader board. There were twenty names in total – with the option to scroll through more of the rankings – and points next to each name.

'Twelve thousand points,' Jake said. 'Ten. Nine. Seven and a half. Four thousand, three hundred and seventy-five.' He paused as his eyes scanned the page. 'Do we know what you get points for?'

Roland moved the cursor and clicked on a link at the top of the page.

'There are instructions,' he explained.

As Jake read through the list, he squinted. Users were able to acquire points based on sexual acts they committed with other members of The Community.

Three hundred for anal intercourse.

One hundred for vaginal.

Fifty for oral.

Twenty-five for anything else.

'Jesus,' Jake said, feeling his mouth become moist with saliva. 'Sixteen thousand points. Who's top?'

'TheTopDog,' Roland replied.

'Can we view his profile?'

'Yes. But there's nothing there.'

Jake leant back in his chair and exhaled deeply. 'Do you know how it works?'

'Unfortunately, I do.'

CHAPTER 41

THE COMMUNITY

'It's called The Community,' Jake said to Drew and Garrison in the MIR. Both men were standing over him, watching the screen. 'And it's essentially an online swinger's forum but with a dark twist. There are just over fifteen thousand members – and it's growing quite rapidly; we've had two people sign up in the past hour – and the aim is to meet up with like-minded people – meaning sadists and masochists. Then you organise what you want to do with them, where you want to do it, and then you go and *do* it. They call it an act of Communion. And you get points depending on which sexual acts you take part in. In order to get the points, you have to document it with either photographs or video evidence. That's the most important part,' Jake explained. 'Members need to have proof that they've done what they claim to, otherwise they don't get the points.'

'Is this legal?' Garrison asked, shovelling a digestive in his mouth. 'Sounds fucked up to me.'

'I mean… if everything's consensual…' Jake responded.

'Who polices it?' Drew asked, his voice sounding intrigued.

'The site's creator. Someone named S. That's all we know about him. Or her.' Jake paused. 'Most members submit videos and put them on the news feed. Sort of like a pornographic version of YouTube. There seems to be a correlation with points and video views too, because people's ranks are changing every second. Instead of being paid royalties for the amount of views they get, they get points that contribute to their standing in the leader board. The more views, the more points.'

'I bet you anything that S – or whoever the fuck he is – is sitting there jacking off to every video he gets ten times a day.' Garrison said with his mouth half full.

'Who's at the top of the leader board?' Drew asked. He grabbed a chair and joined Jake.

'Someone called TheTopDog.'

'Original title,' Garrison retorted over Jake's shoulder.

'Where are Steven and Jessica on the leader board?' Drew asked beside him.

'Fifth. They've got about ten thousand points – a mile off TheTopDog in comparison to everyone else beneath them.'

'How do they communicate with one another?'

'Via message. The platform has a direct chat feature.' Jake opened up Steven and Jessica Arnholt's Community inbox.

Silence fell over them as the three men read from the screen.

'There are loads,' Drew said. 'They've been busy.'

'They've messaged everyone in the top twenty,' Garrison added.

'Including Jessica Mann,' Drew said, pointing at the screen. 'Forty-five days ago. The three of them were together.'

'This is helluva community,' Garrison said. 'You sure this isn't illegal?'

Jake hesitated. 'I mean, there isn't anyone under the age of eighteen on here.'

'How do you know?' Drew asked.

'Roland checked beforehand. As part of the sign-up process you have to select your age – you can't be under the age of eighteen. It's part of the rules.'

Drew sniggered. 'There's nothing stopping a fifteen-year-old from saying they're eighteen.'

'Granted. But when you sign up, you're required to enter credit-card details. On the surface, it looks all above board. But if we began to dig deeper into it, I'm sure we'd unearth a few things.'

'Yeah,' Garrison said, chuckling. He swatted Drew on the shoulder with the back of his hand. 'We'd probably find Drew lurking on the bottom of the leader board, sitting on zero points because no one wants to fuck him. Not even his wife.'

'Fuck you,' Drew spat, giving Garrison the finger.

Jake and Garrison burst into laughter, and for a split second, Jake felt like he was back in the group again. Part of the gang. As though his performance regulation had been completely forgotten about. But that was all over as soon as Drew opened his mouth again.

'What else do we need to know? How's it funded?' Drew asked, restoring balance and calm to the group.

'It's a subscription model. Members pay S a fee of £2 a month.'

'One of the most reasonably priced subscriptions I've ever heard of,' Garrison said. 'Even *The Guardian* charges a fiver.'

'If you're such an advocate, maybe we should sign you up. See what sort of trouble you get up to.'

'You'd like that, wouldn't you?'

'Guys!' Jake said, attempting to restore the peace. 'Come on. Four people are dead and the only thing linking three of them is this Community. If we can work out who the creator is, then he can give us the person responsible.'

'You think S knows who he is?' Drew asked.

'He must do. These sorts of people are committed to getting higher scores. Look.' Jake pointed at the leader board. 'It's midday and people are already rising through the ranks. They're busy. They're at it. They're determined to become the best of the best. That's what the killer is trying to do – he's trying to become the very best. He's meeting up with other members because he knows they'll agree to his demands, and then he—'

'That doesn't explain why he's killing them,' Garrison said.

He was right. It didn't.

'Perhaps with Steven and Jessica Arnholt it got out of hand, and ever since then he's been trying to relive that night. Trying to relive what it was like to spend the first night with the first Jessica.'

'What are you saying?' Drew asked.

Jake shuffled his body around so that he faced them both. 'I'm saying that Jessica Arnholt is the catalyst. There's a reason all the other girls have been called Jessica, and they all look exactly the same as Arnholt. He's targeting lookalikes with the same name.'

'So we need to lock up all the Jessicas in a fifteen-mile radius, keep them indoors between the hours of 9 p.m. and 7 a.m., and make sure they don't speak to strangers?'

Jake scowled at Drew. Why was he being such an arsehole?

'Take this seriously, Drew. These are people's lives we're playing with here.'

Drew folded his arms. 'All right then, *boss*.' The last word was replete with venom. 'What's our next step? What do we need to do?'

'It's like I said,' Jake replied, pulling out his phone. 'Our guy could be anyone of the fifteen thousand accounts left. But the one who'll know who it is faster than anyone else is S. We find him, and he gives us the killer.'

'And how are we going to find him, genius?'

Jake sighed. The personal insults were gradually beginning to wear him down, and he didn't know how much more he could take.

He liked to think he was thick-skinned, but this was something else – throughout college and university he'd been adored and befriended by many. He'd been liked. He'd had friends. And he'd gained even more sympathy friends after he'd nearly died in an avalanche during a snowboarding trip with the university. But he'd never been subject to ridicule and belittling that, he hated to admit, bordered on bullying. It was a completely alien concept to him – one he had no experience of how to handle.

'Fortunately for you,' Jake began, 'Roland's been working on it since we've been talking, and…' Jake looked at his phone. Right on cue it began ringing. He answered. 'Roland! Yes…? Excellent… Hero… Send it to my email. I owe you one. *We* owe you one.'

Almost as quickly as he'd answered, Jake rung off and placed the phone on the table slowly.

'Roland's managed to find S's address. And we're going there now.'

CHAPTER 42

MUMMY'S BOY

Denise Tanner placed a cup of green tea on the coffee table beside Elizabeth.

'I hope it's all right,' Denise said, sitting on the sofa opposite. 'When I was pregnant with Laura, I didn't stop drinking green tea. The small dose of caffeine kept me up all night because I was drinking so many... I suppose that explains why Laura was such a handful and was always awake when she was supposed to be sleeping. Only got myself to blame really.'

Elizabeth chuckled awkwardly. They had just got back from the hospital and she was feeling tired. Her body ached. Her legs ached. Her back ached. Her neck ached. Her stomach ached. She was convinced she was going to be admitted to a bed for the rest of her life due to the toll the pregnancy was taking on her bones and muscles.

'Are you OK?' Denise asked, setting cup on the saucer.

Elizabeth sipped and swallowed. The liquid scalded her mouth, but she tried not to show it.

'I'm just nervous,' she replied.

'Oh, Liz. Everything will be fine. You've been through it once before, so you know what to expect. Besides, I'm here for you if you need help, and so are your parents.'

'I...' Elizabeth hesitated. 'I wasn't talking about the birth.

Although, I am still nervous about that – because I know what's coming it makes me more afraid of the things that could go wrong. I was talking about Jake.'

'Jake?' Denise retorted, her maternal instinct overwhelming her. 'Why are you nervous about Jake?'

Elizabeth said nothing. Instead, she sipped more of her tea, wished she'd said nothing and looked out of the window; a car drove past and a mother pushed a pram while a child skipped by her side.

'Liz?' Denise pushed.

'Nothing. Don't worry. I shouldn't have said anything. Forget I mentioned it.'

Denise lifted herself off the sofa and joined Elizabeth's side. She placed her hand on her daughter-in-law's knee. 'You can tell me, Liz. Especially when it comes to my son. If he does anything to hurt you, trust me I'll whip him back into shape. And that's a promise.'

Elizabeth forced a smile. It was a nice gesture, one that she determined Denise wasn't joking about judging from her tone.

'It's just… It's his work. He's been really busy these past few weeks, and I'm afraid that he's not going to be there for the kids. He's not going to be there for me when I need him. I'm worried he'll prioritise his work over everything else.'

'Do you resent him having his job?' Denise asked, her tone soft and soothing.

'No! Not at all. I love that he loves what he does. And I'm so proud of him. I wouldn't want him to stop because of me. I just want him to be there… I want him to be *here*, you know?'

Denise leant closer. 'I do, love. I do. When Ian and I first started out with Laura, we didn't know what we were doing. We made loads of mistakes. We thought we could just carry on the way our lives used to be. But it didn't work like that. We learnt that pretty early on – well, I say "we", but it was actually me who noticed first… Ian was a little slow. But he got there in the end. He realised that he couldn't spend all his time at work, and that he needed to sacrifice some evenings with his friends to support Laura and me. And if Jake is anything like his dad – and, trust me, I've known him long enough to know that he is – then he'll be the same. It'll just take him a little while to realise it. Obviously, being a police officer is completely different to a physiotherapist – they're at opposite ends of the spectrum – but I'm just trying to tell you to have some patience with him. Trust him. He'll come out all right. And I think you know, deep down, that he will too. I mean, you're having another one of his babies! And if he doesn't sort himself out, then you can always tell me, and I'll kick his arse into gear. He's a mummy's boy – can't say no.'

Elizabeth chuckled, but it was weak. She felt a little better, but not enough for her to be able to forget about it entirely. She loved her husband – would do anything for him – but she hoped he would prove it was reciprocated sooner rather than later.

'Thank you, Denise,' Elizabeth said, squeezing her mother-in-law's hand. 'Thank you. I really do appreciate it. You've been amazing throughout all of this… and with Maisie too.'

'You're welcome, love. I just wish Ian was here to have met you, and to watch you both grow into the wonderful young adults you are.' Tears formed in the corners of Denise's eyes. She avoided Elizabeth's gaze and spotted something on the coffee table. 'What's this?'

Denise rose from the sofa and picked up an orange card.

'I have no idea…' Elizabeth replied.

Denise returned to the sofa and handed it to her. Elizabeth inspected the Congratulations card and read the messages inside. One of them stuck out.

Remember: my mum's name is Ellie. Wonderful name. Wonderful person. Liam.

'How sweet,' Elizabeth said, closing the card and setting it down on the arm of her chair. 'It's from the guys at the station. Bless them. I didn't know they'd given us that.'

CHAPTER 43

ON THE REGISTER

S lived in Bratendon Tower, a high-rise building that was part of the Ruthwell estate in the south of Stratford. The building was tall, narrow, grey, derelict and uninspiring. It stood out drastically against the flatness of the rest of the landscape. It was one of the focal points of Stratford and regularly regarded amongst the community as a shithole.

'Someone would think people live there out of choice,' Drew said. He leant forward in the driver's seat and peered up at building.

'You sure this is it?' Garrison asked.

Jake had been resigned to the back and had given no argument. He was at the bottom of the pecking order and he knew it.

'This is what Roland sent me, yeah,' Jake replied. 'Did anything come back on the PNC?'

Garrison pulled a laptop out of the footwell, opened it up and logged onto the Crimint – the Crime Intelligence System. It was a database that held information on every convicted criminal in the country. Name. Location. Date of the crime. Nature of the crime. Evidence against them. Sentence served. Last known address. Everything. It was like an encyclopedia of crime.

An image of an elderly man appeared in the top-right corner. His hair was long and thinning, his nose pointed and beaked. His eyes were buried deep in his face, the pupils a shade of deathly black. He reminded Jake of Danny DeVito's Penguin.

'Looks like the type,' Garrison noted.

'What does it say?' Jake asked, leaning between Garrison and Drew's chairs. His eyes struggled to read the text on the screen.

'Give me a second.'

Jake waited as Garrison digested the information.

'Sampson Decker. Convicted serial rapist—'

'Rapist?' Drew interrupted and turned back to face Jake. 'Did he show up on your sex offenders search the other day?'

Jake shrugged. 'I don't think so...' The truth was, he couldn't remember the names, and he couldn't remember following up on them either. So much had happened since then that it had completely slipped his mind. But he wasn't about to confess that to them both; he didn't want to add any more fuel to the performance notice.

Garrison cleared his throat, signifying he wanted to continue. 'Says here he was found guilty of raping thirteen women in the space of a month in 1970. He was twenty-seven. He then served thirty years in prison and has been living on the dole ever since. He has biannual meetings with a therapist to sort out – and I quote – "his severe deviant sexual urges"...'

'Christ,' Drew said, thumping the window with his fist. 'He knows that if he can't rape anyone himself, then he can get others to do it instead.'

'That's sick,' Jake said, 'beyond disturbing. Shall we?'

CHAPTER 44

B–A–I–N

Sampson Decker's address was number forty-two on the sixth floor. By the time they reached the front door, waiting for it to open, all three of them were out of breath.

A few seconds later, it did. The man they saw in front of them was not the same man they'd seen on the computer a few minutes ago. He looked older now, and far worse. His skin sagged heavier on his face, and his eyes were buried even deeper into his skull, covered by several layers of deep crevasses in his skin. Two tubes dangled from his nostrils and were connected to a respirator machine on wheels behind him. His breathing was heavy and raspy, and sounded like a dying Darth Vader.

Sampson's expression remained unchanged at the sight of the three men standing outside his doorway. Perhaps it was because he didn't have enough strength in his body to react. Or perhaps it was because it had happened so many times in the past that he was used to it by now.

'Yes?' he said, his voice barely more than a whisper.

'Mr Decker?' Drew said, holding his warrant card in Sampson's face. 'We'd like to come in please, if that's all right? Ask you a few questions?'

'You got a warrant?' Sampson asked.

'Not necessary,' Drew replied. 'Just a few questions. That's all.

Won't take up too much of your time. Not unless you've got something you want to tell us.'

'I didn't forty years ago. I don't now either.'

'We'll see about that,' Drew said, forcing the door open and stepping into Sampson Decker's flat. Garrison followed behind. For a moment, Jake remained where he was, torn between leaving or staying.

As Jake teetered on the edge, Garrison turned back to face him. 'Come on,' he said. 'We need you on this one, mate.'

That was invitation enough. Jake stepped over the lip in the door frame and entered Sampson's flat.

The first thing he noticed was the rancid smell that assaulted his senses. It was inexplicable, like there had been a dog or a cat that had lived and died there... and was still in the property, buried somewhere beneath the mess and rubbish.

The four men moved into the living room at the end of the small corridor. Jake paused and looked around him. There was a box television in the corner of the room, resting atop a stack of magazines and shoeboxes. Beside it was a pile of CDs stacked neatly to the height of the television, and then a handful scattered about the place. Beside the television was an archaic radiator. It was boarded up and shielded by a wall of newspapers. There was an armchair next to the radiator, and Sampson claimed that as his own as soon as they entered. The old man struggled to sit down and was forced to use the arms of the chair for support.

'Is this going to take long?' Sampson asked as Drew and Garrison found seats on the sofa opposite. Jake remained standing.

'It will take as long as it takes... S,' Drew said.

An awkward silence fell on the room as they waited for a response.

Sampson smiled, which turned into a chuckle, then a cough. Globules of phlegm and saliva spewed into his hand and ricocheted back onto his face. He left them there to dry.

'So that's what this is about?' Sampson said, after regaining himself.

'Would you like to tell us what we want to know? Or are we going to have to ask you?'

'The latter. I'll waste your time like you wasted thirty years of mine.' Sampson tried to speak fluently but it was too difficult. He was forced to cough in between breaths, and each cough sounded worse than the last.

'If you ask me, that was time well spent. We managed to keep you off the streets for a very long time,' Drew said. There was venom in his voice, and Jake was quickly realising this was turning into an assault, rather than a questioning exercise.

'Mr Decker,' Jake interjected, pulling his pen and pocketbook from his blazer. 'We wondered what you could tell us about The Community?'

'You already know, otherwise you wouldn't be here.'

'We want to hear it from you. You created it.'

Sampson said nothing. 'I did not create it. It is the vision of someone else.'

'Who?'

'Long dead. You'll never find him. A cell mate of mine. We shared the same views on things. He created it. I fathered it,' Sampson explained. His eyes were cold and steely, giving nothing away. 'You don't scare me. I don't have long left to live, gentlemen. There is no amount of damage that you can do that will frighten or shock me.'

As Jake opened his mouth to speak, Garrison interrupted him. 'What do you know about Steven and Jessica Arnholt?'

Sampson slowly turned to face Drew, smirking. 'There we go, son. A real question. You could learn a few things from your elder, here.'

He sniffed hard and wiped the snot away from his nose with the back of his hand. 'They're members. Good members. They've been a part of The Community for a good number of years now. One of the first to sign up when I began the forum.'

'Did you know they were murdered a few nights ago?' Jake probed.

'I've seen things on the news. Tragic.'

'Tragic indeed. Horrible murders. Truly horrible. But you already knew about them, didn't you? You've been seeing all the footage. So why don't you tell us who's committing them, and we'll get out of your hair.'

Sampson looked into his lap and then slowly raised his head. 'He was the first... The very first after I uploaded the website. Within twenty-four hours he was there, signed up and already paying the reduced subscription of fifty pence. Back then it was just a maintenance cost. I don't know what he was searching for, but he managed to find me so quickly. And I'm glad he did. Without him, word wouldn't have spread as well as it did. He had a tight network of people he trust—'

'What's his name?' Jake snapped, growing impatient.

Sampson slowed. He looked around the room, pausing at each of them for a few seconds. Then he slowly lifted his skinny fingers and pointed one at Jake.

'I don't like this one,' he said.

'Neither do we,' Drew remarked, keeping his gaze focused on Sampson. 'But his question still stands – give us a name.'

Sampson sighed. 'You'll never catch him, you know? He's managed to kill four already and you're none the wiser about who he is. He's too clever to be caught. And he'll strike again before you find him. Of that I'm sure.'

'What's his name, Sampson?' Garrison said.

No response.

'Tell us everything about him.'

Sampson chuckled. 'That's a long story, my friend. How long do you have? He's the best out there. There's a reason he's top of the leader board, and not just because he's been in this business longer than anyone else. He's smart about what he does and who he picks. But it wasn't always like that. When he first joined, he knew nothing. He hadn't even slept with a girl. He'd only ever had fantasies. He masturbated a lot.'

An essence of life and enthusiasm was restored in Sampson's voice; it was apparent he was enjoying himself – speaking about his favourite subject. Jake thought it must have been because he'd bottled it up for so long. He doubted there were many people Sampson had to share this sort of thing with.

'I took him under my wing,' Sampson continued. 'I taught him everything I knew. There were a few things I learnt inside prison. I passed those on to him. He absorbed everything quickly and put it to practice a few weeks later. I organised a prostitute for him. Later that day, he returned a man. But as the number of members in The Community grew, so did his desire. He became obsessed with coming top of the leader board. Besotted with the idea of being good at something. He never excelled at anything as a child. He never won any sports prizes, academically he wasn't smart, and he never won the girl. So when he stumbled upon The Community, he was home.'

'That's some home,' Drew retorted.

'So why's he killing people?' Jake asked. 'What's changed? Why did he kill Steven and Jessica Arnholt?'

Sampson hesitated before responding. 'It was his special Communion. He'd been organising that night with Jessica for so long. It was the time Steven finally let him fuck her. Before then all they'd done was everything other than intercourse. And when he got there, he found out they were going to betray him – he found out they were going to kill him. He had to get to them first. And he did. He sent me everything. And now he's struggling to get rid of the taste from his lips.' Sampson licked his own lips as he finished talking, baring half a set of black and yellow-stained teeth.

'You've been telling him what to do, haven't you?' Jake said. 'He's living out your fantasy.'

'At first, he was. But now he's started down a different path –

182

one nobody will be able to bring him back from. He got a flavour of what it was like to experience those things. Mutilation of a dead corpse. Necrophilia. The taste of human flesh. All of it. And now he's trying to relive it again and again.'

'Do you know where he's going next? Do you know what he's going to do?'

'No,' Sampson said.

Liar, Jake thought. He didn't trust a word the man said.

'You said he sent you everything,' Garrison continued. He leant forward and placed his elbows on his knee. 'Is this through the direct messaging on The Community's website?'

Sampson shook his head. 'We haven't used that for a long time. He doesn't trust it. Too easy to catch him. I told you he was too good for that.'

'How then?' Jake asked.

Before Sampson had a chance to respond, Garrison interrupted loudly and stepped in front of Jake, blocking him from view. 'I wonder, Sampson. Do you have a laptop or a computer round here that we might be able to take a look at? Maybe even some picture albums where you've printed your favourites? I'd quite like to see them.'

As soon as he'd finished speaking, Garrison took it upon himself to turn his back on the three of them and slip out of the living room and into the hallway. Within seconds, the sounds of kitchen cupboards opening and glasses being moved about echoed around the flat.

'Hey!' Sampson said, struggling out of the chair, using his stick for support. 'Get back here!'

Sampson left the room, panting.

Once he was out of sight, Drew reached into his pocket and produced three small black objects.

'What's that?' Jake asked, confused.

'Our evidence,' Drew replied.

He moved about the room and placed the objects in inconspicuous places: on the underside of a lamp by Sampson's chair, the back of the radiator and on top of the door frame that led into the hallway.

'Wait, you can't,' Jake started.

'Why not?' Drew replied, focusing his attention on the arm of Sampson's chair.

'Because we don't have a warrant.'

On the arm of the chair was an old Nokia mobile phone. Drew ignored Jake and bent down to pick it up. He started to scroll through the address book, nodding as he absorbed the names of Sampson's contacts.

'What are you doing?' Jake asked. He leant across Drew and snatched the phone from his grip. 'What are you playing at?'

'I could ask you the same thing,' Drew replied.

'No. That's it. I've had enough. I won't let you do it. We don't even have a warrant to seize anything – not if we want to be able to use it as evidence.' Jake turned and pointed to the lamp by the wall. 'And what about those? Have you got a warrant for those?'

'It's back at the office. This is all part of my strategy. Remember, I'm Deputy SIO when Liam isn't around. Trust me.'

Jake glanced down at the phone. For a moment he wondered what sort of horrors were inside it. What sort of images and indecent messages and videos Sampson had been sent over the years since The Community had begun. But he wasn't allowed to look through it, not without a warrant. Following regulations and procedures was one of the most infuriating things about being a police officer, but they were there for a reason. They helped keep the police accountable as much as they did the victims and witnesses. It was a double-edged sword – one that, sometimes, Jake wished didn't exist.

'What were you looking for anyway?' Jake asked, finally coming out of his thoughts.

'A name.'

'What name?'

'The name of our killer, genius.' Drew snatched the phone back from Jake and began scrolling through Sampson's message. 'And there it bloody well is. Lester Bain. B-A-I-N.'

'How can you be sure it's him?'

Drew spun the phone around and shoved it in front of Jake's face. A few inches from his eyes, on the heavily pixelated screen, was a thumbnail image of Jessica Mann's mutilated and dismembered body. The sight made Jake feel queasy. For some reason, it was worse seeing it on the screen – as though the photographic image of her remains made more real somehow.

'We can use this,' Jake said after Drew lowered the phone. 'He's complicit in all of this. Why don't we arrest him now?'

Drew shook his head and touched the side of his nose with his finger. 'Strategy, Jake. All part of the strategy.'

Before Jake was able to respond, Sampson erupted into the living room, waving his stick around. Over his shoulder was Garrison, standing in the darkness of the corridor.

'Get out!' Sampson pointed to the front door. 'Get out of my house! All of you! You have no right to be here!'

'We can show ourselves out,' Drew said, setting the mobile phone down just as Sampson turned his attention back to Garrison. As Jake and Drew shuffled past Sampson in the door frame, he continued, 'We'll be back soon. Once we've found your little friend, we'll be back for you.'

'You'll never find him,' Sampson gave as his last remark.

All three men stopped outside of the door frame. 'If we don't, we know where to find you. That's good enough for us.'

Drew closed the door behind them.

'Come on,' he said, 'let's get the fuck out of here. The less time I spend in this place, the better.'

As they hurried towards the lift, Jake's phone vibrated. He looked at the caller ID and his eyes widened, his pulse quickening.

'Sorry,' he said, holding his hand in the air as Drew and entered the lift. 'I've got to take this. I'll meet you at the car in a few.'

Drew and Garrison grunted and then closed the lift doors behind them.

'Liz? What's wrong?' he said, answering just as Drew and Garrison disappeared.

'What are you talking about?' a male voice said. 'It's me... Elliot.'

CHAPTER 45

UNEXPECTED SURPRISE

Lester had been in the property business almost all his life. It had been a delightful inheritance from his parents after he'd killed them. He'd received their empire when he was eighteen years old – old enough, in the eyes of the law, to manage the properties and oversee them on a day-to-day basis. And, since then, he'd kept the properties ticking by in the background. It was lucrative, and it was money he didn't have to work hard for. His portfolio consisted of ten houses in the Stratford area that brought in enough capital to fund his camomile lifestyle – eight that the government knew about, registered under his name; two that were off the books, filed under an alias. The reasons for doing so were twofold: it was great for the tax, and it was perfect if he ever needed to escape the mundanity of life. But, in all those years since he'd taken over the business, he'd never experienced something as sudden as this: a tenant wanted to terminate his tenancy with immediate effect, and he wanted Lester to be there to finalise all the paperwork and inspect the property before he left. It was an inconvenience. Not only did it force Lester to spend time away from finding another Jessica – either online or through another pimp – but it also forced him to show his face in public during the day. And that was something he didn't like to risk.

   And there was an additional problem. The Nasties were getting hungry again – he could sense it. Jessica the Prostitute had been a terrible experience. Her attempted escape had ruined it for him. It had thrown him off and put him off from performing at his best. His hand still ached from the multiple stab wounds he'd inflicted on her. He needed to do better next time. It needed to be more controlled, more delicate, and he needed a place to be able to dedicate more time to the Communion. Ever since he started out, he'd always maintained the rule of meeting for a Communion at the other party's location. The reasons were simple. First, and most importantly, it was for security purposes. He didn't want anybody finding out his home address and dobbing him in to the police. Second, it was for the extra points it would garner him on the leader board. On the infrequent occasion that he had been forced to do it at his house, he'd been extra careful and gone to great lengths to make sure they didn't know the exact address: he'd often meet them in a communal place and take them back to his house that way. It wasn't a watertight way to avoid their knowing his address, but it was better than nothing. And now it was time for a change. The past few Communions had been ruined by the threat of a housemate coming home early or somebody walking past in the middle of nowhere. He needed a place. And now that he thought about it, perhaps his tenant's abrupt departure was actually a gift.

Lester wandered up to the front door and knocked. It was a one-bedroom house that he'd completely renovated a few years ago. He'd given it a new kitchen. New bathroom. New living room. New bedroom. It was a steal, and he'd given it to the current tenant on an even better rolling contract that required thirty days' notice for cancellation. It was mutually beneficial for both parties, and he'd never had any issues with them. Except for now.

The door opened.

'Hi, Sampson.'

'Hi, Carl. Good to see you. Are you well?' He flashed a smile, and for a split moment he almost forgot that he was supposed to pretend his name was Sampson.

'Never better, thanks. Would you like to come in?'

Lester entered the narrow hallway without responding. Who did Carl think he was, asking if he wanted to enter the building he owned? It was his house. The scrawny little cunt didn't own any of it.

Carl closed the door as Lester turned left into the living room – and stopped dead in his tracks. Standing in the window bay was a dark-haired girl. She was wearing a tight pair of denim jeans that accentuated her curves and a backpack over her shoulder. She swayed from side to side on the balls of her feet.

'Hello,' Lester said surreptitiously.

The girl spun around. 'Oh, hey.'

'And who are you?' Lester asked, intrigued.

'This is my girlfriend, Jessica,' Carl said.

Lester just about stopped a puff of laughter from sneaking out of his nose. He extended his hand and shook Jessica's. It was soft, warm, moist, perhaps a little sweaty.

'You nervous?' Lester asked.

Jessica's face looked taken aback.

'Don't worry,' Lester continued without realising he'd said it. 'You have no reason to be.'

Carl jumped in, standing between Lester and Jessica like a dog protecting its owner from a nearby threat. In his hand he held a thin folder of documents.

'Everything's in there,' Carl said. 'Final bills. All our previous bills as well. Council letters. And an address if you need to forward anything on.'

'Excellent,' Lester said, taking the folder.

'Is there anything else you need?'

'No.' Lester threw the folder on the nearby sofa. 'I think that covers everything. Do you mind if I just wander around the place... you know, make sure everything's OK? Make sure there's nothing broken. No dead bodies you've got hiding in the cupboard or something.'

Lester chuckled, but his attempt at humour was not well received. Carl and Jessica stared at him blankly.

'Not a fan of dead people jokes, eh?' Lester shrugged. 'Tough crowd.'

'Erm...' Carl said. The excitement in his face had gone. 'I don't have a problem with that. Do you need us here while you do it?'

'Yes,' Lester said abruptly. 'Please. Just in case I need to query anything. Do you mind if I start in here?'

'No, no. Of course not.'

'Great, thanks. You can leave now. I'd prefer if you were in a separate room of the house. You can leave your things here though, just so I can make sure you're not going to go running off!'

Slowly, cautiously, Jessica dropped her bag to the floor and followed Carl out of the living room, holding his hand. As soon as he heard their hushed voices in the kitchen, he set to work. He rushed towards Jessica's bag, reached inside and pulled out one of her debit cards from her purse, sliding it in his pocket before he placed the bag back as perfectly as he'd found it. Then, for the next few minutes he pretended to carry out a sweep of the house, moving from room to room. He didn't care if it was torn to bits or if there were scuff marks on the doors and walls. He had enough money to paint over it, and there would still be people looking to rent it from him regardless of what it looked like. They needed somewhere to live, and he could fulfil that need.

Once Lester was finished, he stopped at the bottom of the stairs and called them back.

'All clear,' he said. 'I couldn't find anything.' He extended his hand. 'You've been a great tenant. I'll be sad to lose the money you've been giving me for the past eighteen months.'

'I'm sure you'll find someone else quickly,' Carl said, forcing himself to smile.

'I'm sure I will.' Lester let go of Carl's hand and moved over to Jessica. He took her hand in his. 'It was a pleasure to meet you.'

'You too.'

'I hope you two live a very long and happy life together.'

'Right,' Carl said, grabbing Jessica's arm. 'We'll get our things and go. We've got somewhere to be.'

'Where you going?' Lester asked as he followed behind them.

'We're going travelling for a while. South America. Then Asia. Might do some work out there while we're gone. The address we gave you was my mum's. She'll be able to take care of anything if you have any issues.'

'Sounds fantastic,' Lester said, feigning a smile. 'I hope you have a wonderful time. Now, don't let me stop you. Go on – get out of here!'

Carl and Jessica disappeared into the living room, returning moments later with a backpack and a suitcase each. They hurried out of the door and over to Carl's Mini before throwing their baggage in the back seat and speeding off.

Lester estimated it had taken them thirty seconds to get out of there. Maybe forty. It was as if they were part of the pit-stop crew for a Formula One team. They'd made it apparent to him that they were in a hurry and that they wanted to get out of there as soon as possible. Which was fine for him, because now he had a reason to call them back. He glanced down at his watch. How long should he give them? Ten? Fifteen? No. Those numbers were too high. He needed to shorten it down to a few minutes. Make it seem like he had only just found it. But he needed to prepare. He needed to ready the utensils for the bloodbath that was about to unfold.

CHAPTER 46

SPECIAL LITTLE PLAN

Elliot didn't know the name of the individual holding the gun at him, but he was fairly sure it wasn't someone he wanted to spend a lot of time with. His instructions had been simple: call Jake and explain everything. But right now, as he held the phone to his ear and stared into the barrel of the Glock 17, he panicked, his mouth frozen open.

'What are you doing, Bridger?' Jake said, slowly bringing him around. 'Where are you? I thought you were supposed to be out of the country?'

'I... I... er...' He held the script he'd been given in his hands. 'I've changed my mind. If I leave, then they'll know something's wrong. It's safer for me here.'

'What's wrong? What's going on?'

'I just need to know you haven't done anything stupid.'

'Stupid. Like what?'

'You haven't mentioned anything about what I told you, have you?'

'No. Of course I haven't.'

'Good,' Bridger replied. He glanced at the gun and then the owner. 'You need to keep it that way, Jake. For your own safety. And your family's. It's too late. The wheels are already in motion. By Friday, Danny and Michael will be in the witness protection scheme.'

'Why are you telling me all this, Elliot? You told me this yesterday.'

'I just need to make sure you understand. These people are dangerous.'

'I understand, but I can help you.'

'You can't help everyone, kid.'

'Not unless you let me try.'

Bridger sighed. The fucking idiot didn't understand what was going on. He didn't understand that he was trying to protect him.

'Promise me, Jake,' Bridger began. 'Promise me you won't say anything to anyone. It's not safe. You've got a family to provide for.'

Jake swore under his breath. The sounds of heavy footsteps echoed through the speakerphone.

'Fine. All right. Fine. I promise. I promise I won't say anything. But it was a shitty thing, playing me like that. Why did you trust me with your life?'

A smirk grew on Bridger's face. 'Because you're a good guy, and I knew you wouldn't do anything with it. But now I just need to make absolutely certain. Because they will find you if you do. It won't be hard.'

'Tell me who they are, Elliot. Give me some names.'

'When one name disappears, another appears in its place. They're everywhere, Jake. Everywhere.'

Bridger rung off and threw the phone into the footwell. The device bounced on the floor and came to rest against his foot. He slammed the steering wheel repeatedly with his palm and groaned.

'Very good,' the man holding the gun said. 'Very convincing. Did he believe you?'

'Yes,' Bridger replied, avoiding the man's gaze.

'Don't worry. This will all be over as soon as the brothers are out.'

'What happens then?'

'You'll get your share. As promised.'

'That's not what I meant.'

'Don't worry,' the man said. 'You're safe for now. If we need you for other jobs, we'll be in touch. But if we find out you've been spilling your little secrets, we'll make sure there's a bullet in this chamber reserved for you. As for the brothers... The Cabal has people who can take care of them. It might not be now. It might be in a few weeks, months, years. All depends on how they fare and what sort of things they get up to. My advice would be to stay away from them.'

'What about Jake?' Bridger asked, slowly turning towards the man. He had thick, blonde hair, a broken nose and an unkempt blonde beard. 'What will happen to him?'

'Tanner's his own man. He can look out for himself. But you don't need to concern yourself with him. The Cabal's got a special little plan for Jake Tanner. We all have.'

CHAPTER 47

BLOODBATH

Fifteen minutes later, there was still no sign of them. After he'd called Jessica, notifying her that she'd left her debit card behind, Lester had used the time expertly. He had ventured into the kitchen, pulled apart the cutlery drawer and laid out six meat knives in a row across the countertop beside the sink. Afterwards, he wandered to the end of the garden and found the gardening tools that had come included with the tenancy. He picked out a pair of secateurs, a hammer, a handful of five-inch nails and a handsaw.

As he carried them to the house, his body tingled again. The Nasties were on their way, waiting to be released as soon as he laid eyes on both Carl and Jessica. It was going to be euphoria. His own home. All the time in the world. His own tools. He kicked himself for not doing it like this before.

And then he remembered. There was soon to be another obstacle he'd need to overcome: the mess that would need cleaning afterwards. Not a problem though. He'd spent enough time on the Dark Web to know that he could ship their bodies off to a pig farm, or maybe he could incinerate their remains in a fire, or perhaps he could chop them up and dissolve their existence in a bathtub full of chemicals. Out of the three, the third seemed the most enjoyable: watching their slow, gradual decay into nothingness.

A car pulled up outside the property, distracting him.

He froze. Held his breath. Touched his penis and rubbed his testicles.

Seconds later, the doorbell rang.

Lester clapped his hands and rubbed them together. He left the debit card in the kitchen and placed the smallest, most inconspicuous blade in his pocket, then rushed to the door.

It was Carl.

'Thanks for coming back so quickly,' Lester said, a smile beaming on his face. 'I hope you weren't too far away?'

'No, it's fine. Where's the card?'

'It's this way,' Lester said, stepping into the house. Carl stayed where he was. 'You can come in, you know.'

Reluctantly, Carl followed Lester inside. He took the young man into the kitchen and paused. Carl's eyes widened as they fell on the apparatus on the surface.

As the realisation that he was in serious trouble dawned on him, Carl tried to make a run for it. But it was too late. There was no time to save himself. Lester removed the blade from his pocket, grabbed Carl's head from behind and held him back. Lester outmuscled and outweighed him considerably. It was almost like wrestling with a child. There was nothing the younger man could do.

Lester plunged the blade into the man's neck and dragged downwards until he reached his Carl's collar bone. A fountain of blood splurged from the man's throat and exploded all over the walls and floor. Lester then let Carl's body flop to the wooden flooring and watched him drown in his own blood.

He licked what he could of Carl's blood from his hands, until they were almost clean, then put them in his pocket as he raced out of the house. It was only a temporary precaution though; as soon as Jessica was in the house with him, he would smother himself in their blood. In the past few days he'd developed a fondness for the taste of it. The metallic tanginess. The thick texture. The sweet aroma.

He skipped to the end of the patio, turned left behind a set of bushes, and slowed as he saw Carl's Mini. The vehicle was facing in the opposite direction, which meant Lester had the advantage of surprise.

He staggered over to the car, feigning injury, and slammed his fist on the passenger-side window. Jessica jolted, her hand flying to her chest in shock. Lester yanked the car door open.

'Jessica, quickly! You have to come quickly. Something's happened to Carl. He's collapsed! He's hit his head! He's bleeding!'

Jessica's face whitened with fear. She unclamped her seat belt, jumped out of the car and followed Lester back into the house blindly. *Ah*, he thought. *The things we do for love.*

Lester made sure she was the first one in. She gasped at the sight of Carl's body lying there, soaked in his own blood. She attempted to scream, but nobody could hear her. Lester shut the door behind him and wrapped his hand around her mouth, stifling her.

As he tried to lift her off her feet, Jessica squirmed under his grip and clamped down on his hand with her teeth, biting into his flesh and bone. Groaning, Lester was forced to release her.

She darted towards the door. But she only made it halfway down the corridor before Lester grabbed her trailing hand and pulled her back. He punched her around the side of the face, felling her. Then, using the knife he'd used on Carl, he tore her shirt open and stuffed the excess fabric in her mouth, silencing her. She gagged and struggled, and Lester gave her another punch, grinning as her eyes rolled in the back of her head.

He estimated he didn't have long until she came to again, so he sprinted to the kitchen, grabbed the knives and the hammer and nails, and returned while Jessica's eyes were still moon white.

She mumbled incomprehensibly behind the rag in her mouth. Lester spilt the nails onto the floor, scattering them across the wood, then grabbed one of her hands and pinned it to the ground, stabbing it with the nine-inch kitchen knife he'd just retrieved. The blade tore through her skin and buried itself in the wooden floorboard.

Jessica screamed, spitting the cloth from her mouth. She danced in and out of consciousness, and Lester wasted no time in pinning her other hand to the ground.

Once the knives were in, he cemented her position using the hammer and nails. In her clothes, in her ankles, in her shoulders, in her thick strands of chestnut-brown hair. Each time the hammer slammed on the nail's head and the metallic sound perforated his eardrums, he groaned. He could feel himself getting excited. Droplets of his phlegm dripped onto her mouth, caressing her, dousing her in his fluids. *It won't be the only fluid*, he thought.

After he'd successfully pinned her body to the floor, he slapped her across the face. He wanted her to be awake for this. He wanted her to witness everything he was going to do to her. With the others it had been over too quickly. He'd been afraid of losing them, of them escaping – and that had been an almost too close reality for him last night. But now was different. This was his own home, his own turf. He could do what he wanted. And nobody would know a thing.

CHAPTER 48

STRATEGY

Lester Bain. Lester Bain. Lester Bain. Jake repeated the name in his head. Their meeting with Sampson Decker had been a success. They finally had a name, a suspect, someone they could begin to investigate with vigour. And it hadn't taken long for them to find something either. After a quick check on the electoral register, and a brief search online, Jake had managed to put together a suspectology report for Drew and Garrison.

'He's a successful property tycoon,' Jake began, reading from a *Stratford News* article dated ten years ago. 'A narcissistic one too, judging by the comments he gave in this piece. He inherited his parents' business after their sudden death when he was twelve. They both perished in a car accident. I looked into and, at first, it didn't seem like there was anything wrong about it. But after I did some digging, it turns out my suspicions were correct. The report says that neither of his parents were wearing seat belts at the time of the accident which, according to witness statements from family and friends, was extremely uncharacteristic of them.'

'So little Lester unplugged them and watched them rocket through the windscreen?'

'Potentially,' Jake said. 'But nothing was ever taken further with it. After their death, Lester went into foster care, where he dealt a lot with social services. They gave him some counselling and, when he was sixteen, one of his therapists made some disturbing reports. He tried to molest her, but in the end, nothing came of it. It was her word against his. But – and this is the interesting bit – Lester recounted several experiences where, as a child, his mum would abuse him – both physically and sexually – and his parents would take him to a caravan site in the middle of nowhere, just so they could do things to him.'

'Now we know where he gets it from,' Garrison added, hovering a biscuit above his lips.

'What about his address?' Drew asked, dismissing Garrison's remark. 'What about his properties? Have we got anything on those yet?'

Jake nodded. 'He's the registered landlord for eight properties. All are currently being let under his management.'

'And his own address?'

Jake held a sheet of paper in the air triumphantly. 'Right here.'

Drew clapped his hands together and leapt out of his seat. 'Beautiful. Get a warrant together, get it approved by the magistrate and get some uniform with you.'

Jake beamed, filled with hubris. 'Already done,' he said. 'Warrant's drafted. I just need to get down to the courts.'

Drew moved to the centre of the Incident Room and scribbled the information on the whiteboard underneath Lester's name at the top. A few seconds later, he turned back to Jake and Garrison.

'I think we need to check out the other properties as well. Just in case,' he said to Garrison.

'I'm on it,' the man said, rising out of his chair.

'And what about you?' Jake asked Drew as he hovered in the door frame.

'I'm going to speak with Liam quickly. It's all part of the strategy, boys.'

CHAPTER 49

CONTINGENCY PLANNING

No names. That was the mantra. No names, under any circumstances. None.

And, for Liam, he'd kept it that way. Elliot Bridger was none the wiser about any of his credentials. He prided himself on being able to keep a secret from those closest to him, and he was even prouder that he'd managed to work his way up through the ranks of The Cabal's criminal underworld. The Cabal was a modern-day enigma, a new version of Voldemort – whose name must never be spoken aloud, especially in public. Partly because very few knew the name – not even those in the higher echelons who Liam had tried to cosy up with – and partly because anyone who did speak it usually found themselves six feet under shortly thereafter.

Liam was seated in the car park of Farnham Golf Club, following his meeting with Bridger. On the phone, in his ear, was that same enigma.

'How did it go?' The Cabal asked.

'It's done.'

'Bridger's aware of what he needs to do?'

'Yes,' Liam replied.

'And Jake?'

'Even more so.'

'Is he a threat to our operations?'

Liam shuffled himself in his leather seat and turned the radio down until it was almost silent.

'Jake Tanner's no threat,' he said. 'He's harmless. He's just happy to be one of the team. He's fresh, beady eyed and still thinks the service is the best in the world. But once he realises that it isn't all it's cracked up to be, he'll come round.'

'And if you're wrong?'

'Then hit him where it hurts.'

'And you know where that is?'

Liam suppressed a smile, even though there was no one in the vicinity to see it. 'I wouldn't be doing my job if I didn't.' He paused. 'Financials. He's always struggled with it. His background in that respect makes for interesting reading.'

Of course there was Tanner's family too – and his kids – but that was a step too far for Liam.

'Don't get attached, Liam,' The Cabal said. 'You remember what happened last time.'

'I'm not. I won't.' Liam reached for the reusable plastic cup in the holder by his side. He took a sip and relished the sickly taste of the whiskey as it rushed down his throat. 'It's going to sound odd, but Jake Tanner has the power to make everything great. He has a lot of potential.'

'Don't romanticise him either,' The Cabal said.

'I'm not. And I'm not the only one who's said it either. Bridger agrees. He thinks Jake has potential to go far.'

The Cabal paused. They were the kind of person who paused just to make the other person on the line nervous about what was to come next. And Liam hated every second of it.

'How are we coming along with everything else?' The Cabal continued.

'Good.' Liam nodded. 'Shipments are coming in fine without delays. The runners are getting the stuff on the streets. And the boys at Flying Squad and Drugs Squad have been keeping me up to date with everything on their side.'

'And what about Henry?'

'Nothing I can't handle,' Liam said.

'We'll see.' There was another pause. It was shorter than the first. 'When can I expect The Crimsons to be operational?'

'Friday,' Liam responded. 'They're due out on Friday. Witness protection. Isaac's in charge of it all. At best, we're looking at a couple of months – wait for everything to blow over first. It's too hot on them for now.'

'And worst case?'

'They open their mouths.'

'Contingencies?'

'Plenty. I know some people. I know some people who know some people. And they know even more people.'

'Good. The last thing I want is Danny and Michael Cipriano – our biggest assets – getting their head filled with more air than it already is.'

'I'll see to it that doesn't happen,' Liam replied and rang off.

CHAPTER 50

EXCEPTION TO THE RULE

Opposite Jake was Lester Bain's house. It was a small, semi-detached property on the corner of Widdin Street. It blended in well with the rest of the houses on the road, and to the untrained eye, looked normal. But there was nothing normal about it. That it housed one of the city's most gruesome and notorious serial killers frightened Jake. How was it possible for Lester to blend in with society so easily? That he could just leave the house, slaughter a handful of unsuspecting individuals and then slip back into normality as though it was nothing? The thought concerned him, and as he sat there waiting for the rest of the uniformed officers he'd requested to accompany him on the search and arrest to arrive, he tried to turn his thoughts into something else.

Excitement.

Anticipation.

Lester Bain was less than twenty metres away. He was within arm's reach. Jake was just a few minutes away from arresting the bastard and adding some credibility and notoriety to his career. But he had to be careful in this situation. He couldn't accept all the praise and recognition. It had been a team effort, and he hoped the rest of the team would realise that. With any luck, Liam might rescind the performance regulation notice.

Jake hoped.

Behind him, a police car pulled over. It was showtime.

Jake climbed out of the car, nodded at the uniformed officers, explained to them what was happening and then, like a small army, they hurried over to Lester's house. There were ten of them in total, and at the back of the convoy, two officers carried a tool known as the Enforcer – a battering ram which was capable of hitting a door with more than three tonnes of pressure.

The search team filtered either side of the front door, giving the Enforcer a clean avenue. Two officers swung the ram in the air and smashed it into the door. It buckled after one swing. Jake and the rest of the officers filtered into the property, immediately spreading out. They were all under strict instructions to search for Lester Bain and any evidence they would be able to seize later on. But for now, Lester was the priority.

Jake waited in the middle of the hallway while he allowed the officers to conduct a full sweep of the house. Less than thirty seconds later, it was over.

'No sign of him,' one officer said.

'He's not upstairs,' another added.

'Nor down here, mate,' a final one added. 'We're checking out the back now but it's not looking likely.'

Jake sighed, dejected. Their one chance of finding him, their one chance of catching him unawares had been squandered.

Just as Jake was about to open his mouth, another officer appeared at the top of the stairs, interrupting him.

'Jake, I think you're going to want to see this. Are forensics coming down?'

'No...'

'They should be.'

Jake ordered someone in the vicinity to make the call and then politely forged his way through the officers in front of him. At the top of the landing, he followed the officer into a bedroom. At first he was hit with the smell of camomile wafting up his nose. And then he saw it.

The table dresser.

The jars.

The tongues.

The fingers.

'Jesus fucking Christ,' Jake said under his breath. He'd been right. Lester had kept mementos. He'd kept their body parts as symbols of his murders.

The sight of them formed a knot in Jake's stomach and made him feel queasy. He turned his attention away from the dresser and focused on the rest of the room. At the tidiness of it all. The banality. The cleanliness.

Lester's bed had been made perfectly, almost military-style. On the bedside table was a small lamp and a flower. On the floor was a pair of slippers with a sock resting in each of them. The walls were bare, painted in a dull cream colour, the windowsill was empty and the washing basket by the door was devoid of any contents. It was almost as if Lester hadn't lived there for weeks. It stood out in stark contrast to Lester's modus operandi, the messiness of his killings, the depravity of his soul. During university, Jake had learnt that a person's bedroom was like looking through a window into their soul, but when it came to Lester Bain, that couldn't have been further from the truth. In this particular instance, Lester was an exception to the rule.

And for some reason that scared Jake most of all.

CHAPTER 51

LISTENING IN

Jake, Drew and Garrison were huddled around Drew's desk, hunched over a tiny laptop screen. In the intervening hours, Jake and the rest of the search team, along with help from the forensics squad, had conducted a detailed search of Lester Bain's property, seizing the most valuable items pertinent to the outcome of the case – including the trophies on top of his dresser. While the forensics squad were conducting the rest of the search on the property, the items they'd already seized had been sent away for analysis, but it would be some time before they received the results.

Next on the agenda, though, was to find Lester Bain. Again. If he wasn't at his house, then it sparked the question as to why. Had Sampson tipped him off? Had he seen the police cars outside his house and bolted? Jake didn't know. None of them did. But fortunately for him, Drew had had an idea.

The three of them were listening to the live audio recordings from inside Sampson Decker's flat in the specialist operations room on the second floor of the building.

'Are you sure we should be doing this without...' Jake began, remembering his discussion with Drew early. The thought that they'd illegally bugged Sampson Decker's flat without the necessary warrants had been playing on his mind.

Without responding, Drew reached into his side drawer and

handed Jake three pieces of paper stapled together.

'There's your warrant,' Drew said. 'Before you start to complain.'

Jake gasped slightly. He was offended by the insinuation. 'Who said I was going to complain?'

'That voice in your head. Now shut up and listen.'

Jake's eyes skimmed over the top half of the intrusive surveillance warrant, noticed that it had been signed and dated correctly by Assistant Commissioner Richard Candy, and then returned his attention to the laptop.

Sound frequencies were displayed on the monitor, and every time Sampson coughed, the frequencies fluctuated and spiked.

'What are we listening for?' Jake asked.

'Anything. Anything he might say to incriminate himself further. He might call Lester, or Lester might call him. And when that happens, we'll be listening and recording every word they—' Drew was instantly cut off by the sound of ringing coming from the computer.

'Someone's calling him,' Jake said, feeling himself get caught up in the excitement of the situation.

The three of them waited in high anticipation for Sampson to answer the phone. Eventually he did. The sound was grainy and full of static but still audible. Drew scrambled across the desk for the mouse and pressed the record button.

'You've done it again?' Sampson asked, his voice quiet, almost like a whisper.

'It was glorious,' a voice said. This one was deep and gruff, heavy and exasperated – full of excitement and happiness. The complete opposite of Sampson's.

'How many?'

'Two. A couple. Her name was Jessica. I couldn't help myself. I hammered nails into her hands and fucked her while she was alive and bleeding. He was already dead by the time anything happened to her. It was her I wanted. I had to get the boyfriend out of the way first. But I did stuff with both of them, don't worry.'

'What did you do to him?' Sampson asked. Jake wasn't sure, but he thought there was a hint of genuine curiosity in his voice, as if Sampson was going to get off on what he heard.

'Everything. His fingers were delightful. And the rest of him tasted delicious.'

There was a light groan coming from Sampson. Then it was a while before he responded.

'Do you have the evidence?'

'Of course.'

'Send it to me.'

'No. I want to negotiate first. How many points will you give me? Second place is only a few hundred behind me. This is unacceptable. I need double what I've had beforehand.'

'Lester…'

'Give me more points!' Lester screamed.

'A thousand,' Sampson said. His breathing was becoming heavy, and with each breath it sounded wheezier and wheezier.

'Two.'

'I'll give you none if you carry on.'

'You do that and perhaps I might have to come for your body. You're lacking a few teeth, aren't you?'

The knot formed in Jake's stomach again, except this time it threw a little bile up his throat. He was experiencing the harsh brutality of the opposite end of the spectrum of human emotion and psyche for the first time, and he didn't like it. He'd studied cases about people like Lester in university, but he felt safer reading about them in textbooks or watching documentaries. This was different. Jake was living it. Jake was experiencing it.

'Fuck… you…' Sampson worked himself into a cough. It was soft and weak.

'Give me my two thousand points!'

'Only if you promise to stop.'

'Stop? I can't stop now. I've got so much more I want to accomplish. You don't know what it feels like. I won't stop. I *can't* stop.'

'You need to,' Sampson said.

'Why?' Lester asked. 'What's happened?'

'The police. They're after you. They came round… to my place earlier.'

'What? No. What did you tell them?'

'Nothing. I told them I didn't know where you are. But you need to get out of the city. Out of the country. Lay low for a bit. Go off grid.'

'No,' Lester said, 'I'm too far gone.'

The line went dead and the deafening sound of silence rung in Jake's ears. He removed his headset and placed it on the table, then stared at Drew and Garrison. They looked angered. Worse, they wore an emotion he'd never seen on their faces before: fear. They were afraid of what Lester was going to do. They were afraid of how he'd managed to slaughter another two victims as though they were nothing but cattle; of how they were going to catch him before he struck again. Fuck, Jake was too. And he knew the fear wouldn't leave him until Lester was caught.

CHAPTER 52

DISPOSAL

The Dark Web was a wonderful place. It was the source of so much information and knowledge that he'd struggled to absorb it all.

After he'd slaughtered and defiled Carl and Jessica, Lester had realised the need to dispose of them in an efficient and effective manner. For that, he needed access to a computer. But neither Jessica's nor Carl's had worked; both had been locked by their passwords. And his was on the other side of the city.

So, as a last resort, he'd stolen Carl's Mini, raced back home, picked up his laptop and hurried back to the house. He was certain nobody had seen him. He'd been quick, discreet and none of the neighbours paid any attention to him anyway, so why would they notice him arriving in a blue Mini that wasn't his?

They wouldn't.

Since retrieving his laptop, he'd managed to source suppliers for large quantities of the hydrofluoric acid that he would need to dissolve Carl and Jessica's remains – and the plastic containers he'd need to put them in.

But it wasn't over yet.

According to his research, it would take days for the bodies to disintegrate, and, in that time, he would need to make absolutely certain that nobody came knocking for them both. Sure, Carl and Jessica had told him that they were meant to be travelling halfway across the world, but what if they were meant to see a friend beforehand? Or pop round to their parents to say goodbye? He couldn't risk it.

He needed a contingency plan to get his name as far removed from the both of them as possible.

Fortunately, he knew just the people.

Lester had managed to stumble upon the Dark Web in an Internet cafe when he was eighteen. It was the first place he'd met S, and it was the first place he'd begun to make some very dear friends. He wasn't very well liked in person, but online, masked by the cloak of anonymity, he was able to become anyone he wanted to be.

And there was one person whom he had bonded with quickly.

Lester knew him only as The Mandate, an alias he'd adopted on the Dark Web. The Mandate was capable of hacking into government websites. He could change names, forge documents, assign new identities, make people disappear – all with the click of a button.

And that was exactly what Lester needed.

As he relaxed on the sofa, staring at the ceiling, he received the message from his companion, confirming everything had been taken care of.

Carl and Jessica had made their flight from Heathrow at 8 p.m. and had already landed in Brazil. Their debit cards were stopped and all history of Carl being a tenant at the property had been rewritten.

It was almost as if neither Jessica nor Carl had ever existed.

And, as Lester eased himself lower into the sofa, he realised that was exactly the same thing he would need to do with S.

| PART 5 |

CHAPTER 53

CHECKMATE

The darkness enveloped him. Stars dotted the sky, flickering like light bulbs on the blink. The air around him was cold, and he felt the hairs on his arms prick up in protest. He wasn't sure if that was because of the chill hugging his body, or the adrenaline that surged through his veins. Sampson Decker – S, his mentor, his good friend – had betrayed him. Sure, Sampson had taught him everything he knew, but there was no doubt in Lester's mind that Sampson had told the police everything: where he was, what he'd done, what he was going to do. To Sampson, Lester was dispensable, another cog in The Community's machine, a means to an end. Lester could be replaced by whoever was in second position, just like that. Nobody would know a thing.

That was unacceptable. Something needed to be done about it.

Lester was standing opposite Sampson's block of flats. The street was poorly lit, and he used the shadows to cloak him. He was beside a bin, just behind a car. In the distance, to the right, was a group of teenagers wearing hoods. Some of them were on bikes, circling one another, pretending they were going to collide and then veering away at the very last moment. Small orange dots glowed against their faces like fireflies, with clouds of smoke lingering in the air above them.

Lester paid them little attention. There were other, more

important things for him to worry about.

He waited there for five minutes, keeping his gaze fixated on Sampson's window. The light was on, and shadows wrapped in a blue glow flashed against the curtain as images played across Sampson's television screen. With every passing second, Lester was aware he was giving himself a bigger obstacle to overcome. He didn't know whether the police were nearby, on their way, or whether they had deserted Sampson entirely. He tried to think about it logically. But there was no rush of logic flooding his brain. There was no hint of calm or precision in his thinking. Instead, it was filled with rage and the desire to maim and dismember. Maybe he would treat Sampson like Jessica Number 5.

Lester crossed the road and dived into the block of flats. He climbed the building's steps and slowed as he reached the sixth floor. The wind picked up and whistled quietly as it whipped around the avenues and stairwells. The cold worsened his goosebumps.

Lester paused at the top of the flight of stairs and waited. Listened.

There was silence.

He rounded the corner and wandered along the outside of the building. A concrete wall came up to his hips on his left. London's lights sparkled in the distance, and from up here he was able to see any cars passing by. For now, there were none. But he made a mental note of the cars and motorbikes that were visible: three of the former, one of the latter.

His breathing was steady, and as he came to Sampson's flat at number forty-two, he held his breath and knocked on the door. The noise of his knuckles on wood echoed around the estate, amplifying exponentially as they reverberated on the different buildings and walls. He stopped again and listened for any unwanted and undue attention he may have just caused. He was going to have to be silent if he wanted to remain unnoticed.

The door opened.

'Lester?' Sampson said, rubbing his eyes. 'What are you—? It's nearly midnight.'

Lester barged in, ignoring the man standing in his way, and rushed to the living room.

'Lester!' Sampson cried as he slammed the front door shut. He hobbled into the living room after him, stopping in the door frame. 'What are you doing here?'

'I've come here to talk,' Lester said, his voice calm. 'I just want to know what you told the police. That's all.'

'Nothing,' Sampson said, shaking his head. The tubes that hung from his nose swung from side to side.

'You're lying.'

'I'm not. I promise. Lester, come on. Why would I tell them anything?'

'Then what did you say? You didn't just sit there in silence.'

Sampson's breathing was almost non-existent as he gasped for breath every second. 'I told them nothing of what they wanted to hear. I told them about The Community. What it was. How it came about. How good you are. How they'll never find you.'

'And it'll stay that way, won't it, Sampson? You'll make sure of that, won't you?' Lester took a step closer to Sampson and moved his hand behind his back. 'You'll make sure they don't know where I'm going and what I'm doing next.'

'What will you do next?' Sampson asked, pleading for information. There was still a note of fear in his voice.

'Wouldn't you like to know.'

Sampson shook his head again. This time he moved the oxygen tank from one arm to the other. 'Don't do anything stupid. You need to get away. They're close, Lester.'

'How can they be? I thought you didn't tell them anything.' Lester waited for a response, but when one didn't come, he continued. 'What did they say about me? Did you ask? Did you ask them how much they knew?'

Sampson shrugged. 'They came here asking that very thing. They don't know where you live. They don't know who you are in the leader board. They don't even know your name. But you need to lay low for a while. Especially on The Community. They'll have access to it no doubt.'

Lester smirked. 'I'm branching out of The Community now. Bigger. Better.'

'Where? What are you going to do?'

Lester opened his mouth but hesitated. His suspicions were rising. Sampson was asking too many questions. He took another step closer towards S. As he approached, his mentor coughed and wiped away the mucus and saliva from his face. It was laced with a darker, crimson colour.

'Why the sudden interest?' Lester asked. 'Why do you want to know?'

'You're being paranoid.'

'Did they put you up to this? Are you wearing a wire?'

'You need to lay low, Lester.'

'Don't say my fucking name.'

'I'm not... I didn't mean to... I...'

Lester took another step closer. They were separated by a few feet. Sampson's sweat and bad breath assaulted his senses, then a smile grew on Lester's face. At first he chuckled, and then it developed into a sinister laugh. He could see the fear in his mentor's eyes. But it wasn't enough to make him sympathetic. Nothing was.

'Why would I betray you like that?' Sampson begged, spluttering more phlegm and blood onto his hands. 'I've made those mistakes before, and I suffered as a result. I'm not about to make them again.'

Lester looked down at the floor and shook his head in disgust.

'You're a good liar,' he said, 'but I've had enough of your bullshit. I can't believe a word you say. You've betrayed me. I know you have.'

Here they came. The Nasties. In full swing. Lester removed the blade he'd used on Carl from his pocket and screamed in anger and frustration. His body was layered with sweat.

'I can't listen to your shit anymore. You've ruined' – his heart pounded, and his chest heaved – 'you've ruined everything!'

At the sight of the weapon, Sampson began to clutch his chest. His breathing switched to short, shallow breaths and the colour left his cheeks. Then his legs buckled and he collapsed to the ground, still holding on to his chest. Sampson opened his mouth to speak but nothing came out.

Lester approached slowly, carefully. He didn't want to disturb the beauty and serenity of what was happening right in front of him. He wanted to savour the moment. It was precious. He'd always thought of Sampson as a father figure. Sampson had guided him from the beginning of his time with The Community to where he was now, and the man had done a good job. But there was always something lacking, always something that felt not quite right. Perhaps it was the fact that Lester felt like he was a pawn in Sampson's own game of sexual conquest across the city.

And now Lester had made his final move. He stroked Sampson's face and stared into his eyes as he left the man to die on the floor in the chill; it was a longer, more prolonged suffering for him that way. The Nasties could wait.

Check... mate.

CHAPTER 54

HABITS

Jake yawned as he entered the office. In his hand he held a cup of coffee. It was already his second of the day and it wasn't even 8 a.m.

Jake sat at his desk and waved good morning to Lindsay. She was already typing away on her computer and paid him little attention. Last night had been another late one. They'd stayed in the office till 11 p.m., listening to Sampson move about the flat and watch reruns of *Only Fools and Horses* on the TV Channel 'Gold'. Between the three of them, they'd decided – after a game of rock, paper, scissors – to leave Drew in charge of monitoring the recordings while Jake and Garrison went home for the evening.

There was no sign of either of them.

The double doors to the office opened and Jake's eyes flickered to the person who had just entered. As soon as he realised who it was, he leapt out of his seat.

'Guv!' Jake asked, rushing towards Liam's office, trying to get there before Liam did. 'Can I speak to you?'

'Not right now, Tanner. I've got things to do,' Liam said as he shouldered past Jake. He threw his keys into the office door, unlocked it and entered.

As he closed the door, Jake placed his foot and hand in the way.

'Please, guv. It's important.'

'If it's about your performance review, you know I can't discuss it with you. You'll have to wait until our meeting.'

'I just want to know why now? After it feels like you've finally let me into the team, you go and throw this at me. I feel like I'm pulling my weight. I'm doing my job. Yeah, I've made a few mistakes, but who hasn't in their time? I'm still learning, and I'm still absorbing everything I can from you guys. You're all excellent and I envy how close you are. I envy how successful you all are too.'

Liam said nothing. He set his plastic coffee cup on the table and approached the door. He pulled it open slightly, away from Jake's foot, and leant against it.

'Do you want to know what I think, Jake?' Liam asked, his voice stern.

For a split second, Jake contemplated saying no. There was an inflection in Liam's voice that forced Jake to second-guess whether he wanted to hear it or not.

'I don't think you're right for the team,' Liam continued. 'I mean, it seems to be all about you, doesn't it? Jake, Jake, Jake, Jake, Jake. I assume Drew told you where I was yesterday? He has a habit of sharing things that aren't his or anyone else's business. Did he tell you?'

'He kept the details to a minimum, but I guessed the rest.'

'Yeah, well. And what's the first thing you say to me after I get back? You want to talk about *your* issues, something that affects *you*. Nothing about me. Not even a "morning, boss, how are you feeling today?"' Liam hesitated. His chest rose and fell heavily. 'Nothing. You only seem to care about yourself, mate. And I don't think you'd be a good part of the team. This performance review is completely separate, but they both work in tandem with one another.'

Jake stood there for a while, silent. Words escaped him.

'How are you feeling?' Jake asked hesitantly. His mind took over and ran on autopilot.

Liam scoffed. 'Few minutes too late for that, don't you think? Get yourself in the debrief room in a couple of minutes. Everyone else will be here soon. You might be able to redeem yourself in there.'

Liam shut the door on Jake's face.

At that moment, Garrison arrived. He passed Jake and slammed his bag on his desk, crushing a half-opened packet of biscuits. Then he moved into the debrief room.

Jake followed.

CHAPTER 55

MISTAKE

'Right then,' Liam said, closing the door behind him. He moved across the room and stood beside the whiteboard. 'Where's Drew?'

Before either Jake or Garrison were able to respond, the door was flung open and Drew stumbled in with a beaming smile on his face – as though he'd just returned triumphantly from losing his virginity. 'Sorry I'm late, guv. Been sleeping in the Incident Room all night.'

'You fell asleep?' Jake asked, sitting upright in his chair.

Drew shrugged. 'I can't help being tired, mate.'

'We're gonna have to assume your middle name is Incompetent from now on,' Garrison retorted.

'Enough!' Liam held a hand in the air, placating both men. 'I can't be arsed with listening to any of your shit today. There's still so much we have to do, and I don't want to have to put up with your bollocks.'

Shuffling in his seat, Drew cleared his throat. He asked, 'How you feeling, guv? Treatment go OK?'

'Yeah it was all right, thanks. Doctor's said I've started responding well to it. Cheers for asking.'

Liam shot Jake a sideways glance and then moved to the nearest desk. He perched himself on the end of it and wrapped his arms across his chest. 'What's been going on then?'

'Lots, guv,' Drew said, resting one leg atop his other knee. 'The man we're looking for is a Lester Bain. Property owner. Some call him a tycoon. I call him a ty*cunt*. We've searched all the houses that he's the registered landlord for, and nothing. Nobody knows where he is. Not even his tenants – they all say they haven't seen him in a while either. Apparently that sits all right with them – the last thing they need is a pissy little landlord breathing down their neck every two seconds.' Drew paused. 'Jake and a group of uniform raided his house but there was nothing there. Except for his trophies... tongues... fingers.'

'What about Lester? Was he there?' Liam asked.

'No, sir,' Jake responded.

'What are uniform doing now? They need to be outside those properties waiting for him.'

'Already done, guv.'

'Good. Why do I get the feeling there's something else I need to know?

'Another two dead,' Drew said, taking it upon himself to be the suck-up with all the information. 'We don't know who and we don't where, nor do we know when. But we do know how. This time it was another couple.'

'Steven and Jessica Arnholt volume two?

'We—' Drew began.

'No,' Jake interrupted. Now was a chance to redeem himself and he wasn't going to let it slip. 'I've been doing some thinking. The girl was called Jessica, but from the sounds of it, the boyfriend had nothing to do with any of it – he was just in the way. Regardless, he's still trying to satisfy his obsession with women named Jessica. But I feel like this one was random. There was nothing pre-emptive about it. On the phone to Sampson Decker he sounded almost surprised that he'd managed to do it. But I don't think it was random insofar as he stumbled upon them on the street. Rather, these were people he might have known, or people that he'd met in the past.'

'How so?'

Jake shrugged. 'It's entirely possible he's got a list of properties that we don't know about. Either not under his name or registered in an offshore account somewhere. Maybe they were tenants.'

Liam nodded as Jake spoke, inspiring him to continue.

'It would follow the pattern of his last kill with Jessica-Anne: moving away from The Community. So long as they look like Jessica and have the same name as her, he's coming for them.'

Liam nodded in approval then turned and scribbled a few notes on the whiteboard behind. Returning his attention back to the team, he said, 'Good work. I'm impressed. It would appear you lot *can* pull your fingers out your arses when you're not in the middle of taking the piss out of each other. The only question now is: we know who Lester is, we know what he likes and what he's looking for, but how the fuck do we find him?'

A moment of silence fell on the room as they contemplated. It was the question that had been at the forefront of Jake's mind ever since he'd stormed Lester's uninhabited home. And he had just the answer.

'Lester knows we're after him, right?' Jake said rhetorically. 'Sampson told him to lay low for a while. So that's what he's going to do. He's going to stay indoors. He's not going to venture out very far, not if he knows we're after him. So his only two options to find his next kills are either returning to The Community and finding someone there that he can Commune with, *or* getting another prostitute. If he goes with the latter, it'll be difficult for us to manage and find him. But we need to...' He paused for effect. 'We need to bring him back to The Community somehow.'

'How would we communicate with him? We can't use Steven and Jessica's account. He knows they're dead,' Liam said.

'And,' Garrison added, swinging a pen in one hand and half a hobnob in the other, 'after reading through Lester's messages with the Arnholts, he likes to take things offline. He did the same with Jessica Mann. He's never given a single piece of information about himself away. He always asks for their mobile number first and then contacts them that way. More than likely he's been using a pay-as-you-go-phone as well, same as Sampson. Unregistered. And a bitch to trace. I don't even want to begin to think what would be on there. There was enough filth on his chat with Steven and Jessica.'

Garrison took a final bite of the biscuit as he finished speaking.

Liam turned his back on them, scribbled a word on the board and underlined it several times.

MISTAKE.

'Just because he hasn't given his address out to anyone yet doesn't mean he won't,' Liam said, slapping the lid on the end of the pen loudly. He began to pace from side to side.

Slowly, Jake raised his hand as though he were in a classroom.

Liam stopped pacing. 'You don't have to do that here, Jake.'

Jake lowered his hand awkwardly. 'I have an idea, guv. I thought ideas always warranted a little bit of hand raising.'

The sides of Liam's mouth flickered. 'Let's hear it then.'

Jake cleared his throat before beginning. 'Maybe we can tell him where to go.'

'What do you mean?'

Drew and Garrison turned round in their seats to face him. He felt like he was being summoned to read to the rest of the class.

'I suggest we make an online profile on The Community. Call ourselves Jessica. Set up our location to the local area – in the epicentre of where the other girls have died – and then message him. Ask him to meet. There's no guarantee he'll even see it or read it, but we can try. This is probably the best opportunity we have of finding him right now. Lure him into a trap he can't resist.'

'Jake...' Liam began as Jake prepared himself to be chided. 'Brilliant idea. Let's get to it.'

CHAPTER 56

ONLINE PROFILES

The four of them were hovering around the laptop in the debriefing room. Jake was in charge of the mouse and keyboard, while the rest of them watched. In front of them, on the left-hand whiteboard, was a map of Stratford. Pins were placed in each of the locations where Lester's victims had fallen, with two extra pins placed to the side for last night's unidentified victims, and in the centre of the map was the location in which they would set up the trap: Maryland. It wasn't definitive, but it was the best educated guess they could take.

On the right-hand whiteboard were the profiles of Lester's victims, headed by mugshots taken from driving licences or their social-media accounts. A lot of work had gone on in the background to profile and learn as much information as possible about them all, not just by Jake but the rest of the team too – and now he was pleased to see it being put to good use.

Jake opened TorBrowser and waited for the status bar to move all the way across the screen. Once the network has been securely connected to, Jake loaded The Community's web page in the knowledge that their connection was masked several times over and cloaked in anonymity. Then Jake scrolled to the bottom of the screen and hit the link that led them to create a profile.

'We need a picture,' Jake said. 'Where can we get one from?'

'I have an idea. Give me a minute. Someone owes me a favour,'

Liam said, staring at his phone's screen. He lifted the phone to his ear and stepped out of the room and out of earshot.

'Name...' Jake said aloud. The cursor hovered over the Name field.

'Richmond,' Garrison said. 'Jessica Richmond.'

'Fuck you,' Drew spat, 'that's my sister's name.'

Garrison chuckled. 'How would she like to become Mrs Jessica Garrison?'

'I swear to God,' Drew began, clenching his fist. 'You're old enough to be her grandad.'

'Experience comes with age, son.'

'Shut up, the both of you,' Jake snapped.

Both men fell silent and returned their attention to the laptop. Jake had already entered a surname into the field.

'Tanner. Jessica Tanner?' Drew said. 'You sure you want to do that?'

'Yep. Any issues?'

'Hey, it's your family name.'

Jake ignored the comment and continued filling out her profile.

'Age...'

Drew consulted the board of Lester's previous victims. 'Twenty-four. Twenty-seven. Thirty-one. Twenty-nine. Average age seems to be mid-twenties.'

'Let's go twenty-five,' Jake said, filling out the information as he spoke.

'Anything else?'

'Hobbies and interests.' Jake paused a beat. 'I assume this means sexual hobbies?'

'Leave it blank,' Drew said.

'What about personal info?' Jake hesitated. 'How about: "Live at home with my mum still but she's always out at work. I work as a hairdresser. I have a cat, and my other pussy needs some excitement in its life."'

Jake felt a nudge on the back of his shoulder. It was Garrison. 'Do we need to be worried about you, mate? You sound like you've done this before.'

Jake ignored him. Carrying on, he said, '"I've never been in a committed relationship, but I've had a few flings in the past. My ex got me into this sort of stuff and I've never looked back since. Open to anything."'

Jake finished typing and hit the full-stop key hard. 'That's our alibi. Someone in The Community gave her the details.'

At that point, Liam returned. He pocketed his phone and wore a smile on his face, flashing the left side of his teeth.

'Done. Check your emails.'

Jake did, on his phone, and loaded up a selfie of a young, attractive woman in her mid-twenties. She had brown hair that flowed past her shoulders, her nose was small and her eyebrows were thick. Jake took one glance at Jessica Arnholt on the whiteboard and noted it was an almost perfect fit. It would be too irresistible for Lester to refuse.

'Who is it?' Jake asked, pretending he hadn't already realised it was the BBC News reporter that had launched a scathing attack on him following the press conference the other day.

'That doesn't matter,' Liam responded. 'She's given us permission to use her image. That's all you need to know.'

'Does *she* know what it's for?'

'Yes.' Liam was abrupt and straight to the point. 'I told you, she owes me one. Everything's all above board. Trust me. You've got nothing to worry about.'

'I wonder what she did to make you use this as her favour towards you. It must have been something terrible,' Drew added, rubbing the underside of his nose.

'Nothing that hasn't been done to me before.' Liam lifted the laptop screen so that it was in his eyeline. 'Is everything ready?'

'One last thing,' Jake said. He hit Continue and the screen loaded onto the next step. 'Just the payment. We have to pay the subscription of £2 a month.'

'Is there no fourteen-day trial period? Sleep with as many people as you want in that time and decide if you want to pay for the same privilege in the future?' Drew's face beamed as his class-clown persona came out again. Nobody paid him any attention.

'How are we going to get round this one?' Liam asked as he pointed at the screen.

'We're not,' Jake said. 'Not unless we give Sampson a call and get him to waive the fees.'

'No time,' Liam said. He placed his hand firmly on Jake's back. 'Looks like you're up.'

'What?' Jake swivelled on the chair and craned his neck to look up at Liam.

'We're using your name… we might as well use your card details. You've got to go all-in if you're doing this, Jake.'

Jake opened his mouth, but nothing came out.

'We can't use the Met's card – the name on it is different, and you don't have one of your own. If anyone asks, just pretend you're Jessica's brother or something and she's using your details.' He squeezed Jake's shoulder. 'Don't worry, you'll get the money back.'

'I'm not worried about the money,' Jake replied. 'I'm more worried about putting my details out there on the Dark Web. What if it gets cloned?'

'We'll sort you out. I'm sure Roland can make sure that doesn't happen. As soon as you enter the details and pay for the first month, we'll block the subscription.'

Jake looked down at the table. What was he doing? He'd always been warned about putting his details out there online, and it would be ten times worse on the Dark Web. What if someone hacked into his account? What if someone stole all his money? The risks outweighed the gain. Or did it? Lester Bain was going to kill more and more people if they didn't do anything about it. And if he did this for Liam and the team, did that mean they might accept him a little more?

Before Jake was able to think about it further, Liam spoke. 'This all hinges on you, mate. You want to catch him, right? Then you know what you have to do.'

'Rather you than me, mate,' Drew added.

Jake stared into Liam's eyes for a moment. They were unrelenting, powerful. And he had given Jake the reaction he hoped for: a slight smile. Nothing that gave away too much, but just enough to hint that doing this *was* a step in the right direction towards healing the situation between the two of them.

Jake reached into his pocket, pulled out his wallet and removed a silver Barclays VISA debit card. He entered the relevant information and hit Submit. The web page went blank for a brief moment, and then a swirling circle icon appeared. A few seconds later, they were greeted with a page that confirmed they had completed registration

Liam clapped Jake on the back again. 'Good work, lad. Now find this prick and message him.'

CHAPTER 57

INBOX

Lester was hungry. A different type of hungry. And it was worsened by the regret in his stomach. Not even the emergency camomile he'd bought from the supermarket could soothe him. He should have killed Sampson, slaughtered him, made him suffer a painful and satisfying death – rather than letting his heart give up on him. Lester didn't care whether the man had given him everything, taught him everything – it wasn't enough to surpass the betrayal. And now it would be too dangerous to return to the flat. Sampson's estate would be swarming with police, no doubt. It was too hot.

He needed to shower – while sharing the bathroom with Jessica and Carl's disintegrating remains. He needed to take his mind off everything. He needed to let the sin wash out of him and sink down the drain.

As Lester lifted himself out of his chair, his computer chimed. It had been in sleep mode all of last night and this morning, only disrupted every now and then when he wanted to check his inbox. Even though he knew nobody would be messaging him, it didn't stop him from checking it every ten minutes.

But now somebody *had* messaged him.

Lester unlocked his laptop, clicked on the red notification by his inbox and paused.

'Jessica Tanner,' he said as his eyes fell over the new message. He bypassed the content and clicked on her profile.

Her image intrigued him. She was pretty, young, with brown hair and brown eyes. Smiling. Happy. She looked almost like a perfect embodiment of Jessica Arnholt.

He read her profile.

'Young, dumb and living off mum. Single... and looking for some fun, I hope.' Lester cracked his knuckles. 'Well, Jessica, I'm sure I can teach you a few new things.'

He turned his attention back to his inbox.

Hey, how r u? Nice 2 meet u. This is really awkward cos this is my first time I've ever dun this and I have no idea what I'm doing or if I'm doing it rite, but I saw ur profile and I saw u were @ the top of the leader board, and I wondered if u could show me a few things? I'm very eager 2 learn.

Lester grinned. Usually, he hated all that text speak. He had no idea how anyone understood it all. For a while he'd tried to adopt it, to see whether it was quicker. But it wasn't, so he'd reverted back to the correct way of spelling and communicating. There was no excuse for bad grammar.

He typed his response.

Lovely to meet you, Jessica. You have a lovely name. Of course I can teach you a couple of things. I don't usually allow myself to mingle with newbies – there aren't enough points in it for the both of us. But for you, I can make a special exception. We all have to start off somewhere. Not to mention, you're a very pretty girl, and I wish you'd joined earlier so we could have spent a longer time getting to know one another.

Lester hit send and waited. He didn't know how long he would have to wait for a response. It could be now. Later tonight. Tomorrow. A week. There was no knowing, and he hated the uncertainty of it all. What was he going to do to fill the time now? He couldn't get in the shower; he was too excited. He needed a release.

While he waited, Lester grabbed a toilet roll from the downstairs bathroom and masturbated at the table over Jessica Tanner's profile picture. He envisaged what she looked like naked, and what he would do to her in the bedroom – before he ripped her apart. It titillated him, and a few minutes later, as he cleaned himself up, a message appeared in his inbox.

'Yes!' he whispered, clutching the paper in his hand.

He opened it and read.

Oh gd! I was paranoid I was cummin off as really dumb and stupid! I really am new 2 all of this, so how does it work now?

In the top-right corner of Jessica's page was a small green dot, indicating that she was online. If he messaged her immediately, he might be able to organise the meet as soon as possible.

It's fine. I like it when girls play dumb. It makes them endearing. All we need to do is organise a time and place, and that's it. We meet up, do our thing, and then we get the points for it. Obviously, I'll take it easy on you, seeing as you're new to this whole thing.

Lester signed off the message with a winking emoticon. He hit send, and straight away, he saw the message had been read by his next victim. This was perfect. Within a few hours he would be able to meet her and satisfy The Nasties.

Another message came in. Jessica was good at this. Keen. Eager. She wanted to be shown the ropes. *Oh, mother, the ropes.* All the things he could do to her with ropes. Lester groaned and wiped the excess saliva that was drooling from his mouth away with the back of his hand. And as he did so another message arrived.

U can cum to mine if u like? It'll have 2 b later though. I don't finish work til 18, but my mum's gone away for a cuple of days and I want us to b alone, does that sound OK?

Lester replied.

Sounds perfect.

Less than a minute later, Jessica responded with her home address and told him to be there around 8 p.m.

'Yessir,' Lester said, grinning at his laptop. He closed the lid and went to the shower to clean himself up.

CHAPTER 58

DOG

'Done,' Jake said, clapping his hands together. 'I think he's taken the bait.'

'You'd better hope he has. This is the only chance we've got.' Liam scribbled the time that they'd agreed to meet Lester on the board and circled it several times. 'Otherwise he'll get wise to our methods and disappear into the unknown for a while.'

'We'd best prepare then,' Drew said.

'What do you need us to do?' Jake asked.

As soon as he'd said it, an idea popped into his head. It was something he'd thought of earlier but hadn't been able to consider further. Jessica-Anne and the prostitute at Archie Arnold's house. There was a distinct possibility they were both from the same organisation. And there was an even higher possibility that, if their plan failed, Lester would return for some repeat business.

'I want AFOs from SO19 stationed in the house, around the street and in the neighbourhood,' Liam ordered. 'I want an army of uniforms – and plainclothes – to be on the scene, prepped and waiting. Some of them can be with us. Strength in numbers and all that. We've got less than four hours to prepare. Reckon we can get it done by then?'

'Yes, guv!' the three of them said in unison.

Liam adjourned the meeting and ordered them to carry out their tasks. As they filtered back to their desks, Jake made a left turn and headed towards the exit.

'Where are you off to?' Garrison called from his desk, which was situated right by the double doors.

Jake smirked. 'I've got to go see a man about a dog.'

CHAPTER 59

GOOD EGG

'Where's he going?' Drew asked, leaning against Garrison's desk.

Garrison shrugged and thumbed another biscuit into his mouth. 'I don't know. He said he's going to see a man about a dog.'

'Shall we follow him?'

Garrison shrugged again.

At that moment, Liam exited the debrief room and marched across the office. Drew whistled for Liam to come over and explained the situation to him.

He whispered as he spoke. 'What you saying, guv? Good egg gone bad?'

Liam gave a quick glance at the door and shook his head. 'No. He's not going anywhere we need to be worried about. This time I think he's being a good egg.'

CHAPTER 60

BARGAINING TOOL

Jake slowed his car to a halt in a lay-by outside a Co-op convenience store. The high-street chain bustled with life and patrons carrying bags of shopping and newly purchased bottles of alcohol by their hips. Jake killed the engine and hopped out. A few metres behind him was a phone box on the corner of the High Street and Carpenters Road.

Jake observed his surroundings, turning his head left and right, studying the characters around him, making sure he wasn't being followed or interrupting anything – or anyone. Then carefully, with his hands in his pockets, Jake approached the phone box. As he neared the object, the smell of urine and alcohol rose up his nostrils. It made him grimace, and for a moment he wondered how many people had used the phone box as shelter for the night.

Jake closed the door behind him and looked at the corkboard of business cards above the phone. There were dozens. Builders looking for work. Casinos that had just launched down the road. And the ones that most caught his eye: local gentleman's clubs with pictures of provocatively dressed women on them with their mobile numbers plastered in solid white lettering beneath. Jake searched for the one Archie had recommended – Diamond Geezers. He found it on the bottom of the board, picked it up and dialled the number.

The tone sounded in his ear.

'Yes?' a voice asked. It was Eastern European, although Jake was unable to discern exactly where. Possibly Russian. Possibly Latvian. Possibly Romanian.

'Er... Yes...' Jake said, stammering. He'd never done anything like this before. 'I was... I was wondering if I could make an appointment for tonight?'

'Sorry, we don't have any of those left. Goodbye.'

'Wait! Please!' Jake said. He rested against the side of the phone box and pressed the phone tight to his ear. The person on the other end of the line was still there. He could still hear their breathing. 'This is important. Sorry. I've never done this before.'

He hesitated again, trying to think of the best way to proceed. 'I need to know if you received a call the other day – on the twentieth. A man asking for a prostitute called Jessica?'

There was silence on the other end, and for a moment, Jake panicked. He thought the call's timer had run out.

'What is this?' the voice asked. 'Who are you?'

'Please. You're not in any trouble or anything. I'm investigating Jessica-Anne's murder. We're really close. We just need your help to catch the guy.'

'Police? You must fucking joke! We don't talk police!'

Shit. This wasn't going the way he'd hoped.

'Don't you want to catch him? Don't you want to find out what happened to her, help us arrest the man responsible?'

'No. We don't trust police. Don't call number again.'

'OK,' Jake said calmly. 'I won't call this number again. I'll call the other one instead. And then the one after that. And the one after that. We're the police. You think we won't be able to contact you again? We'll keep calling, and the next time it won't be as friendly as this.'

The voice chuckled deeply. 'You think you find us? You can't find fucking killer.'

'With time we will. With time we'll find you *and* the killer.'

'If that's right, why you need us?'

Jake swallowed. This was it. The bargaining tool.

'We need your help. I need to ask a favour. You don't need to tell us anything. We don't need to meet. I just need you to do something...'

Jake let that hang in the air. He hoped there had been enough intrigue in his voice to arrest the man's attention on the other end.

'What you need me do?'

Jake sighed an exasperated breath. 'We think he's going to try and make contact again,' Jake lied. 'We think he's going to order another girl to use soon. If he does, I want you to let me know. That's it. You just need to tell me where he's meeting the girl and when. Simple.'

'That's it?'

'Yes,' Jake said. 'You can call on a different number if you'd like. It won't be traced.'

The man coughed. 'OK. For Jessica.'

'And one other thing,' Jake added.

'What?'

'If he calls someone else – a competitor of yours perhaps – get them to call me too. The killer is going to use all the channels available to him. We need to make sure we find the right one. We can't afford to let him kill another person.'

'And what I get out of this? What in it for me?'

Jake sighed silently to himself. 'I can assure you the police will leave you alone. We won't interfere with your business. You go your way and we go ours. Simple.'

'Simple.'

'Agreed?'

'Agreed.'

Jake gave the man his work mobile number and hung up. He sighed heavily as he placed the phone on the receiver. It was done and he was grateful it was over.

Jake closed the phone box door and waited, holding his breath.

His senses heightened and he suddenly felt very vulnerable. As though he was being watched. He flicked his gaze from the man carrying the bags of shopping walking away from him to the couple crossing the street arm in arm, then to the kid on the scooter a hundred yards away. None of them were watching him; none of them were even looking his way. He was just being paranoid – afraid that it was either Lester in the distance observing him, or the people Bridger had warned him about, calculating his every move.

In the end, he decided he was being stupid and headed back towards his car. But as he went to start it up, he was interrupted by the sound of his phone ringing. It was his personal mobile.

Jake answered without checking the Caller ID. He didn't need to; he knew exactly what it was about.

'E-Elizabeth?' he asked, stammering, struggling to get his words out.

'Jake! Jake! Jake! I'm on the way to the hospital. Come quick. I'm with your mum. I'm having the baby!'

CHAPTER 61

GREEN ZONE

Jake's momentum was so strong that he stumbled and almost fell to the ground as he burst through the revolving doors of Croydon University Hospital. The A&E section to his left overflowed with people waiting patiently in the seating area while their relatives paced from side to side, launching torrents of verbal abuse at the nurses and support staff trying to help them. Jake paid them little heed and hurried to the reception desk, slamming his hands on the surface. He was out of breath, and his nose was running. 'My wife,' he began, gasping between breaths. 'Elizabeth Tanner. She's just gone into labour. I need to find her.'

The woman behind the desk gave him a blank look. He supposed it was because she was used to seeing his type – mad and frantic. And, in a weird way, he found that it calmed him down.

'Let me just check that for you,' she said.

She started typing on the keyboard. Slowly. Jake had seen Maisie type faster than that and she was only two years old. He silently willed her on in his head.

'Here we are,' the woman said after what felt like a lifetime. 'Elizabeth Tanner you said?'

'Yes.'

'OK, she was admitted to the Lucina birthing centre. Green zone. Ground floor. Over an hour ago.'

'Thank you.' Jake gave her a thumbs up as a sign of his gratitude before heading off down the corridor. He sprinted from one end of the hospital to the other, weaving his way in and out of nurses and patients and doctors and cleaners and medical staff and family members. By the time he arrived at the Green Zone's entrance, his legs burned and he was out of breath, his body consumed by a potent combination of fear, adrenaline and pure excitement. In that moment, nothing else occupied his mind except for the rising pressure of exasperation and emotion in his chest. He slowed to a halt, bent double and rested his hand against the wall for stability.

Without warning, his vision turned to white, and his body went numb, cold. Visions of snow and the mountains from when he was trapped in the avalanche appeared in his mind. He couldn't breathe, and the room spun. The walls began to close around him, inching closer with every exasperated breath. Then his head hit the floor. And when it did, the white wall relented, changing to black.

CHAPTER 62

C-ZONE

Jake awoke to the sensation of touch. His body felt like it was being moved, poked, prodded. In the distance, faint, almost as if they were only figments of his imagination, he heard voices. They were muffled at first, but then, as his consciousness slowly clawed its way back to him, they became clearer, more distinct.

'Sir!' It was a soft voice. Calm. Soothing. Like Elizabeth's when she tried to get him back to sleep after he'd had one of his episodes.

Elizabeth!

Jake's eyes shot open, revealing the world to him. He was surrounded by three nurses, trying to nurture him back to reality. One of them had a finger on his wrist, checking for a pulse; another was by his waist, the other by his head.

'Elizabeth,' he said, lumbering himself up onto his elbows. 'Elizabeth.'

'Sir, you need to stay still,' ordered the woman attempting to cradle his head.

'I'm fine. I'm fine. I need to find my wife.' He felt like shit. The fall had made him feel sick, and now a nauseating sensation permeated through the rest of his body.

'I'm sure she's fine. I'm sure you'll get to see her. I'm sure she's still in here somewhere.'

The nurse situated beside his waist stood and got him a cup of water. She returned and handed it to him. 'Drink.'

Jake didn't need telling twice. He downed the water.

'She's giving birth. I need to... I need to find her.' The sudden rush of cold water numbed his brain, inciting a headache, and he winced in pain.

'We need to make sure you're all right first,' one nurse said. He moved to Jake's back and supported him.

'You're not listening,' Jake said. 'I'm fine. It's happened before. It's just an anxiety attack. You don't need to help me. I need to see my wife.'

Jake staggered to his feet, despite the nurse's protestations, and stumbled towards the birthing centre.

The ward was twenty yards from where he fell, yet, before he'd passed out, it had seemed much further.

'Sir!' the nurses called, but he ignored them. He'd experienced anxiety attacks all too frequently to become worried by them anymore. They were a part of his life, and he'd grown to live with them. At first, after the accident, they had been frequent. And if it wasn't an anxiety attack, then it was severe dizziness, nausea, claustrophobia. But in the last year or so, he'd learnt to control them, thanks to his own self-guided recuperation and the help of a therapist. After several successful attempts at abating them, Jake had soon realised his episodes only came when he was placed under immense pressure and stress. And he was prepared to fight against them. He didn't want his life to be shackled and dictated by his everyday actions and processes.

Jake opened the ward door and was greeted by another long, seemingly never-ending corridor. Along the right side was a row of benches, which knots of people – families, friends, partners – occupied, and along the left was a series of birthing rooms.

Twenty yards away Jake saw his mother, Denise, bouncing Maisie on her knee.

He beamed as he approached them.

'Where is she?' he asked, taking them both by surprise.

Denise dropped Maisie from her knee, hugged Jake and then lifted Maisie into her arms.

'She's in there.' Denise pointed to the room opposite.

'Is everything OK? Any issues?'

'She's gone in for a C-section.'

'Oh my God,' Jake said, throwing his hand to his mouth.

'Don't worry. Everything's going to be fine. They've put her under now. They said it shouldn't be too long. All we can do is wait and wish her well.'

CHAPTER 63

ELLIE

'You can see her now,' the doctor told him. 'She's awake… but tired.'

At once, Jake erupted out of his seat and rushed into the birthing room, gripping the door handle tightly. There, resting on the bed with her head against the pillow, was his wife. Her face was covered in a thin layer of sweat that shone in the fluorescent light, and her body was hooked up to four different IV drips and machines. The ECG monitor beeped monotonously beside her.

'Hello, Nelly,' he said, smiling uncontrollably.

Nelly was the nickname he'd given her after she'd told him that the narwhal was her favourite animal. She loved them so much – and he loved her so much – that, on her birthday, he'd found a company that allowed him to sponsor a narwhal in her name. He called it: Nelly the Narwhal.

'How you feeling?' Jake asked, taking her hand and kissing her forehead.

'Tired,' she replied, blinking slowly. 'Is… Is she OK?'

'Yes. The doctors have taken care of her. They're cleaning her down now. I'm sure we'll be able to see her soon. I'm so proud of you.'

Jake gave her another kiss on the forehead and held her tightly in his arms. Her skin was warm. It felt brittle and delicate, as though if he touched it, it would break and tear. Elizabeth was one of the most precious things in his life, and he would never do anything to hurt her. He'd made that vow three years ago, and it still meant as much now as it did then.

'I love you,' Elizabeth said.

As Jake opened his mouth to let her know he loved her too, the door opened. A midwife entered, carrying their newborn girl in her arms.

'Here she is,' the midwife said. 'She's just catching up on some sleep.'

'No, she's wide awake,' Jake said, pointing at Elizabeth, who slapped him on the arm disapprovingly while the midwife suppressed a smile.

Elizabeth stretched her arms out and took her daughter from the midwife. She moaned softly as she stroked the little girl's face. Jake leant across and did the same, stroking both the baby's and Elizabeth's brows. Pure joy and happiness – an emotion he'd only ever felt when Maisie was born and on his wedding day – flowed through him. It was incredible. Invincible. Nothing could beat it. All the stresses of the past week – Lester, Bridger, the Jessicas, Liam – they all disappeared from his mind, as though they had never existed.

'Have you thought of a name yet?' the hospital staff member asked, breaking the silence.

Jack glanced at Elizabeth just as Denise and Elizabeth's parents entered the room.

'No,' he said, feeling distracted. 'We haven't, not y—'

'Ellie,' Elizabeth said, taking Jake by surprise. Where did she get that name from? And then he realised: Liam. She must have seen it on the card the team had given them.

'Ellie?' Jake squeezed her leg with a grin.

'Ellie.'

'Ellie.' Jake nodded. He liked it. It was simple and beautiful. Just like their gorgeous girl.

Their families swarmed them. Martha and Alan joined one side, while Denise the other. They hovered over the baby, touching her cheeks and holding her tiny hands. Alan moved across and shook Jake's hand, and as soon as they'd finished, Denise rounded the bed and gave him a hug. She squeezed him tight.

'I'm so pleased for you both,' she said, tears forming in her eyes.

'Don't start, Mum. You'll set me off.'

'Crying's OK, you know. It's OK to cry sometimes. Your father used to.'

'I'm not in a crying mood.'

Denise smirked. 'I'm sure we can change that. I mean, you only have to look at her for a second before you start tearing up and going all gooey.'

'I think that's just you, Mum.'

Denise reached into her purse and removed a camera. 'Do you mind if I take a few photos? Everyone needs new baby photos.' Before Jake could answer, she took it upon herself. 'Martha, Alan – do you mind if I take a couple of pictures for everyone's photo albums? I can get them made up and put into frames for you both.'

Elizabeth's parents nodded and said, 'Yes, that'd be lovely.'

As Denise left Jake alone to snap photos on her camera, Martha shuffled around the bed and decided it was her turn to speak to him.

She placed her hand on his arm, letting him know she was there. 'Jake, I was wondering if I could have a quick word outside?'

His body turned cold. 'Yeah, sure,' he replied, his brow slightly creased.

The corridor was quiet, and all Jake could hear was the sound of Denise instructing Elizabeth and Alan to pose for the camera. The smell of sterile air, laced with a hint of cleaning chemicals and antibacterial spray, lingered.

Martha Clarke was a beautiful woman, even though she was more than double his age. She wore her hair short, in a bob that flicked up around her ears and underneath her jaw. Her lashes were heavy with mascara, her lips darkened with a vibrant shade of red lipstick. She wore a dark blue blazer and a pencil skirt that reached just above the knee. She was a member of the government as the Secretary of State for Housing, Communities and Local Government, but the lack of shadows beneath her eyes suggested the complete opposite – as though she had an exotic job in an even more exotic country.

'Is everything OK?' Jake asked.

'I'm happy for you two. I'm just… *concerned*, that's all,' she said with a hint of discontent in her voice. He was going to hate this, he could tell. As part of her governmental responsibilities, it seemed it was necessary to come across as intimidating in every facet of her life. At least, that was the way Jake felt around her.

'What about?' he asked.

'Why didn't you tell me Elizabeth was going into labour? I thought we'd agreed that I would take her.'

'I didn't know she was going into labour until she was already on the way. Besides, none of us were expecting this. Ellie's a couple of weeks early – you were probably busy at work or something,' Jake said, his back already up. Martha knew how to get under his skin, and she always did it with success. No matter how many times he tried to defend himself against her, it was no use, and she always managed to leave him with scars.

'And where were you?' she asked, folding her arms.

'At work. The same as you.'

'And how's that going? I hear you're getting put under a lot of pressure.'

'Who told you that?'

'My daughter. She does still talk to me, you know.'

The muscles in Jake's shoulders and arms tensed. 'What else did she tell you?'

'Is there anything *you* want to tell me?'

Jake paused.

'Work's been a struggle recently,' he said slowly.

'Why?'

He sighed before responding. There was no point keeping secrets from her – she would find out sooner or later. 'I'm being put on this performance review,' he said. 'My supervisor served me with a Regulation 13 notice the other day. It means—'

'I know what it means,' Martha snapped. 'What did you do? Why are you on it?'

The way she said it annoyed Jake. She made it seem like he was the one to blame, like it was all his fault. When it wasn't. She was jumping to conclusions prematurely, just as she always did – and he didn't appreciate it.

'Nothing. I'm trying to do my job,' Jake said.

'Come on, Jake. It's you – you must have done something for them to hand it to you. These things don't just happen.'

'Are we done?' Jake asked, placing his hand on the door.

'I want to know what you're going to do about it. Don't forget that I was the one who helped you get into this position at MIT after your little fiasco with Surrey Police and all the shit you decided to accuse people of afterwards. And if something happens to your career now, I might not be there to pick up the pieces – not that I should have to anyway – and I need to know how it's going to affect my little—'

Jake puffed out a dissatisfied grunt. 'Hey,' he said, taking a minute step closer towards Martha. 'I made a promise to your daughter a long time ago that I would provide for her and protect her. And I'm going to do exactly that. Don't think I've forgotten about it. I love that woman more than life itself. I love my family more than life itself. I'm going to fight this, and I'm going to resolve it, OK? And I don't need you or anyone else to tell me how to do my job – either as a father or a husband.'

CHAPTER 64

SECRETS

'What's going on?' Liam shouted into the Major Incident Room where Drew and Garrison were working. It was almost 7 p.m., and Jake was nowhere to be seen. 'Does anyone know where the fuck he's gone?'

Both men shrugged.

'I've tried calling him but he's not picking up,' Liam snarled.

'I told you we should watch him, guv,' Drew said quietly. 'I knew the guy was a snake. He better not be getting cosy with the IPCC lot. Otherwise I'll—'

'What?' Liam replied half-closing the door behind him. 'You'll what exactly, Drew? Beat him up? Kill him? The days of police brutality are gone, pal, so you're going to have to be a lot smarter about it if you want a certain someone to take any notice of you.'

Liam sighed and coughed repeatedly until his chest and his lungs hurt. As he finished, he inspected his hand and wiped the small piece of blood he found on the back of his trouser legs. 'Now shut up, and one of you call him again – I don't care who. Just make sure he's here within the hour.'

Drew reached for the phone on his desk and dialled Jake's mobile. Meanwhile, Liam returned to his office and shut the door behind him. He leant against the wood and rested his head against the door. His mind began to wander into a forest of paranoia where each tree was a separate debilitating thought. What was Jake playing at? Where was he? Was he assisting with the case or was he working against them? Was he with Bridger? Was he working with the IPCC? Had he worked out what was going on?

No. Of course he hadn't. Bridger had told him to stay away. And Jake was a good detective, but he wasn't an idiot. Naïve, yes. A rookie, yes. Oblivious to the realities of Major Crime, yes. But Jake knew what was good for him, and he knew when to follow advice. At least, that's what Liam tried to convince himself of, but it didn't work – it didn't stop the thoughts from entering his drink-addled mind and plaguing it like the cancer that was eating into his lungs.

As Liam wandered back to his desk, the phone in his left pocket rang. It was the burner phone that he kept for all of his illicit activity. His personal phone was in the right, and on this occasion he didn't pay attention to which phone was ringing.

'Tanner?' he said without looking at the Caller ID.

'No. It's Martha.'

The name took a while to register in Liam's mind. 'I thought we'd agreed I wasn't dealing with you anymore?'

'Plans change.' She spoke with her usual steely, stern resolve that made the hairs on the back of his neck threaten to stand and piss themselves in the form of sweat.

'What do you need now?'

'It's my son-in-law,' Martha said. 'He—'

'Where is he? We've been trying to contact him.'

'Let me finish,' Martha snapped. 'He's at the hospital. My daughter's just given birth.'

Liam swallowed, stalling for time to try to think of what to say. 'Oh… I see… congratulations.'

'I won't pass on the message, but thanks for the sentiment.' Martha paused. Through the phone it sounded as though someone had just walked past and she had politely said hello, more out of necessity than anything else.

'Is everything OK with the baby?' Liam asked.

'Yes. They're both fine. Jake can tell you all about it when you see him. But for now I need you to explain something to me.'

Liam gurned. 'What?'

'How someone in his position can be served with a Regulation 13 notice, even though he's in training?'

'I… he…'

'You know that's bullshit, Liam.'

'Your son-in-law doesn't,' Liam replied, feeling his voice come back to him. 'For someone who likes to keep everything by the book, he's surprisingly clueless about the Police Performance Regulations Act.'

'He's got a growing family to provide for – he's got a lot on his mind, and he doesn't need you adding to his stress.'

Liam stopped talking for a moment. A knock came from the door and Drew entered, hovering in the door frame with his body weight against the door.

'Still nothing, guv,' Drew whispered.

'OK,' Liam said, conscious of the woman breathing down his ear. 'Leave it for now. We'll get hold of him soon. There's still time until the meet.'

Drew nodded and closed the door.

'Meet? What meet?' Martha asked as Liam opened his mouth to speak.

'The serial killer. We've lured him into a trap.'

'And you need Jake there?'

'Ideally.'

Martha sighed through the phone. It was so loud it sounded like a gust of wind had just entered his office and billowed around him.

'Right,' she began, 'here's what I want to happen. I want you to call him and ask him to come back. He'll probably say no, but I'll convince him to go. I'll make sure everyone understands that it's necessary. Then, the lot of you can go and do whatever it is you need to do. Once that's all been put to bed, I want you to rescind the regulation notice you gave him. Tell him it was a bad joke or something, or that you made a mistake.'

'It was,' Liam interrupted. He enjoyed interrupting Martha and knocking her off her pedestal; it was an infrequent victory that he liked to savour.

'It was what?' Martha asked.

'A joke. I gave it to him to give him a massive kick up the arse. We needed to solve this case, and I thought this was the way to do it. It was part of his initiation.'

'Christ, Liam,' Martha said. He could almost feel her rolling her eyes through the phone. 'You need to get some lessons in humour. Now go. Don't make me call you back, because next time the consequences will be worse.'

Liam's eyebrow flickered. 'What's the consequence now then?'

'There isn't one. That's exactly the point. This is your free pass. And who knows how much information I can spill. All it takes is one *mistake* and everyone's little secrets will come tumbling out.'

CHAPTER 65

BINGO

Lester impatiently counted down the hours, minutes, seconds in the house. He'd tried to pass the time by stirring the contents of the plastic tubs he'd bought from the Dark Web that contained Carl and Jessica's bodies, but he'd soon become bored. And then he'd had a brilliant idea. He could do a recce of Jessica Tanner's house. Maybe even catch a glimpse of her from a distance, see what she was like in the flesh. It had been a risky endeavour – leaving the house in broad daylight – and an unsuccessful one. Not only had he not seen Jessica at all, but he was beginning to feel like something about the Communion wasn't right. It felt staged. Too good to be true. And if there was one thing Lester had learnt in his time, it was that if it was too good to be true, then it generally was.

Yes, the address had checked out. And, yes, he'd seen a figure floating about the windows. But there was still an issue. There was still a small part of him – the rational side that hadn't been completely devoured by the monster within him – that suspected there was foul play.

Jessica Tanner. Jessica Tanner. Jessica Tanner, he repeated.

He played his suspicions through in his head. One: Jessica had messaged him first. She'd been the one to initiate the conversation. Two: she was new – brand new, in fact – and had no points. So why was she messaging him straight away? Why had she tried to attack the biggest fish in the pond when she should have started off with the little ones?

And then there was suspicion number three: the surname. Tanner.

It rang too many bells for him to be comfortable with. But he couldn't quite put his finger on why.

He knew it was familiar, recent, a name he'd either read or heard in passing.

And then it came to him.

Lester opened his laptop and went onto the BBC News home page. The top news article was about him. His face had been released to the general public – a screenshot taken from a CCTV still of him outside the coffee shop where he'd bumped into Jessica Mann – and the journalist writing the article had called him the Stratford Ripper. Lester didn't want to be in close proximation and in the same esteem as Jack the Ripper, mostly because Lester deemed himself to be better. He was smarter about everything he did. More technical. More logical in choosing his victims. More advanced in his methods. Nevertheless, Lester had resigned himself to the fact that, after all of this was done, he was going to live in infamy; that he was going to be in the history books as one of the worst serial killers London had ever seen.

It'll look quite good on the CV, he mused.

Lester read the rest of the article, brushed over the images the journalist had lifted from the victims' social-media profiles, and then found a video embedded at the bottom. The thumbnail displayed three men, dressed formally in suits, sitting at a table. The Metropolitan Police Service's crest was emblazoned on the backdrop behind them. A microphone had been placed in front of each of them, and the man on the left had his own placard.

Bingo.

Lester watched the video. It was the press conference that had been televised a few days ago. He remembered it fondly; the man on the right, DC Jake Tanner, had been left to answer all the questions. And he had done so poorly. The man had highlighted the police's ineptitude, and how they were no closer to finding him.

It was at that moment that Lester knew it was too much of a coincidence that Jessica and Jake shared the same name.

This was a set-up.

CHAPTER 66

COMING BACK

Nothing could distract Jake right now. He was in his own state of happiness, holding Ellie in his arms, his body surging with warmth and joy. She was precious. And he was so proud of her for surviving a premature birth. It was a miracle she'd even been born in the first place; according to doctors, Elizabeth wasn't able to conceive a child, and that made Ellie's birth all the more special. Both Ellie's and Maisie's.

But when Martha called from the other side of the room asking to speak with him, he knew that he needed to pay attention.

For the second time, they stepped out of the maternity room and into the hallway.

'You need to get to work,' Martha said, cutting straight to the chase. Jake supposed that was her only saving grace.

'Why?'

'Your manager called. He told me to tell you "it's time".'

Jake looked at his watch. It was 7 p.m. Where had the time gone?

'Why did he call *you*?' Jake asked.

'He didn't,' she replied, looking sheepish. Although, when it came to Martha, it was difficult to tell what she was thinking at any given moment.

'How did you find out then?'

'He called the hospital, and they put it through to someone here.

You were too busy so I took the call for you.'

Jake paused a second and scanned Martha's face. He wanted to see if there was any hint that she was lying. But there was none. Her pupils didn't dilate, and she didn't avert her gaze. She was a master at controlling her own facial expressions.

'Thanks for letting me know.'

'Go. I'll tell Elizabeth.'

'No,' Jake said, holding a hand out to Martha's shoulder. 'I can tell her myself, thank you. I'd like to say goodbye to my baby as well.'

'You make it seem like you won't be coming back.'

Jake opened the door. 'Well, let's hope I do.'

CHAPTER 67

SOON

On the way back to Stratford, Liam and Jake had agreed to meet a half mile down the road from Jessica Tanner's fake address. It was 7:45 p.m., and the rest of the team were in position. Members of SO19 were armed and operational, patiently waiting in the back of an inconspicuous white van, while other plainclothes officers had been deployed around the area. Liam's car was parked by the side of the road, sheltered by an overhanging tree. As Jake stepped out of the car, he felt an ominous gust of wind brush past his feet and climb up his leg.

'I suppose congratulations are in order,' Liam said, shaking Jake's hand as he closed the door behind him. 'How is everyone?'

'They're good. Fine. Healthy. Beautiful. Incredible.' Jake ran out of adjectives. He was truly on another level of emotion, and he just hoped it wouldn't come crashing down in the next twenty minutes.

'I'm pleased for you,' Liam said.

'Where are the others?' Jake asked, bringing his attention to the present.

He wanted to focus. Shit, he *needed* to focus. He needed to push all of his thoughts and feelings about Elizabeth and Ellie away so that he could concentrate on the present. One of London's most sadistic and vicious serial killers was on the loose, and it was his opportunity to catch him.

Jake couldn't allow himself to be distracted by anything.

'They're in the property now. Drew, Garrison, a whole army of

AFOs. As soon as Lester Bain rings that doorbell, they'll be on him.'

'What do we do now?' Jake asked.

A smirk grew on Liam's face. 'Follow me.'

Liam turned on the spot and started towards the meeting point. Jake's body was on high alert. His gaze darted left and right, constantly searching for any signs of life on the other side of the street. He was conscious of the fact that he'd been cutting it fine. It had taken him just over forty minutes to arrive, and he was all too aware of Lester's timekeeping. In the back of his mind he hoped Lester wouldn't be early. Jake knew it would be a part of the serial killer's nature; that he would be impatient; that he would want to get to the kill as soon as possible. As far as they knew, it had been over thirty-six hours since his last one... and he would be hungry.

They stopped outside a house on their right. It was an old Victorian building, built high and narrow, and it reminded Jake of his own home. In fact, it was almost identical, except that Jake's looked more modern and was built with brick that wasn't crumbling away. They climbed a small flight of steps and passed through the door using Liam's key. The inside was flooded with officers, many of whom Jake didn't recognise. The majority of them were standing in the hallway, keeping themselves out of view.

Liam led Jake into the living room at the other end of the corridor. A knot of officers was huddled around a coffee table in the middle, light from overhead bouncing off their reflective strips. Standing by the window was Garrison, peering through the curtains.

'This is where we're controlling everything,' Liam said. He pointed at the computers on the table.

'Where did we get the house from?' Jake asked. 'Not another person who owes you a favour?'

Liam chuckled. 'Not quite. This was the former house of a drug dealer. He managed to get himself in a lot of debt with some even worse people. We seized the house and everything inside it, and it turned out the guy didn't even own it in the first place. He wasn't paying any rent, and nobody's been able to get a hold of the landlord.'

Maybe it's Lester, he thought, immediately regretting it.

CHAPTER 68

HUN

Lester stalked the streets like a stray dog. Nobody gave him a second look; the first was all it took for something innate inside passers-by to fear him and move across to the other side of the road. The wind whipped between the terraced houses and narrow streets, buffeting the bottom of his jeans and his coat. It was beginning to get colder outside, and the humidity in the air had dropped drastically. He craned his head skywards and lost his gaze in the sky. The clouds were pitch black and thick.

Rain was imminent.

Perfect, he thought.

He was less than a mile away from Jessica Tanner's house. Despite coming to the realisation that he was being set up, part of him wanted to see what he'd created. It was the monster inside him speaking. The Nasties. He wanted to see how much effort the police had gone to in order to catch him. He wanted to laugh as he watched them wait for him and then panic when they realised he wasn't showing up. Call it narcissism. Call it sociopathy. Call it whatever the fuck you want, but Lester just wanted to show them that he was still one step ahead, one body in front of them.

He rounded Colegrave Road with his hands in his pockets. It was a mile long, and at the other end, on the left, was Jessica Tanner's supposed house. Twenty yards in front of him was a tree.

He stopped beside it and made a call.

'Stratford Cabs,' the female operator said on the other end.

'Good evening,' Lester began. 'I'd like to get a cab please. The corner of Colegrave and Dunmow. One person. As soon as you can.'

'Where to, love?'

'Missoula entertainment centre, in town,' Lester replied.

'I know the one. Not a problem. Someone will be with you in about five minutes. What's your name, hun?'

CHAPTER 69

OPPORTUNE MOMENT

It was a long five minutes. In that time, the sky had darkened, the clouds with it, and a light shower of rain had started to fall, gently sprinkling his face. As he waited at the side of the road, he folded his arms to keep the heat in his body. He tapped his foot against the pavement and shuffled from side to side. The excitement was building. The adrenaline was building. The anticipation was building. The Nasties were building. So what was taking the cabbie so fucking long?

Just as Lester was about to call the taxi company to chase them up, a car pulled over. It was clad in Stratford Cab banners and graphics and looked like something out of a Hot Wheels set.

The window rolled down and Lester leant through.

'All right, mate?'

'Cab for Jake Tanner?'

Lester smirked. 'That's me.'

The cabbie thumbed Lester to get into the back and he did as instructed. The interior of the vehicle was made of leather, and it smelt strongly of strawberries and raspberries; a Jelly Bean air freshener dangled from the rear-view mirror and swayed as Lester closed the door behind him.

'Where you going, mate?' the driver asked.

'Town centre please,' Lester said with a forced smile.

The cabbie made a right turn onto Colegrave Road and started down the street. Lester tapped his leg voraciously as they drove closer and closer to Jessica Tanner's house. His pulse squeaked and echoed in his ears, his heart beat furiously against his chest. He licked his lips, savouring the taste of his own sweat.

'How you doing tonight then?' the cabbie asked, rudely interrupting him from his stupor.

'Fine,' he replied. The last thing he wanted was to make unnecessary conversation.

Lester continued to stare out of the window. He observed the houses and counted down the numbers. Forty-nine. Forty-seven. Forty-five.

Something piqued Lester's interest on the right-hand side of the road. It was a small detached place, ten house numbers down from Jessica Tanner's alleged residence. Inside the front window, through a thin veil of material, was a petite woman tending to a baby in a high chair.

Before he was able to focus any more on the woman in the window, Lester's attention was distracted by Tanner's house. As they neared it, he noticed a stationary car that hadn't been there earlier in the day, occupied by two people in the front seats. He knew exactly who they were and what they were there for.

'Not today,' Lester whispered to himself.

'What was that?' the cabbie asked, slowing down as they came to a speed bump. His eyes flickered into the rear-view mirror.

'Nothing.'

The cabbie had one more chance. If he spoke one more time, Lester would slice the man's neck with the same blade he'd used on Carl and Jessica. He needed to shut up if he wanted to survive. It was that simple.

As the cab drove past the Tanner house, Lester beamed. It was on his left, and he was sitting on the right-hand side. He leant across the seats to get a better view. It was beautiful. The police had gone to a considerable amount of effort. They had set up a red room, with red ambient lighting, in the top-left window and had turned all the other lights off.

They assumed it would act as a beacon for him – a lighthouse of lust amidst the overwhelming sea of black and blue.

They were wrong.

Lester gave a small wave to the house, a final mockery, before it eventually passed out of sight.

At the end of the road, rain began to lash at the windows, creating a thin sound on the roof of the car. Lester closed his eyes and embraced the therapy of it.

The cabbie turned left onto Major Road, drawing them closer to the town centre. But there was a problem. Lester wasn't satisfied. It wasn't enough. He didn't feel content with just seeing the house. He didn't feel content with waving at it either. He wanted to be near it. He wanted to be as close as possible to it. He wanted to give the police one last middle finger.

Less than half a mile away from Jessica's house, he pretended his phone had gone off.

'You all right, love?' he said into the phone, putting on his best cockney London accent. The cabbie glanced in his rear-view mirror and they both locked eyes. 'Yeah. Oh my God, are you OK? No. Yeah sure. Of course I can. I'll be right there.'

Lester placed the phone in his lap.

'Sorry, mate, but could we go back? The missus has just cut herself and I think I need to take her to A&E.'

'What?' the cabbie asked, disinterested.

'It's a ball-ache, I know. But you don't need to hang around. I can take her to the hospital myself.'

The cabbie swerved the car into a U-turn. 'Not a problem,' he said.

They drove in silence as they started back towards the Tanner house.

'Which number was it, mate?' The cabbie leant forward and craned his neck to see out of the front window.

'Forty-one,' Lester said, just as the house came into view. The light was still on, but thankfully, nobody was there.

The cabbie pulled up outside and stopped the meter – £5.60.

Lester threw him a tenner, thanked him for his trouble, told him to keep the change and then exited. He stepped out onto the pavement and – carefully – approached the house, psyching himself up. It was all about the act. It was all about confidence – making it look as though he knew what he was doing, as though he had every right to be there.

Lester ambled slowly towards the house with his arm shielding his face from the rain and any possible method the police might have that would identify him. By the time he reached the door, the cab had disappeared out of sight and out of earshot.

He waited. Frozen. His body began tingling. His pulse bounced out of his skin. His muscles went taut. His mouth dripped with saliva and the rain hammered at his face. Within a few seconds of standing there, he was drenched. His hair. His shoulders. His legs. His feet.

Lester knocked on the door hard, ignoring the numbing sensation that coursed through his body.

There was no response.

He knocked again, this time even harder. On the other side of the door came the sound of a baby crying.

Still no answer.

Lester tried again. He entertained the idea of screaming for help but knew that would draw unwanted attention; even though he understood there were police stationed inside vehicles, he didn't know how many there were, and he didn't know how close they might be. At least the sound of his knocking was drowned out by the rain bouncing off the surrounding cars' roofs.

As Lester raised his fist to knock again, the door opened wide.

Lester gave the woman in front of him no chance to react. He charged in, pushed her against the wall and slammed the door shut. Before she could open her mouth to scream, Lester's hand smothered it. He then pressed his other arm against her throat and pinned his body against hers, immobilising her legs with his thighs. Her eyes bulged, revealing the shock and horror that appeared in someone's face moments before they realised something bad was about to happen to them. He loved that look. The whites of the eyes. The pupils growing smaller and smaller and smaller. The exasperated breath. The heaving chest. It all worked together harmoniously in a choir of death. And he was the conductor.

Lester sniffed and smelt fear oozing from her pores. He leant closer, and as soon as he did, her eyes closed. Smiling, he licked her forehead, moving from left to right, and then right to left. The woman screamed beneath him and wriggled. She tasted good – not the best, but good. Satisfactory.

'Shh,' Lester hushed, placing his finger against her lips. In the other room, the baby's crying worsened. 'If you stop, everything will be OK, all right? I don't want to hurt you. I don't. Honestly. You just need to calm down. Nod if you understand what I've just told you.'

Eyes wide, the woman dipped her head.

'I'm going to take my hand away from your mouth now, OK, and when I do, I want you to stay quiet. You can manage that, can't you?'

The woman dipped her head again, and Lester eased the pressure on her mouth but maintained it everywhere else on her body.

'Is anyone else home?'

She shook her head frantically; Lester believed her.

'The baby… I need you to make it quiet. Please.'

The woman groaned, opening her mouth to protest, but nothing came out.

'Ple… Please…'

'It's OK,' Lester said, placing his arm around her. 'You don't need to be afraid. We're only afraid when we reach into the unknown. Look at me – am I scared?'

The woman didn't know how to react, so Lester answered for her. 'I'm not afraid because I know exactly what's going to happen, and you don't need to be either.'

The baby was still in its high chair in the kitchen at the front of the house. The infant's little face had turned red and her mouth was covered in remnants of food and drink. As soon he loosened his grip on her, the mother rushed to the baby and picked her up. She cradled her in her arms and stroked her cheek.

'Give it to me,' Lester said. '*Please.*'

The woman retreated, clutching the baby against her chest until she bumped into the wall. Lester smiled. There was nowhere for her to go. He stood in the doorway between her and the exit. His gaze fell on the baby. He'd never done anything with one before. That was an experience he was looking forward to.

'Please,' she said, pointing at him, as if that would keep him at bay. 'Please take what you want. Money? We have lots of it. Please, just don't hurt us.'

Lester shook his head. 'Your insurance would pay you back for all the damage. No... I want something more special than that. I want your cunt.'

Lester grabbed at the child, yanked her free from the mother's grip and threw her to the ground. The baby bounced on the stone floor and lay still. The mother screamed, her pitch piercing his ears. He had to silence her.

Lester punched her in the stomach, smashed her face against the kitchen surface and let her fall to the floor. He stood there with his chest heaving over the two still bodies.

| PART 6 |

CHAPTER 70

GHOST TOWN

In the last hour, Colegrave Road had been a ghost town. The only thing they'd seen on the road that was of any interest had been a taxi that had come and gone. Liam, as the SIO and the officer in charge of the investigation, had quickly disregarded. At first, Jake had protested, claiming that it should be investigated, but after they'd witnessed a man sheltering himself from the rain enter a house down the road, Jake and the rest of the team had dismissed it.

'I don't fucking believe it,' Liam said, checking his watch as he paced around the kitchen. He waved his finger about. 'This was our *one* chance to catch him and we've blown it. How? What stopped him from coming? What tipped him off? More importantly, *who* tipped him off?'

Everyone in the room fell silent. A response escaped them, and nobody was willing to chase it and bring it back.

Liam threw his hands in the air. 'Am I just talking to myself?'

'He's smart,' Jake jumped in. 'Smarter than we gave him credit for. He must have realised it was too good to be true. Jessica Tanner – she'd come out of nowhere, and amidst everything else that's been going on, she still wanted to sleep with him. I think he saw through that straight away.'

'Well I'm glad you're piping up now,' Liam said.

'It was my idea, guv. I don't understand why you're—'

'Because he's still out there, and he could be killing someone right now and fucking their skull as we speak!' Liam slammed his hands on the kitchen surface. The cutlery that was in the drier beside the sink shook from the force.

At that moment, the kitchen door opened, and a uniformed officer entered, panting heavily.

'Sorry to interrupt,' he began, rain dripping from his cap. 'Guv – you'd better come see this. He's taken another one.'

Jake watched Liam's eyes widen. He mirrored him.

'You've got to be shitting me,' Liam said. 'Another woman?

'Sorry, guv, but it's better if you see it. Especially DC Tanner.'

The officer said nothing else and left the room. For a long moment, Jake and Liam stared at one another, horrified. What did he mean? Why Jake specifically?

He and Liam followed the uniformed officer out of the house and into the rain. At the end of the pathway, they turned right and sprinted down the road. In the distance, fifty yards away on the other side of the road, three police vehicles were stationed outside a house. Uniformed officers had already set up a perimeter and were beginning to roll out the white tape across the middle of the street.

Jake didn't like the look of this.

He swallowed hard as they reached the first step, where they were met with another uniformed officer holding a clipboard, sheltering it from the elements by hiding it inside his mac. Jake and Liam signed in their attendance and made for the front door.

As he climbed the small flight of steps to the property's entrance, something in the window caught Jake's eye. Light burst from inside the room, and there was a thin net curtain distorting his visibility of what was inside. From his position, he saw droplets and smears of red adorning the windowpane and curtain. But there was more on the other side. A lot more.

Tentatively, Jake entered the house. All he could hear was the heavy sound of his breath and the flashing of the forensic team's camera lenses.

He stopped at the threshold of the room. Before him was a massacre. On the floor, naked, was a woman and a baby. Both had been heavily mutilated – the mother more so than the little one. She was missing her limbs and the contents of her stomach had been flung across the kitchen counter and the floor. On the lower half of her body, incisions had been made around the vagina and thigh area. Blood still continued to drip down her body and pool onto the floor. The baby, lying a few feet away from her, was almost untouched, save for her missing fingers and tongue.

A lump swelled in Jake's throat.

'This is what I wanted you to see,' the officer said, pointing to the wall directly opposite.

Jake's eyes rose from the dead bodies and fell on the wall. His mouth fell open and his skin went cold.

Inscribed on the wall were five words:

BETTER LUCK NEXT TIME TANNER

Jake's mind went blank. He felt dizzy. Disorientated. Weak. Nauseous. Like he wanted to be back in the avalanche where the wall of snow was trapping and suffocating him. This woman had died as a result of him.

'Oh my God,' Liam said. He removed his phone and called Drew, told him to get down to the property immediately and then hung up. To the uniformed officers, he said, 'How long ago was this?'

'The blood's still wet,' the officer began.

'Their bodies are still warm,' came another voice from behind them. The owner walked up to them and introduced herself. 'Forensic pathologist Olivia Tointon.'

'Where's Poojah?' Liam asked.

'Day off. I'm filling in for her. We're both equally qualified, don't worry.' She hesitated, shot Liam a derisive look and then twisted towards the dead bodies. 'Judging by the state of this crime scene, I'd say he came in, and then—'

'What's the time frame?' Liam interrupted.

'It couldn't have been more than thirty, maybe even as little as twenty minutes ago,' Jake added, bringing his mind to the present. And then he realised what house they were in. 'Guv,' he continued. 'This is the house... the guy that got out of the cab. He came here. It was... it was Lester. He wandered into the house without us even realising who he was.'

'Right under our fucking noses.'

'Who found them?' Jake asked, turning to the uniformed officer.

'The husband. He came back from work late. He's round the next-door neighbour's house now,' said the officer.

'Did he witness anything? See anyone coming out of the house?'

'I don't know. But the back door's been smashed open and there's traces of blood in the garden and along the fence.'

'Bloody hell,' Jake said. He turned out of the kitchen and headed outside through the front door. The rain continued to fall, and he slipped on the final step. Catching himself on the metal railing, he steadied himself and ran into the road. He looked up and down, left and right.

Nothing.

They had lost Lester. And what was worse was the fact that Lester knew who Jake was. He was mocking him. Rubbing it in his face. Using his own name against him.

Lester had just made it personal.

CHAPTER 71

HIDEAWAY

Lester's muscles ached. He was fatigued and mentally exhausted. The Communion had been over quickly – too quickly. Much quicker than he would have liked, but he knew it was necessary. The longer he spent in the house, the longer he drew attention to himself and the more he risked being caught. In fact, he'd been cutting it fine as it was. That bastard husband had come within seconds of walking in on him. During the Communion, his victim's husband had texted to say he was round the corner, running late from work. Lester had seen the message and left through the back garden. He'd been forced to rush through the message he'd left on the wall. He wanted to take more time with it, more care, more precision. But instead he'd had to sacrifice the luxuries and hurry it. The message remained the same.

Darkness had swept through the streets of Stratford and the roads were dimly lit, tinged a deep orange and yellow. Lester headed west on Temple Mills Lane, crossed the bridge over the railway lines and waited by the nearest bus stop, sheltering himself from the elements. He leant against the narrow bench, his weight bowing the plastic advertisement for erectile dysfunction behind him. Overhead was the digital timetable displaying the schedule for when the next three buses were due to arrive. The number seventy-three – the one that would take him to his next location – was only a few minutes away.

As he waited, he relived the Communion, re-experienced the short time he'd spent in the woman's company. The look on her face as she'd regained consciousness just before he'd slit her throat. Her soft skin. The baby's, even softer. How little they'd protested. The Nasties had been satisfied. But only for a short while.

By now, he was certain the police would have found the bodies and would be looking for him, which meant he couldn't afford to slip up. Not now. He had to think calmly, rationally, logically. The majority of murderers and rapists and criminals always made their first mistakes within the first couple of hours following a crime. Lester wasn't about to become another statistic.

A minute later, the bus arrived. Double-decker. Lester lifted his head, glanced at the driver and boarded the bus. He paid using a five-pound note and climbed to the top level, finding a seat at the front. His favourite. Now he could see everything in front of him.

As the bus swerved in and out of lay-bys and streets heading north on the A112, a dozen police vehicles charged past, their sirens blaring and lights flashing.

Lester needed somewhere to stay nearby. Urgently. Somewhere he could lay low, somewhere under the radar. Carl and Jessica's property was off limits for now; it was too far away. And the longer he spent out in the open, the more he risked being seen.

But he had the perfect answer: the other property nobody knew about. The semi-detached two-bedroom in north Stratford. His little secret. The one he kept unoccupied all year round for this exact purpose. On one occasion he'd even invited someone round for a Communion. It even had its own red bedroom that had been inspired by Jessica and Steven Arnholt's.

Lester disembarked the bus a hundred yards from the house on Nutfield Road, wandered up and down the street, recceing the road and the house, before doubling back and inserting his key into the lock. As he entered, his senses and body were on high alert for any unwanted signs of attention.

There was nobody – and nothing – in sight. Nobody knew he was there. Nobody knew the property existed. It was perfect.

Lester was greeted with the smell of damp; the house hadn't been used in a long time, and it was beginning to show. He entered and eased the door shut behind him. Beside the door was a two-metre-long mirror. Lester paused and looked at himself. His hair was wet and dishevelled, and thick caterpillars of blonde hovered centimetres above his eyes. His skin was red, rouged with excitement and adrenaline, and his eyes had turned black. Lester grinned at what he saw. He wasn't a monster. He wasn't an animal. Of course he wasn't. He was a normal human being leading a normal life. *And fuck anyone who says anything different.*

'One last time,' he told himself. 'One last time. One last time never hurt anybody. And then after that, lay low. They're onto you. Just now was too close. One last time.'

Lester leant closer to the mirror, his breath fogging the underside of his face. 'But if you're going to do this, you need to make it a good one. Make it one you'll never forget.'

CHAPTER 72

EVERYTHING IS READY

Lester stepped out of the shower and placed his feet on the bath mat. Steam clawed its way up the bathroom mirror slowly as he wrapped his towel around himself. The shower had helped him relax, calm himself before the next visit from The Nasties.

With his towel still around him, he dropped down and did some push-ups, placing his feet on the toilet seat for better development and growth in the upper region of his pectorals. After cranking out fifty, he wiped away the steam from the mirror and stared at the enhanced muscles that the short bout of exercise had produced. He was a specimen – a fine specimen – and he intended to keep it that way.

He left the bathroom and headed to the bedroom. In the middle of the room was a large double bed that had never been slept on. A thin layer of dust carpeted everything in sight. Beside the bed was a table. He ambled up to it, opened the top drawer and took out a mobile phone and a business card.

He sat on the bed and twirled the business card in his fingers. It felt old and soft, as if the prolonged shelter from oxygen in the drawer had weakened the material. But still, its contents were visible.

It was the number for a brothel. One that he'd used years ago after he'd celebrated the tenth anniversary of his parents' death.

He'd needed a release of excitement then, and he needed one now. In fact, Lester had loved their service so much he'd kept their details.

He switched on the phone, waited for it to load and then dialled the number. The SIM card was registered to him, but the usage was so infrequent, and the deal so cheap, he seldom received any marketing or sales calls asking him to upgrade and change tariff. It was almost as if the number didn't exist. So long as he continued to pay the bill every month, there was no issue – the service provider got their money, and he got their service. And he liked to keep it that way.

Lester stared at the silhouette of a woman on the card and licked his lips. It conjured images of his last experience with them. Martina. That was her name. She was beautiful, and she had made the evening all the more beautiful for him. He remembered the look of surprise and mild excitement on her face when he'd showed her the effort he'd gone to in the bedroom. He wanted her to feel comfortable, for her to be able to enjoy their first time together. He'd wanted it to be memorable. And, to his surprise, it was. For both of them. Martina had told him that it was the best experience she'd had with a client. Still, to this day, it was one of his finest accomplishments.

'Martina,' he whispered, getting a hard-on as he said her name.

For a moment Lester wandered if she was still there, and whether he could get her to come to his. But he knew that wouldn't be possible. She was the opposite to Jessica, and he couldn't tarnish his experience with someone who looked different. The red hair. The curvy hips. The freckly face. The green eyes. It wasn't right. No, if he deviated from the pattern now, then everything he'd worked for would have gone to waste – and he'd leave The Nasties unsatisfied.

She had to be perfect. Anything else wouldn't do.

Lester dialled the number.

It went through to voicemail.

He tried again.

This time, somebody answered.

'Yes?' This time it was a woman.

'I'd like to book a hair appointment,' Lester said. He hoped the catchphrase hadn't changed since he'd last used the number.

'When?'

'Now. As soon as you can fit me in.'

'Where?'

'My place. I'll text you the address after we've finished the call.'

'OK. Let me see if we have someone available. Do you have any specific requirements?'

'Yes,' Lester said excitedly. 'She has to be tall, tanned, skinny, and brown haired. Her eyes must be brown, and she must be called Jessica.'

'One moment,' the female voice said. There was a long pause, and Lester tried to keep calm, but it was difficult. With every passing second, his breathing rate increased, as did his blood pressure.

'Hello?' the voice asked after a while. 'Yes. We have a girl that is suitable for you, and she is available straight away, but her name is Jennifer. Is that OK?'

'No,' Lester snapped. 'Jessica. It has to be Jessica. It would be wrong if it was any other name. I'm sorry, but I hope you understand. Her name must be Jessica.'

Lester touched himself as he called out the name.

'One moment please.' The woman disappeared again, and Lester waited. His moment of erotica subsided, and his penis quickly went flaccid. The sensation had been fleeting, but he knew it was building to something larger.

The woman's voice distracted him again. 'I've just found someone for you. She's exactly what you're looking for. Tall. Dark hair. Slim. And her name is Jessica. But it will take her an hour to get to you. Is that OK?'

Lester checked the alarm clock on the bedside table. It was just after nine. An hour would do.

'Yes,' he said, trying to hide the excitement in his voice. 'That will be fine. Tell Jessica I look forward to seeing her. I'll text you my address now. I'll be waiting for her. I hope she's ready. Tell her she doesn't need to bring anything. I have everything here already.'

CHAPTER 73

NO NAMES

Jake, Liam and the rest of the Major Investigation Team were still at the crime scene, trying to piece together what had happened. In the past half hour, they'd made little progress. Except for the call they'd made to Stratford Cabs, enquiring about Lester's trip. Jake – and the rest of the team – learnt that Lester had used Jake's name for the booking. Hearing the news made him feel even more sick than he already did. Now Lester was mocking him, and Jake wasn't about to stand for it.

He was standing in the middle of the kitchen doorway, unable to tear his eyes from the dead bodies. The victims' names were Nina Deckart and her daughter Maxine. The sight of the small baby on the floor horrified Jake. It made him think of Ellie. How she'd been ripped out of Elizabeth as a way of bringing her into existence; how, paradoxically, another baby had been ripped from existence on the same day.

'Where's he gone?' Jake asked, turning his back on the kitchen and focusing on his colleagues in the hallway. Liam, Drew and Garrison stared at him blankly.

'Well, shit me,' Garrison said. 'I hadn't thought of that. Why didn't we think to ask ourselves where he is? We could have saved ourselves a whole lot of time if we'd just thought to ask it sooner. Absolute genius over here.'

'Shut up,' Jake said, still aware that he had a Regulation 13 notice looming over his head. He wasn't back in everyone's good books just yet. 'I mean... *where* is he? *Where* would he have gone? Where *could* he have gone? Eh?'

Silence.

Jake pondered aloud, letting his mind run away with itself, regardless of what the others thought or said. 'Lester would need to be looking for somewhere secure. Somewhere he knows. Somewhere he feels safe... comfortable. Somewhere nobody else knows.' Jake paused. 'He's just attacked again. He's on a high. He's excited, pumping with adrenaline. His mind is too clouded to think rationally. Like a frightened animal he's running back to somewhere safe. Maybe even paternal. Maternal. He needs somewhere he can calm down and think. He needs somewhere to recuperate. Where?'

The three men looked at him, devoid of any expression.

'The last one was an actual question...'

'Oh,' stuttered Garrison.

'He... he...' muttered Drew.

'A home,' Liam said. 'He needs a home. His home. One of them.'

'Which one?' Garrison asked.

'It can't be any of the ones we're watching – I've not heard anything from uniform to suggest he's gone back to any of his registered properties.'

'It has to be one we don't know about,' Jake added. 'The place he killed the unidentified victims the other day? Somewhere near. Somewhere still in the city. If he's gone on foot, it'll be even closer. If he's gone by public transport, that stretches the radius, but only marginally. It's going to be a place he can reach quickly.'

'How do you plan on finding it, genius?' Drew asked derisively. Jake sensed he wasn't committed to this plan. 'We've been through all the records, we've cross-referenced the databases – we've found all of the properties that he's the landlord for.'

'Perhaps he's used an alias. Perhaps it's a family member's that he never changed the name on. Perhaps he's used Sampson's name. We all know how much he idolised that freak. It could be any name, I guess.'

'That narrows it down,' Drew retorted. 'Anyone. It could be anything. It's like the press conference all over again – absolutely clueless.'

'I mean, you can either help,' Jake said, 'or you can go home and let us finish the job without you. It's pretty simple. If you've got nothing better to do than just insult me and take the piss out of my suggestions... If you think you're such a hero, Sherlock, then why don't you come up with one of your own?'

Drew fell silent, his face turning pale. He looked down at the table as a response escaped him. None of the three men said anything. Jake wondered if it was because they were intimidated by him suddenly or whether it was because they were all deep in thought. Jake thought neither situation likely.

'Widen the search,' Liam said, taking them all by surprise. 'See if any of his family members or friends have any properties lying around the place.'

'He inherited the business from his dad – that's got to mean something.'

'We'll get to it,' Drew said.

Jake stepped out of the hallway and moved into the living room. He checked the time – 9:55 p.m. Nina and Maxine had been killed just under two hours ago, and they were all still twiddling their thumbs. And it was getting late. Elizabeth and the baby would be sleeping, exhausted after the events of the day, but he wanted to hear his wife's voice – or at least know that she was OK.

Jake called his mum.

'Jake?' she began. 'What's wrong?'

'Nothing. I'm fine. I just wanted to check up on everybody. Where are you?'

'At the hospital still. I'm with Martha and Alan.'

'Elizabeth? Ellie? Maisie?'

'They're all OK, Jake. They're sleeping at the moment. Elizabeth's been out for hours already.'

'Good.' A smile grew on his face. 'I just wanted to know they were doing all right.'

'How's work? Should you be calling?'

'Probably not. I can't explain—'

'That's fine. I understand. So long as you're keeping safe.'

'Of course I am,' Jake said. 'Isn't it past your bedtime?'

'Funny. Although I think Martha's trying to have a competition to see who can stay the longest. She's wrong if she thinks she can beat—'

At that moment Jake's work mobile started to vibrate. He looked at the screen. It was another call from an unknown number.

'Listen – Mum – sorry, I've, eh… got to go. I'll speak to you later. Love you. Bye!'

Jake hung up the call with his mum and answered the other phone.

'Hello?' he said.

'Detective Tanner? I was told to get in touch with you if we received another call…'

CHAPTER 74

22:03

'Are you sure about this, Jake?' Liam asked as they hurried towards Liam's car.

'One hundred per cent.'

'Why didn't you tell me about this earlier?'

'I'm telling you now…' Jake said sheepishly.

Liam sighed. 'If this doesn't work, it's on you.'

Jake was completely aware of the ramifications of his actions and decision-making. If he turned out to be wrong – and they let Lester slip through their fingers again – he was prepared to accept the Regulation 13. Until then, he'd have to have the courage of his convictions.

'How reliable is the intelligence?' Liam asked as they hopped in.

'That's open to interpretation, guv,' Jake replied. 'Lester used an agency when he killed Jessica-Anne. Diamond Geezers – the same as Archie Arnold. I noticed they had tattoos on their wrists that were almost identical.'

'Maybe they were really close friends,' Liam said. Jake was unsure whether it was intended as a joke or a legitimate suggestion.

Either way, he chose to ignore it. He continued. 'But this time I got a call from another agency, Rough and Tough, saying that someone had requested a prostitute meeting Lester's specific requirements. It's too much of a coincidence for them not to be related. I can't imagine they're in the position to be making prank calls to the police.'

'You'd better hope not.' Liam thrust the key in the ignition and started the engine. 'What's the address?'

Jake gave it to him and watched Liam plug it into the satnav. The device's screen turned black and then switched to a street-view map of east London. Their destination appeared as a small red pin less than half a mile away. According to the device, it would take them five minutes to get there through all the traffic. That was too long.

As they bombed it to the other end of Colegrave Road, bouncing over speed bumps and potholes, Jake redialled the mysterious number.

'It's me,' he said. 'What's the girl's number? We need to tell her not to go into the house.'

'I can do it,' the Eastern European voice on the other end said.

'No,' Jake replied. 'This is a police investigation. I might remind you of that. You've been more than helpful.'

A silence ensued.

'Pen and paper,' the gruff voice said.

Jake grabbed Liam's phone from the centre console, unlocked it and entered the prostitute's number.

'She'll be there by ten, yes?'

'Yes. Maybe just before.'

Jake's eyes glanced towards the dashboard clock.

'It'll be tight. We'll get there as soon as we can.' Jake hung up and looked at Liam. 'It'll be cutting it fine. She's due at the house by ten.'

'Our ETA says 10:03 p.m.'

'Reckon we can shave off three minutes?'

'We can die trying.'

Liam floored the accelerator and propelled the car forward, throwing Jake deeper into his seat. His hand launched towards the holder above his head by the passenger window, and his knuckles whitened.

As they sped along the A112, Jake dialled the prostitute's number.

CHAPTER 75

BATHROOM

'Is this it, love?' the man in the driver's seat asked.

'Yeah. Here'll be fine thanks,' she replied.

'You sure? I don't mind dropping you off right outside.'

'It's fine. Here'll do.' She made it a custom to always get out near her next appointment but never directly outside. It was a superstition of hers that had stuck. That way nobody knew where she was going, just in case she was being followed. She'd had a stalker once, and that was enough for her to triple-check every time she went to visit a client – old or new.

'You're the boss,' the cabbie said, pulling to the side of the road.

She reached into her purse for the twenty quid it had cost her, leant forward and handed it to the driver.

'Pleasure doing business with you…?'

'Jessica,' she said.

The cabbie gave her a wink as she left the car and her skin crawled. She hated creepy old men. And she hoped her next client was someone younger, more mature, different to her other clientele. She didn't know why, but she found that they always seemed to favour the younger girls. Perhaps it was a manifestation of a complex they'd developed in adult life.

She'd almost told the cabbie her real name – Jennifer. But she'd stopped herself when realised that tonight, she was Jessica. That had been the client's specific requirement. Dimitri was insistent upon that point. No matter what, her name was Jessica.

It should have sounded odd to her, but it didn't. It wasn't the first time she'd had an unusual request. In her experience, she'd seen the darker side of human nature and, specifically, men. When it came to sex, there was a completely different side to them. Animalistic. Ritualistic. Sometimes it frightened her. Sometimes it didn't. It was all part and parcel of the job; something she'd come to accept over the years.

Jessica idled along the street, her high heels clacking on the pavement. She held a clutch bag under her arm that carried the essentials: her purse, phone, house keys and several condoms. It was a rule of hers to check over all her clients before she engaged in any physical activity with them. It was for both their benefit and made good business sense – the less likely she was to catch something, the more clients she could have, and the more money she could make.

As she walked, she adjusted her thong to stop it riding up. She was wearing her favourite underwear, after her boss had told her this was a very special client. He had particular requirements and was prepared to pay the top price for them. And she was more than happy to reward him for it.

She checked the address on her phone and counted down the house numbers.

When she finally saw the door emblazoned 126, she hurried towards it and rattled her knuckles against one of the wooden panels.

As she waited, her phone rang. She glanced at the screen, realised it was an unknown number and ignored it. She was working; it was unprofessional to accept calls. The front door opened as soon as the phone was back in her clutch bag.

'Jessica?' came a soft voice. It was endearing and sounded almost afraid. Like this was her client's first time.

The door opened wider and revealed to her the man she would be spending the next hour or two with. He was dressed in shorts but was missing an item of clothing on his top half, revealing a surprisingly well-sculpted body. She estimated that he was in his mid-forties, and he was looking good for it. He clearly took care of himself. His face was relatively handsome – acceptable, considering she would have her eyes closed for most of it anyway – and she didn't get the impression that he was a creep.

'And what do I call you?' she said, after realising that she'd spent a considerable amount of time staring at his face.

'You can call me Steven,' he said, stepping aside. 'Please come in. You must be getting cold. And wet.'

Steven closed the door behind her and took her hand. It was

warm and soft, and slightly damp. A smell of shower gel and shampoo lingered in the air and enlightened her senses.

'Hope you don't mind,' she began. 'I'm a little early.'

'Not at all. Not at all.'

'Nice place you have here,' she said, observing her surroundings.

Steven smiled, disappeared into the kitchen and returned with two wine glasses and a bottle in his hand. 'I hope you like red?'

'Are you trying to get me drunk?' she said before giggling playfully. She didn't know what was coming over her. She was never usually like this; it was always 'get straight in, and then out again'. But there was something about this man that was different. Perhaps it was his charm. Perhaps it was the disarming smile. Or perhaps it was because he came across as so sweet and innocent that she almost felt sorry him.

'Perhaps I am.' He blushed. 'What will you do to me as a punishment?'

Jessica flicked her eyes at him. 'Whatever you want me to.'

'I was hoping you'd say that.' He hesitated. 'You know, I was round someone's house recently, and they didn't even give me a tour. Would you like one?'

Jessica looked up and down the stairwell. 'I don't see what harm it could do. So long as you're quick. I'm hungry.' She winked at him.

'Right this way then.'

Steven poured the wine into their glasses, handed Jessica hers then led her into the living room before showing her the kitchen. It wasn't anything special. It had all the utilities and the amenities that she had in her own kitchen. It was the same with the rest of the house – a small office, an airing cupboard, a bathroom. None of it was that spectacular. After the sheer number of houses she'd seen, the novelty of them wore off after a while – eventually they all began to look the same.

Finally, Steven showed her the bedroom.

'You ready?' he asked, standing with his hand wrapped around the door handle.

She nodded.

As Steven opened the door, her phone vibrated again. She quickly looked at the Caller ID and hung up on it.

'Someone important?' Steven asked, his demeanour changing slightly. He became more rigid, concerned.

'My manager. He likes to make sure I get to my appointments OK.'

'That's cute,' he said. 'You can take it if you like?'

'No, no. It's fine. I'm a big girl. I can look after myself.'

Steven smirked again, bearing his white teeth. 'Do you get a lot of clients?'

'I have my fair share.'

'Have you had anyone like me before?'

She moved closer to him, pulling her skirt higher up her thigh. Inches separated them, and then she placed her arm on his shoulder and moved it down to his chest.

'Darling, I've never had a client like you before,' she said.

Steven pressed the handle and opened the door. A wall of red hit her in the face, and from the outside, she saw a series of whips and chains and sex toys on the wall and on the bed.

'There's a first time for everything,' Steven said, and before Jessica could react, he grabbed her elbow and nudged her into the room.

Her senses were on high alert. She'd never experienced anything sadistic or even masochistic in her life. Other clients' fantasies had been tame, reserved – usually involving the feet or putting her in awkward positions. Never anything like this. Never this perverse. Jessica sensed this was going to change her sex life forever. And, right now, standing a few feet away from the instruments, she didn't know whether it would be for better or worse.

Lester closed the door. The room darkened a deeper shade of red. 'What do you think?' He held his glass in the air.

'I... I...'

'Speechless. I thought you might be. Please make yourself comfortable. We have a long night ahead of us.'

'Ah, yes,' Jessica said. 'About that—'

Lester reached into the bedside-table drawer and produced a wad of money.

'I know – you want the money upfront. That's fine.'

He handed it to her; this was her favourite part of the job.

'That's for the first few hours. There's a little extra than your usual rate. And there's plenty more where that came from, depending on how long our evening together lasts.'

Jessica placed the money in her bag. 'I hope for your sake it lasts a long time.'

Lester set his glass on the table. 'I'm going to introduce you to a world of pain and pleasure – one of the deadliest combinations ever experienced.'

'I can't wait—'

Jessica's phone started ringing again. Lester's face fell. His brow furrowed and his eyes narrowed.

'Sorry,' Jessica said, feeling slightly intimidated. 'It's my boss again. I should probably take it. Just to get rid of him.'

'Fine. But be quick,' Steven snapped. His entire demeanour had turned sour.

Jessica rushed out of the bedroom and headed into the

bathroom, where she pulled the door to and sat on the toilet seat.

'Hello?'

'Jennifer – this is Detective Constable Jake Tanner from the police. Act normal.'

She paused a second, taking in the instruction. 'Oh, eh… hi, babe. You all right?'

'The man you are currently with is incredibly dangerous.'

'Yeah, yeah. Everything's fine.' Jessica hopped off the seat and tip-toed closer to the door. 'I got here all right, although the cabbie was trying to flirt with me on the way down.'

'You have to keep as far away from him as possible.'

Holding her breath, she cautiously slid the bolt into position. She exhaled heavily as she heard it lock.

'Are you in a safe place?'

'I don't know how long I'll be,' she said. 'I've just popped to the toilet before we begin.'

'We're on our way, Jessica. You have to stay out of sight and make sure he doesn't come anywhere near you.'

'I think you're going to have to cancel my other clients for tonight.' She spoke loudly, in case Steven was eavesdropping outside the bathroom. 'I've got a feeling this is going to last all night. He's even got toys and weapons for us to use…. No – I've never tried them before either.'

'Just hold on tight, OK,' Jake said. 'We're one minute away.'

'Don't worry, babe. I'll be safe. I've been in this business long enough to know what I'm doing.'

Jessica hung up the phone. Her body had been running on adrenaline throughout the entire conversation, and now that it was over, it completely disappeared. Her body froze in shock, and her mind dissociated itself from everything. She wanted to breathe, but couldn't. She wanted to move, but couldn't. She wanted to scream and run away and wish that she'd never come here, but couldn't.

Her hand loosened its grip on the phone, dropping it to the floor. It smashed on the solid tile flooring. Splinters of glass ricocheted into the air and bounced off her leg. Jessica let out a small gasp and bent down to pick it up.

Within a split second, there was a knock on the door.

'Is everything all right in there?' Steven asked. She could almost feel his breath on her, crawling up her neck, moving around her ear to the side of her face.

'I'm fine!' she shouted. 'Fine. Fine. I j-just dr-dropped my phone, that's all.' She stood, reached into her bag and found a small lipstick and mascara. Her hands shook violently. 'I won't be long – I'm just adding s-some make-up.'

Silence. She thought she'd heard his footsteps moving away

from the door, but over the deafening sound of her heart and frantic breath, she couldn't be sure. She undid the cap on her lipstick and pressed the stick to her lips. Her hands continued to shake uncontrollably, smearing the red wax over her mouth.

She paused and froze. Slowly, her head turned towards the door. The thin line of light that ran along the bottom of it distorted and changed. Now there were two dark shadows a few inches wide. He was standing on the other side. He was there, ready, waiting.

It didn't bear thinking about. He'd been so calm and reserved yet quietly confident. He had seemed charming and charismatic – and good-looking!

She remained perfectly still and strained her hearing. Steven's breathing had increased, and with every passing second it was becoming heavier, and heavier, and heavier, until it turned into a hollow growl.

'What are you doing in there?' Steven asked, his voice deeper than the darkest depths of the ocean.

'I–I…' Jessica stuttered.

'Have you heard the story of the three little pigs?'

Before Jessica could answer, a loud bang shocked her into falling backward onto the toilet. A piece of the door caved in, revealing a slither of light coming from the landing.

The sound was followed by another bang.

And then another.

And then another.

And then Jessica saw it. The hammer, and the mountain of evil in her client's eyes. He repeatedly bashed down the door, sending pieces of woodchip and plastic into the bathroom. Jessica crawled over the bathtub and cowered in a foetal position, hoping it would protect her. She tried to scream, but her lungs wouldn't function.

A few seconds later, Steven threw his arm through the gap he'd created in the door and turned the handle.

CHAPTER 76

HISTORY

'Get out! Get out! Get out!' Jake screamed as the Liam skidded the car to a halt and the tyres finished kissing the pavement.

Liam and Jake were the first to arrive, followed immediately by Drew and Garrison and a convoy of firearms officers in the back of a white, unmarked armed response vehicle.

Jake leapt out of the car and sprinted towards the house. Screams and shouts came from the armed officers behind him, ordering him to stand aside and move out of the way. It was procedure for the AFOs – authorised firearms officers – to enter and clear the area first so that he and the rest of the team could inspect the damage. Panicked by their loud voices, Jake jumped to one side and allowed the members of SO19 to pass. Each member of the team was clad in Kevlar vests, helmets and carried a SIG MCX 556 Carbine in their arms. All of their sights were trained on the house.

They fanned out either side of the front door. One of them – the furthest on the right – shuffled towards the door. In his hand he held an Enforcer. On the count of three, he swung the ram into the door and buckled it, splintering the lock into a dozen pieces.

'Armed police! Armed police!' they screamed as the rest of the team fell into the house, spreading across the width of the property.

As soon as they were in, Jake entered behind them. Something in his mind had forgotten the procedures. He didn't care if he was supposed to wait for the all-clear. Rules weren't important right now. His only focus was on saving the victim's life. On the phone she'd sounded distressed and afraid, and as soon as she'd told him she was in the bathroom, Jake had grown worried.

He rushed up the stairs. As he climbed the steps, he listened for any signs of Jennifer screaming – any sign that she was still alive amidst the shouts and chaos coming from the armed officers.

There were none.

The stairs twisted left, and as he came to the top step, he froze. The bathroom. Lester. Half-naked. Standing over Jennifer's body. Holding a hammer in his hand. Blood gushing from her head.

Two armed officers were in front of Jake, either side of the bathroom door. They screamed at Lester for him to lower the weapon.

'Put the weapon down!'

'Drop it, or we will shoot!'

Lester's chest rose and fell like a trampoline as he stared at the mayhem he'd caused. Before he did anything, he laughed. He twisted his body slowly and, facing the armed officers, lowered the weapon, dropped it to the ground and raised his arms.

Within seconds, he was pinned to the tiles and cuffed. Jake watched, paralysed.

The armed officers hefted Lester to his feet and dragged him out of the bathroom. Jake retreated at the sight of him. That smile, those teeth, the hair, the eyes – they would all burn in his memory for a very long time to come.

'Better luck next time, Tanner,' Lester said, his mouth dripping with saliva.

'Shut up!' the armed officer closest to Jake said. Then he grabbed Lester's head and thrust it down into his chest.

As soon as they were out of sight, Jake rushed into the bathroom.

Jennifer's body still lay there, limp. Blood continued to gush from her head.

'Jennifer! Jennifer! Jennifer!' Jake bent down by her side and felt for a pulse on her neck. It was faint. 'Wake up! Come on!'

He turned to the door and screamed for help. A second later, Liam and Drew arrived. They swore aloud as they saw Jennifer lying in the bathroom.

'Get a medic!' Jake barked, spittle flying out of his mouth.

Drew disappeared, headed downstairs and called for assistance. While he waited, Jake tried to staunch the blood erupting from Jennifer's head and keep her alive.

After what felt like an eternity, Drew returned with two paramedics in tow. They carried an emergency travel pack with them. As they entered the bathroom, they ordered Drew and Liam outside, and moved Jake out of the way. He was useless and covered in blood.

'Give us some space please,' one of the paramedics said, while the other spoke into the radio on their shoulder.

'Jake!' a voice called from somewhere. 'Jake!'

It was Liam, beckoning him to get out of the bathroom.

'Leave them to it, mate. Get out. Let them do their job.'

Jake ignored him, and it wasn't until Liam grabbed him by the arm and pulled him out of the room that he finally lost sight of Jennifer. She was dying. And it was his fault. He'd been too slow.

Jake stopped at the top of the stairs, crouched down and burst into tears, smearing them away with his bloody hands.

'Come on, lad,' Liam said, crouching by Jake's side.

'It's my fault,' he said between breaths. 'I fucked it all up. Now three other people have died.'

'We got him. *You* got him. He can't hurt anyone else ever again. He's done. History. And it's thanks to you. If you hadn't called the pimp in the first place, we would never have known where he was – we would have had to start from the ground up again.' Liam reached across Jake's back and eased him to his feet. 'Come on, mate. Lester won't be able to touch anyone else. I think we should get you home.'

'Jennifer…' Jake said, looking up towards the bathroom door. As they reached the bottom step, another duo of paramedics entered the property and raced upstairs.

'There's nothing you can do for her. You've done everything you could, mate.'

Somehow, Jake didn't believe any of what Liam had just said.

CHAPTER 77

DANGEROUS GAMES

The following afternoon – just after Jake had woken up at midday –
Bow Green bustled with people Jake didn't recognise. Many were
carrying lever-arch folders and cups of tea, jostling and talking
excitably to one another. There was a furore of excitement that
permeated and bounced about the place. It was so unusual to him. It
was as though he'd stumbled upon a completely new team.

Jake moved across the floor to Liam's office, minding the new
faces that shot past him from every angle, and knocked.

A couple of seconds later, Liam's face appeared.

'What's all this then?' Jake asked, pointing at the room.

A smile grew on Liam's face. 'Well, since you've decided to sleep
for half the day, we needed to replace you.'

'This many?' Jake asked, his eyebrows raised.

'Consider it a compliment.' Liam stepped aside. 'Please come in.
I've been waiting for you to show up.'

Jake entered Liam's office and, at once, he noticed something
different about it. Or perhaps it was something different about Liam.
He didn't know. But there was a nice smell that lingered in the air.
As though the years' worth of sweat and alcohol abuse from
previous occupants had disappeared in one clean sweep.

Before he could give it any more thought, he was ordered to take
a seat.

'How are you feeling?' Liam asked.

'OK,' Jake said. 'I've been trying not to think about it.'

'It'll take some time to get used to, but you will eventually.'

'How is she?'

'Critical. But stable. Lester crushed her skull and bruised her brain. She was lucky a piece didn't pierce any of it. It's too early to say what state she'll be in when she wakes up... *if* she wakes up.'

Jake hung his head low. Visions of Jennifer's head resting in his hands flashed in his mind. The blood. The weight of her body. The small dent in her head from where Lester had caved it in with his hammer.

'And Lester?' Jake asked, looking up at Liam.

'Talking. Surprisingly. Or rather, unsurprisingly. He's giving us every little detail. He's getting some sort of kick out of it all.'

'He's a narcissist. He wants to satisfy his ego. He's probably jacking off in his head about how good he is and the fuss we're all making over him.'

There was a pause.

'He confessed to something none of us knew about,' Liam began.

'What?' Jake asked, his intrigue rising.

'Sampson Decker. He killed him the night you guys went and spoke to him.'

'Wait,' Jake said, dumbfounded. 'The night Drew fell asleep when he was supposed to be listening to the surveillance?'

Liam held a hand in the air, pre-empting Jake's protestations. 'Don't worry about that. I'm dealing with DS Richmond as we speak.'

Jake sighed and looked down at his lap. He breathed in through his nose and out through his mouth in an attempt to calm himself down. 'How many more victims do you think we'll find after all of this is done?'

'I hope none. He's going to spend the rest of his life in prison, regardless. But if you ask me, that's not enough. For what he did...' Liam paused a beat. 'For what he did, we should bring the death penalty back.'

'Bit too political for my liking,' Jake said. 'Maybe he'll suffer more by rotting inside a small box.'

Outside Liam's office, laughter erupted.

'You never told me what was going on out there,' Jake said.

'We've enlisted help in filing everything and getting the evidence together for the CPS.'

'A confession's not enough?'

'Not if there's any chance he could try and get the insanity plea or something like that. He and his lawyer are going to try that route, I think. They're in the interview room now... You fancy speaking with him?'

Jake shook his head. 'I'll pass thanks. I have nothing to say to him. And the questions I do have, I think I'd rather not know the answers to.'

'Sometimes it's better not to know anyway – that way you can never get hurt.'

Liam paused a moment; Jake could see that there was something he wanted to say.

'Listen...' he began, 'we need to talk.'

Jake didn't like the sound of that.

'I'm sure over the past few days you've had enough stress and things to worry about without the added pressure of the Reg 13 notice you were served. I know you've been meaning to talk to me about it, and I know I haven't been the most cooperative, but I wanted to let you know that it's no more.'

'Excuse me?' Jake said. The tension in his back and shoulders and neck and fists subsided.

'There never was a Reg 13. It was a test. A practical joke. I wanted to see how you'd react to it, see how you'd improvise and begin to prove yourself.'

'But... I...'

'You don't need to say anything. But you can at least rest easy that there won't be a meeting, and your record isn't going to be tarnished... for the time being.' Liam gave Jake a little smirk.

'I... I...' Jake sighed heavily and shook his head. 'That's some fucking dangerous game to play, sir, if you don't mind my saying so.'

'I had every faith you'd be fine. Although I don't know which I admire more: your tenacity to prove yourself, or the fact that you had the balls to try and argue the toss. You're a good egg, Jake. And it's good to know we've got loyal people within this team who are willing to fight it out to the end – no matter the cost. Now, what are you doing for the rest of the day?'

'Well,' Jake said, 'if it's all the same to you, sir, I'd like to go and see my wife and newborn, and maybe take my paternity leave while I'm at it.'

'I can't see a problem with that.'

'That is, if you don't need me for the investigation anymore?'

'I think you've earned it. Have you decided on a name yet?'

Jake smirked. 'You won't like it.'

'What is it?'

'Promise you won't let your head swell?'

Liam's nostrils flared. 'You did it, didn't you? You chose Ellie.'

Jake nodded.

Liam erupted out of his chair and extended his hand. 'I knew I could always rely on you to do the right thing, Jake. You won't regret it, trust me. Now why don't you get out of here and take as much time as you need.'

CHAPTER 78

PERFECT

Jake skipped down the steps and jogged to his car. He couldn't wait to get out of the building and forget about everything for the foreseeable future.

His job was done. Lester had been arrested and would soon be sitting in a prison cell like he deserved. Jennifer was in a hospital bed, recovering. And he had his job back. He had his job security. And, he knew, this meant he would be back in the team. He would be respected again. He would be able to join in the camaraderie, the banter, the loyalty that each member showed to one another.

Then a thought hit him.

As he reached his car door, he opened it, hopped in and leant across to the glove compartment. The £500 the team had given him earlier in the week was still there. He pulled out the wad of money and flicked the notes through his fingers. It felt good. It had been a long time since he'd held that much money in his hands.

And he had the perfect idea on how to spend it.

On his way to the hospital, he drove into Stratford Shopping Centre, hurried into a PC World and made a purchase.

He rushed back with the bag in his hand and a sense of accomplishment in his heart.

As he returned to the car, he called Elizabeth and told her he was on the way.

'I'll be about an hour,' he said. 'Which room are you in now?'
'The same one as before.'
'Perfect. I can't wait to see you.'

CHAPTER 79

FINGER

Elizabeth's face beamed as Jake entered the hospital room. She was sitting upright in the bed with the sheet pulled up to her chest. She spread her arms out as he approached her.

'I'm so glad you're OK,' Elizabeth said. 'I've been worried sick.'

Jake set the PC World bag on the floor, reached across Elizabeth and hugged her. He wanted the moment to last a lifetime, but he was overpowered by his sudden urge to kiss her. He pulled away from her and gave her a kiss on the lips, forehead and cheek.

'I told you I'd come back safe.' Jake sat by her side and stroked her face. Her skin felt soft under his, but, as he sat there, the sensation was tarnished with flashbacks of Jennifer's bloody head last night. He tried to shake them free from his mind. To his surprise, they disappeared. But he knew it would only be a temporary solution.

'How was it?' Elizabeth asked, squeezing his leg.

'Horrible. But you don't need to worry about that – nor me. I don't want it to stress you out. It's done. It's over. I'm here now. I'm all yours.'

Elizabeth held out her hand. 'I'm Elizabeth. Nice to meet you. I don't think we've been introduced.'

Jake took her hand and kissed it. 'The pleasure is all mine, Miss.'

She flinched and flashed her left hand, twirling her wedding ring on her finger.

'Mrs,' she corrected.

'Apologies. He's a very lucky man.'

'Meh, he's all right.'

Jake chuckled. He enjoyed their sense of humour – the fact that they could still act childish and get away with it, even though they were both in their mid-twenties and had just had their second child. Every other aspect of their lives was serious, so why couldn't their relationship and their family be their escape from that?

Jake leant down by his side and grabbed the bag.

'I bought you a little something.'

'When? Why? With what money?'

'What's with the interrogation? Isn't that my job?'

Elizabeth scowled. 'Answer me.'

Jake knew better than to argue. 'When? Today. Why? I wanted to treat you, and it's a little apology for my absence these past few weeks. And with what money? The guys at work gave us some as a small congratulations for Ellie.'

'How much?' Elizabeth said. She had entered concerned and serious mode.

'Five hundred quid.'

'What!'

'I forgot to tell you the other day when I brought the card home.'

'And you spent it all?'

'On an investment,' Jake pointed out.

'What do you mean an investment? You could have used that to pay off the car insurance that's overdue. Or the other bills that we've got piling up.'

'It's an investment,' Jake repeated, handing her the bag.

She reached in and pulled out a box. As soon as she saw the branding on the side, she gasped.

'Oh, Jake!' she said, holding the gift in her hands.

'Is it the right one?'

Elizabeth nodded. Tears formed in her eyes.

'It's the one you said you wanted, right? And hopefully you'll be able to take better pictures with it. And with those better pictures, you'll make more money. And with that money, it'll pay back the money spent on the lens in the first place. See… an investment!'

'This is not how you treat an emotional woman!' she said with a catch in her throat.

'You can use it on Ellie. Test it out on her. Make sure it works all right. Do you like it?' Jake asked with a smile on his face that he hoped would never end.

'I love it. It's perfect. Did you bring my camera with you?'

Jake's smile dropped immediately. It told Elizabeth everything she needed to know.

'Idiot,' she said, chuckling.

'Sorry.'

'Don't be daft – it's fine.'

'How is she?' Jake finally asked.

'She's doing fine. Doctors have been looking after her all night. They say she's in perfect condition.'

'Where is she?'

'Sleeping at the moment. My mum's with her.'

Jake stood and brushed his legs down. 'You want to come with me?'

'Not right now,' Elizabeth replied. 'I will later.'

Jake bent down and kissed Elizabeth on her forehead again. He'd read somewhere that it was common for mothers to suffer from postnatal depression. And Elizabeth had reacted the same way when Maisie was born – as though she felt some sort of resentment towards the baby. Jake knew her well enough to avoid pressing her for a response. In time, it would come.

He said goodbye, told her that he loved her and hurried down to the baby room. There, he found his mother-in-law sitting on a chair, thumbing away on her Blackberry.

'Fancy seeing you here,' Jake said.

'Sorry I'm not your actual mother,' Martha replied, keeping her eyes fixed on the screen. 'She left a few hours ago.'

'She can look after herself.'

Martha raised her gaze to him. 'I heard about work. Congratulations. The Stratford Ripper's finally off the streets.'

'Just another day in the office,' Jake replied smugly.

Martha placed the phone under her leg. 'Speaking of the office – will you be staying there?'

Jake nodded. 'They dropped everything. They said they were just testing me to see how well I coped under the pressure.'

'And I suppose now that you've arrested Lester Bain, you passed with flying colours?'

'A little hyperbole, but I'll take that.'

'Good,' Martha said. 'We're pleased for you. Keep up the good work.'

Jake knew deep down she was being genuine, no matter how sarcastic it came across when she said it.

'It's nice having you around,' Jake said sarcastically, hoping she recognised it. Their relationship was amicable though; they had both mutually – and silently – agreed to respect one another.

Martha gathered her things, shoved them under her arm, gave Jake a brief hug and then left to rejoin Elizabeth.

As soon as Martha moved out of his field of view, Jake

completely disregarded her from his mind. The only thing that was important right now was his beautiful little girl, wrapped up in a blanket, sleeping.

He placed his hand on the glass. A midwife entered through a door on the other side of the partition. Jake recognised her as the one who had helped deliver the baby. She wandered over to Ellie, lifted her out of her bed, disappeared through the door on the other side of the glass and returned through the same door Martha had just left from.

'Would you like to hold her?' the nurse asked as she appeared.

'More than anything,' Jake said, already holding his arms out.

Ellie was heavier than he was expecting, and he had to adjust his position as he took her. She awoke in his arms, her eyes blinking open to reveal a stunning hazel brown. Jake gave her a kiss on the forehead and then buried his nose in her cheek. He held out his finger for Ellie to grab, and she took it, swallowing it whole in her fist.

'Hello, Ellie,' he said, overcome with emotion. 'I'm your dad. And I'm going to make sure nobody ever hurts you. Promise.'

CHAPTER 80

THE CABAL

Later that evening, the doctors had given both Ellie and Elizabeth the all-clear to leave the hospital and get themselves fully set up at home. Jake was in the middle of carrying Ellie to the car when his phone rang. He glanced at the Caller ID while juggling the car keys.

He opened the door, placed Ellie in the back seat and instructed Elizabeth to plug Ellie's seat belt in.

'Sorry, I have to take this,' he said, stepping away from the vehicle and answering the call. He kept his voice quiet, out of earshot of Elizabeth. 'Hello?'

'Did he tell you my name?' came a machine-automated voice.

'Excuse me?' Jake asked, glancing back at Elizabeth and the girls, making sure they were OK.

'Did he tell you my name?'

'Who?'

'Your friend, Elliot Bridger. Did he tell you my name?'

Jake hesitated a moment before responding. 'No...' he said quietly, afraid of what might happen as soon as he said it.

'Then let me tell you,' the automated voice said. 'That way you won't forget it. My name is The Cabal. And consider this your first warning.'

'First warning for what?'

'You won't be hearing from Elliot for a while.'

'What? No. I haven't said anything to anyone. I promise.'

'He's been taken care of for the foreseeable future.'

'I haven't said anything to anyone. You have to believe me.'

'It was long overdue. Elliot was a problem, and we've eradicated that problem. Just like we can do with you. So let Elliot Bridger be a shining example to you of what will happen if you choose to ignore his advice. It's very important that you don't interfere with things you don't understand, Jake Tanner. We are bigger than you can even comprehend. You can trust no one. Not even your wife and two little girls. How is the little one, by the way? If you want to keep her – and the rest of your family – safe and secure at night, then you'll do well to remember what I've told you. We've given you fair warning. This is your first and last. You will not be told again.'

EPILOGUE

Lester Bain pleaded to being insane at his court hearing. His claim was rejected and he was sentenced to fifty years in prison. He will never set foot out of prison again.

Michael and Danny Cipriano were released from remand and entered into the Witness Protection Scheme on 21 May 2010. Their exact whereabouts are only known by a few individuals.

Lester's last victim, Jennifer Warren, sadly lost her life after months battling her brain injuries in intensive care. Her parents initiated a charity aimed at stopping young girls entering the world of prostitution. Jake Tanner is one of the faces of the campaign.

DS Elliot Bridger subsequently retired from Surrey Police at the age of 40, and is living off his pension in his home in the Surrey Hills.

After several attempt to shut it down, The Community continues to exist, although its users are painfully reminded of the effect it had on some of their members every time they sign in. A dedicated police team are monitoring any significant deaths relating to The Community's members — in particular, the top of the leaderboard: Handsome Mike

* * *

All potential charges against Archie Arnold were dropped, while he was subsequently questioned in relation to human trafficking and prostitution rings in the Stratford area. No lines of enquiry were taken any further.

Enjoy this? You can make a big difference.

Reviews are the most powerful tools in my arsenal when it comes to getting attention for my books. They act as the tipping point on the scales of indecision for future readers crossing my books.

So, if you enjoyed this book, and are interested in being one of my committed and loyal readers, then I would really grateful if you could leave a review. Why not spread the word, share the love? Even if you leave an honest review, it would still mean a lot. They take as long to write as it did to read this book!

Thank you.

Your Friendly Author,
Jack Probyn

ABOUT JACK PROBYN

Jack Probyn is a British crime writer and the author of the Jake Tanner crime thriller series, set in London.

He currently lives in Surrey with his partner and cat, and is working on a new murder mystery series set in his hometown of Essex.

Keep up to date with Jack at the following:
- Website: https://www.jackprobynbooks.com
- Facebook: https://www.facebook.co.uk/jackprobynbooks
- Twitter: https://twitter.com/jackprobynbooks
- Instagram: https://www.instagram.com/jackprobynauthor

Printed in Great Britain
by Amazon